M000201285

THE
POLICE REVOLT
OF 2016

LAWRENCE C. MACKIN SR.

"A Great civilization is not conquered from without until it has destroyed itself from within."

Ariel Durant

"As for what is not true, you will always find abundance in the newspapers."

"Nothing can now be believed which is seen in a newspaper. Truth itself becomes suspicious by being put into that polluted vehicle."

Thomas Jefferson

WEDNESDAY, AUGUST 12, 2015, 09:00

Despite the occasion, it was actually a beautiful day. The sun was warm on Sean's face, and there was just enough wind to allow the flags to wave. As he often did, he gazed intently at the American flag and thought of those who had suffered, bled, and died for that flag and the country it represented. He lowered his gaze and glanced across at the obviously pregnant widow and small son of murdered Officer William Dillon. So young to be a widow with two children who will never know their father.

He was trying to remember all of the police and military funerals he had attended in the last few years when the order "Attention" was given, and instantly, with a sound like a crack of thunder, 5,000 Police Officer's snapped to. Taps began to play as Officer Dillon's casket was lowered into the ground. The casket flag was presented to the widow by the honor guard, and "Amazing Grace" sounded on the Bagpipes. Secretly, every officer there, and in the country for that matter, was wondering, "What if that were me? What about my family?"

When the last notes sounded, Mrs. Dillon was helped to the limo. In order to face the limo as it drove by, every officer present made either a left or right turn, while holding their salute. The command, "Order Arms," was given, the salutes came down, and the parade was dismissed. In a somber mood, all of the officers began making their way back to the hotels that they were staying in. By pre-arrangement, Sean met a group of senior officers from various departments across the country at the gravesite. They had first met several years ago at a police officer's funeral and, unfortunately, had met at many others in the last few years. On top of this, they had also gotten together at professional schools and conferences for senior police officials that were held across the country. Sean had had many conversations —both individually and in groups— with these men and women. And, from what they said, they were as passionate as he was in their desire to save the country.

Out of all of them, he knew he could count on Sara Mahoney. More than just count on...she actually scared him. She wanted to hang every member of congress from a tree with a sign around their neck that read:

"I Betrayed the Constitution." Sean believed that, given her way, she would actually do it. The other certainty was Joseph Annino, an amazing man. A graduate of West Point, an MBA from Harvard, a Major on the Virginia State Police, and best of all, a full Colonel in the Virginia National Guard. "Lot's of firepower there!" thought Sean. Annino's plan was simple: march on Washington DC, arrest all of the traitors there, declare an interim government and correct all of the unconstitutional actions taken by the government in the last forty years. As Annino stated on many occasions, he had taken an oath to "Defend the Constitution against *all* enemies, foreign and *domestic*," and in Annino's opinion the domestic enemies were far more dangerous than any foreign. Yes, Annino was that ready to fulfill his patriotic duty. Well, that pretty much was exactly what they were going to do.

As they stood there in a group, before any preliminaries, Sean asked, "Well, who is ready for a revolution led by us, the police?"

To Sean's surprise, none of them looked shocked. On the contrary, they were all nodding and smiling.

Sara was the first to speak. "Let's do it. How and when?"

One by one, the others joined.

"Count me in."

"It's about time."

"I guess we were all just waiting for a leader."

Sean smiled to himself; he had picked the right group of friends—no, the right group of patriots! Annino was practically crying, he was so happy.

"The 'when' is during the Law Enforcement Memorial week in DC, May, 2016."

Edward Larkin, a Captain Detective from the Chicago Police and an expert in surveillance and counter surveillance, spoke up. "Pretty much everyone else is gone, and we look funny standing here. Let's not attract any attention. I say back to our hotel, change, and we meet in the bar in an hour."

Everyone quickly agreed and Sean issued his first order. "Ed, you are going to be in charge of security for this. Brian, you are in charge of communications. You and Ed are to work closely together."

In unison they both answered: "Yes sir!"

When they met in the lounge, Sean said to them, "Before we go any further, this is your last chance to get out of this. There is no turning back from this point forward. Once in, never out." They all knew exactly what he meant. No one left.

"So, why during the Memorial week?" asked Audrey Lapaglia. Besides Sara, Audrey was the only other female in the group, and was also an Inspector on the NYPD.

"That's easy" said Larkin. "Ten thousand cops from all over the country come to DC for the Memorial. Our police army will invade and assemble in DC without anyone thinking anything of it."

"Don't be too sure of that," cautioned Sean. "We have a lot of planning to do and will have to bring in a lot more people to coordinate this. Rule number one is no one, I mean no one, who is not personally known to us, is told anything about this. As a matter of fact, before any of us talk to anyone else we are going to set up a vetting unit, comprised of ourselves for right now, to decide who we admit to our circle. Let me remind you all of our history as Americans. Our nation was established by a revolution to right the wrongs of King George and his government. What the present U.S. government has done to the American people is far worse than what old Georgie did. Remember Thomas Jefferson stated: 'God forbid we should ever be twenty years without such a rebellion?' Well, it's been about 150 years since the end of the last rebellion, so I say we are way overdue. And, furthermore, the Declaration of Independence states that, 'It is the Right and the duty of the people to rise up and abolish a government that oppresses them.'"

"Yeah," Tony said, "Talk about no representation, the Constitution states that there should be one Representative for every 30,000 citizens."

"How did we end up with only 435 Reps?"

"It's a lot easier to bribe 435 people than it is to bribe thousands" said Brian.

"Anyone ever see a poor Congressman, or Senator for that matter?" They all just thought about that.

"Political correctness, conflict resolution, lawyers and lawsuits have all combined to remove courage from Americans, especially American males. The people have not acted, the military has not lived up to their oaths to protect the Constitution, so now it is up to us."

Brandon Robinson, a Captain on the Philadelphia Police Dept. in command of SWAT and a ten year veteran of the Marine Corps, did not like that. "Sean," he said, "It was up to the generals, admirals and," glancing over at Annino, "Even the colonels to act. You can't expect the non-coms and privates to issue orders like that. Maybe that's why Obama relieved all of the generals and admirals that did not agree with him. Kind of like what Obama's hero Stalin did to the Russian army before WWII."

"Well, thank GOD for the Second Amendment and the NRA, of which I am a proud life member," added Annino. They all laughed at that.

"All right," said Sean, "That's enough for now. The next round is on me. We will all meet back here at 0800 tomorrow. As a test for operational security, none of us will speak about this tonight, but I want each of us to start really thinking about key people we can trust. Anyone in our departments that we can bring down here such as SWAT teams, which I happen to command in Boston. Not to mention every member of which is a military veteran, handpicked by me no less."

Audrey, who had in her command the NYPD SWAT team (ESU), spoke up. "No problem" she said, "Them and around 30,000 other NYPD would be racing down here to help, whether or not they are ordered. Don't forget all of the officer's we've had murdered. And not a sincere word from our Mayor, DiBlasio, Obama or racist Holder. In fact, it's just the opposite. They call us stupid and racist! We risk our lives and make decisions in seconds that they would not have the courage to make in a million years, and then they judge us! I actually feel sorry for some of these liberal maggots when the NYPD gets ahold of them. Well, not really sorry," she added.

Sean smiled. "Don't forget that our departments get along very well. Marching in each others St. Patrick's day parades, playing sports and drinking together. Brandon, what about Philly SWAT?"

"Same as you" smiled Brandon, "All handpicked men. Trust me, they will be all for this!"

Sean started to hear the ancient Irish rebel song, *The Rising of the Moon*, playing in his head. "For the pikes must be together at the rising of the moon!"

THURSDAY, AUGUST 13TH 05:00 HOURS

Sean was wide awake at 5 AM. He tried laying in bed until 6:00 am, trying to calm himself down and running over in his head what he would say at the meeting. He thought of calling home to check in with Shannon, then he remembered that it was not advisable to call her before 6:30 AM, even then it was risky, that Irish temper!

Sean got up, started the coffee pot in his room, showered, and noticed that the time was 7:30 AM. He thought, "Might as well head down to the lounge now, be early to greet the group." However, he was shocked when he entered the room— he was the last one there. The news was on and everyone looked very serious. Sean noticed that Audrey had tears in her eyes. "What happened?"

"Two more NYPD Officers were ambushed and murdered, about 3AM" she said.

"They got a call for a women having a baby on the sidewalk when they arrived they were shot down, never had a chance. Not a word from DiBlasi expressing his sympathy!"

Brandon walked over. "I think I have an idea, a way of getting something good from the murder of these officers and unfortunately any future murders."

"What's that?" Ed Larkin asked. "These funerals, It gives us a perfect excuse to meet face to face in the open, so to speak, and plan without being obvious. And to meet any possible new members of our group."

"I hate to say it but that is a great idea" said Sean.

"Yeah," said Ed, "The plans for the re-birth of our nation are born from the blood of our fallen heros."

Sara then spoke up. "By the way, should we have a name for our group?"

Everyone was quiet for a moment. Then, Al looked up and noticed that the sun was shining through a gap in the curtains, directly on the American flag. He remembered his history lessons back in his school days, and how Paul Revere and the founding fathers had called themselves the *Sons of Liberty*. "Look at the sun on the flag," he said to everyone, "How about we call ourselves the Sons and Daughters of Liberty?"

A second or two went by as Sean looked around the room. Everybody seemed to agree. "All right then, the Sons and Daughters of Liberty it is.

"Ok", said Sean, "let's get to it, I know we all have planes to catch. Ed, you and Brian are to have a means of us securely communicating with one another worked out by the next meeting, which I guess will be next week in New York at the funerals. Everyone think of others we can trust, especially at the Federal level. And remember, we are actually in a war here— with the liberals and the media, among others. Don't forget, they will not hesitate to kill us. Think of Obama's buddy Bill Ayers, Waco, Ruby Ridge and all these other groups that are cop haters. Obama signed an executive order, which Holder condoned as legal, giving him the authority to launch missile strikes from drones on terrorists within the U.S. They wouldn't hesitate to consider us terrorists. The media would praise them forever for whacking us! Be safe, GOD Bless, and why don't we all try to stay at the Marriott uptown for the funerals."

FRIDAY, AUGUST 14, 10:00 HOURS

Sean's three hour flight back to Logan airport in Boston seemed to be over in the blink of an eye. After picking up his bag, he walked over to the state police barracks where he had parked. He thought about going into the barracks to see if his friend Major Jeffrey Clark was in, but then decided that he just wanted to get home to see Shannon and the girls. He called Shannon and told her he would be home in thirty minutes, and that he would like to take a family walk out to Castle Island at Fort Independence.

As he pulled up to his house on East Broadway he could not believe his luck, there was actually an open parking spot right in front of his house. Shannon, who heard the door open, came running up to him. She jumped into his arms, exclaiming, "I am so glad you're home, I missed you so much! Sean, I want you to retire. Things are just getting too dangerous for police officers; it's open season on cops." At that she started to cry. "I can't take it anymore!"

"Shannon, let me change. We will go for a walk and talk, but you and I both know that we cannot afford for me to retire. I've only been on the job 27 years, I have at least six more to go." As he said this, Sean thought; "That will make 33 years as a cop, and for what, a 66% pension? Make a career in the military and you might get a 40% pension, but," and his blood boiled at the thought, "serve two years as a congressman and retire for life with a full pension, COLA and medical included. Unreal. Well, that will be coming to an end."

As he always did, Sean scanned up and down the street as they came out of the house. On an impulse, rather than turning to his left to walk out to Castle Island, he took Shannon's hand and walked to the right. She glanced up at him.

"I just want to walk by the Vietnam Memorial." It was only a two minute walk, past St. Brigid's Church where they were married, and where their kids were later Baptised, and received all of the other Sacraments of the Catholic Church. He thought to himself, "I guess my funeral will be here also."

At the memorial Sean read and counted the names, as he had done so many times in the past. So many lives from such a small section of Boston. South Boston, or "Southie, " as it was known, had always sent more of her son's per population to serve in the armed forces than any other place in the country. Sean looked at the names, then turned to Shannon. "They did not die, they did not give their young lives for, for what these liberals are doing. Destroying their America."

They then walked down Broadway and began to walk along the beach to the sugar bowl. At the beginning of the causeway was the South Boston WWII Memorial. The name of Shannon's uncle, who of course she had never met, Lt. John P. Mulkern,U.S.A.A.C. was one of the many names engraved on the Memorial. Shannon had told him that Lt. Mulkern was 21 years old on his first bombing mission over Germany, just two weeks before the end of the war in Europe, when his plane went missing. No trace of the plane or the crew had ever been found.

While walking along the causeway, Sean said to Shannon, "Look at that fort. You know, the British troops who killed the Sons of Liberty in the Boston Massacre were quartered out here after the massacre." Walking around the back of the Fort along Boston Harbor, they came to the South Boston Memorial dedicated to her sons who gave all they had in the Korean war. For the third time that day, the amount of names on the memorial amazed him. Out loud, he said, "No they have not died in vain." Shannon looked up at him, but just kept silent.

As they rounded the corner of the fort, they gazed out into Boston harbor. Sean thought of the time, so long ago, when the harbor was filled with British warships. Sent from King George, the ships were meant to enforce his rule, as well as crush the spirit of liberty that was growing in the hearts of the colonist. George failed. But history repeats itself and once again a foreign despot, this one from Kenya, was, along with his leftist allies, trying to crush the spirit of liberty within America. For the thousandth time Sean said to himself, "No, we are going to stop them."

Shannon interrupted his thoughts. "One day I would like to take another day trip out to George's Island. I know the forts are the same, but I like it out there." During the American civil war high ranking confederate prisoners, and other domestic enemies, had been imprisoned on Georgia's island by President Lincoln. Sean kind of liked the idea of imprisoning Soros,Bloomberg, and many others out there.

They stopped on another corner of the fort, opposite Logan airport, and Shannon knew what was coming. Sean had said it to her and others many times before. This time, however, was the first time she had seen tears roll down his cheeks. "Look," he said while pointing down the harbor towards downtown Boston, "there you see them, the Masts of the U.S.S. Constitution, Old Ironside's. Look right above the masts, there's the Bunker Hill Monument, and there's the Steeple of the Old North Church. Paul Revere's house is right there too, and over there that monument is Dorchester Heights, were George Washington placed the cannons brought down from Fort Ticonderoga, during the dead of winter by Ethan Allen and the Green mountain boys. Forcing the British to abandon Boston. So much history! So much of the birth of America right here! Right there next to the silver building the site of the Boston Tea Party, think of all those who fought and died right there on Bunker Hill, or on Old Ironsides to give us our Freedom. A freedom that so many don't even think about, or know that they are losing.You know Lexington Green and Concord are what, 40 minutes from right here. Plymouth rock where the Pilgrims first landed is not even an hour away. No Shannon they are not going to get away with it, we will stop them!"

FRIDAY AUGUST 21ST, 09:00 HOURS

Once again they assembled to honor two more fallen heros, Joseph Murray and Anita Hicks. The two officers were murdered while racing to help with the birth of a child. St. Patrick's Cathedral was filled with blue, the streets were filled with brother and sister officers from all over the country. Within nine days, seven police officers had been murdered. Four others had survived assassination attempts. Obama urged restraint on the part of the police, and the officers who had survived the assassination attempts by defending themselves and shooting their attackers were now being investigated by Holder's justice department for possible civil rights violations! Cops across the country were in a foul mood! The media had even published the names and addresses of the Officers in the paper's, probably hoping someone would finish out the job.

The funeral Mass concluded, and with more precision than he had ever seen before, the two caskets were carried from St. Patrick's, placed in the hearses, and driven to separate cemeteries for burial. Sean went with Audrey to the burial of Officer Hicks.

At the cemetery, Sean noticed that the brass of the buttons and badges of the officer's seemed to shine more brilliantly than usual. The leather gear, gun belts,and boots were all shining black. The flags were held higher. It was as if the officers were saying to their brother, "You made us better, you have brought out the best in us and we will not forget you." Tap's sounded, and Amazing Grace was played on the bagpipes. So many times Sean, Audrey, and the assembled officers had witnessed this honor given to the fallen. Yet each time it was more meaningful than before.

Sean walked with Audrey back to her unmarked and was about to get into the passenger seat when he looked over and saw the tears in her eyes. "I'll drive" he said. They had to wait as the many police cars from all over the country drove from the cemetery. After a few moments Audrey, with venom in her voice, said, "Notice how Holder, Obama, Sharpton, Jackson or any other of the civil rights leaders have not attended one funeral for a fallen officer? Obama did not even go to Paris for the march against terrorism. Why would he, it was only French cops that were murdered by his Muslim brothers and sisters. No loss to him. Imagine how the U.S. looks in the eyes of the world, thanks to the Kenyan. All these countries that stood by us after 9-11, that fought on our side in the Gulf Wars and Obama can't show support for them. What a group of incompetent misfits we have running our country!" Then, looking at Sean she vowed, "Not for much longer though!"

They arrived back at Audrey's home; several of the group were already there waiting for them. Audrey apologized, "Sorry we got tied up in the traffic, please come in." She quickly opened the door and, acting as a perfect hostess, took their coats and showed them where her bar was. "Help yourself guys, I will be right back".

It only took about 20 minutes for the rest of the group to arrive. After several minutes of talk, mostly about the funerals and Paris, Sean called the meeting to order.

"Ok, we are all ticked about what is going on, but lets put our emotions aside and get down to Business. First Ed and Brian, what have you come up with for a way for us to securely communicate with each other?"

Ed and Brian looked at each other and Ed gave Brian the nod to proceed. "Well first, we are going to communicate out in the open at public events using our department or private cell phones and emails. We are going to make it appear to anyone who happens to look at us that we are just a good group of friends who enjoy hanging out with each other. Also, it's a good way to arrange a meeting, out in the open. We all know that if, say, Ed, invites us to his house for a cookout, it's a summons for a meeting. We can all email or phone back our acceptance or not. Also don't forget that the FBI and Secret Service monitor police communications, both radio and electronic. A couple of my guys thought it would be funny to run the license plate on the presidential limo. The Secret Service flipped out, called the officers, myself, and a few others in for an 'interview,' and threatened a full scale investigation. After a few apologies they calmed down, but just remember: they do watch.

"Now, in layman's terms we are working on a low level, low band radio network that will enable us to communicate real time with a great deal of security. These bands have not been used in a long time and not too many, if anybody, bothers to monitor them nowadays. For right now though, we have bought disposable phones that as we know, are untraceable. I put 10 hours of time on each phone. Do not program any names into the phones and if you lose your phone send out an email to the group and we all stop using our phones and pick up new ones. Any questions?"

" Yeah" asked Al, "who might monitor the low band radio channels? If anyone does, it would be the military, NSA, ours or any other countries. But these lowbands have relatively short range—- say 1500 to 2000 miles tops. So, to send a message from Boston to San Diego myself or Ed, may have to relay the message." But no one thought of the message traveling west out into the Pacific from San Diego.

"Great, now the next order of business— new members. Any nominations? And why." Again Al spoke up first, "Yes, I would like to nominate Sheriff Joshua Denver from Arizona." They all knew him and everybody just laughed.

"Great pick" said Sara, "just in keeping with the rules, why him?"

"Well, Joshua is now President of the National Sheriff's Association, so he has direct access to every sheriff in the country. We all know that he is a man of courage and he has a long record of speaking out against Obama and illegal aliens," at that Brandon Robinson gave a growl. His wife, Jess, had been killed following being hit in a car crash by an illegal alien, driving drunk. This left Brandon to raise their then 5 year old daughter by himself. "Also, Joshua has openly defied Obama, Holder and every other liberal in the world."

"Just one thing about Joshua" said Anthony, "for those very reasons, the Feds are definitely watching him. That could be an advantage though, get the Feds looking left while we fake right, could work."

"Let's not be too hard on the Feds, I think we will all be surprised at how many of them are with us."

"Ok a vote, all in favor of Sheriff Joshua." The vote was instant and unanimous. "Great," said Al, "I will see him Friday, let you all know then. But I think we all already know his answer."

Next, Joe Annino spoke up. "I have a list. You ready? Now don't be shocked. First, a very good friend of mine. We were both housed on the same base in Afghanistan and Iraq, we play golf together, our wives are like sisters–"

"Ok, ok who is it?"

"Wayne Kelly, the Commandant of the U.S. Marine Corps." There was absolute silence in the room. Finally Audrey spoke. "Well, that sure takes this to another level, but are you crazy?"

"Not at all. Wayne has said to me on several occasions how concerned he is for the security of the country. Obama has hurt the military more than anyone knows. Now Obama even wants to bring illegal aliens into the military before U.S. citizens. Wayne has stated to me that the country cannot survive much longer under Obama, and he does not think we could fight a major war now against a first rate enemy. He has even stated to me that he should do what his oath requires of him and save the country. Several of his top generals have all been retired by Obama. Wayne is not sure why he has been spared so far, but he thinks that in Obama's eyes he is only a figurehead, and that Obama thinks his political appointees will follow Obama's orders, and not his."

"He really said that?" the others asked.

"Yup," Wayne affirmed.

Again there was dead silence, "Well as Audrey said, he would bring this up to a new level to say the least.... All in favor?" Again, the vote was unanimous.

"Who else Joe, Santa Claus?" everyone laughed.

"No Obama is a Muslim, he does not believe in Santa."

"Maybe he will if Santa is in a flight uniform and flying a marine attack helicopter." More laughter.

"No, not Santa, but I want to invite the commanders of the Maryland, North Carolina, South Carolina, Pennsylvania and West Virginia National Guard to join us. I know them all, served with them and they all are extremely patriotic Americans. I think that all of them just like we were, and probably everyone across the country is, just waiting for a leader." At that he looked over at Sean, "Thanks for being that leader, Sean." Up until that moment, Sean really had not thought of himself as the leader. All of a sudden he felt crushed with responsibility.

"All in favor" he said. Again, everyone voted in favor.

It was Tony Lee who spoke next. "Yeah, well, I want to talk to the number three man in the ATF, Joe Garcia. He is a career man and not one of Obama's political appointees. He is really still ticked about the "Fast and Furious" gun scheme. When we are playing golf he is always telling myself and Joe about how demoralized the ATF is. I can think of several ways he could help. What do you think Joe? I think we both should talk to him again, get a more solid feel about whether or not he is willing to act."

"Ok by me" said Tony. "This Saturday when we play golf together, we'll talk to him."

The vote on Garcia was postponed until after they had a chance to talk with him.

"Anyone else?" asked Sean, "Not in particular," said Brian, "but in general, has anyone given any thought to who will be the interim president, vice president, secretary of defense etc.?"

"Yes" said Sean "I have but, before I say anything I would like each of us to read the biographies and public positions of the leading U.S. Senators and Congressman. I think our president and vice president come from there. As far as Secretary of Defense, if General Kelly is with us, I think he should be the next one, at least until the president appoints a new one. Another very important position we have to fill immediately is the Secretary of the Treasury After we do this there will be a run on the banks, I mean by countries, and we do not want the financial integrity of the U.S. damaged any further than what the Kenyan has already done. I also want to stop the wire transfers of cash out of this country by individuals such as Soros, Bloomberg, and Turner. We will tax their billions, might help to pay for some of the damage they have caused.

"After all, they believe in redistribution of income, right? So we will assist them in redistributing their money, see how they like that. Plus, Obama said no one needs more than three million dollars."

"I figure any money made in this country by illegal aliens is our money. They made it illegally and we will seize it just like we would seize the cash from any crime. Well, maybe not seize it all, but we would charge them an exit tax. When it comes to the illegals we are not going to play around with them. Just as Presidents Eisenhower, Hoover and Truman did, illegals will be ordered out of the country immediately. You know, several times during the American Civil war the U.S. Supreme court informed President Lincoln that some of the wartime measures he was implementing were unconstitutional. Lincoln replied that what might be unconstitutional in time of peace becomes legal in time of war, in order to save the country. Lincoln also asked the court if they had an army to enforce their decrees!"

There were no more names put forward for now, there was talk about the latest attacks on police in the country and in Europe. After a couple of drinks Anthony stated, "You know, there will have to be many pre-emptive arrests. Has anyone thought about who we arrest, who makes the arrest, where they are held–"

"Good point" Ed interjected. "Lets think that over for the next meeting. But I believe the officers from the Waynesboro, VA police department should be allowed to arrest Holder. Don't forget that on Feb.1st, 2014, Officer Kevin Quick of that department was kidnapped by four black males while on duty. They took him to several ATM machines where they forced him to withdraw his money, then they executed him. They were arrested within several days and Holder jumps right in and orders no death penalty for the four. Of course the maggots of the media don't report on the murder. Yes, I think Waynesboro will like the honor of arresting Holder." They all gave a sinister laugh at that. Holder, after all, has a special place in the hearts and minds of every police officer in the country.

"If that's all, food's ready" announced Audrey. They all put their thoughts on the back burner for the moment.

While they were eating, Sean mentioned that there were only nine months until police week in DC, and of bringing as many members of their departments as possible down with them.

After a few drinks, Brandon blurted out, "You know we should have a list of grievances against Obama and congress, to explain to the American people why we are doing this."

"I don't think that the average working American needs to be convinced. Look at the taxes, local, state and Federal, not to mention the additional taxes from Obamacare. Nowadays both husband and wife have to work full time to support a family, mainly due to taxes. I think the average working American has to work almost six months just to pay taxes."

"I thought the medieval serfs had it bad when they had to work one day a week on their masters land. But our masters in congress, like Rangel, don't even pay taxes; they are too busy hiding $50,000 in cash in their freezers. Don't forget the Reverend Al Sharpton, I think he owes around four million in back taxes, what a poor man of the cloth, makes you sick!"

"What about Jesse Jackson, anyone read the book 'Shakedown' about him?"

"How about the attack by the government on religion in the country? Christians anyway, not Muslims of course. They're protected, they can pray in public or do anything else they want, like praying in Arabic on the White House lawn with Obama laughing about it. I remember when I was a kid shows such as *Romper room*, *Leave it to Beaver*, and *Andy Griffith* all talked about GOD –and even prayed on the shows– and it was normal then. People seem to forget that America was founded as a Christian nation, where quotes from the Bible were engraved on our monuments and schools. The Ten Commandments were displayed in court houses and in the Supreme Court. The National Anthem used to play on television everyday at 6AM. Truth, honesty, hard work, patriotism –not to mention courage– were all admirable qualities that made America great, made us exceptional. Now, we have let our elected rulers turn their backs on GOD and, even worse, won't let us talk publicly about HIM. Now our veterans, our real patriots, are called possible terrorists by Obama and his gang. Well to them they are; our domestic traitors know full well they have to fear armed patriotic Americans.

"That's why Obama proposed an internal military as strong as our regular military: to defend the U.S. internally. Defend from who? No other president ever said such a thing. No other president has stockpiled so many rounds of ammunition, weapons, streetsweeper armored cars inside of the country, under Homeland Security and FEMA instead of the military. Why? Who is he trying to arm? His Muslim friends, illegal aliens, welfare parasites?"

"Hey, did you see overnight Obama freed five more terrorists from Guantanamo Bay?"

"Yeah, that's great. He let's them go free so that they can kill more Americans."

"Yeah and to top it off, the soldier he was trading them for was a deserter; eight brave men died trying to save him when they thought he was captured."

Sean sat back, listening and letting them vent. But what they were saying was the exact same things that he had heard Americans from Boston and other parts of the country saying for a long time now. America had gone horribly wrong. Things were totally upside down. The ship of state had capsized, and it was up to them to set her floating right side up again

"Ok guys, let's calm down a little, a few more drinks and we will end up attacking them tonight. Might work though. When myself and my family went to France a couple of years ago we took a trip to the Palace of Versailles. I remember learning there that at the beginning of the French revolution the farmers, armed just with pitchforks and shovels, went up to the palace. They told the soldiers on guard there to either shoot them or get out of the way. The soldiers had no loyalty to such a corrupt king and were not about to fire on their own people. The soldiers just melted away and the people went in, caught King Louis and Queen Marie Antoinette, hung them and many of the other society members, looted the place, and began to clean up their government."

"In Cuba, Castro and only about 50 in his merry band of commies marched into Havana and took control."

"The same thing happened to the Russian Czar. He and his family were captured when his soldiers failed to protect him. Then later the commies killed him, his wife and children. Lenin had no mercy and believe it, Obama will have no mercy on us!

So history repeats itself. What we are going to do is very possible. "

"So, you think with about 10,000 cops, the marines, national guard we might get it done?"

"We will have more than that. Let's think about our allies, the NRA, what are there, six, seven million armed freedom loving Americans? That's it right there; the NRA could do this on their own. And we will have how many other gun owners standing up with us? Veteran's groups. Remember the WWII vets, when Obama tried to stop them from visiting the WWII Memorial in DC? They tore down the barricades and went to the memorial. The guys who took Iwo Jima, stormed ashore on Omaha beach on D-Day, stopped the German SS at the Battle of the Bulge. The men who, after Pearl Harbor, sailed out and destroyed the Japanese navy, the men of the "Mighty Eighth Air Force", they still know what it is like to have courage, to be a man in America."

"And woman!" yelled Sara and Audrey at the same time. "Sorry ladies, you are absolutely correct. Without women building our ships, tanks, planes, guns, and manufacturing ammunition, we could not have won WWII. Without women handing their husbands, sons and brothers their rifles and telling them to stop the British army there would never have been a Lexington Green, or shot heard around the world at the Concord bridge. Sometimes I think that women, especially today, have more courage than men."

"I think my favorite story of female bravery is Dolly Madison, refusing to leave the White House, even with the British troops marching towards her, until she had saved the portrait of George Washington during the War of 1812".

"You know we keep talking about cops, but don't forget the fireman. Many vets there. And construction workers and postal employees –now they're a scary group with lots of vets."

"Our Vietnam vets, they were treated awful by the country when they came home, but I bet you they will answer the call. Vets from the Gulf wars, they know first hand what they are fighting for, they have seen the Muslim terrorist up close and personal. Our country's active military have a morale rate of about 17%. They live with what Obama and these leftist pukes, these domestic traitors, have done to them and our country. I really think that the 99% of them that can come, will come.

Then we have the average American citizen, hard working, law abiding, GOD fearing. They are seeing the country fall apart. They know what is going on, just listen to any talk show, but they feel alone, power-less, leaderless.

"I know who will come to our side. But I do not underestimate Obama and what tricks he might have up his sleeve. I feel it deep in my bones he will arm the illegals if he can. He probably has a communica-tion system in place to contact all of the radical Muslims, both U.S. citizens and the ones he is letting flow into the country daily. No we have a fight on our hands. But as the saying goes, freedom isn't free, better to die a free man with a rifle in your hands than a slave with a chain around your neck."

"We are risking it all, but that is what the Founding Fathers did when they pledged their lives, fortunes and to them most importantly their sacred honor to establish this country. Don't forget the men and women who risked it all on Lexington Green and at the Concord bridge for our freedom. Or Nathan Hale, who, when he was about to be hanged by the British, stated: 'I regret that I have but one life to give for my country.' That history, our history, is not even taught in our schools anymore. Let alone civics. God forbid children grow into responsible citizens who hold their elected responsible for their actions and votes in congress. Nope, can't have that."

"We could go on and on about the sacrifices made by Americans from the beginning of our country until now, but let's talk about our potential opposition. One, I think we will have some problems with the Department of Homeland Security and FEMA. But not all of them mind you, certainly not Customs and Border Inspection. They are totally demor-alized, having had to watch and take care of all the illegals flooding over our Southern Border since Obama announced his Amnesty plans. A plan which he did not have the courage to sign.

The DEA and ATF will probably be with us. The FBI... I think that with all the political correctness, the Muslim group CAIR going through their offices with Obama's permission, I think the vast majority of them will be with us."

"Yeah CAIR, you know that they were actually designated a terrorist organization by the United Arab Emirates?"

"Remember how they tried to take 'assault weapons', especially the AR15, away from American citizens? Only to have Janet Napolitano wanting to buy an AR15 for every government employee as 'personal defence weapons.' I wonder how many personal defense weapons they did buy and who has them?"

"What about the Secret Service? They are among the bravest people I have ever met, each and one of them ready to step in front of a bullet to save the life of the president or any other dignitary that they are assigned to protect. However, they too are demoralized. Look at all the missteps lately: allowing a felon with a gun on an elevator with Obama, letting people with forged invitations into White House events, and on and on. Remember the Clinton's called the Secret Service,"personally trained pigs" you don't think that the Obama's, with friends like Bill Ayers, treat the Secret Service any better, do you? Also there are armed marines stationed the White House, a lot more of them than people think. When Commandant Kelly issues his orders and the marines arrive at the White House with us... well I don't think that the marines will fire on other marines."

As an aside Brian added, "I read on the Drudge report today that the terrorist group ISIS has starting executing people who feed birds."

"*What?*" said Ed. "You sure?"

"Yeah I couldn't make that up, they are totally whacked. And the media, liberals and Obama all want to cuddle them and bring their Sharia law here, unbelievable!"

"I have a great idea" said Audrey. "We deport all of the Hollywood fruitcakes, commie liberals,democrats, media, ACLU members, defense attorneys, college professors among others, to Iran. They can live under the Muslims, let the Muslims give them a Muslim version of a fair trial."

"Both they, and the Muslims would deserve each other. Imagine the Mullahs trying to teach the ACLU about Allah. The ACLU informs them that due to the mythical Constitutional Separation of Church and State they cannot talk about Allah and besides, there is no GOD. The Muslims will be busy cutting off heads for the next hundred years! Yeah, I would like to see Hillary and the other one, the Indian girl from MA, you know Warren, yeah, imagine them having to wear veils, walk five steps behind their husbands, get slapped if they speak without permission? I kind of like the thought of that, but would that be cruel and unusual punishment to send Hillary and Warren to Iran. Are the Iranians that bad?" Lot's of laughter from everyone .

It was getting late and they all had to fly home in the morning. Last thing Ed said, "At 23:00 hours tomorrow night, August 22nd, I will send you all a "test, test," message on your phones; let me know if you do not get the message. At 23:00 hours on the 23rd I will send you the low band frequency number that we will communicate on. Again, let me know if you do not receive it. Oh that is 23:00 EST. Since DC is in the EST zone, let's use that time as main time format."

Sheriff Al then spoke up. "I don't know about all of you but I really think that we have to tell our spouses about this. I have been married to my wife for 31 years, I can't keep this a secret from her any longer. What do you all think? Besides, I can think of a hundred ways that she can help in the background. And if we fail, and retribution comes, do you think anyone would ever believe that our spouses knew nothing of this? They will be punished the same as we will be".

There were several minutes of silence. Everybody knew what Al said was true, they were all just thinking about how to tell their spouses and what the reaction would be. All except Brandon... he sat there remembering his wife. Jess was the best friend he ever had and he knew she would be all for this. Hoping no one noticed, he quickly wiped a few tears from his eyes.

"Alright, I guess you are right, Al. But if any of our spouses flip out, threaten to inform on us, can't be reasoned with, you have to tell me right away. At that point your active participation is over. However, you are still sworn to this cause. Once in never out, remember. We each know our spouses, and we each have to decide how and when we tell them."

They finished their drinks, said goodnight and made their way back to their hotels.

Saturday August 22nd.

At precisely 23:00 hours EST, all members received a "test test," message on their phones. In addition to the text being recorded by computers of the NSA, it was also recorded by the spy satellites of The People's Defense Agency and relayed to the computers in Beijing,China.

SUNDAY AUGUST 23RD.

At precisely 23:00 Ed and Brian sent out the low band radio frequency of 30.125 khg. Again, unknown to them the computers in the NSA
and Beijing recorded the transmissions.

TUESDAY, AUGUST 25, 06:00 HOURS

At 6AM, Joe Annino drove the two miles to the municipal golf course.

He noticed that Tony Lee and Joe Garcia's car's were already there. He still did not know who was the fourth member of their group today. He opened his trunk to get out his clubs. As he did so he happened to look through the space between the trunk and rear window and saw Garcia, Tony, and to his mild surprise Sheriff Al.

After quick hello's, they boarded two golf carts and headed out to the first hole. It was there that they decided the teams, Joe and Joe would play Tony and Al. The usual bet, losers bought lunch.

There was the usual friendly banter back and forth for the first few holes. On the third hole Joe Annino casually mentioned that there was another attack on two officers in Zanesville, OH last night. Both officers were shot when they stopped a car for speeding, a second vehicle pulled up, opened fire on the officer's and then the passengers in the first vehicle opened fire on the officer's. Both officer's, air force police veterans by the way, were able to return fire. They are both in critical condition but expected to live.

Garcia shook his head, "How can everything be unraveling so quickly?"

"Police Officers being hunted in the streets. Every time I hear of it, it reminds me of my guys, murdered by the Mexican cartels with the rifles given them by Obama and Holder!"

"You know the very fabric of our country is unraveling, I don't know what to do, the guy's I work with, my wife, people in the supermarket, everybody is asking, 'What's happening, what can we do?'"

Joe, Tony and Al just looked at each other and at Joe Garcia. Al was first to speak, "Joe, what if some people, people who think just like you do and are planning to do something, what if these people asked you for your help in trying to save our country and–"

Garcia quickly interrupted, "You're talking about a revolution, count me in!"

"Joe," Al said, "you know what you just said. You know a man in your position, like anyone else, is risking it all. You could be a huge asset, but once in never out, do you want to think about this?"

"Al, myself and some other friends have been thinking about this for a long time. I take it that this is why we got together today, to talk?"

"Well what do you want me to do?"

"Think about in general what you can do to help, who you can both trust and who can contribute, obviously people high up in their agencies are who we need the most, just be patient for a week or so and one of us will get back to you."

Garcia just smiled. "You mean I have to be ok'd. Fine with me, I will put it in writing and sign it just like John Hancock, if you want me to."

WEDNESDAY, AUGUST 26TH.

Sean woke up early, 5 AM. Actually. he did not really sleep. When he received the message from Ed and Brian last night, it was if a dream of his own creation was coming true. He had no regrets, but it was almost unreal. He looked down at Shannon, sleeping next to him, his wife and best friend of almost 30 years. What was he doing to her, taking a chance like this? Then he remembered his history, like when American soldiers and sailors were imprisoned on the prison ship JERSEY, during the revolutionary war. The conditions were barbaric, but none of the captured Americans betrayed the country and neither did any of their families, they sacrificed their lives and their sons lives for freedom, he could do no less. For he knew that if the liberals were not stopped and stopped soon, the last vestiges of freedom would soon disappear from America.

He decided that this morning was the time to tell Shannon everything. He got quickly out of bed and started the coffee, took out a couple of frozen bagels from the freezer and even took out the cream cheese to let it soften the way Shannon liked it.

When he went back into the bedroom he stayed on top of the covers and gave Shannon a big hug, he started playfully nibbling on her ear and whispering "wake up," she opened her right eye a little, looked at the alarm clock and gave him a not so playful whack on the side of the head, "are you crazy it is 5:20 in the morning." " Come on get up. I already started the coffee. Let's drive out to Castle Island, sit on a bench and watch the sunrise, I even have the bagels ready." " What's up?" she said. "Let me tell you over coffee," "This better be good, if it's another history lesson, I swear...".

Sean quickly poured the coffee, after all these years he knew exactly how to make it for her, one and a half sugar's, a third of the cup with low fat cream and the rest coffee. He smothered the bagels with cream cheese and when Shannon came down, they were out the door and sitting on a bench at Castle Island within 5 minutes, looking at the sun rise over the islands of Boston Harbor, the sun glinting off of the water, a freighter coming into the harbor and maybe a dozen small boats heading out for a day on the water. It was just so peaceful.

He was too quiet, Shannon knew something big was coming. Sean had been acting weird, even for him, for a good month now. "Ok, you have me here. It's beautiful, but the last time we were here this early was for Sunrise Mass at Easter. What's up my love?"

"Shannon, you know how I feel about this country. You tell me all the time I sound just like your father. And I know how much you love our country."

"What is it, Sean? No games, what are you up to?"

"Forgive me for not telling you sooner, but myself and some friends, actually I started it, are organizing, have been organizing a revolt. A second American revolution, led by the police to restore freedom, full freedom, the way the Founding Fathers intended it to be .." "Oh my GOD Sean," she dropped her coffee put her face into her hands and started crying, "How far along is this?"

"Pretty well along honey, the marines are even on board!"

"Why you, why us?"

As soon as she said, "Why us," Sean knew that Shannon would support him. "It is not just us, my love, there are millions who will be with us. Why me? Someone had to organize this."

He then went on to tell her everything from the beginning to now. "Well what do you think?" "You know we have always stood by each other, I am with you of course, but for GOD's sake Sean! Do we tell our kids?"

"No not yet, but soon enough. They will have to be on their guard for their personal safety, maybe we should all get to the gun club to brush up on our shooting." They sat in complete silence for awhile, Shannon afraid, proud and incredulous all at once. She listened and on the breeze she could hear mother singing her favorite Irish rebel song "The Bold Fenian Men."

AUGUST 26TH. 06:00 HOURS

General Kelly's car approached the main gate of Marine Base Parris Island, South Carolina. The Marine MP's had been told to expect him. At the gate they snapped to attention, saluted smartly and as required, asked the driver for identification. Kelly smiled to himself; the MP a kid of maybe 20 was obviously nervous. Not only did he have to ask the Commandant of the Corps for identification, but the base commander, Major General Paul McDonald Jr., and a marine honor guard were standing just feet away. Despite being nervous, the MP did everything required of him. "Well that is a good sign," Kelly thought, "Marines obeying orders." The car passed through the gate and the honor guard opened ranks for inspection. Kelly walked up and down the ranks, very pleased with what he saw, his marines, the thought still gave him goosebumps.

The band played the Marine Hymn, "First to fight for right and freedom, and to keep our honor clean." Well, they would possibly soon be fighting again for freedom, in a place none of them could imagine, but it would be in keeping with their honor and their oaths of allegiance to the Constitution!

After the inspection General McDonald escorted General Kelly around the base for an inspection. Again Kelly was very pleased with what he saw. After the inspection they went back to McDonald's secure command post, secure against both land and aerial attack and any attempt at electronic eavesdropping.

Wayne already knew the answer, but he asked anyway,"Paul how long have you been in the Corps for?", "I was lucky enough to enter Annapolis right after high school, September of 1987". "Tell me where you served, what action you saw and how has the Corps' changed, for the better or worse since you joined"? "Wayne what's up, we have known each other for what 29 years, what are you up to, you know my record as well as I do! Both Gulf war's, service in Iraq and Afghanistan. But, as far as how the Corps has changed, well we have gotten softer, I suppose all old timers in any military feel that way, but we have! Running in sneakers instead of boots, hiking with only 30 lbs of equipment instead 75 and on and on, why?" "What about the country Paul how has that changed?" A suspicion was beginning to grow in Paul's mind, but no it couldn't be, he could only hope, but could it be?

"The country that we grew up in is almost gone, the country our fathers grew up in is gone. I remember a story my father told me about when he came home from the Korean war, (Paul's father won the Navy Cross, the country's second highest decoration for bravery at the Chosin Reservoir). He took some time off to travel in the U.S. along with his dog, he fished, hunted," at that Paul pointed to an Remington bolt action .308 that his grandfather had given to his father and that was now Paul's. He would be passing it down to his oldest son, Paul the fourth soon. "All without any licences, permits, camping restrictions, try doing any of that now. I guess what I am saying is that there was a lot less government then and a lot more individual freedom. Today there is a lot more government and a lot less individual freedom. Come to think of it dad said he did not even have to have a dog license then."

"Paul, remember our oath of Allegiance, to defend the Constitution against all enemies, foreign and domestic?"

Paul no longer had any suspicions, not even a doubt, he knew it was a certainty, just say the word general he thought. "I do Sir, and I am ready to honor that oath, that is what you wanted to hear, correct? Give me three hours and I can move 6000 marines". Wayne held up his hand, " Stop Paul," "Let me fill you in." Over the next hour Wayne informed Paul of all he knew and most importantly the date, the second day of the Law Enforcement Memorial week in May 2016. "You say a police officer, a Deputy Superintendent from Boston is starting this, organizing it?"

"Yup".

"Can't wait to meet him."

"You will soon enough, for now we have plans to make. Paul, this is going to go just like any other military action we have ever taken, we need complete secrecy. Nothing, I mean nothing, in writing for now, think of what officers you want here with you, anyone we have any doubts about we will transfer overseas. I am also going to transfer the base Commander's of Camp Lejeune, Quantico and Cherry Point, they are all Obama's boys. And I want to make sure that someone we really trust is assigned to command the Marine detachment at the White House and the Washington Navy Yard."

"Yes Sir, but can I suggest that we not arrest Obama's boys? We bring them to say your office the day before things start, arrest them and hold them until this is over. If we transfer them they will call Obama, have their transfers cancelled and people might start asking questions."

"OK,we can do that, get going on your logistical needs, call me to play golf when your plans are finalized, I have some other officer's to talk to, Carry on General."

Aye aye Sir, with pleasure."

THURSDAY, AUGUST 27TH 05:00

Sara was up early; she had to be. She had coast guard reserve's today. Just a training class, but, she thought, it should be very interesting. The class was being taught by a regular Navy Lt. JG, and was on the subject of the alliance of the drug cartels, Mexican army, Al Qaeda and their use of American ports to smuggle drugs into the country. "Just up my alley," Sara thought. "Might help me as a cop." She left a note for her husband, Daniel, reminding him of where the kids had to be today, picked up her coffee and headed to the door, just before opening the door she gave herself one last look in the mirror, liked what she saw and walked out.

She stopped at the entrance to the San Diego naval base, showed her Coast Guard ID to the Marine MP and drove over to the lecture hall. She spotted several friends that were up at the brunch table, walked up and joined them in getting breakfast. She caught a few words of the conversation and chuckled to herself, same old same old, "Obama has cut the military budget and especially the guard budget so bad we could not stop a row boat full of kids from landing anywhere in the country, let alone the cartels using submarines to transport drugs".

"Morning Thomas, Morning Andrew". Both of them beamed. "Morning Sara, come sit next to me" said Andrew. "As usual Tom did not shower today." Boys will be boys she thought.

A polite silence filled the hall as Lt. JG Susan Nguyen,U.S.N. walked up to the microphone.

"Good Morning, my name is LT. Nguyen. I am honored to be speaking to you today about the dangers our nation is facing from the almost unchecked smuggling of drugs into our country. America is under attack! The attack is just as real, and maybe even more fatal, than an attack from any foreign military. Those of you who are recruiters, how many potential enlistees do you have to turn away because of drug problems? Masters at arms, how many case's of drugs do you come across on our bases or ships? Each case, each individual, we lose to drugs is a victory for our enemies. I know that some of the reservist that we have here today are police officers in their civilian career; how many times have you personally seen the effects of illegal drugs on our youth? The strain on our hospitals from treating overdoses, the crime driven by drugs, our courts are overloaded by drug cases, in many neighborhoods our kids cannot walk to school without being offered drugs. Our streets are like a war zone, in some cities they *are* war zones, and who benefits from this? Well our foreign enemies of course, but also our domestic enemies".

At those words Sara immediately thought, another member of our group? The talk went on for another two hours; the end brought thunderous round of applause.

While others in the hall were saying their goodbyes and filing out Sara walked up to Lt. Nguyen, gave a fairly formal salute, which Lt. Nguyen returned. Sara then introduced herself, shook hands and stated, "Your talk was great. Not only very informative, but strongly patriotic, as it should be from a member of the military."

"Well I am very patriotic, my father raised me that way. I am a first generation American of Vietnamese descent. My father was only 15 when he served in the South Vietnamese Army, he was lucky to escape Vietnam and get a green card. He worked 16 hours a day, seven days a week to both learn English and start his own floor sanding business. He always told us that we were very lucky to become Americans, to have all of the opportunities that democracy and hard work bring. He would not even speak Vietnamese until he had completely mastered English. Listen to me going on and on! But as you heard from my presentation, I am afraid that our country is in terrible danger. Mainly from within, but once we are weak enough our enemies will not hesitate to attack."

On an impulse Sara asked, "Want to take direct action to help save the country?" Susan thought for only a few seconds before nodding yes. "Tell me how."

"Let's exchange phone numbers, I will call you soon."

"Ok, I will wait to hear from you."

On the drive home Sara wondered if she had been reckless in talking with Susan. "No," she thought, her cops instinct taking over, "she is going to fit in just fine."

SUNDAY, AUGUST 30TH 09:00 HOURS

For many people labor day weekend was a time to relax, drink beer and hang out with friends and family. For Wayne Kelly, it was one less day, weekend, month that he had to get the Marines ready for what was coming. As his private Marine plane approached the runway at Marine base Pendleton CA, he glanced out the windows; it was truly amazing. Tanks were maneuvering and firing over an obstacle course, attack jets screamed low on a strafing run, marines on a dozen ranges were firing artillery and machine guns. The power, his power to use, to wield in the defense of the country, was truly awesome. Not to mention the men themselves.

General Kelly had ordered that he be greeted only by the base commander, who was also an old friend, Lt. General Patrick Carpenter; and several of his staff officers. Carpenter figured that this was not a social call. After salutes and hello's, they got into the waiting cars and drove to the secure HQ.

General Kelly then informed the staff officers that he would like to speak with General Carpenter alone— the officers could go over to the officers club to relax, but be back in two hours. They knew two hours meant exactly two hours.

Pat poured drinks for both of them. "So what's up Wayne?"

"Well Pat, remember last year when you wanted to move your marines to seal off our southern border? Still want to do it, as a part of something much bigger?"

Pat almost crushed his glass in his hand, "Yes sir, as soon as you order it!"

"You did draw up plans to do just that didn't you, on your own I mean?"

Laughing, Pat nodded yes.

"Oh, wanted you to know that Paul McDonald is all in on this." At that he gave a very thorough military style briefing to Patrick.

"Wow, we really gonna do this?"

"Yes but as I said for now your job will be to seal the Mexican border, using whatever force is needed. You are to cooperate with local law enforcement, local national guard units, and if needed plan on having an army of armed civilians coming to help. By the way, how do you get along with Admiral Cleburne? We will need the help of the U.S. Navy, Army and Air Force. As of now I see the role of the Navy and Air Force to be keeping the Russians and Chinese at a distance. Never can tell what will happen, though."

"I really do not expect any appreciable resistance, I just don't see anyone standing up for Obama. On the other hand Sean Dominguez has identified some possible resistance from Muslims and any sleeper cells that are in the country. Whatever comes we are going to crush it hard and fast; no PC rules of engagement, no quarter, we are going to do this and do it right!"

"Yes sir!"

"Are we going to tell our staffs? I trust them all but it is up to you, now or later they will have to know."

"Yeah, you're right, I trust my guys too. If we don't tell them, it is as if we don"t trust them, and we do need their full help."

In exactly two hours there was a knock on the office door. The staff officer's entered. General Carpenter invited them to sit, offered drinks and then said, "Listen up." It was a trust that would not be misplaced, SEMPER FIDELIS!

At approximately 14:00 hours, Sara sent the first low band group message:

"Have found another member for our group, a reg. Navy LT. Jg. I have not told her anything specific but she really seems like one of us. Can I talk with her further? Please advise."

This message was followed up by AL. "Our ATF friend is in, can we proceed with a full briefing?" The NSA and Peoples Defense agency satellites duly recorded the messages and stored them in their database. Several hours later, the response from Sean was brief: "Proceed if you are sure."

About 6 pm Al phoned his friends Joe Garcia, Tony and Joe, and invited them and the wives to the house for a cookout on Sunday. They all quickly accepted.

On the flight back from Pendleton, General Kelly and his staff officers were having the exact conversation that General Carpenter and his officers were having. Like any military operation they identified the target, which in this case was the Congress, the President, VP and Cabinet of the United States.

"Sir, as far as the Congress goes, on any given day at least half of them are not in their offices. Between playing golf, going on junkets, meeting their lovers and who knows what else, how will we round them up? And the ones that are there will bolt into the escape tunnels, like the rats they are —sorry sir— and head for their secure bunkers."

"Deputy Superintendent Dominguez has already thought of that, and I must say his idea is brilliant, appeals right to all of those megalomaniacs, lets their own ego be the undoing of them. Dominguez plans to invite both houses of Congress to have their pictures taken with hundreds of police officers, from around the country, you know flags flying on the Capitol steps, and when they are assembled on the stairs the police will arrest most of the Democratic and Rino members. They will then be immediately sent to Sheriff Joshua's desert holding facility. Whoever is chosen as our next President and Vice President will be taken to the White House; hopefully after everything is explained to them they will take up the Office of President and Vice President. The Secret Service will be on board with us; if not the Marines at the White House will disarm them and, along with a battalion of Marines flown up on copters, will establish a defensive perimeter around the White House for several blocks. The police will also be involved in securing the perimeter. National guard units from the surrounding states will be on hand to assist local police in the event that they are needed and will be stationed at bridges, key intersections.

Counter espionage specialist from the military, NSA, FBI and CIA are going to go through all of the files, computers, phones and other electronics of members of congress and, of course, Obama's Czars. We will see what they were up to and we will tell all to the American people. I am especially curious as to the activities of any Muslim members of Obama's staff and the White House visitor logs."

"I want to emphasize that this is not a military coup. We will have a new President, VP and Cabinet and we will take our orders from the new President. As far as possible we, the military, will remain in the background."

"Won't that be kind of hard to do general with Marine helicopters landing on the White House Lawn, our tanks on the streets and jets overhead?"

"I said as far as possible. Oh, and believe me, I will insist that the new President give a complete and total pardon to all military, police and civilians involved in this."

At that they all grew quiet, "We need a pardon for saving the country?"

"Sir, what about Obama and his family?"

"The new President can determine his fate. There was talk of seizing Obama's millions, along with the fortunes of other liberals. As far as his wife, I heard she and Obama both lost their licenses to practice law; if not, she can go back to being a lawyer and supporting her family. No way is he going to get a pension though."

"Seizing his millions is fair, reimburse the taxpayers for all of those vacations".

"There will have to be special attention paid to locations such as the UN. My thoughts, and mind you only my thoughts is that for their own safety, is that all members of the UN are sent back to their own countries. That will disrupt the intelligence gathering of many nations and give us both a chance to go over their computer files, and shut the U.N. down for good, at least in this country.

TUESDAY, SEPTEMBER 1ST 14:00 HOURS, AT AL'S HOUSE

Joe Garcia and his wife Kay arrived first. Al introduced them to his wife, Carol Ann and went to get drinks and appetizers .

"Would you excuse me?" Carol Ann said to the Garcia's, "if I don't help him he will either drop our drinks or forget the appetizers. Honestly after 27 years together I still don't have him trained!"

"No problem, just yell if you need a hand, in the meantime I want to look at your garden."

"Do you have a garden at home?"

"Oh yes, but I cannot get my azaleas to grow anywhere near as nice as yours".

While they were talking Joe Annino, his wife Margaret, and Tony and Nancy Lee arrived.

"Hello everyone happy labor day weekend! Isn't it great to be old and have kids out doing who knows what?"

"Yeah, well it's the who knows what that scares me."

Kay noticed that Joe Annino called all the guys together to a corner of the yard. She also noticed nervous looks on the faces of the girls.

"It is a pleasure to meet you, Joe."

"The pleasure is mine" said Joe. Right away they knew that they would be good friends. "So Joe, Tony and Al tell me you want to help save the country, I mean by taking direct action."

Joe looked very serious and looking them in the eye replied, "If not us, who?" That was good enough for them.

"So, did you guys tell your wives?"

They both answered, "yes." Turning to Garcia, "Joe, how will your wife take this?"

"We have to fill you in, would you like me to fill your wife in at the same time?"

"Discretion is the better part of valor." They all laughed.

"You sure that she will go for this, at least not say anything?"

"Yes I am sure, did you know that both of our son's are on active duty in the navy? Kay, talk about a mother bear, as far as she is concerned trees should be painted red, white and blue and Obama....."

They walked over to where the girls were sitting and after some small talk, Joe Annino started the conversation. "Joe and Kay, welcome aboard. Kay, in Joe's defense he has had only one brief conversation about this."

"About what?"

Joe looked her right in the eye and said, "Well darling, it is about saving our country from destruction, the same destruction me and you have talked about a thousand times. Only these people and a lot of others, me and you included I hope, are going to do something about it. We are going to have a revolution with the goal of restoring our country to the Republic, which our Founding Fathers intended. Did you guys know that when Benjamin Franklin was leaving Independence hall in Philadelphia a woman asked him, 'What kind of government have you given us?' He replied, 'A Republic, if you can keep it.'"

"Over the years, especially since the 1960's, the American people have let down their guard. We have let a small number of domestic traitors come very close to ruining the Republic and the American dream. Now, we are going to help these people and a lot others save and restore our Republic. Joe here, and I guess Al and Tony, will tell us how." Kay was dumbfounded, she just looked from face to face . Carol Ann, Margaret and Nancy just looked at each other and then at Kay.

"It's alright Kay, we all felt the same way, but we are all for it now . We are going to stand with our men and stand up for our country."

"I am in too, that was just quite a bit to digest, though. I guess it will have to sink in over a couple of days."

Everyone smiled, they were getting stronger person by person . "Ok and a reminder to everyone, this is an absolute secret, we do not talk about this with anyone. We will maybe tell our kids the day before this happens, but none of us will know all of the plans. It will be on a need to know basis. So here goes, this is what we are going to do and why we do it."

Joe talked for the better part of an hour; no one interrupted or disagreed with what he said. When he had finished he asked, "Any questions?"

Al spoke up. "Can I add something?"

"Of course."

"One subject that you did not bring up is race relations and the damage that liberal Democrats have done to the American people by dividing us along racial lines. As both a sheriff and a reverend I have seen the destruction of the Black family caused by the welfare state. Teenage girls having multiple children out of wedlock with multiple fathers. No fathers in the home to help raise the children as GOD intended. The use of racial quotas for everything, basically telling Blacks that they are not as intelligent as Whites, Asians, Hispanics. Blaming every failure of Blacks on the monster of racism— a monster that, by the way, was killed years ago in this country when the civil rights battle was won. Now, egged on by racial hucksters like Jackson, Sharpton, Holder and yes, Obama and a boatload of others, Blacks actually believe that all their problems are caused by racism. That's why we are seeing a rise in racial hatred on the part of blacks. Look at the knockout game, where Blacks cowardly attack White people, usually females or defenseless males, film it, and without fear of the police put it on Youtube. Did you know that under Holder the U.S. Dept. of Justice has not prosecuted one, not one, Black for a civil rights violation against a White person? Not one!"

"Now please calm down honey, remember your blood pressure." Turning to the others, Carol Ann continued, "Sometimes I get nervous when I am watching him and listening to his sermons, that vein on the right side of his temple starts bulging out about six inches."

They all looked at the bulging vein and laughed.

"I just watched a youtube video by a man named Bill Whittle titled something like, 'Republicans, Democrats and racism,' it was a real eye opener."

After a couple of minutes Joe again excused himself and the other guys and went inside to talk.

"Well guys, let's start with the FBI. I know a few agents and Ed Larkin has some contacts there, do you guys know anyone there?"

Tony spoke up. "Yes I do, as you know I am my department's liaison officer with the FBI and ATF. Most of the people I know are supervisors, although I do know some field agents. The FBI is as demoralized and as screwed up by political correctness as is the rest of law enforcement. I would not feel real comfortable, at least not right now, in approaching anyone there and trying to recruit them. With a few exceptions they are real quiet about what they are thinking."

"Ok Joe, I work more in the streets and on interstate investigations with a lot of FBI agents, most of them, the guys who get their hands dirty, they are like us. I can think of several in particular who might be with us."

"Great you guys work on the FBI, I will ask Ed to feel out the agents he knows. Now let's rejoin the girls while they are still talking to us, after all this is a party".

"Almost forgot– Joe, here is a throw away phone, and a list of phone numbers. Do not program any names or numbers into it. Also here is the low band radio frequency that we will be using, you will need to pick up a low band radio transmitter and receiver. Remember no names, if you have to call someone on the list you will identify yourself by the number your name is listed under on the list, such as #4. Got it?"

"Yes I do."

The rest of the evening passed pleasantly enough, mainly with talk of the kids, sports and cooking, but no talk of revolution.

THURSDAY, SEPTEMBER 3RD. 08:00 HOURS

Colonel Annino contacted his chief of staff in the national guard, Major Johnson. "Chris, please call to arrange a social meeting with Colonels Palmer of the Maryland National Guard, Jackson from the PA guard, Patterson from North Carolina and Thompson from SC," and as an afterthought, "May from West Virginia. See if they can meet me here on the 9th into the 10th. Schedule the meeting for 10:00 hours. Oh, and let them each know that the others have been invited."

"Yes Sir, right away."

"Chris, I want you to attend also."

"Thank you Sir, I would be honored."

Back in Virginia, Major Annino made the same phone call to his friends on the PA, NC, WV, SC and MD State Police.

At about the same time Deputy Superintendent Dominguez was on the phone with Inspector Audrey Lapaglia of the NYPD.

"Hello Audrey this is Sean Dominguez from Boston PD. How are you, how's the family?"

"Great Sean, everyone is fine thank GOD, how is your family?"

"We are all doing well thanks, Audrey. I won't keep you long but I was wondering if you would like to get our SWAT teams together to do a little practicing. You know, have a friendly competition. Let the guys get to know each other."

"How about we expand it a little. We invite the Philly, Chicago, DC, Richmond and any other PD teams that you want to."

"Good idea Audrey, let me make some calls and get back to you within the week. If we are going to expand this any idea's of a location?"

"How about the DC area, it is getting cold up here all ready and all of the guys seem to like going to DC."

"I have a friend on the VA State Police, maybe we could use their range."

"Let me know, hope to see you soon'.

At approximately 8PM that night two messages went out and were recorded.

FRIDAY, SEPTEMBER 4, 09:00 HOURS

Sean was sitting at his desk on the fifth floor of Boston Police HQ, gazing down Tremont Street at the minaret of the mosque of the nation of Islam. An unsummoned memory of the Boston Marathon bombing came to him. He remembered the carnage and chaos that two, just two, Muslim terrorists caused. A city shut down, a nation on alert, of course Obama did not call the bombings and murders an act of terror. No, to Obama, bombings, the cutting off of heads, murders of police officers, were not acts of terror here or anywhere else in the world, they were "crimes" carried out by criminals. A sudden thought occurred to him how much damages could be caused by thousands or even hundreds of thousands of terrorists in the country? All carried out at once! on command.

09:20 hours

After calling Sara Mahoney to see if her SWAT team was interested in a shooting competition, Sean then placed another call to Major Annino of the VA State Police. The phone was answered by a secretary who put Sean straight through to the Major.

"Sean how's it going."

"Great Joe, all is well with the family, everyone is healthy, and yours?"

"Likewise on my end, so what is up my friend?"

"Well you know I think that my SWAT team is the best in the country. Audrey Lapaglia, thinks that her's is the best and so on with a few other depts. So, I was wondering if your guys would like to—"

"Yes definitely! And we are the best." They both laughed.

"Well there is obviously only one way to settle this."

"Exactly."

"Ok I would like to do it soon, within the next month anyway. The where is Audrey's idea, somewhere near DC."

"Oh, so I have to host this, ok, ok but I am not buying all the beer for that many guys. Hey, a good friend of mine is Wayne Kelly the Commandant of the Marine Corps, would it be ok with you if I call him and invite some of his guys to compete? Who knows, he might buy the beer."

"That would be great, I would love to meet him."

"OK, let me call him, see what he says, if not we can shoot on the VA National Guard ranges."

"That's great Joe, I will wait to hear from you and then call the other depts."

" Good talk to you soon".

Without wasting any time Joe immediately called his golf buddy, Wayne Kelly on his personal cell phone. Wayne didn't answer, so Joe left him a brief message about the SWAT competition and asked Wayne to give him a call back.

16:00 hours

Joe heard his phone ringing with the personal ring that he had pro-grammed in his phone for Wayne; Mickey Mouse, which was a favorite of the marines.

He answered with a jovial "Wayne how are you Sir?"

"I think your idea of a SWAT competition is great, but could we expand it? I would like to invite the air police, navy seals, green berets... you know, get a real competitive group together. Maybe invite the Joint Chiefs to watch."

"That would be something a lot bigger than even I imagined, could you host it?"

"If we limit it to say 20 men per team, I could provide housing in the barracks. Then the guys could really get to know each other.

"I like the way you think sir, how soon could you host us?"

"Saturday Oct. 10 and Sunday Oct 11, with the awards being given out on Monday the 12th, so the teams can arrive anytime Friday the 9th.

"That's great Wayne let me make the call's, get a firm number for you and get back to you in a few days. Oh and I have a friend of mine, a Deputy Superintendent from the Boston Police, Sean Patrick Dominguez coming down. I think you two will hit it right off."

"I look forward to meeting him and any other friends of yours."

"Thank you Sir, talk to you soon."

20:00 hours

The Officers Club, U.S. Naval Base San Diego.

Ensign Michael Wong was not happy. Earlier in the day he had gone on a first date to see the movie "American Sniper". While Ensign Wong loved the movie, his date thought that it was too violent, and that no American's should shoot women and children. Wong tried to explain that by arming a young boy and then picking up a bomb herself and attacking Americans the women made herself and, unfortunately, the young boy, enemy combatants. The sniper had no choice but to save the life of his fellow Americans!

His logic did not impress his date. The date ended early, and that was why he was drinking in the officer's club— not that he really minded being there with his buddies.

"Then you know what she said to me?"

"Mike you have told us ten times or so."

"Yeah well, no second date for her."

With a big smile on his face and a wink at the other guys, Lt. Paul Edwards could not resist saying, "Mike I should have warned you, she drives a small car,which has a 'make love not war' and an Obama, Biden bumper sticker on it.'" The other guys let out a roar and sat back to watch the show.

"Obama," screamed Wong, "do you know what he did to my graduating class at Annapolis? I'll tell you, he would not let us graduate wearing our dress swords, imagine that! Officer's without dress swords! U.S. Navy Officer's could not wear swords because our so called commander in chief was afraid that one of us might stab him, run him through. That says it all about Obama; he does not trust the military. But, at the West Point graduation the doggies, GOD Bless them, got it right . They refused to stand and clap for Obama!"

"That's enough Mike, we are all on active duty, quiet down."

"Yeah, fine."

Two very attractive young ladies were listening from a nearby table: Naval Officers LT. Jg. Susan Nguyen and her friend Ensign Amanda TI. They were both first generation Americans of Vietnamese descent, both had a strong love for America, and both detested Obama.

Susan gave Amanda a look and said "What say we go make some new friends, they're kind of cute!" Amanda nodded and to Susan's surprise and embarrassment yelled over to Wong's table, "Hey sailors, do you just drink with boys, or are girls welcome too?"

The response was instant; chairs fell over backwards, as did Ensign Wong. Susan and Amanda just looked at each other and began to laugh hysterically, and Susan actually had tears in her eyes while trying to catch her breath. "That wasn't funny, oh, it hurts, my poor stomach!" Susan exclaimed.

Looking like he wanted to sink into the floor Wong got up, pulled his chair back to his table and sat down. He could not even look at Susan and Amanda.

Paul and the other guys made it over to the table. Susan just looked over at Mike, she could not help but feel bad for him. "So girls, I'm Paul, and this is Frank, Tom, and Billy."

Susan leaned over to Amanda, "Can you handle the four of them?" Amanda just laughed, "The stories I could tell you!"

"Hussy, if you get into any trouble just give me a yell!"

"Will do, but don't hold your breath!"

Susan got up and walked over to Mike's table. "Do you mind if I sit down? Actually, first, have you really been drinking that much? Was that an accident or were you just trying to get my attention?"

"No, that was an accident, and if it got your attention it was certainly worth it. Please sit down, my name is Michael Wong". "Susan Nguyen, Mike, pleased to meet you, let me get us a drink." "Ok but I buy, you fly" "Deal." In the blink of an eye Susan was back with two rum and cokes, one with a lemon, one with a lime, "OK, Mike, this is a test, lemon or lime, you choose, but think of this, our future depends on your choice."

"You are messing with me, right?" Susan gave him a beautiful smile turned around and said "left hand or right hand?"

"Left." Laughing at the look on his face she said "Jerk!"

"I wanted the lemon" Mike started to stutter, but Susan could not do this to him any longer. "I'm just busting them on you, so tell me what is your M.O.S. and what else do you think of Obama?"

"My M.O.S.?"

"Yes, your Military Occupation Speciality."

"I command a hovercraft, you know we work closely with the seals and marines, dropping them and their equipment where and when they need to be and picking them up, all depending on the mission of course! We can provide suppressing fire if needed I also maintain and relay communications for them. In the event of casualties we provide basic field tirage, quick clot and Israeli tourniquets, bandages, plasma and lots of prayers."

"Wow, I really admire that."

"You do?"

"Yes, now tell me about your feelings for Obama,"

"You mean Barry, or whatever his real name is." Susan knew she had found a friend, a comrade . But, she thought to herself, still no Mr. Right.

SATURDAY, SEPTEMBER 5TH. 07:00 HOURS

General Wayne Kelly entered the Pentagon for his meeting with the other members of the Joint Chiefs of Staff. Both for tradition and added security, each branch of the service provided two armed, uniformed members of their police to stand outside of the door. Today it was two MP's from the air police, without breaking stride Wayne inspected them as he approached. "They look good," he thought to himself. "Nice creases, brass, boots, helmets shining, leather gear flawless... not bad." They snapped to attention and both gave a perfectly timed salute. The door was opened for him, and when he entered he noticed that the Chairman, Admiral Fletcher of the Navy, General Stewart of the Air Force and General Quinn of the Army were already there, picking at the breakfast buffet that had been set out for them.

After a friendly good morning and a casual salute, Wayne walked over to his seat, put down his briefcase and went to get some breakfast.

When the food was finished, the door was opened by the air police. Wayne could not help but notice that General Stewart was inspecting his men, looking for but not expecting to see any flaw in their uniforms. Just to annoy him, he was almost going to tell Stewart that his men looked good except for the scuff mark on the left boot, just by the foot arch, on one man. But instead he said, so all could hear, "Your air police look very sharp General Stewart."

"Thank you General Kelly."

The briefings began, there was not to much new going on in the world's military that would present a danger to the U.S.

There was, however, the continuing problem with the Chinese Navy. China had claimed a large area of the China sea as her own, and had begun building an island as a military base. DIA and CIA briefers agreed that China would probably place their long range missiles that were specifically designed to destroy U.S. Aircraft Carriers on the island.

It was President Clinton who, after receiving large campaign donations from China, transferred our super CRAY computers from under the authority of the Defense Dept, from where they could not be exported, to the authority of the Commerce Dept. where they could be. The computers were purchased by China; the Chinese military was then able to much more accurately program their missiles to target both American ships and cities.

For at least a decade now China had been pouring billions of dollars into their navy; their nuclear submarines were the most advanced in the world. While the Chinese navy was modernizing and expanding the U.S. Navy had atrophied. Carriers had not put to sea in months, not only were the carriers themselves rusting away but skills, once the best in the world of the men and women who served on the carriers were growing rusty.

Something had to go, there simply was not enough money in the three trillion dollar a year federal budget to support the welfare state and the military. Everyone knew it would be unfair and mean to cut the welfare budget, so the military just had to suffer.

Vietnam, South Korea, India, Taiwan and Japan had and were continuing to dispute China's claim to the area. There had been several incidents where shots had been fired, boats rammed, hoses used by the Chinese against those they termed trespassers.

As the meeting was breaking up General Kelly asked his fellow Joint Chiefs if they were up for a little friendly shooting competition that he was hosting at Quantico. They all readily agreed to send their 20 best men to compete in the various events. Wayne filled them all in on the logistics, admitting that the only area he thought the police teams might have an edge would be in house to house operations, but that would remain to be seen. "Lastly gentlemen, a bet between us."

"Ok Wayne what do you have in mind?"

"I have an empty shelf on my wall and I have always said to my staff how nice it would be to have all of your uniform hats on that shelf. So, whatever military team scores the most points wins for your offices the hats of the rest of us. Any takers?"

No one wanted to lose their hat to the others, but no one was about to back down.

"Ok I'm in."

"Me too"

"And me."

"Great we have a bet. Oh the winner must be there to claim the prize." They all nodded their assent and rushed off to assemble their teams.

09:00 hours

Sean and Shannon were on their third lap of speed walking around Castle Island. They decided to do one more full lap around Pleasure Bay Lagoon. They were coming up to the statue of Admiral Farragut. Sean started laughing to himself, another piece of American history right at his doorstep.

Admiral David Farragut was the first man to achieve the rank of Admiral in the U.S.Navy. During the Civil War, at the Union attack on Mobile Bay, Admiral Farragut lashed himself to the rigging of his ship and yelled "Damn the torpedos, full speed ahead!" A navel legend was born. Supposedly Admiral Farragut came from South Boston, VA. The people of South Boston VA commissioned a statue of the Admiral to be placed in VA. An understandable mistake was made, the statue, in error was delivered to the City of Boston, MA. The then Mayor of Boston, James Michael Curley, refused the request and demands of the people of VA to return the statue. He wrote them a nice thank you card, placed the statue by Marine Park, facing out towards Boston Harbor and Castle Island, and named the street Farragut Road. The Irish sense of humor.

Sean thought, "Just a small piece of American history, but how many people remembered that history, or ever learned it to begin with? Probably not someone from Kenya who came here VIA Indonesia." If even that was true.

Every Immigrant to America came here for a better life, some voluntarily, some, like many Irish, involuntarily. The Irish came here on the "coffin ships;" old condemned slave ships. The slaves had value, the Irish did not. They say that you could walk across the Atlantic on the corpses of the Irish. No, no immigrant group has had it easy, yet most, including Cubans, Jews, Vietnamese and on and on became successful through hard work. No whining, no excuses, all they asked for was a chance. But if you listened to some...

For the millionth time Sean asked himself, "What happened to America?"

"Sean, I did not want to tell you, it was supposed to be a surprise, but the kids, including Sean Jr. will all be home for your birthday next week."

Like himself and his father, Sean Jr.was on active duty with the U.S.Army. He was serving with one of America's elite units, Delta Force, at the rank of staff sergeant. He tried to call them as often as possible, but he was never able to tell them where he was. Sean understood this. from his own time in the army. Sean was very proud of his son, and all who served. "Freedom isn't free," he thought to himself.

12:00 hours

They were just coming in the door when the cell phone starting ringing. He noticed that it was Joe Annino calling, and his breathing quickened. "Joe, how are you?"

"Great, let me give you the dates for the SWAT competition. Wayne Kelly has kind of upped the antes; he's including the green berets and/ or delta force, navy seals, air police and, of course, marine snipers. He's also inviting the Joint Chief of Staffs. The event will be held at marine base Quantico, here are the dates, would you mind making the calls and get back to me with who is coming?"

19:00 hours

Sean was very satisfied. He thought to himself, I have to remember to get out a press release announcing the SWAT competition and get on the invitations for the congressional pictures in May.

MONDAY, SEPTEMBER 7. 11:00 HOURS

Sean and Shannon had slept late. As they were sitting down for coffee, Shannon turned on the morning news. The news was from Dearborn, MI. Apparently a Police Officer had shot several men, recent immigrants from the Middle East, who had attacked two employees of the City of Dearborn who had been changing the street signs from Arabic back to English. It seems that residents of the predominantly Middle Eastern neighborhood had, on their own, been switching the signs from English to Arabic and renaming the streets. The two employees had been stoned by a large crowd chanting in Arabic. When the police arrived, the crowd had turned on the police and began hurling rocks at the officers and EMT's attempting to render medical aid to the employees. The employees had been transported to a local hospital and were in critical condition. The "victims" of the police shooting were transported to a separate hospital for treatment. Large crowds were gathering at the scene, and President Obama had promised a full federal investigation of the incident.

Sean and Shannon just looked at each other. Finally Sean was the first to speak, "Well he is certainly doing everything he can to turn the police against him."

"This helps us though?"

"Yes, in a sad way, this helps us."

13:00 hours

Joe Annino was thrilled. He had been called back by all of his friends, and all of the people from both the state national guard and police that he had called earlier in the week. With only two exceptions, everybody could come to his little hunting cabin in the woods on Friday and stay for a long weekend till Tuesday. Joe had not even realized it, but that would be over 9/11. A good or bad omen?

Although easily accessible, his little cabin actually sat on 12 acres of secluded woodlands in the middle of nowhere. The main cabin had four bedrooms, and several years ago Joe and Margaret had actually added a second cabin.

Joe thought about sleeping arrangements. He was 95% sure all of them would be on board with the,"housecleaning," he laughed out loud at the phrase. Yes, he liked that, the "house cleaning." It made him think of the time that Ronald Reagan, while holding a broom, was giving a political speech. Ronnie held the broom on high and said "clean the house, clean the house!" The crowd loved it so much that the chant was not only repeated by the present crowd, but became a national chant for all Americans.

Anyway, maybe the best thing to do was to just let the guys figure out who they wanted to bunk with. Joe figured Saturday night or Sunday night would be the best time to introduce them, at least as a group, to what the "Sons and Daughters of Liberty" had planned. Joe thought of inviting Sean, but then decided it might be too obvious to anyone who may be watching them.

15:00 hours.

The situation in Dearborn had not gotten any better.

The news media, sensing an opportunity to create another Ferguson, or even better an LA Rodney King incident, were flocking to Dearborn. Their game plan was obvious from the beginning: the poor Middle Eastern immigrants, many of whom were "undocumented", were just trying to bring a little bit of home with them. They were just trying to keep in touch with their homeland, they were practically unarmed, they had no guns, could not the police have had a community meeting with them prior to invading their neighborhood? After all, the Middle Eastern immigrants were willing to tolerate American culture.

However, on the first day the media made a huge mistake. They broadcasted live the crowd chanting in Arabic, with raised fists, the faces contorted in hate, the burning American Flags. The plaid face masks and the ISIS flags in the background told the story. A story that Americans saw and were shocked by. This was not the West Bank, or Iran, this was here in America! What was happening to our country?

As promised by Obama, the FBI and a team of special prosecutors from Holder's Justice Dept. arrived in Dearborn to investigate, *the police*.

The media joyfully speculated on the possible criminal charges and penalties that the officers could face. The media then not only publicized the names, photos and addresss of the officers, but they also showed pictures of the officer's wives and children; after all, "the public had a right to know."

By 7pm that night, Muslims had begun sympathy protests in many cities across the country.

The terrorist organization,CAIR had issued a statement condemning the persecution of innocent Muslims by the U.S. and Israel.

There had been incidents of looting, of course, how could you protest injustice without looting?

All in all, not a bad days work for the media.

TUESDAY, SEPT.8 . 08:00 HOURS

Ed Larkin sat with his wife watching the morning news of Dearborn.

Ed was considered an expert in Muslim Terrorism. He lectured on the subject at the FBI Academy. However, lately with all the PC at the FBI, ordered by the White House with CAIR's approval, he had been getting fewer and fewer invitations to speak at the academy.

Ed had always began and ended his talks by saying, "Remember not all Muslims are terrorist, but all terrorists are Muslims".

Ed explained to his wife Haley that what they were watching happening in Dearborn was the exact same script employed by the PLO, Hamas, Al Qaeda and ISIS in the Middle East and around the world. But this was in America, obviously ISIS and company, by staging this type of demonstration, was feeling pretty strong. They were flexing their muscle and showing their brethren around the world how they were here in America, beginning their conquest of "the Great Satan."

"I wonder when they will start cutting off heads". "That is disgusting, that can't happen in this country". Ed just looked at her. "Are you kidding me what about the beheadings last year in Oklahoma by Muslim's, ever hear of 9/11 and the World Trade Towers? No one ever thought that would happen here. The Muslims felt so bad about 9/11 that they wanted to build mosques at the sight! Thank GOD for the construction workers in NY who put a quick stop to that".

Then Ed remembered something, and he groaned out loud.

"What?"

"Brian Olofoson, I have to work with him all day. Every time an incident involving the Muslims happens, which is almost everyday now, he flips out".

"Well darling don't forget that he was on the U.S.S. Cole when it was bombed by terrorists."

"Oh yeah, he was the communications specialist on duty when the bombing happened. He was lucky to escape with his life, only lost 60% of his hearing in his left ear.

"I can't understand why he never got married".

"Why would he, at 6'3', 230 lbs, built and looking like a Viking, he has no trouble meeting girls!"

She just glared at him. "Well, I have to go now." "Please be careful."

WEDNESDAY SEPTEMBER 9. 07:00 HOURS

Joe arrived at his cabin nice and early . He figured the other guys would be arriving anytime after 10 AM. He had a lot to do to make sure that everything would be perfect for his guest's. It was almost like he was conducting a psychological op. Well, in a way he was. First things first, turn on the water, hoist up the flags, bring in the groceries, get out the right patriotic movies,etc. He had also brought several documentaries on the American Revolution, along with some of their favorite war movies.

He was glad to see that the first to arrive was his chief of staff from the VA . National Guard, Chris Johnson. Chris was a known quantity, known to Joe since the second Gulf war. Chris was one of the first marines to enter Baghdad, literally on the first humvee.

"Chris".

"Yes sir".

"I told you before that when we are alone, or up here especially, it is Joe."

"Ok, thanks, sir".

"Is there anything that you would not do to protect, save the country?"

For a split second Chris thought that was a funny question, but the look on Joe's face let him know that there was nothing funny about it . Then a light went on in his head and he remembered who else was coming to the cabin for the weekend.

"Respectfully,sir, I think you already know the answer to that question, or else I would not be here".

"Yeah that's true enough. This is what we are going to do and how you can help".

Chris had always had the greatest respect for Colonel Annino, not only as a military man, State Police Major, but more than that, Joe was just an old fashioned gentleman. A true Patriot! Now, Chris had the feeling that he was standing in the presence of someone who was more than just a man. Any order that he received from Joe would be carried out.

Chris sat in awe as Joe talked. The sheer audacity of it, the moral and constitutional right of it and, most importantly, the simplicity, beauty of it, left him speechless. The only minor negative to it was that a yankee was the one who had put this into action and was, according to Joe, in command, which made that that. Oh well, aside from the yankee, it was perfect. With just the national guard units they could bring in an army of two divisions, plus air, with the marines already on board, well...

But, his job in the military was planning and logistics. He, and whoever else he was authorized to bring in, would assign roads, possible targets and on and on to the units from the VA guard that would participating in the operation. He reflected that this same function would be being duplicated by each state national guard staff, the marines, army, navy and air force, not to mention police units that were being brought in. Although the police were semi military in nature, Chris did appreciate the difference between them, and he hoped the public perception of having the police lead the "cleaning" as opposed to the military would be less threatening.

At about 11:00 hours the rest of the guests started to arrive. The hello's, firm handshakes, and back slaps were all completely genuine. These were men; they were not afraid to look into anyone else's eyes when speaking with forthrightness and sincerity. They trusted people with a firm handshake who would look them right back in the eye. Men who said what they meant and meant what they said. On the other hand, limp wristed political types who could not look you in the eye when talking to you, well...

Joe was a perfect host, inviting his guests to choose a bed based on their order of arrival. Sparking up the grill and getting each of his friends their first drink, which Joe believed was his duty as a host, everyone was to help themselves after that.

These men were all cut from the same cloth. Most of them had not only served in the military, but had seen combat, either in the military, police or both.

"So what's for lunch Joe?"

"We have venison, steaks, chili, and sausage, baked potato's, Boston baked beans, hot wheat rolls and salad for any vegans."

They all laughed at that. They were hunters, carnivores, warriors. Men who kept their country free and the streets of the country safe.

"Anyone up for doing any hunting or fishing, you're welcome to use my rifles and rods. Make yourselves right at home, relax."

"Joe, what are you up to? You're being too nice, not like you at all." This brought another round of laughter. "Nothing at all, just with the way the country is going, things are changing, it is good to be around my friends, like minded Americans, that's all".

"Here here, to like minded Americans". At that very second the wind blew through the trees and the American and POW flags snapped open .

Like everyone else, Joe looked up at the sound. Both the flag he loved and the flag that represented so many that had made the ultimate sacrifice for America. Joe was not superstitious, but he could not help shivering.

"Hey Joe, I myself haven't sat around a campfire in awhile, I feel like being lazy, any chance I could get a fire going?"

"Of course Pat, sitting around a fire with my friends, having a drink and smelling the venison cooking is not a bad way to spend an afternoon."

"Nope, what more could a boy ask for!" more laughter.

Someone mentioned the movie *Lone Survivor*, and they all just stopped to listen. "You know those kids would have all been ok if it were not for Obama's PC rules of engagement. Yeah, don't hurt the enemy, don't tie them up and for goodness sake don't kill them". "Yeah, then Obama will give you a medal for restraint, imagine that, giving soldiers a medal for not fighting". "What about the movie American Sniper, all the Hollywood maggots wondered if it was ok to make a movie about a killer, do you believe that the men who defend their freedom of speech, are called killers, anyone ever hear them call ISIS or Al Qaeda killers?"

"Obama is of course responsible for the decline in our military, but don't just blame him, what about our gutless wonders in the senate or congress? Mainly Democrats, but also some Republicans. They have a duty to the military and the country, why are they all just keeping quiet about what is going on?"

"One possible reason is that before any of us heard a word about the NSA reading our emails and listening to our phone calls, Obama had them all under surveillance. He found out all about their kickbacks, girl and boyfriends, secret bank accounts and who knows what else. Then he had someone, maybe Pelosi, show them all their files, tell them if they kept quiet and voted the right way they could continue to do what they want. You know, 'you have to vote for it before you can know what's in it.' If not Holder would reveal the files as part of an undercover investigation, and they would threaten them with indictment and jail. Maybe that's one reason congress has done nothing to stop Obama!"

Joe and Chris just looked at each other. Joe was not about to contradict anything that had been said. The conversation was going just fine without his help.

No one even attempted to refute the theory. It just sounded too plausible, too believable.

"Remember that video that was going around on the internet awhile ago? You know, the man dressed as John Adams, I think it was, talking about how dangerous Obama and the democrats are. At the end he said 'if you don't own a gun you better get one, because you are going to need it!' "Obama wanted to talk to him, and the guy refused to speak with Obama."

"Good for him, someone still has some guts". "Lots of the American people have guts, look at everyone who wears any type of uniform and serves his country, both in and out of the military. They are too busy trying to make a living to support themselves and their families, not to mention the parasites that won't work. But look at all the people with disabilities working in supermarkets to support themselves."

"What do you suggest, Walter?"

Walter just looked around at the faces of his friends, his brothers, really, all just waiting for him to answer. "Did anyone watch the mini-series, *Sons of Liberty*?"

Almost everyone nodded yes.

"Well that is what we need, a revolution".

"You know how many times a day I hear that on talk radio, in restaurants?"

"Yeah, just talk."

"People are smoking mad,and where there is smoke there is fire."

"Well, maybe we just need someone to light the match."

14:00 hours

The phone was answered on the third ring. "Sheriff Joshua Denver's office, Peggy speaking".

"Hi Peggy, this is Sheriff Al Thomas from DeKalb County GA, how are you today?"

"Just fine sir, the Sheriff is expecting your call, let me put you right through."

"Al, this is Joshua, how are you doing?"

"Just fine Josh, GOD is good to me."

"Yes HE has been good to me also". "Well that is because you have confessed HIM before man, JESUS will remember and confess you to the FATHER".

"Reverend, imagine if the ACLU heard us proclaiming GOD on tax-payer time".

"Me, I do it all the time, don't really care what the ACLU think, they are on one side and I am on the other and their is no middle ground."

"Amen to that. What can I do for you?"

"Well I was wondering if either I could come out to see you or if I could invite you here to talk a little politics and the role of the sheriff's association in supporting conservative candidates".

" I think I would enjoy that talk, but if you don't mind, would you come out here?"

"I was hoping you would say that, I would love to see some of Arizona, when is good for you?"

"How about next week, the 14th ok?"

18:00 hours

Sean was still in his office, watching the evening news. Of course the news was still focused on Dearborn, the night was falling and the media was fervently talking about the possible burning and looting. They were speculating on whether or not civil unrest would spread to other cities in the country, or maybe even the world. They could only hope.

Sean picked up his office phone and set up a conference call with Sara, Audrey, Brandon, Ed and Tony. Fifteen minutes they were all on the phone together.

"Hi guys, not to be rude, but this is official, have you all been watching the situation in Dearborn"? A chorus of "yes's" answered him.

"Things are pretty quiet in Boston, but I have personally noticed, from looking out my office window, that a large amount of men seem to be entering the mosque of the nation of Islam and no one seems to be coming out. Anything like that happening in your cities"?

Ed spoke first, "Yes. Well, not a mosque, but my Officers have reported large numbers of males entering the Rev. Wright's "church". They are not coming out either".

"Hmmmm".

"Any ideas why"?

Audrey spoke up. "I don't have any information right now Sean, but let me contact some of the precincts that have mosques in them and see if there is anything unusual going on, then I will get back to you".

"OK great, thanks". Sara was next, "Hi Sean, like Audrey I have not heard anything but will get back to you".

"Great "

Tony was the last to speak. "Sean, there is one thing unusual going on. Members of the new black panther party have been observed driving quickly up to the Homeland Security warehouse, you know where they keep the armored cars, guns, ammo and who knows what else. Almost like they are timing themselves on how quickly they can get there. Then they just drive away."

"Tony, will you please write that up as an official police communication and send it to all depts.? Include the FBI., and ATF."

"Will do Sean."

"What are you thinking, a dry run, training exercise?"

"Exactly."

"Call Ed and Audrey, speak to them personally. I know that Homeland security has warehouses in NY and Chicago. You know what, they also have one outside Atlanta. Call Sheriff AL, ask him to let us know how things look in Atlanta."

Sean was walking out the door when he remembered that he had to send a press release regarding the SWAT, military competition. He quickly wrote the release, emailed it to the depts. official press liaison and asked that it be sent out in the morning.

20:00 hours

Pat, well you could not just blame Pat, but mainly Pat had the flames going 15 feet in the air. Joe had had to beg the guys to stop putting wood on the fire. The whole forest was in danger of burning down! But, he had to admit, things were going great! Everyone was relaxed and discussing the current state of the country. It might already be too late, but if something was not done soon, it would be all over.

21:00 hours The White House

Mohammed Ali Kalaak was very pleased. As a special advisor to the president it was his job to maintain a liaison and of course that required a communication system with the faithful. Tonight's "call to prayer" had been particularly pleasing. As usual he met for prayers in the Oval Office. They had given thanks to Allah and to the prophet for showing his presence in Dearborn, then at the suggestion of the president he had partially tested the "call to the faithful" in six different cities; the results had been most satisfactory. None of the faithful had reported any problems at all, not one! How could there be problems when they were doing ALLAH's will? Yes, Obama will stay in the White House for the rest of his life!

San Diego; 18:10 hours, 21:10 hours EST

It had been a long and aggravating day, Sean's call was a welcome distraction. Sara had contacted all of the various districts and commands with the San Diego Police dept. She was both relieved and annoyed that no one had observed anything unusual involving mosques or Muslims. Oh, she needed to clear her head. On an impulse she called Susan Nguyen and made plans to meet her for a drink.

As usual every male head turned when Susan walked into the club, she had that effect on men, she was really quite stunning. She spotted Michael Wong and some of his friends at the bar, and though she wanted to go right to a corner table, thinking that might be rude she decided to walk over and say hello. While walking she heard Thomas say too loudly to Mike, "Here comes your girl friend." Susan decided to put Thomas in his place, so she walked up to Mike, gave him a kiss on the cheek and ignored the other guys, who were all speechless. "I missed you Mike where have you been?" Mike just mumbled something, Susan flashed a beautiful smile and said "sorry I have to meet my friend Sara, oh there she is now, I will call you later". Susan did not have Mike's phone number, but Thomas and the other guys did not know that!

Susan pointed to the corner table and Sara headed right over. "So what's causing you to have such a rough day, my friend?"

"Oh, nothing and everything, let me grab us drinks, what will you have?"

" Rum and coke with a lime please." She had no sooner said this when a waiter arrived with two rum and cokes, one with a lime and the other with a lemon, Susan laughed and gave Mike a thank you wave and that smile of her's.

"So, who is your friend, kind of cute, anything going on with him?"

"Noooo."

"Welllllll, he wants something to be going on." They both just laughed.

"Congratulations," Sara said, "you have been accepted by the group. I think we are lucky to have you, but before I tell you anything you have to understand, we are playing for keeps. Should I proceed?"

"This is about saving the country right, protecting the Constitution?"

"YES it is."

"Then yes I am all in."

"Ok, here goes, but let me tell you first I do not know every detail like any military operation we all only know what we need to know."

"Makes sense." Sara talked for the next 90 minutes with Susan occasionally asking questions. when she was finished Susan sat there stunned. "The marines are already in?" "Yes and while I do not know for sure, I expect that the other services are all in too." "Well what do you want me to do"? "For now think about how you can help, I think that maybe if we get get you transferred to Admiral Fletcher's staff, you would be in an important position to act as liaison, monitor communications, lots of things, and from what you tell me of your admirer Mike, well, guys like him and his friends could come in real handy."

"Will do, let's have one more drink and get home."

THURSDAY, SEPTEMBER 10. 08:00 HOURS

Joe and Chris were both in the kitchen starting coffee and

mixing up pancake batter when Pat walked into the room. "One look at him and it was obvious that he was suffering from a massive hangover.

"You don't look very good, want a coffee?"

"Please and a soft drink and beer, I am serious, I would have been ok if Piffer had not brought out the moonshine, what the heck is wrong with him, he is a State Police Major from SC, he should know better than to have that stuff." Both Joe and Chris just laughed, "well Pat you are a Colonel in the MD National Guard, you should know better than to go near that stuff." Pat just stared at them, what they said just did not make any sense, all he could mutter was "we do not have moonshine up north ."

The rest of the guys came stumbling in all seemed to be suffering hangovers to one degree or another. If the public could see them now!

They all just looked at each other grinning, all knowing that they had a great time last night but not really believing their own memories of the night.

Walter May vehemently denied stripping down and while holding a flaming branch, the size of a tree,giving the speech from the movie Gladiator "I am Marcus..."

Conor Evans called them all liars when they reminded him of his moonlight walk through the woods pretending to be bigfoot.

But everyone who could remember and even those who could not agreed,that the best one of the night was when Colonel Edward Jackson, soon to be General Jackson, from the PA National Guard, 28th mechanized Infantry division, swore that he was actually the reincarnation of the famous Confederate Cavalry General Stonewall Jackson, jumped on the back of Major Stephen McCain of the WV State Police and with McCain screaming "get him off of me" rode him around like a horse screaming "charge!"

At that everyone quickly forgot about Palmer and Evans' exploits, nicknamed Jackson, "Stonewall" and nicknamed McCain "Trigger" they all roared with laughter, all except, McCain for some reason he did not see the humor in this. He seriously wanted to know " why when he was kidnapped, forced into servitude as a horse " at that Palmer yelled, "You were not kidnapped, you were rustled!" This brought on hysterical laughter from everyone, McCain realizing that there was no point in debating with an intoxicated group of morons, opened a beer and wished he was elsewhere, for the moment anyway.

They heard the car doors bang shut, Frank Wickens and Vince Gibson arrived at the same time, shook hands surveyed the scene of the fire, shook their heads and walked into the cabin. It had been awhile since either of them had seen so many grinning hungover men in one place so early in the morning.

Joe came to greet them, informed them that the second bedroom on the right in the other cabin was theirs, handed them a beer and let them know that breakfast was ready.

Breakfast was delicious, Joe and Chris had outdone themselves, the pork and maple sausage, made from a boar Chris had shot, eggs and blueberry pancakes smothered in freshly harvested syrup and home-made whipped butter, with biscuits and gravy had them all in a great mood.

Frank and Vince went to their room,

"Well, it's obvious they haven't been watching the news."

Overnight two bombs had exploded in Dearborn MI. One was at a checkpoint manned by both Dearborn and MI State Police; at least two officers were reported killed, with another four taken to the hospital. The second was outside of a church just as people were entering for 7 AM Mass. The pressure cooker type of bomb malfunctioned, so no fatalities as of now, but most of the people attending were elderly and were taken to area hospitals.

"Yeah, they will soon enough, did you see them, they are like a bunch of kids having a great time on a camping trip, I don't want to be the one to ruin it for them."

"Me neither." "In any event they will find out soon enough."

About 11AM Pat's wife called him, "have you seen the news" "no, and hello nice to hear from you to" "Pat two bombs went off in Dearborn, at least two cops are dead, some channels are saying three are dead and a bunch of seniors were hurt when a bomb went off at a church, a church." "Let me get the news on, see what's up I will call later, love you."

"Hey guys can we turn on the news, my wife said two bombs went off in Dearborn."

"You are kidding right"

"No, afraid not."

There was absolute silence in the room as the news came on, the jovial mood, the boys' weekend away festivities were over.

The news, that is to say FOX news, they could be trusted a little bit, the other networks could not be trusted at all,was turned on. The scene from the church was gruesome, the glass doors of the church had been blown apart and the flying glass had caused many injuries, mostly severe cuts, but at least one elderly woman had her arm severed from the glass. The scene then switched to the police checkpoint where, it was now confirmed, three police officers were dead from the explosion and another five injured. Apparently a suicide bomber, wearing Middle Eastern clothing, had rode a bicycle packed with explosives up to the checkpoint. The officers, not expecting a bike bomb, got too close to the bike and then the bomb was detonated.

The bomb at the church was confirmed as a pressure cooker, with a timer on it set to explode at 7 AM.

The broadcast was then interrupted by special report from the White House where President Obama was giving a speech to the nation. "These criminals will not escape justice, there is no where for them to hide, the full power of the Justice dept. and law enforcement will be brought to bear, in addition to the ongoing FBI investigation, I am sending a team from the ATF, to assist in the investigation. I am also dispatching my advisor, Mohammed Ali Kalaak, to meet with community leaders in the area to try to understand the reasons that would lead to such a terrible crime."

It was Edward Jackson who spoke first. "Criminals, community leaders, FBI investigation, they were there investigating the cops, did, did I hear that right, his advisor, Mohammed Ali Kalaak! GOD what is happening, churchgoers, Christian, not Muslim, church goers being bombed!' He looked around the room, all eyes were on him. "What do we do?"

Joe took his cue, "Ok gentlemen, aside from friendship, the real reason, that I invited you all here this weekend is that there is a well thought out, well organized mission underway to remove Obama from office, the mission is being organized by the police, with major military support, before I go any further a real simple question, are you in or out?"

No one objected; no one even raised an eyebrow. Jackson looked at Joe and all of the others "I'm in and I thank GOD that someone with intestinal fortitude has finally come forward to organize and lead this. I am ashamed of myself for not having had the courage to do this".

One by one everyone agreed; they were in. While his aides, Vince and Chris, cleared a table and began laying out maps of their respective states indicating lines of advance, checkpoints, temporary fuel depots, objectives and a multitude of other military needs, Joe, assuming the role of colonel began the briefing. Gone were the men who for a night got to be carefree boys again, here again were the warriors the men who once again would answer their country's call, the men who would lead other men and women, who would command awesome power in the service of their country, not to seize power for themselves, but to defend the republic from all enemies and "TO SECURE THE BLESSINGS OF LIBERTY FOR THEMSELVES AND THEIR POSTERITY!"

13:00 hours

Joe Garcia, sent out a quick message to the group over the low band channel, "Being deployed with my group to Dearborn, message regarding mosques and warehouse's seems to be on spot, will communicate with FBI friends on scene.

Again the satellites recorded the message.

14:00 hours

Joe finished the briefing. "Any other questions?"

"Yes Sir, a good side of my questions is that police officers, citizens volunteers,you name it are going to be coming to DC as quick as they can. We are going to have too many people—granted a nice problem to have—but how are we going to get the word out to them to stay where they are, and begin making arrest in their home areas, and who is going to organize and command them".

"Great question Conor, the answer is that we will activate the EBS, Emergency Broadcast System, effectively taking over all radio and TV stations. We will inform all patriotic Americans to report to their local sheriffs who will deputize citizen volunteers, such as NRA members in their counties. Known members of anti American groups such as the ACLU and traitors such as Jane Fonda, who are always saying they will leave America because they hate it here will be immediately arrested."

"Yeah but they never leave do they!"

"Police officers, city,state, and universities, aside from those already in DC for Memorial Week, will be ordered to remain at their posts, ready to assist if needed.

Remember, this is not a military coup. We want to cause as little disruption in the lives of the American people as possible. We want them to immediately begin to feel the yoke of liberal democratic laws and regulations lifted from their lives, to feel freedom once again. But the cancer of liberalism will be cut out now, once and hopefully for good . All opposition will be crushed, gentlemen, by whatever force is needed to crush it. Is that understood?" A chorus of, "Yes, sir" answered him. "Now lets eat and talk over anything that any of you might want to review."16:00

General Wayne Kelly sat in his office watching the news of Dearborn. Not only was he outraged about the bombings happening at all, let alone in America, but also as a military historian he saw all too well that history was again repeating itself both in Western Europe and now in the United States. Another invasion of the West by Muslim armies was underway, he reflected to himself. When people talk of the crusades they always mention how the Christians armies attacked the Muslim's;

most forgot to mention that the crusades were a counterattack against Muslim armies that had invaded and conquered western lands, including the Holy Land.

He reached into his desk drawer and removed his low band transmitter,

All branches will attend the event at Quantico."

The listening satellites duly recorded the message.

FRIDAY, SEPT. 11TH 07:00 HOURS

Joe Garcia could not believe it, here it was Sept. 11, of all days, and he was in Dearborn, MI, investigating yet two more bombings which, while yet to be proved, appeared to be the caused by a Muslim suicide bomber and possibly at least one other suspect. In his heart though, Joe knew that there were many more than just one suspect.

As his car was passed through the security entrance he noticed the armored cars, SWAT Officer's carrying rifles, and evidence collection teams hard at work. "My poor country," he thought.

He walked over to the command post, a large tent that had been set up about a block from the scene of the police bombing. The entire area, for blocks around, was cordoned off. This was done as both as part of a crime scene, as well as to provide security to the investigators, ATF, and FBI who were and would be combing the area, reviewing security video of the police bombing, attempting to locate witnesses and a thousand other details required on an investigation of this magnitude.

A second smaller, but no less sophisticated, investigation was simultaneously being conducted at " Our Lady of Peace and Mercy Church," the site of the second bombing.

With relief both personal and professional he noticed that his friend, Special Agent Nathan Green, seemed to be in command. Nathan looked up and also felt a sense of relief. Inter-agency investigations could be very tricky, to put it mildly. Sometimes there was a lack of information sharing, and in all honesty Nathan had to admit to himself that the FBI was probably more guilty of not sharing information than other agencies.

With Joe heading up the ATF end of the investigation Nathan knew that not only was one of the ATF's best on scene, but also that there would be no secrets between agencies.

As if to send a message to all who were present, skipping a handshake,Joe and Nathan gave each other a huge bear hug. And if that was not message enough to their teams, in a loud enough voice to be heard by anyone in the tent, Nathan stated "Joe, thank goodness you are here. Let me bring you and your team up on what we have so far. I mean everything that we have."

12:00 hours

Audrey Lapaglia was standing at the site of the World Trade Center. The names of the victims of the attack had just been read. Her command, along with agents from the FBI, ATF and Secret Service, was on an unannounced high alert.

No particular threat had been made and there was no credible intelligence regarding any proposed attack today. But given the day and the bombings in Dearborn, you just could not be too careful.

Thinking of Dearborn, she and some of the members of the NYPD command, along with many of her officers, would be flying out there for the funerals of the murdered officers. She asked herself, "How many more times is this going to happen ? Memorial Week can't come quick enough." As she stood there she saw her old friend, actually an old boyfriend, Carl Brown, walking up to her. Carl had done well for himself. After serving four years active duty in the army, where he obtained his undergraduate degree, he went on to NYU and obtained a Masters in conflict resolution. He was hired by the Secret Service and now he was the regional director of NY. He was here today to personally supervise his agents who were guarding dignitaries from various countries allied with the U.S.

Carl came up and as he always did gave her a kiss, which lingered just a second too long on the cheek. "Audrey, how are you? Did I ever tell you that you are the only girl who ever broke my heart?"

"Yes Carl, every time I see you." With smiles on their faces they just looked at each other. Not for the first time, Audrey wondered what life would have been like if she had married Carl when he had asked her. Oh well, water under the bridge.

"So Carl, right from the shoulder what is your evaluation of the state of the country? And don't lie to me!"

"The truth? We are screwed. You would not believe how messed up things are not only in the White House but also in the congress, senate, and from what I've seen state and local governments. I am petrified for the future of my kids!"

"Yeah, do you want to help do something about it?" "I know that look Audrey, what are you thinking of?"

"Just a little corrective action."

"Audrey, I know that you are only kidding. I have to go now, talk to you soon."

Well that did not go as well as I hoped, Audrey thought to herself, but the seed is planted; let's see if it grows. As Carl walked away he was thinking to himself, "She was serious, yeah, something has to change, but 'corrective action?'" He would be wrestling with himself for days.

14:00 hours

AL called Sheriff Joshua's office himself. Peggy answered the phone and once again put him right through. "Josh, Al here, how are you?"

"Fine Al, couldn't you wait to talk to me on the 14th?" "Well actually I still hope to talk to you on the 14th, but at the funerals for the Dearborn Police Officer's. I feel that I have to attend. We do need to speak and I am pretty sure that there will be some people there that you will love talking to."

"I will be there Al, looking forward to seeing you and your friends."

"Great, I believe that I will stay at the Marriott. Hopefully you can stay there also."

"Let me see if I can get a reservation, see you there."

SATURDAY, SEPT. 12TH 11:00 HOURS

The investigation was proceeding slowly. It is amazing how many small pieces, be it glass or metal from a bike, not to mention explosive residue and on and on that had to be collected at a crime scene. For instance each piece of glass, no matter how small, was placed in it's own plastic bag, numbered, and would have to be examined individually piece by piece. One could never tell where a vital piece of evidence might be found.

Joe and Nathan looked up from the mock up of the crime scene. The large crowd that had been watching and filming them since their arrival began to clap, dance and give thanks to Allah. His second in command, Peter Callahan came into the tent. Joe and Nathan just looked at him.

"Sorry to interrupt sir, but you are not going to believe this. President Obama's aid, Muhammad Ali Kalaak, or something like that, is here. Just arrived with a Secret Service escort no less; he is demanding access to the crime scene and he wants to bring in community leaders right now to monitor your investigation. Joe and Nathan just looked at each other.

"We will go talk to him Peter, thank you."

"This ought to be good."

"Yeah, probably wants to make sure that no one jumps to any conclusions about a man in Middle Eastern clothing riding a bike that blew up the cops."

As Sean and Nathan walked over to Kalaak, they observed that he was giving a speech to the crowd in Arabic. For some reason, the many TV reporters and cameras on scene were not recording Kalaak's speech. But the FBI cameras were.

The crowd seemed pleased with whatever Kalaak was saying; Joe distinctly heard Obama's name several times.

Kalaak observed them coming up to him, and immediately switched from speaking Arabic to speaking English. It was then that the TV cameras started to roll. In a very condescending tone, Kalaak informed

Joe and Nathan who he was and that he was sent directly from the president. Kalaak then demanded that the spiritual leaders of the area be allowed into the command tent so that they could observe the investigation first hand. Additionally, he wanted the spiritual leaders to view and handle any evidence that they wanted to; this, of course, would aid in the investigation.

Nathan acted as spokesman. "Well Sir, first no one is coming into our crime scene."

"I told you who I am."

"Yes, but regardless, no one will be entering this crime scene."

"And if I do, what will you do about it?"

"You, or anyone else, will be arrested."

"I am a special advisor to the president." At this point an FBI agent came up to Nathan and handed him a lab report on the rocks that had been thrown at the city workers and at the police. The report stated that a total of eleven distinct DNA samples had been found on some of the rocks; three of the samples were from one of the police officers, and two from the city workers. Therefore, the other six samples were from possible suspects in the attack on the police and city workers.

Nathan read the report, handed it to Joe to read, and then addressing Kalaak said, "Sir, the lab report that I just reviewed stated that in addition to DNA samples, blood that's actually from the police officer and two city workers who were attacked, six other DNA samples have been recovered from the rocks used in the stoning attack. I would greatly appreciate it, and I am sure that the president would also appreciate it, if you would use your obvious influence with the crowd to request that all males give a voluntary DNA sample so that we can eliminate suspects in this attack."

"Well sir, will you help us?"

"Infidel!" screamed Kalaak. He was about to scream more when he realized that the TV cameras were recording his every word; he quickly turned and walked back to his Secret Service SUV. Once inside, Kalaak then dialed Obama and informed him of the lack of cooperation from the FBI, and also how he had called the agent an "Infidel." Obama just laughed. "Oh well, he is an infidel. And don't worry, the media will never report on this. Come back to Washington, your mission has been a success."

Nathan and Joe walked back to the secure command tent without saying a word. Once inside, Nathan exploded. "Did that advisor to the president really just call me an Infidel?!" The electronics tech who had been viewing the talk then interjected. "Yes sir he did, we have it on tape!"

"I want a copy of Kalaak's speech to the crowd, the one in Arabic, now. And send a request for an interpreter to translate the speech for us. Last thing: do not tell anyone that you gave me a copy, understand?"

"Yes sir."

Nathan just glared at him. "Joe let's call it a day and go somewhere to talk." As far as Joe was concerned, that was a great idea.

"Sure Nathan, lets go." As they were leaving the tent Joe looked around at the faces of the other FBI and ATF agents who were still inside and had heard Joe called an "Infidel." They all looked rather angry.

15:00 hours

They decided that given the area, the best place to have a drink was back at the hotel. They ordered and went to a corner table.

"Joe, I've been an FBI agent for 23 years, and five years in the navy before that. I have never seen, I don't know how to even say it, except that with what's happening to America, everything is upside down. I feel helpless. I want to stop what is going on but I—"

"Nathan, a lot of people feel that way. We all see ourselves as just individuals, but what if their was a group who had made up their minds to do something about the state of our country?"

"Do you mean that? Do you really mean that something is being planned?" Joe just took a drink and looked at Nathan. After a few minutes Nathan said, "I'm in."

"What about other FBI agents?"

"They are as disgusted as I am. We all know what happened in Dearborn, but who gets investigated? The police. And this has happened how many times? Did you see the media, they didn't even turn on their cameras to film Kalaak. Imagine if I had called him an atheist or something! I would be fired fast enough for the media to make it a national story."

"Nathan, there is going to be a revolution. To restore America to the vision of the Founding Fathers, to greatly diminish the size of the government, to give people back their freedoms, to again make the U.S. military the strongest in the world, should I go on?" With a look of hope and determination on his face Nathan said again, "I'm in."

Joe spoke for quite awhile, telling Nathan everything he knew. Nathan asked a few insightful questions and then said, "Ok, let me tell you what I and my FBI can do to help." Now it was Nathan's turn to speak, while Joe asked a few questions.

" I never knew, even dreamed that the government could do all that."

"Yeah, well, they put all that in place because they don't trust the American people, military, police or, come to think of it I suppose, the FBI. It's like something out of Communist Russia where everyone is watching everyone. But it will be great to turn the tables on them!"

"A toast to that! Actually, a lot of the people involved will be here for the police funerals. Do you want to meet them or do you want to stay in the background?"

Nathan thought a second, then responded, "To quote Benjamin Franklin, We all hang together or we all hang separately. I would like to meet them!"

SUNDAY, SEPTEMBER, 13TH 11:00 HOURS

Without realizing it, Sean and Sara arrived at the hotel two cabs apart and went to separate lines at the receptionist desk. The hotel was packed with police officers arriving for tomorrow's funerals of the three murdered officers. After checking in, Sara looked around the lobby and spotted Sean, Sheriff Al, Audrey and some of the other group.

She took it upon herself to approach each of her friends and ask them to meet in an hour at the poolside bar. She was wondering if they all had the same nervousness in their stomachs as she did. Things had really progressed since their last group meeting. She supposed that they were all questioning what they were doing, wondering how much they could really trust each other. Has anyone that has been brought into the group had second thoughts, had they been betrayed? Sara was an expert on reading body language, and she intended to practice her skills while both talking to and watching members of the group.

Everyone readily agreed; the bar sounded like a great idea. Al informed her that he might be a little late, as he was going to have a talk with Sheriff Joshua. Sara wished him good luck and with a smile on her face said, "I will say a little prayer for the success of your talk, Reverend."

Al laughed. "Thank you, I can use all of the prayers I can get."

"Ok, see you when you get there."

Sara unpacked quickly, went poolside, and ordered her favorite summer drink. She figured that this would be the last one till next summer, not that it got that cold in San Diego. The bartender quickly delivered her rum punch. Before she even had a sip, Ed Larkin and Brian Olofson came up to her asked if she was buying. "Just the first dozen or so," she said. "After that it's your turn." After a chuckle Brian said "No problem. For some reason a couple of dozen drinks sound just fine."

One by one the Sons and Daughters of Liberty arrived at the bar, greeted each other, bought drinks and settled in to wait for their leader, Sean. Joe Annino arrived with several men that no one recognized by name, but whose identity could not be mistaken. The way they carried themselves when they walked, stood with their legs apart, and held their drinks in their left hands, keeping the right gun hand free, left no doubt; they were cops alright. And by the look of them, they occupied positions of authority. These were men who, like the rest of the group, had looks of determination on their faces.

Sean was heading out to the pool bar when he heard his name called by Sheriff Al. He quickly walked over to Al and instantly recognized the man who was with him, Sheriff Joshua Denver of Apache County, AZ. "Al, how are you? And Sir, my name is Sean Dominguez. It is an honor to meet you Sheriff."

"The honor is mine Sean. Al has mentioned your name to me several times, and from what Al has told me we have a lot in common."

"Well Sean, as of now I have not had an opportunity to have a private talk with Josh. I was just going to invite him back to my room for that talk, care to join us?"

"Most definitely; lead on, Al."

They entered Al's suite and Sean and Joshua were both impressed. "How come you rate a suite? The Boston Police Dept. would only pay for a no-view room with a queen size bed for me. I even have to buy my own meals." "Well, when I was checking in, my wife made the reservation under the name of Reverend Al, not Sheriff Al. I guess the girl at the desk is a good Baptist, because she upgraded me to this room. See, being in good with the LORD has it's privileges." This brought on a chuckle. Al then asked if he could offer them a drink— water, pepsi, or juice. Sean and Joshua just looked at each other, hoping that there was a beer to be offered, but no luck. Al was a teetotaler. In his opinion prohibition should be brought back, and he was not about to aid the devil by providing alcohol to GOD's children.

Realizing that a beer was not on the offering, both Joshua and Sean accepted a water.

"Well Josh, Sean being here is providential. You have been one of the few people in this country that has continuously stood up for America first. You even gave the Governor of AZ, Jan Brewer, the courage to fight Obama and Holder and company in the courts, as well as to stand up for the independent rights of the state of AZ. against the onslaught of federal tyranny."

"Stop Al, you are making me blush what's up? What are you leading up to, and why is Sean being here providential?"

Al just looked at Sean, Sean nodded and Al began, "Sean has been busy organizing a revolution, led by the police, to defend the Constitution, greatly reduce federal power, remove illegal aliens from the country— forcibly if necessary, strengthen our military, hold Obama and a lot of other people accountable for their treason....So before I go on, are you in or out?"

"I hope that your room is not bugged Al, but I am in, so how can I help?"

At this point Sean began. "Sir we need you to hold and house, many members of congress, some left wing billionaires, left wing hollywood losers, and others that are dangerous, that are a cancer to our country, will you do it?

Joshua looked as if he was witnessing the coming of the LORD. "Congress you say? I assume my girl Nancy Pelosi will be among those arrested. Sure, I will do it. Imagine Nancy hot bunking with one of the poor illegal aliens, who I am sure, I can arrange it, will be a member of one of the Mexican gangs. I can't wait to let Nancy and the rest of them put their liberal beliefs to the test! You know, practice what they preach. Pelosi actually said that illegals were the real patriots, sorry, now I'm going on. Tell me what else you need me to do."

"This is all going to happen on the second day of the Police Memorial Week, May 2016 in DC. I need you to not only organize your own county, be prepared to swear in as many people as needed as deputies, house the prisoners, but most importantly this has to be done in every county in America. I think that you are the only man who knows every sheriff in the country, who we can or cannot trust, who will be with us or not, the ones who will cooperate with the state national guard units, who by the way, will all be federalized by the new president, and a hundred other things that will have to get done. Joshua, I know that you would probably want to be in DC when this happens, but you can't be, you are just too well known, especially in the Southwest. You are highly respected, your influence in this critical area of the country cannot be underestimated. Sorry, but you are needed there."

"Not my will, but HIS be done, I will do it."

"There was never a doubt in my mind, your name was put forward at our first meeting, we were just waiting for Al to talk to you. Congratulations, you are now a member of the Sons and Daughters of Liberty."

"Can I ask a couple of questions?"

"Go ahead."

"Well who will be the next president?"

"Someone asked that at our first meeting. I have my own idea, but I asked everyone at the meeting to consider the voting records and known history of members of the U.S. Senate and Congress. Most likely our next president will be a real Reagan Republican. I will include your vote as to who it will be, the majority will rule. Oh by the way, I will insist that the next president give a full pardon to all who are involved in saving the country."

"Second question, what happens to Obama, and his family?"

"That will be up to the next president. In my opinion his daughters are innocent and should not be harmed in anyway. Michelle on the other hand, well that will be up to the next president. I love history though, and at the end of the Civil War, General Grant asked that very question of President Lincoln concerning Confederate President Davis. Lincoln strongly implied that if Davis managed to flee the country, he should be allowed to go. Maybe that is what the next president will decide about Obama. Send him back to Kenya along with his illegal alien aunt and uncle. But, that might depend on what is learned about him and his private actions while president, which are probably much worse than his public actions."

"Don't forget that for years after he was elected Obama kept threatening to have a special prosecutor investigate President Bush. So he can't complain if a special prosecutor looks at Solandra etc."

"Next question, what about the military?"

"Right now the marines and many state national guards are in. We should know about the air force, army and navy in about a month."

"Wow."

"Any other questions?"

"I am sure I will have some but let me think for awhile please."

"No problem, lets go outside and join the others."

The Reverend Al was shocked. There were at least 200 semi to fully intoxicated people, who were all probably police officers, drinking, dancing too closely, throwing each other in the pool...by most people's standards pretty normal, but to a man of the cloth, it was a vision of Sodom and Gomorrah. He was most shocked by Sara Mahoney, a married woman no less, who had that giant, Brian, trapped in a corner looking like she was going to attack him. The poor man had a look of horror on his face, and Al could only imagine how hard he was trying to get away from Sara. What Al did not realize was that the look of horror on Brian's face was caused by Sara's repeated telling him that she had found him the perfect wife, a stunning girl by the name of Susan. They could meet soon; if it was not for the approach of his friends Joe Annino and Joe Garcia, along with another man he did not know, he would have fled to his room to pray.

"Sean, Al, I would like you to meet two of my friends and the two newest members of our group, Joe Garcia of the ATF and Nathan Green of the FBI."

"Pleasure to meet both of you and welcome."

"Thanks Sean, but the pleasure is ours ."

"Sean, Joe and Nathan are heading up the investigations of the bombings in Dearborn. You would not believe what they have been telling us about the Muslim reaction here; they are all in favor of the bombings." "Yeah I saw the news, the ISIS flags."

"Yes, but even though they were there the news media did not report how Obama's special advisor, Mohammed Ali Kallak, came with a Secret Service escort, spoke to the crowd in Arabic, got them all fired up, and demanded access to the crime scene for religious leaders so that they could monitor the investigation. And, when Nathan refused and threatened him with arrest if he tried to enter the scene, Kalaak called him an Infidel! And not one word about it from the media."

"Boy, I would love to have a tape of that."

"Well, we do, the FBI recorded it."

"GOD Bless them. Nathan, we are going to get along just fine."

Cops are notorious gossips. Within an hour, every cop in the hotel and then the surrounding hotels had heard about Kalaak's comments. They of course had to call back to their own departments all over the country and tell their friends of Kalaak's calling the FBI "Infidels." It did not take long for every cop— local, state and federal, to hear that they were infidels in the eyes of Obama. Their anger grew.

MONDAY, SEPTEMBER 14, 06:00 HOURS

Wake up alarms were ringing at dozens of hotels and motels in the Dearborn area. Police were getting up, showering, shaving, repolishing boots that had already been polished 10 times, and pulling imaginary strings from perfectly pressed uniforms. More ominously, they were opening cases and removing AR 15 rifles, checking the magazines, and making sure they were full. Normally only the honor guards would carry non-firing rifles. But times were not normal anymore; American police officers had once again been murdered by Islamist terrorist here in America, and the police were in no mood for any nonsense today. Especially after learning that they were infidels. Somehow, copies of the FBI surveillance video had been shown to the officers. Yes, they were in no mood. Technically it might have even been illegal for some of them to have private rifles with them, but who was going arrest them, their brother and sister officers?

The three murdered officers were all from the same neighborhood, all had attended the same schools, played on the same ball teams, and today they would all have their funeral Mass at Our Lady of Peace and Mercy Church. The same church where the second bomb exploded. At the request of the families, the glass church doors that had been destroyed in the bombing had not yet been repaired. They would all be buried at the New Calvary Cemetery.

The funeral Mass was to begin at exactly 9AM. There were so many officers who had come from not only the United States, but also Canada, Israel, France, Russia and Saudi Arabia present, along with military police units, that there was no way they could all enter the church. Officers stood shoulder to shoulder on both sides of the road, the entire mile and a half distance from the funeral parlor to the church. The honor guards lined up both inside and outside the church.

Hundreds of police motorcycles and cruisers led and followed the procession. The twenty three flower cars, filled with flowers sent by mourners from all over the country and the world, were a tangible expression of grief for the fallen officers and their families.

There had been a rumor that protesters from the community were going to heckle the funeral, but for some reason, they decided against it.

MONDAY. SEPTEMBER,14TH 10:00 HOURS

Not only were no television cameras allowed in the church, but also, at the request of the families, no members of the media were allowed in either. The hundreds of officers and friends of the families in the church were only too glad to help honor the wishes of the families by pushing the media out of the church and closing the doors in their faces. Outside of the church the media screamed that they were the victims of police brutality, that the public's "right to know" was being violated, they threatened lawsuits, fumed about the separation of church and state, threatened to go worldwide with the way they were being treated, but not once expressed any sympathy or any remorse for the murdered Officers or their families.

The funeral Mass concluded and, with a tangible feeling of grief, the flag draped coffins were carried out of the church by police. The flags of the State of MI and of the many various police departments present were dipped in honor as, one by one, the coffins passed by and were placed into the hearses.

It was only a quarter of a mile from the church to the cemetery. The sky itself seemed to reflect the blues, reds, and yellow colors from the lights of the many police vehicles in the procession. While the motorcycles and cruisers led the way officers, hundreds of them carrying AR15 rifles, marched at a full step pace alongside of and behind the hearses.

The streets were lined with mourners, citizens, everyday hard working people from all over MI and surrounding states. People who trusted and respected the police and were grateful that men and women were willing to do such a thankless job.

Several governors were present, ambassadors from seven different countries attended, but noticeably, no one from the Obama administration was in attendance.

Upon arrival at the cemetery, the hearses stopped one behind the other. All three officers, were now to be buried next to each other.

Except for the tramping of thousands of feet as the officers marched in and assembled into perfectly aligned massed ranks of blue, there was absolute silence.

The bagpipers began to play Amazing Grace. Upon the last note being played, with a sacred reverence, an international honor guard, The Dearborn PD and MI National Guard began to remove the coffins from the back of the hearses. The command "attention" rang out and thousands of feet slammed together while flags were lowered in salute.

With a precision that was unequaled, the coffins came out, and in perfect step were carried and placed down over the graves in unison.

Father Ciccone, who had administered the Sacraments of First Communion and Confirmation to all three, began the graveside prayers. After the prayers, the MI State Police fired a twelve gun salute. A bugler began to play taps, the notes were picked up and played by a dozen different trumpeters spread throughout the cemetery. When taps ended the bagpipes began to play Danny Boy, and without a command being needed, every officer then raised their right hand in salute. As the last note sounded the salutes came down. The families were escorted from the cemetery, and then something unusual happened. Despite not a word being spoken, and no command given, not one officer made a move to leave. Instead they took the ropes and lowered the caskets into the ground. One by one, each of the thousands of officers walked by and threw a handful of earth onto each casket. Once the gravesites had been fully filled in, the Officers reassembled into massed ranks for a last minute of camaraderie with their fallen brothers. They all gave a last salute, and marched in silence from the gravesite.

14:00 hours

Back at the hotel Sean spread the word for the entire group to meet in Sheriff Al's suite. One by one they assembled in Al's room. Something different had occurred today; it was as if the legions of police had crossed some Rubicon. No one knew how to articulate it, but they all knew something had happened. Sean called the meeting to order and asked Joe Annino to introduce the newest two members of the group.

Joe started with Joe Garcia. "My friends, this is Joe Garcia. He is third in command of the ATF. Joe was standing right there when Kalaak called our next member, Nathan Green of the FBI, an Infidel." All faces bore looks of both disgust for Kalaak, as well as determination to remember him.

Joe introduced all of the members to Joe and Nathan. Sean then asked Nathan to speak first and to advise them as to what assistance Nathan could provide to the cause.

Nathan began by telling them that there were many FBI agents who were just as worried about the state of the country as they were. He then went on to fully explain how under Obama's orders the FBI could not even investigate a Muslim individual, let alone a Muslim group, unless they had clear verifiable proof that a crime had been, and not might be, committed. An obvious example of the handcuffs that Obama had put on the FBI was the Boston Marathon Bombing. "We had information that the bombing was being planned. But under Obama's rules, we could not investigate, much less arrest, the two Muslim brothers who committed the bombings. Obama wouldn't let us investigate the attack on our embassy in Benghazi, either." They all stirred, unable to speak. The resolution in their hearts had turned into an iron conviction that they would not, could not, fail.

"The FBI can help in lots of ways though. We can interrupt and communicate on any police frequency in the country; that might help in issuing orders if needed. We also have a list of all the secret bunkers, as well as their locations and the codes to access them, that any senator, congressman or Obama or Biden might use. We have the home address of all elected politicians in the country at every level of government, we know the address of every member of any potentially violent group, the address of all members of the media, movie stars, athletes, reporters, ACLU members, you name it. We can instantly freeze bank accounts and cancel passports, stop airline flights from taking off, or order any plane in the air to land. We also have access to all NSA recordings of emails, telephone conversations, instant reports on where a credit card is used, you name it Big Brother has it."

"My GOD, the KGB or old Gestapo would be green with envy. The American people have no idea of the electronic police state that they are living in; no one is safe."

"Maybe the best thing to do is to wear your tinfoil hat when you leave the house." They all chuckled sadly at that.

"Nope, no one. Oh also, just like the Secret Service, we always know where the President and Vice President, Speaker of the House,and others are at all times."

"Joe Garcia, please tell us how the ATF can help."

"Well, we have many, not as many as the FBI, but still a fair amount of resources. We also have list of all gun purchases, so if needed we can cross reference any firearm purchases with, say, the list of possible terrorists in the country, both American Citizens and foreign nationals. Sadly, we have much more information on the average loyal American citizen than we do of the illegals in the country. "

"Joe, there are reports and rumors that the Dept. of Homeland Security and FEMA have been stockpiling ammunition, guns and armored cars for use against the American people. Do you know anything about that?"

"Yes, but not much. Obama signed an executive order allowing Homeland Security and FEMA to buy an unknown quantity and type of both guns, ammunition and armored cars without the serial numbers being sent to the ATF, which is a Federal Crime. Also, with the huge cutbacks in the military, there are lots of rifles– and who knows what else– that again, under Obama's executive order, have been sent to Homeland Security and FEMA. But we have no idea of what quantity of weapons has been sent to them."

"Could the military find out?"

"Maybe. Someone, somewhere, has to know, Maybe the FEMA governors."

"You know that Obama has appointed a governor in each of the ten FEMA zones, similar to his Czars that report directly to him."

"We might have some idea of where the weapons are stored though. Last week I myself observed a large number of men entering the Mosque of the Nation of Islam in Boston. I then called some of our group, and— actually guys, why don't we each say what we learned about what happened in our various cities at the same time as Boston? Sara what about San Diego?"

"As far as I could tell, nothing unusual occurred and as far as anyone in my department knows there are no Homeland Security or other warehouses in the San Diego area."

"Audrey, what about New York?"

"Yeah, as you know, our dear Mayor Diblasi had ordered us to stop surveillance of all Muslim groups. Some of the guys have been able to find a couple of minutes here and there to keep half an eye on known or suspected Muslim extremist. We observed that at two different mosques, and an old warehouse in the Bronx, many vehicles with multiple occupants arrived. The men, no women were seen, all entered the mosques, but they just drove up to the warehouse and left. Funny thing, later on the guys took a closer look at the warehouse and area and observed numerous security cameras, placed as inconspicuously as possible. From a distance, the doors of the warehouse seemed to be old and falling apart but close up, they're solid steel. Windows have security bars and alarm sensors could be seen on the windows. So something is going on there."

"Yeah, but at least we know of that site now. Audrey, you know what do?"

"Yes; there will be an increase of surveillance in the area. By the way, when we do this DiBlasi will be arrested also."

"Fine with me."

"Brandon, anything going on in Philly?"

"Yes, not as bad sounding as New York yet, but a similar thing occurred at a parking garage. One of our cars attempted to stop a vehicle for running a red light and speeding right in front of him. The vehicle wouldn't stop for the officers, a short chase ensued and then the rocket scientist that was driving the car pulled up to an old underground parking garage that we thought was closed for years. Then the officers notice that there were already four cars with four or five guys in each car already there, so we have about ten units there. Our guys start checking the occupants of the other cars, and while they are doing that they observed numerous other vehicles, all with multiple occupants, driving by the garage. No one in the vehicles even looks at all the cops, just stare straight ahead and keep driving. We have a bunch of license plate numbers. I'll have to see what progress has been made in the checks on the owners of the vehicles. Oh, and the guy who was driving the speeding vehicle had a lengthy arrest record but nothing currently open, the same for his friends in the car. All long records, but all of them had cleared up any warrants within the last year."

"What a nice group of fellows, now why would they all clear up their warrants at the same time? They obviously want to make sure that they are on the street and not locked up for some reason. We have the gun shot sound location devices in that area of town and surveillance cameras in the streets, on lights, telephone poles, etc. I have already redirected the cameras so that they monitor the garage and street in front of it. I was able to do that on my own authority, so hopefully no one notices— unless of course they shoot out the cameras and sound devices again."

"Ed, what about Chicago?"

"As soon as I got your call I had the local mosques checked and reviewed the daily field observation reports from the officers. The only suspicious event, at least that was reported anyway, was the amount of males arriving at Wright's Church with a special guest, Bill Ayers, the great bomber himself.

"Ayers, going with the rest of them? Why, a night call to prayer from the Minaret?"

"No, something else is up."

"Ok Tony, anything in Richmond?"

"No Sean, nothing that was reported. We do have a large, basically abandoned warehouse district. I will have my guys give it a thorough patrol. There is an old underground parking garage there. We will check on that also, and let you know what we find."

"Al, what about your county, anything unusual there?"

"No Sean, I have not heard of anything. But there is one similarity; I have noticed that some of my regular guests in the County jail have not been inside for awhile. I was hoping that they found GOD. But given the fact of so many other bad boys squaring away their warrants and keeping out of trouble, or at least not being arrested, staying on the street, I don't know."

"Well like the rest of us, do your best to find out." It was Nathan that spoke up next. "Excuse me, but when did this all happen?"

"I think it was on or about September 9th."

"You know, the FBI should have been notified of this right away."

"The FBI and ATF were. Tony wrote up an official report. Sent it out to all police Depts. as well as the FBI and ATF."

"The ATF, got a copy. I had my assistant send it out to all of our offices, with an order that all agents read or be informed of the report. Why didn't the FBI get it?"

Nathan was fuming. "It probably arrived in our Washington office, let me explain again, CAIR has access to all of our communications. They actually have the authority, from Obama, to read our bulletins and pull the ones they don't like. They can remove mugshots and whatever else from our office bulletin boards. Police depts. or anyone else for that matter might think that they are sending an email, fax etc. to, say, the New York FBI office. But everything is first sent to the Washington office. There CAIR can review, delete, and edit anything they do not like. I'm not saying they are there 24 / 7, or that things don't get by them, but...."

"You know what guys, we might not be the only ones planning a revolution! I am going to brief the military and state national guard units that are with us about this possibility. We may need to have military units with us when we take these warehouses and mosques down!"

"What did everyone think of the funerals today? I, for one, cannot describe it in my mind right now, but there is a noticeable change in the police, they were acting more...aggressive. All those rifles, the silence."

"Ya, first time I've ever seen officers walk by a grave and throw dirt down on the coffins."

"Maybe it's from talking to all of the cops from other countries. The Saudis, for instance, boy can they drink! They were telling us that it's shoot first in Saudi Arabia. They actually built a state of the art fence around the country to keep out terrorists. When the alarms go off they not only train cameras on the area, but respond in full battle gear. Anyone who runs, gets shot. They recently lost several officers to ISIS fighters who were trying to sneak into Saudi Arabia. Funny thing is the ISIS fighters were Saudi citizens.

The Muslim madness is happening all over the world. It turns out that one of the Muslims who shot that French Police Officer in the head while he was lying wounded on the ground, was a woman. The Russian Police have their hands full with the Chechen Muslims, and in England the Muslims are so aggressive that the guards at Buckingham Palace have been moved inside of the walls. I think we all know what the Israeli police go through!"

"I guess that we are just catching up with the rest of the world."

"I don't want to catch up, or even run in that race. We have enough problems here. Look at Los Angeles, did you know that 75% of all homicides are committed by illegal aliens? Usually, even if we can obtain prints or other evidence from the crime scene, we don't have the suspect prints in our system. And of course the Mexican Police won't cooperate with us; we don't even know these people's real names! But it doesn't matter anyway, because Mexican counsels in our country, the USA, are giving out birth certificates and other documents to illegals! Making it easier for them to change their identity, obtain driver's licenses and everything else."

"Moving on, have you all been thinking about who you want to be our next president? A good reference for helping you decide whom to elect is the Heritage Foundation; they have the voting records of all senators and congressman available online. Judicial watch is another good source. I'm going to want your votes right after the first of the year, I want everything to be in place for when we do this. Oh, Ed, make sure you give Nathan the list of our phone numbers and radio frequency. Bring him up to speed on how we have been communicating."

"Yes Sean, will do."

"Anyone have anything else?"

"Yes Sean, can I give Susan Nguyen a list of our phone numbers and radio frequency?"

"No offense, but I rather that you hold off on that. We're trying to keep this central group as small as possible, so any orders or information that she has or needs can be relayed through you for now?"

"Yes Sir."

"Stop calling me Sir!"

"Like it or not Sean, you are in command and giving orders. That makes you *sir*!"

"Keep your eyes and ears open and report anything that you feel is important. Our next get together will probably be at the shooting competition at Quantico. If that's all, tomorrow is my birthday."

They all yelled "Happy Birthday *sir!*" and then smiled like kids who know they are being fresh.

"Thank you all. My son, Sean, is coming home on leave; I haven't seen him in quite a while. My daughters and of course Shannon will be there...can't wait for us all to be together again!" Sean looked around and smiled.

"Ok, I am off to the airport, be safe see and talk to you all soon." A chorus of "see ya's" and "till laters" came at him as he left the room.

Sara was whispering with Audrey. "I think I'll go back out and mingle with the guys and girls. Anyone want to come?"

"Sounds good to me!"

"Yeah lets all go. We should listen to them, and also mingle with any members of department command staff that we can find to get the opinion of the various leaders. We pretty much know where the officers stand."

As the group circulated around the lounge they learned that the officers were both standing in a political position far more radical than any of the group members had dreamed, and that they were also an unforgiving bunch of people. Some of them overheard comments that ranged from an outright rebellion to assassination, seceding from the country, a work stoppage.

The officers' imagined penalties for their enemies were truly scary. The various forms of execution and torture varied from one region of the country to another .The Texans favoring staking members of the press and politicians naked over an ant hill in the hot Texas sun. New England officers favored something called keelhauling, where a prisoner stood at the very front of a ship with a rope tied around their waist, hands tied behind their back, and the rope running underwater beneath the ship. Crew members that were standing at the very back of the ship holding the other end of the rope then ran forward, pulling the prisoner the length of the ship, underwater. The prisoner usually died either from drowning or being cut to ribbons by the barnacles that were growing on the bottom of the ship. Of course, there was always the chance of the prisoner being eaten by a shark. For those who were not keeled hauled, tarring and feathering would be ok. Sara and Audrey had to laugh at that. In their mind's eye they saw billionaire liberals, along with multi millionaires like Harry Reid, Pelosi, and Hillary looking like chickens and running around Sheriff Joshua's desert holding facility, covered in tar and feathers. The thought was hysterical!

Hawaiians, on the other hand, favored tying members of congress, liberals, reporters, cop killers and other vermin by their hands and feet and then laying them down in front of a slow moving stream of molten lava. Of course, some suggested the routine methods of execution such as firing squads and hanging. Fairly hum drum, but all lethal.

From what was overheard, and from casual conversations, the senior members of the various departments felt the same as the rank and file officers. All in all, things were looking great for the rebellion, but not so good for a lot of people on the radical left. Just because an enemy had retired or was no longer in office or on the 6PM news, did not mean they were forgotten...far from it. After all, liberal politicians and news anchors had been making up lies and omitting facts to the American people for years. Now they would all have to finally answer to the people.

A main topic of conversation was Kalaak calling the FBI and, by extension, all of them "infidels." One of the Saudi Police Officers heard the talk and informed them that an infidel was a nonbeliever and, under Islamic law, could be legally enslaved, beaten, or murdered.

"What else did Kalaak say?"

"Well, we heard he gave a speech to the crowd, who were all from the Middle East by the way, in Arabic. The TV crews and reporters would not film it or report it, and when the FBI walked up to him Kalaak he switched to English. That's when he called the FBI infidels. I would love to know what he said in Arabic to the crowd."

"Us too."

Suddenly, a voice spoke up. "Well, I just happen to speak Arabic, and if you had a recording of—"

"I do!"

"Who are you?"

"Robert Smith, I'm an electronics expert with the FBI. I was actually on duty in the command tent, recording Kalaak."

"Go get the video. Hey, everyone, quiet down. We are going to watch a video of Kalaak talking in Arabic to the crowd, and our Saudi brothers are going to translate for us."

The lounge grew very quiet, with everyone just looking around, waiting for the video to play. Then whispering started. Voices were getting louder, but then, as Smith came back into the lounge, absolute quiet settled in.

Sara and Audrey were standing together waiting for the video to play when Audrey glanced over her shoulder and saw Carl Brown looking her way. She and Carl both smiled at each other, and Audrey turned away with a smile on her face. Sara, looking at Audrey, guessed right away and asked Audrey, "Well who is he?"

Audrey just gave a shrug and said "You know, an ex boyfriend from long ago. He's a supervisor for the Secret Service now."

"Well we could use his help, maybe you should get friendly again."

"I'm married! But I did briefly talk to him at the World Trade remembrance...I wonder what he' doing here?"

"Probably figured you'd be here at the funerals and came to bump into you."

The video started. The Saudi Police were watching intently as Kalaak's motorcade arrived. A Secret Service agent, was opening the door for Kalaak, who began to walk over to the crowd. Upon seeing him, the crowd starting chanting.

Every officer in the room was staring in silence at the television. As the crowd chanted and Kalaak spoke, the Saudi Officer began to translate.

"Praise be to Allah and his prophet, Praise be to their servant Obama." Over and over came the chant, "MAHDI, MAHDI, MAHDI!"

Kalaak held up his hands, and the crowd became still.

"My brothers, my fellow servants of Allah, Praise his name, this is a great day. Islam has begun to slaughter the servants of the false western GOD. From here in Dearborn, we will spread jihad across America; we will kill or convert all who do not believe in Allah. Obama is proud of you, I am proud of you, and, most importantly, Allah and his holy prophet Muhammad are proud of you. Death to the infidel non believers. Obama has said the dar al Islam prayer in the White House. A servant of Allah has said the dar al islam prayer on the White House lawn, on their national television. The White House now belongs to Allah and we will take it for him. We will throw the Jew out of Washington and into the sea; we will avenge the martyred believers in Palestine." With covered and uncovered faces contorted in hate, the crowd raised their fist, and erupted in shouts of "Allah Akbar, Death to Israel, Death to Christians."

It was at this time in the video that Nathan Green walked up to Kalaak. Every officer in the room was staring at the television, and, mirroring the mood in the video, the crowd in the video quieted down. They watched as Kalaak made his demands to enter the crime scene, was refused by Green, screamed "Infidel!" and stormed away.

There were some shouts in the lounge, some "I can't believe that" but mostly the officers in the lounge were silent. It was unimaginable, but yet they had heard and seen it, the Saudi Officers had translated for them and they had no reason to doubt the accuracy of the translation, especially when they observed the look of shock on the Saudis, they had seen the look of hate on the faces in the crowd, They had heard Kalaak, a representative of The President of The United States scream "Infidel". Heard Kalaak refuse to assist in the investigation, if there was ever any doubt in their minds that something had to be done, that doubt had been removed by Kalaak forever.

Carl Brown walked up to them from behind, "Hi Audrey, that was quite a show."

"Yeah it was, whoever would have believed that?"

"I would, the Secret Service knows a lot about what happens in the White House. For instance, would you believe that since Obama has become President over 400 individuals on the terrorist watch-list have been admitted to the White House? I'm not saying they all met with Obama in the Oval Office, but someone allowed them to enter and have meetings with Kalaak and company. Who knows what they were told or what documents or secrets they were given to take with them when they left. Or who they might have given them too!"

"Carl, this is my friend Sara Mahoney from the San Diego PD. She is a captain there."

"A pleasure to meet you Sara."

" The pleasure is mine."

"Sara, would you excuse me for a minute or two? I would like to have a talk with Audrey."

Sara gave Audrey a quick look, saw that it was ok and said, "Ok I will be over there with Al and the guys if you want me."

"So, want another drink?"

"Not yet maybe in a while."

"I have been thinking a lot about what you said at the World Trade ceremony, and coupled with what we saw and heard today, what I told you about the White House visitors, I would like to know more about what might be being planned. You know, the corrective action."

" Are you in favor of a corrective action, willing to help? Can I trust you?"

"Yes to everything Audrey, especially the part that you can trust me. You knew that, or you would never have broached the subject with me. You know how I still feel."

"Stop Carl, I am married, and this is serious business."

"Ok sorry, what can you tell me?"

"There is a plan in place, actually pretty far along in the planning, for the police to revolt save our country. You still want to know more? Are you in ?"

"Yes, I guess I just needed a little time to think and a little more incentive to join; Kalaak was that incentive. As a Secret Service agent I have protected both Republican and Democrats and I have noticed a tremendous difference in both. The Republicans have such a love for GOD, our country, its history, and a true desire to serve the people and promote individual freedom. The Democrats seem to only want power for the sake of power. They divide people by race, income, gender and any other way they can. You know, divide and conquer. I never thought I would like to go back to the days of the Clintons, but Obama is truly against us. He makes the Clinton years look like the good old days."

"Ok, I don't know everything; we are trying to keep things on a need to know basis. You know, that both protects the group and the mission. So here's what I do know."

After about 45 minutes Audrey finished speaking and asked, "Any questions?"

"Yes, are you sure the new president will come from either the congress or the senate?"

"Absolutely."

"He or she will be sworn in right away?"

"That's the plan."

"There will be no summary executions?"

"No one other than the people in this room have mentioned anything about executing anyone, just the opposite. Aside from incarcerating them and holding them without bail until the investigations are over, no one has talked about summary judgement. Unless you consider removing them from office a summary judgement. There will, however, be a thorough investigation of their finances and their actions while in office. Whatever charges may come from the investigation, time will tell."Ok, I am in, what do you want me to do?"

"Can you get yourself assigned to the White House? That might be the best place to have you and from there you can accomplish the rest of your mission."

"Well the morale in the Secret Service, especially in the uniformed branch, is very low. That, along with my rank, should give me a good chance of transferring from New York to The White House. I'll start working on it!"

"Excellent, I knew I could count on you." Carl loved to hear that; Audrey could count on him all right. He just had to be a good revolutionary, do what he was asked, be patient, and who knows!

22:00 hours

Most of the Officers in the lounge had cleared out.

Sara, Audrey, ED, Brian and Brandon were the only members of the original group still there. Audrey told them all about her conversation with Carl and how he wanted to help. They were all pretty excited to have the Secret Service on their side.

22:00 the Dominguez residence in South Boston.

Sean was in such a hurry to see his family, especially his son, that he practically tripped running up the stairs. He knew from all the lights that were on that everyone was up. When he opened the door and yelled "I'm home!" they all came rushing to see him. Father and son quickly gave each other a warm embrace, more like a wrestling hold really. The Dominguez's were an openly affectionate family, both in public and private. They even called themselves "the herd," as a herd sticks together, takes care of each other, and protects each other. They did truly enjoy being with each other. Sean could not get over how good his son looked. He was in amazing shape, muscle on muscle, tall, and tanned. If not for the difference in years, they could have been twins. Next came the family hug; as they had been doing all their lives, they all got close in a circle and stretched their arms around one another.

They sat up talking for hours, telling each other about all that had been going on in their lives, reliving old family memories and really enjoying each others company.

After a couple of hours Sean and Shannon excused themselves so that the kids could catch up, as they were sure that the kids told each other things that were not shared by them. Upstairs Sean and Shannon just smiled at each other as they heard their kids voices laughing and talking; it was a sound to make them proud.

"So, do you want to know what happened in Dearborn?"

Shannon replied to Sean's question with, "No not now, in the morning, lets get some sleep."

TUESDAY, SEPTEMBER 15TH 11:00 HOURS

Sean and Shannon woke up feeling very contented. They were together, the kids were all home, and life was good.

Sean jumped up. Shannon did not have to ask where he was going— to the kitchen of course, to make mounds of pancakes. Plain, chocolate chip, blueberry, bacon... everyone had their favorite and Sean would make them all. On the way down he smelled the coffee and knew that Sean Jr. was up. As he entered the kitchen he was a little disappointed to see a note, "went for a run be back around 12:00."

Sean started making the pancakes and frying the bacon. One hour should be just about perfect timing to have everything ready.

Shannon came into the kitchen, poured her coffee and said "Ok, tell me about Dearborn."

"You are not going to believe what happened." Sean gave a very detailed account to Shannon, leaving nothing out. "Then, Kalaak called Nathan Green an infidel."

"You're kidding, that's something you here in old movies."

"Yeah, well, we and the rest of the world will be hearing it a lot more I'm afraid."

Neither one of them had heard Sean come in from his run, he was standing at the door looking at them with a protective look on his face.

"Believe me, in some of the places the Army has sent me I hear the word infidel quite a bit."

"Can you tell us where, honey?"

"No mom, you know I can't, but I do have some good news, by the way, Happy Birthday."

"Yes, happy birthday my husband."

"Thank you."

"So what is the good news Sean?"

"It seems that all of those hours you and grandpa spent teaching me how to shoot when I was a kid have paid off. I have been selected to be one of the Delta Force members to represent the Army shooting team at a big competition in October at Quantico. Seems the Army Chief of staff is taking it very seriously, there is a rumor that he bet his hat that the Army would win. For the next three weeks I can be home, I have to go to the gun club to practice a lot. But," I will be around!"

Sean and Shannon just smiled at each other and replied together, "That's great, we are so happy to have you home."

Sean laughed, "You two, after almost 30 years of marriage you not only think the same, you say the same things at the same time. Weird."

Finola and Heather came into the kitchen with a big "Goodmorning all, what's for breakfast dad?"

"Your favorite pancakes and bacon."

"Oh sorry daddy, happy birthday, what would you like to do today?"

"Thanks girls, I would just like us to be all together, doesn't matter what we do."

They said Grace and sat down to their favorite breakfast.

"So dad what were the funerals like, how was Dearborn?" Sean noticed that as Heather asked the question a strange hard look came into his son's eyes.

"Well the funerals were very sad." Sean spoke for a while keeping an eye on his son. "But the worst part was that no one from the Obama White House bothered to attend, though Obama sent his special advisor, Mohammad Ali Kalaak, to inflame the crowd while speaking Arabic to them. He tried to interfere with the investigation and enter the crime scene, and when the FBI refused him admittance called the FBI agent an 'Infidel,' Oh yeah, he had a Secret Service escort with him."

They all just sat there and listened. They knew that Sean, their father would not lie, but it was almost unbelievable— an advisor to the president acting that way.

After breakfast Sean said, "I know, for my birthday present can we all walk around Castle Island together?"

Shannon and the girls just looked at each other and said, "Why don't you and Sean go for a walk dad, you can catch up we have a couple of things to do."

Sean knew that they would be baking him a birthday cake. "Sure that would be great ok with you Sean?"

"Of course dad just give me 20 minutes to clean up."

They walked in silence for a couple of minutes, both remembering all of the hundreds of times they had walked together and all of the father son talks they had while walking.

Even though it was September there were still quite a lot of people on the beach, including a lot of local pretty girls. Sean noticed his son looking at them and said, "If your mother saw you looking at the girls the first thing she would ask is why you are not married or have a steady girl yet?"

"It is hard to have a regular girlfriend, let alone a wife, when you get moved around as much as I do. Not that I do not want one."

"So how is the army."

"I love it, but things are going downhill so fast, with all of the downsizing and cutbacks. Half the time we do not even have enough equipment, like helicopters, for our missions. While Russian bombers and nuclear submarines are coming right up to if not into our territorial boundaries, the Mexican Army crosses into our country escorting huge drug conveys from the cartels, and no one in a position to do something about it seems to care. In fact, I think it is being done deliberately. Sorry."

"No I asked. I myself, and a lot of others, think you are right that it is being done deliberately, we are going to try to change things."

"*How*?"

"By doing what the Founding Fathers did: throwing off the yoke of tyranny, restoring the balance of power that was given to the Federal Government and the states in the Constitution. Living up to our oaths to

Protect, Defend and Preserve the Constitution against all enemies. In this case, domestic enemies!"

Sean was just looking at his father. He could tell that the hot Cuban blood that was in his fathers and in his veins also was beginning to boil. He knew from past experience that when his father got this angry or passionate about something, action of one type or another usually followed. Yeah, the Cuban blood and insanity, combined with the Irish blood and Irish insanity, actually made Sean Jr. a little nervous. Oh, it's a bad combination!

"So dad, what do you and your friends have in mind?"

"We are going to have a revolution, to take back our country."

Sean Jr. could hardly speak. "You are kidding right? How dad?"

"Let's sit here on a bench my son and I will tell you everything, including, by the way, how I organized the SWAT military competition. Did I tell you that the marines, FBI, ATF, and five state national guards are already in on this?"

Sean was incredulous. He just looked at his father in awe. In the language of Southie he always knew that his father was whacked in the head, but this!

"You, dad, you started this, you are the organizer? You have been starting, organizing a revolution?" Sean just looked at his son with a pleased smile on his face. It was then that Sean Jr. was absolutely certain that his father was telling the truth.

It was then that the Irish in him, the love of mischief, took over, and he started to laugh at the impossibility of this. "So dad tell me how."

Sean Sr. talked for a while. He did not have to convince his son of the need for a revolution or the justification for it; it was more of an operational briefing than anything.

"So dad, at the competition General Wayne Kelly, the Commandant of the United States Marines, will recruit the other Chiefs of Staff?"

"Correct."

"And if they do not go along?"

"Well, I don't know for certain, but the match is being held on a marine base my son."

"Ok lets assume they do go along with this, what will their role be?"

"Well I am not a general or admiral but I think that the navy and air force will have to keep any enemies in line, namely the Russians and Chinese, who might attempt to capitalize on what they believe is a vulnerability on our part. Who knows, invade Taiwan, the Baltic States, I would not put anything past them. The marines will seal off the Mexican Border and help the police to seize DC. The army and national guard will probably have to help seize the homeland security warehouses and, along with the local police, put down any civil unrest. Oh, national guard units will be federalized and the units in the states surrounding DC will be moved, at least at first, into DC. Maybe help with transporting congressmen, oh excuse, me congresspeople, and senators, to AZ." They both laughed at the PC .

"You mentioned that there is a strong possibility of hostile action by Muslims, both immigrants and American citizens. With the military so weakened and spread out all over the world we might be short handed."

"The sheriffs will deputize loyal patriotic citizens, who will be used if needed to supplement police and or military units."

"Dad, right now I cannot think of a thing that has been overlooked, does mom know?"

"Yes I told her a while ago."

"How did she take it?"

"Oh just fine, your mother is whacky you know!"

With a mixture of looks on his face— pride, bewilderment, and determination Jr. said, "Let's walk dad, we should be getting home."

As they walked one of Sean Jrs. favorite Irish rebel songs, On the one road, came unbidden into his head. He started to sing and his father quickly joined in, "We're on the one road, maybe the wrong road, but were together now who cares, singing a soldier's song."

They opened the front door both Sean's were greeted by all three girls with a "Happy Birthday Daddy!"

After cake and presents they all went in to the living room. Finola said, "One more present Dad, we are making your favorite supper, so you will have to excuse us for a while."

"That's ok. Favorite supper, hmmm, what could it be?" He wanted seafood, but would not say anything. Sean said, "Dad, when will the Boston Police SWAT team start really practicing for the competition?"

"I will probably have them start the day after tomorrow, pistol and shotgun at our range. For rifles we will have to go out to Fort Devens, the military ranges out there are I think up to four thousand yards long. In the city my guys ever get to shoot at anything that far away. How far away are the targets that you guys practice on?"

"You mean the moving targets, through brush, up partially hidden trails, behind walls, at night? "

"OK, how far?"

Teasing his father Sean replied, "Father that is a closely guarded military secret, but I think the longest shot so far was by a Canadian sniper, about one and a half miles. We of course use the same basic type of rifles, he was using our .50 cal ammo."

".50 cal we use only 223 or maybe 308 sometimes."

"Well dad this is war you know."

"What events will you be competing in?" "Sir, I will be on the long distance competition team and rapid fire handgun. By the way have you been taking care of the guns, cleaning them?"

"Sure want to see what I just bought?"

"Yes lets go down to the safe and you can show me, I love it when you buy new guns dad!"

They both just laughed. It was a standing joke that, with the passage of time, was not quite so funny anymore. When Sean was about 13 years old and he and his father were looking into the gunsafe, Sean looked up at his father and said, "Hey dad, when you're dead these are all mine right?"

When they opened the gun safe Sean Jrs. eyes were immediately drawn not to the guns, but to a radio transmitter receiver that was capable of storing all messages that were both sent and received.

"Dad why do you have the model T18-6 all-weather radio in there?"

"How do you know what that is by just looking at it, without even holding it?"

"Army training dad. We have to be familiar with all kinds of communication and weapon systems, both ours and any potential enemies."

"This, along with burner phones, is how Ed Larkin and Brian Olofson have arranged for us to communicate with each other."

"The phones maybe dad. I guess these are not bad, but not really used by anyone and usually have a short range. Atmospheric conditions could send the signal halfway around the world and any messages will be picked up and recorded by satellites."

As they were looking at the radio a message was received from Audrey. "A high ranking member of The Secret Service is in." Just as they were designed to do, both the American and Chinese spy satellites recorded the message.

"Dad, please understand I am not doubting you, but if this and everything else you told me is absolutely true, you should not wait till May to act. Do it ASAP. I mean that the longer something like this is in the works, the greater the chance that for a hundred different reasons operational security will be jeopardized. You have to act soon!"

Sean thought for a second. "I know what you are saying is correct from a security viewpoint. But the Army, Navy and Air Force are not on board yet."

"Look, according to Colonel Annino, General Kelly is sure that the other Chiefs are in. We have to wait, we do not want a civil war. Imagine if we acted too soon and the troops at Fort Bragg came to DC to save Obama and congress and started fighting the marines, police national guard units? Besides, after all the wrongful persecution, prosecution, verbal abuse and everything else that the police in this country have suffered, it is their right. They are owed the honor of arresting, handcuffing, searching and transporting all of those incompetent parasites in DC that call themselves our leaders. No, the police have to have a major role in this. Also, the average citizen trusts the police; they are used to seeing the police. They love the military, but in their minds the military is over seas somewhere, destroying our enemies and protecting the country. Not patrolling our streets."

"What you say makes sense dad, but please think about acting sooner. So let's see the new gun!"

Shannon yelled down, "Guys 20 minutes till supper."

"Ok mom, we'll be right up!" Sean called. "Lets go up dad. I think I know what we are having for supper."

"Yup smells like your mom's homemade chicken parm to me to... hope she made fettuccine alfredo with it."

FRIDAY, SEPTEMBER 18, 09:00 HOURS

Sean and Sean arrived at the Boston Police range on Moon Island. The island belonged to the City of Boston and, in addition to the police range, it was home to the Boston Fire Academy.

However, gaining access to the island required passage through the City of Quincy. Over the years, there had been several instances of the City of Quincy blocking the streets which led to the Boston range due to Quincy residents' complaints of gun-fire late at night. The Boston Police, not willing to surrender, had responded by having the Boston Police boats land officers on the rocky beach by the range. The officers of course thought that this was funny and made the most of it— charging ashore just like marines taking Iwo Jima, firing guns at imaginary enemies and sending ricochets into the surrounding Quincy neighborhood. A compromise had had been worked out so that no one would shoot on the range after 8PM, and the Boston Police could now drive on Quincy streets to the range.

With obvious pride Deputy Superintendent Dominguez informed the SWAT team and range Officers that his son, a member of the Army's elite Delta Force, would be one of the soldiers representing the U.S. Army in the competition at Quantico. Sean also explained that his son would be participating in the long range sniper and rapid fire pistol events. Several of the SWAT Officers gave a good-natured groan.

While chuckling, Officer Daley just had to say, "Come on boss I thought we were your guys, that you liked us. Bringing a DELTA force sniper here, your son no less, to spy on us, does not seem fair. Good thing we like him. And you too I guess."

Sean liked Daley; he was also from Southie, always had a smile on his face and a heart of gold.

"Ok guys, lets go out and show Delta force what we can do with rapid fire handguns. I think he is going to teach us something on the sniper firing line."

SEPTEMBER, 18TH 09:00 HOURS, ABOARD THE CHINESE SPY SHIP, "BEIJIXING."

Chinese Naval Intelligence Officer, Captain third grade, Xu, could have been up on deck, in the galley or even in bed if he wanted to. He could have been playing cards with his fellow officers. No, it was not that he was anti-social, he just preferred being alone with his computers. He knew that the others considered him a geek or nerd, but he enjoyed having such power at his command, which made him a priceless gem to the intelligence unit. One of his favorite pastimes was listening in on American cell phone calls and even short wave radio messages. After graduating Cum Laude from MIT, he said goodbye to his American life and classmates in perfect English and joined the People's Navy. It would be treason to say it outloud, and even his skills would not save him if he did, but he really liked, no loved, America! So much freedom, go where you want, become what you want...the only thing that limited you in America was yourself. Unlike in China, in America you were only limited by your own work ethic and abilities. He reflected that he missed walking the Freedom Trail through Boston— so much American history there. Tonight he would use the power of his computers to listen in on for a while to some of his old classmates' conversations. He was glad that his friends were all doing so well. Then, he might even spend some time searching the low band radio channels, see if he could pick up that couple in Iowa again who seemed to be having an affair. Yes, it would be a most relaxing evening.

MONDAY SEPTEMBER 21ST 08:00 HOURS

Sean was just walking into his office when Police Commissioner Turner spotted him and called him, along with other members of the Boston Police command staff, into his own office.

"Goodmorning all two FBI agents will be joining us, but let me fill you in. You may have already heard on the news that last night was a very bad night for police across the country. About 5pm CA time, 11pm EST, two LAPD motorcycle officers were deliberately rammed and run into a wall along a freeway by a stolen van. There is video of the attack. Both officers were pronounced dead at the scene. In Chicago, at 10 pm, 11pm EST, an officer was stabbed while he was in a deli waiting for a sandwich. His attacker yelled, "Death to cops night," which is significant. Other patrons of the Deli grabbed him and held him for police. The attacker, a youth of 16, had a phone number in his pocket that belonged to the Reverend Wright's church. In the town of Binghamton New York, you guessed it, about 11pm another officer was just about to get off duty. She went to her personal vehicle in the station parking lot and was hit with a bat by two unknown assailants. The Chicago and Binghamton officers are hurt, but will be ok. There is also security video of each attack. Now, in all three cities, and also in Boston, although none of our officers here were attacked, are numerous instances of tagging. All read, 'Death to cops night, Halloween.'"

The office door opened and Turner's secretary entered. "Excuse me sir, the FBI agents are here."

"Please show them right in."

"Yes sir." The agents entered and Turner, being a perfect host, got them chairs and introduced them to everyone in the room. When it was Sean's turn to be introduced, both agents had a smile on their face. They informed Sean that they had heard a lot about him from a mutual friend at the FBI, Nathan Green, and that they "look forward to working with you, sir." To anyone in the room who listened, the agents were just being friendly to the friend of a friend. But to Sean, they were members of the Sons and Daughters of Liberty!

Agent McNally started to speak, "Last night there were three separate attacks on police officers in LA, Chicago and NY. We believe that all three attacks were deliberately timed to occur at 11PM EST. One of the attackers, a 16 year old, recent immigrant from Palestine, was captured by citizens who witnessed the attack. But it appears someone was keeping an eye on him. Before he even made a phone call, lawyers from CAIR quickly arrived at the Chicago station where the attacker was being held. They have refused to allow him to be questioned. All three attacks took place in locations that are known to most people to be under constant video surveillance. Which means they wanted them recorded, obviously for propaganda of one kind or another.

Also, here in Boston, along with LA, Chicago, Binghamton,Detroit, Dearborn, Atlanta, NYC and other cities, graffiti has been sprayed painted in prominent locations, reading, 'Death to cops night, Halloween.' Obviously, this graffiti appearing all at once in so many locations is not the work of a small number of people, and is not a coincidence."

"That is all we have right now. We will keep you updated on any developments, but for now I think it is obvious that police are being targeted. Be careful and, let your officers know that they should be especially alert and aware of their surroundings and safety. Any questions?"

"Yes, are you part of an organized Federal task force? Is the Justice Department looking into this?"

"No, at this time there is no task force being organized; frankly I do not think that Mr. Holder is placing a very high priority on this. Our presence here and in some other cities is the result of a decision arrived at by the special agents in charge of the field offices. They are acting on their own authority and initiative."

Someone had not only declared war on the police, but also had taken offensive action in three different cities. And the Attorney General of the United States did not consider this a priority.

"Is there any racial aspect to these attacks?"

"I would say definitely not. The two LAPD Officers are both of Hispanic descent. The Chicago Officer is white and the Bingingham

Officer is black. No gender bias either, since both males and a female were targeted. The only color here is blue."

"Another aspect of this is the attacks were unannounced and cowardly. In Dearborn armed police officers were the target; the bike suicide bomber was obviously not afraid to die. But the other attackers were all aware that they could have been shot and killed by the officers, yet they went ahead with the attacks. We are dealing with a hardcore group of either religious or political fanatics, maybe a combination of both."

Commissioner Turner listened with a grave expression. "I see gentlemen. Thank you for being here. Please thank Special Agent Coburn for his concern and for sharing this information with us. I will alert not only the BPD but every Dept. in MA."

"Very good Commissioner. Here are our cards and numbers; please feel free to call us if we can help in anyway."

"Will do. Guys if you will all excuse me I really want to start contacting other departments."

It was as all the others were getting up to leave the office that Sean asked the agents to join him in his office.

Sean closed the door. "So, you are friends of Nathan's?"

11:00 hours The White House

Morning prayers had just ended. Kalaak got up off of his prayer mat and sat in his desk chair. The office door opened and his secretary, wearing a full burka –which was only appropriate– entered. She proceeded to place on his desk multiple articles from newspapers around the country reporting on the attacks on the police, as well as the graffiti warning of more attacks on Halloween. Maybe he had been premature in ordering both the warehouse drills and the attacks.

"Let the unbelievers wait for, think and fear of Halloween night. Let us see how they react, yes another pleasing day."

13:00 hours

Sean had a lot to think about. If the agents were right, then the FBI was more fragmented and demoralized than Nathan realized. Both agents had, over the course of the conversation, mentioned Kalaak. Apparently, his radical views were known to the FBI agents assigned to the White House, and his having called Nathan an infidel was known coast to coast. Anyway, it was good to know that Nathan's recruiting efforts within the Bureau were being so successful. Partly thanks to Kalaak.

Sean picked up the phone and dialed Sara's office number, but her office voice message came on. Sean left a message informing Sara that he could not come out to LA for the funerals.

MONDAY, SEPTEMBER 28TH 09:00 HOURS. THE FUNERAL OF THE LAPD OFFICER GARCIA, ST. CATHERINES CHURCH.

The funeral for Officer Barry Garcia was held first. Tomorrow would be Officer Stephen Vega's. Although both officers' funerals would be from separate funeral homes, they would both be buried in the same cemetery. Officers from all over the county would be attending the funerals. Most Canadian Police departments. were also represented.

Officer Garcia had been a first Lt. in the CA National Guard. His unit's primary mission was supply. Both on a battlefield or in the event of a natural disaster, he was there to help feed and shelter his fellow soldiers and civilians. At the request of the CA National Guard, Barry's wife Beth had given her permission to have Barry's casket carried to the cemetery on a monster army transport truck. Barry would have liked that. Barry would have also liked the dozen other army vehicles, mainly humvees, that would, along with a massive amount of police motorcycles and patrol cars, escort him to the cemetery.

Sara, Brian Olofson, Tony Lee, and Sheriffs Al and Joshua were the only members of the Sons and Daughters of Liberty that were present at the funerals. There was just no way for the rest of them to get the time off from their departments to attend all of the recent funerals.

As they were standing outside of the church waiting for the honor guards to carry out the casket, Sara could not help but notice the police helicopters circling the area. The copters were far enough away not to be heard, but close enough to monitor the roads leading from the church to the cemetery. "Is this what America has come to? We have to fear attacks on police funerals...almost seems like the level of security needed in Israel for the funerals of their fallen officers."

The church doors opened and a dozen officers of the CA National Guard, wearing dress uniforms and carrying dress swords, slow-marched in perfect silence from the church. Sara was watching closely, inspecting them, comparing them to an honor guard unit of naval officers. Counting their steps, she estimated that in twenty steps they would come to a halt, wait five seconds and then turn inwards. Facing each other they would raise their swords, making an archway for the casket and mourners to pass under. Sara was slightly ashamed of herself. She knew it was childish, and maybe even a little disrespectful, to let interservice rivalry surface at a time like this. She did admit to herself that the soldiers looked good. She glanced to her right where members of the U.S. Navy, including Susan Nguyen and Amanda Ti, were standing at attention. Next to the navy came the Air Force, then the Marines, and at least a full company of soldiers, who were standing by the army vehicles.

The coffin was carried out by both police officers of the LAPD and soldiers of Garcia's national guard unit.

An army drummer beat a slow march as the coffin was carried to the transport truck. As the front of the coffin reached each row of massed officers and military personnel, they raised their right hands in salute.

Barry's wife Maria, his mother and father, brothers and sisters all followed closely behind the casket. As Sara watched she was struck by the fact that, despite their suffering expressions, the entire Garcia family refused to cry and show any public weakness. It was as if they were refusing to let the murderers of Barry have any satisfaction in seeing them suffer, the Garcia's were a strong and proud family.

The coffin was placed on the transport truck, the Garcia's entered the limos, the motorcycles were started with a roar, police cars turned on all of their lights and the procession, with it's escort of helicopters began the drive to the cemetery.

The LAPD and CA Highway Patrol blocked off every intersection that the funeral procession would pass through, white gloved officers at the intersections saluted as the procession passed by.

It took 45 minutes for all of the police, military and civilians mourners to get arranged around the grave. Once again, as she had witnessed on too many occasions, they were here to say a final farewell Not a goodbye; that implied that the officer would be forgotten. No, far from it. Barry's name would be engraved on the monument in DC for fallen police officers. In a sense, Barry and every other fallen officer would be with them in DC for the police revolt. In addition, the names of fallen officers would be engraved on plaques in their police stations. Many departments would remember the fallen by announcing at daily roll calls and reading over the dispatch channels the names of officers who had been murdered that day, whether two hundred years ago or just last year. No it was not goodbye, just farewell.

The priest finished his graveside prayers. Barry's wife was presented with the casket flag, taps began to play, the military Honor Guard fired a twelve gun salute. The Garcia's and other civilian mourners began to leave the cemetery, but the Police and Military just remained at attention.

When the Garcia's family limo exited the cemetery, the bagpipers began to play *Danny Boy* and *Amazing Grace*. Officers and military, as they had done in Dearborn, lowered the casket into the ground and began to file by, each taking a handful of earth and throwing it down on the casket. Once the grave had been filled in, a final salute was given.

Officers from the LAPD had attended many police funerals, both in and out of state for fallen officers. Wherever they had traveled they were always treated as honored guest by the local depts. and individual officers. They were going to go above and beyond in hosting the officers who were paying respects to two of their own. The LAPD had quietly "rented" a convention center as close as possible to the hotels that the visiting officers were staying in.

Restaurants from all over LA had agreed to donate food and refreshments for two days. It was not only a kind gesture, but sent a clear message to cops all across the country that they were appreciated and supported by the people.

Sara entered the center with Susan and Amanda. They had driven to LA in Sara's dept. car and were sharing the same hotel room. She scanned the crowd and noticed that Sheriffs Al and Joshua were huddled in a corner table with the Sheriff of LA County, Daniel Henderson. She could guess what they were, or soon would be, talking about.

They walked over to the buffet that had been set up, picked up a plate and got into line. She heard Susan and Amanda talking about some guy and how handsome he was and just had to ask, "Who are you two checking out?" They both laughed and reminded her that she was married.

"That big, tall, good looking, muscular blond giant standing right there and grinning at us. Oh no, he's coming over!"

Sara just had to laugh, there could only be one guy here who matched that description. She remembered in Dearborn how she had been telling Brian all about Susan and what a good wife she would make. Well, maybe she did have a little cupid in her.

Sara watched Susan's face as Brian approached. They both had a radar locked onto each others eyes, and she wished she had a movie camera to record the stupid grins on their faces. Amanda too had instantly picked up on the radar lock, and stepped back to watch the show.

Brian came right up and said "Sara, will you please introduce me to your friend?" Susan just had that grin on her face and stared at Brian. Amanda was envious, but happy for Susan, and Sara could not resist. "Brian, this is Susan Nguyen and Amanda Ti. Susan is the girl I was telling you about in Dearborn, remember? She is also a member of our group."

Brian did not even answer, but just took Susan by the hand, which she willingly gave, and led her to a table to talk. Amanda and Sara just watched them walk away, "Ah, young love."

"Do you have anymore friends like that, you know, one for me?" Sara laughed and said, "Maybe, but let's eat right now."

They walked over to a table where Tony was sitting talking to three men and one woman that Sara did not know. The conversation looked relaxed so Sara thought that it would be ok to ask if she and Amanda could join them. "Hi Tony, if I am not interrupting could we join you?"

"Sara please sit down, this is Jacquelyn Wang, Corey Phillips, Justin Anderson and Mark Hayes. They are all with the FBI. Guys, this is Sara Mahoney; she is a Captain with the San Diego PD and an LT. in the Coast Guard Reserve. And I have not had the pleasure of meeting this young lady yet."

"This is Amanda Ti. Amanda is an Ensign in the Navy, she's here with another mutual friend, Susan Nguyen, who is a Lt. in the Navy."

As they were sitting down, Tony casually mentioned how the FBI agents were all good friends of Nathan Green. Sara took her cue right away, saying, "It's always a pleasure to meet others who are Nathan's good friends."

"By the way Sara, have you seen Brian? I lost him somewhere, we flew out here together from Chicago and are sharing a room. I wouldn't care, but he has the keys to the rental car." Sara and Amanda just laughed,

The night was coming to an early end. Everybody knew they had another funeral tomorrow. Sara walked up to Brian and Susan who were still lost in their own world.

"Time to go kids. Oh and when is the wedding?" Before he even realized that he was saying it Brian, the confirmed bachelor with a million girl friends said, "Soon I hope!" Susan just beamed.

"Well did you two figure out that you are both in the same group?"

"No, what are you talking about?"

"The Sons and Daughters of Liberty!"

"Your kidding, talk about the perfect girl!"

TUESDAY, SEPTEMBER 29TH 0900 HOURS CHURCH OF THE IMMACULATE HEART

The scene was surreal. Here they were, standing for the second day in a row outside of a church, for another murdered police officer's funeral. Officer Stephen Vega's funeral would be just as solemn, and filled with as much pomp and ceremony, as that of Officer Garcia's. Sara was pleased to note that even though Officer Vega had not been a veteran, all of the military that had been present for Officer Garcia's funeral were also here today. As she looked up she saw that the helicopters were on station high above.

The Church doors opened and the Honor Guard of Army Officers, with swords drawn, stepped out of the church and slow marched 20 feet. They stopped, turned towards each other with parade ground precision, and, as one, lifted their swords high to form an arch for Officer Vega's coffin and family.

Today's funeral was much sadder than yesterday's. While Officer Garcia had no children, Officer Vega had four. His eldest, Nancy, was a girl of about thirteen who was having a hard time trying not to cry. She was walking between her mother, who was in a state of shock, and her younger brother. Stephen Jr, who was trying to fight back the tears and be brave. The other two boys appeared to be about seven and eight years old. Both were dressed in blue suits and had LAPD badges on their chest. Nancy, in an amazing act of courage, had given her father's eulogy on behalf of her family. She spoke of how her father was always there for them, coaching softball teams, going to parent teacher conferences, playing catch, or any other game with them that they wanted to. Dad had to work a lot to support his family, most cops did, yet he always called home to check on them, wish them goodnight, ask about homework, and a thousand other things. He would be a father when he had to be, but usually he was more like an older big brother. He kept them and many people who he did not even know safe from the world. Yet he could not keep himself safe, it just was not fair!

Officer Vega's coffin was placed in the back of the hearse. The motorcycles and police cars started their engines. The procession drove through the streets that were blocked off. White gloved officers saluted as the hearse passed by. The repetition of it, the reliving of the previous day, caused heightened emotions. For many, it was too much.

The hearse arrived at the cemetery. The coffin containing the remains of Officer Vega was reverently carried over to the grave. Uniformed officers and military personnel formed ranks. Taps played. The Vega family said there last farewell and left the graveside, officers and military saluting the family as they passed by.

Dannyboy began playing on the bagpipes as the officers passed by next. Each picked up a handful of earth and threw it into the grave, thinking of their own families. Why were they doing this job? Not to get rich, that was for sure. No one really cared. Make a mistake, an honest mistake, and too bad, you go to jail. Why? Accidentally violate a guilty suspect's civil rights, and the charges against the suspect would be dropped, the ACLU would sue, the suspect would receive millions, and you might go to jail. Why do this?

As the last officer passed the grave, the salutes came down, the formation was dismissed, and they all headed back to their hotels and then on to the convention center.

11:00 hours Chicago

Captain Ed Larkin had not slept more than three hours a night since the attacks of the 20th. Two LA Officers were dead. By the grace of GOD both a Chicago and Bingingham Officer would live. Nathan Green was absolutely correct, these attacks and the Dearborn bombing were related. They all believed they knew the how of it. They had quietly reached out to their friends on the RCMP and asked them to increase their monitoring of known radical Islamist in Canada. The Canadian laws regarding wiretapping were much more pro-police than American laws.

Nathan Green had even reached out to his contacts in the Israeli Mossad, asking them if they had any information, but nothing yet. At Nathan's suggestion the picture of the 16 year old was sent to Mossad and Interpol, hoping that their facial recognition computers would give them a name, identify any associates, anything at all. His detectives were conducting one of the largest investigations in years. For days and nights everyone on the streets leading to the deli was being approached and shown a picture of the 16 year old, which, since he was a juvenile, was technically illegal. Security footage had been requested and freely given to the police by the business owners. The search had been expanded block by block. Obama's buddy, the self-proclaimed wounded Israeli war hero and Mayor of Chicago, Rahm Emanuel, would hit the roof when he found out how much money was being spent on police overtime try-ing to solve this case. The knife used in the attacks had been sent to the FBI crime lab, where to their credit the the FBI techs, who were among the best in the world, found one piece of DNA evidence from an unknown black male under the handle of the knife. Evidence that may or may not prove to be of value at some point. In addition, the fingerprints and DNA of the 16 year old suspect were found on the knife.

The ACLU lawyers were still refusing to let the 16 year old speak with the police. No parents or legal guardians could be found, and it now appeared that the 16 year old was in the country illegally. This of course delighted the ACLU lawyers, who were now arguing that the youth should be released to a foster home pending his application to remain in the country. Apparently, the attorneys had forgotten the fact that the "youth" had attempted to assassinate a police officer by stab-bing him in the back, and had shown no remorse. It even took a special ruling from the Chicago Juvenile Court to force the attorneys to tell the police the name of the juvenile—Saddam Uday Daher. At two separate juvenile hearings Daher had refused to speak. His attorneys had argued for a complete medical exam, including a psychological exam, at the taxpayers expense. The court of course promptly agreed to this, and the attorneys, in a further attempt to stall proceedings, vehemently argued against what they just argued for.

Under a heavy police guard Daher was immediately transported to Chicago General Hospital for examination.Captain Larkin himself had twice called Wright's Church to request a meeting with Wright. On both occasions he was informed that as soon as the reverend had an opening in his busy schedule they would contact him.

Today one of his detectives let him know that the phone number that had been found in Daher's pocket had been disconnected.

The phone number...obviously it was for Daher to contact someone in Wright's church, but who? Larkin remembered that the Obama's themselves were members of Reverend "GOD damn America" Wright's flock. Larkin wondered if Daher called the number, would the call have been forwarded to Obama?

If only the media had investigated and reported the truth about Obama when he was running for office, what a stronger country we would have. Instead the media had shielded and lied for Obama. They destroyed anyone, such as "Joe the plumber" who dared to question Obama.Over and over during the campaign, the media kept reporting that "Obama was an attorney, a professor of Constitutional law." Of course the media would never report that both Obamas, like both Clinton's had had their licenses to practice law revoked! Wonder why that was?

Larkin knew that he was going to get into some trouble, but he was running out of options. So this coming Sunday he and his detectives would stand outside of Wright's church before and after "services" and show Daher's picture to members of the congregation. More than likely nothing would come of it, but you never could tell. The more Larkin looked at Daher's photograph, the more he doubted that Daher was only 16 years old. In a warped way it made perfect sense to have a juvenile, or someone *claiming* to be a juvenile, commit the attack. If arrested and convicted, a juvenile would serve much less time in jail or prison than an adult would. Now who associated with Wright's church and Obama played with bombs....?

16:00 hours. The LA Convention center

Sara, Susan and Amanda entered the center. Oldies music was playing over the sound system. This was not a party, but a get together after the cemetery where families gathered to take comfort in each others' company.

They were immediately waved over to a table by Brian, who, judging by the silly expression on his face, was even more infatuated with Susan then he was yesterday. As they walked over to the table Sara and Amanda both just looked at each other, Susan had the same silly look on her face as Brian did. Sara also noticed that the members of the group had staked out two corner tables, and their new friends from the FBI along with Sheriff's Al and Joshua's new friend were sitting at the tables.

Brian got up and met them halfway. He and Susan gave each other a big smile, big hug and a little kiss on the cheek. "Ah teenagers," thought Sara. The Reverend Sheriff Al was also watching, and was relieved that Brian had found a girl who appeared to be single. Maybe his prayers had been answered and now Sara would leave Brian alone!

Brian graciously offered to get drinks for them. The girls made it simple; three rum and cokes with lime. As Brian went to get the drinks, Sara, Susan and Amanda approached the tables. All the men rose to greet them, and they all sat down together. The only person there whom they had not already met was Al and Joshua's friend. Al quickly introduced them, "Ladies I would like you to meet a close friend of ours and a new Brother in the Sons and Daughters of Liberty, Calvin Childs, or C.C. as we call him. Calvin is the Sheriff of LA County."

Tony began the conversation. "I have been listening, eavesdropping, on comments from all of the officers yesterday and today. They come from all around the country, but are expressing the same frustrations, fears, anger. They are tired of the stress on their families and themselves. They are resentful that in a nation of 300 million people, less than one per cent of the population is defending the country." Sara, Susan and Amanda all just shook their heads and said,"It's the same in the Navy. Obama keeps committing us to missions that continue to demoralize and wear out the military, we get no new ships or equipment, the Army gets no new tanks, Airforce no new planes, just more and more missions."

"I am sure that Sean has already heard all this but it can't hurt to remind him. I think that one, the military is ready for a corrective action. By addressing these concerns we will not only gain their further support, but are actually strengthening the military. Two, as an amateur historian I am always awed by the strong similarities between the Roman Empire and the United States. Rome never should have fallen. Just as is happening to the United States, they were so internally weakened and fragmented, there was so much political corruption, that they could not only no longer expand, they could not eject the foreign tribes from the empire. Towards the end of the empire the soldiers would often sell the office of Emperor to the highest bidder. Compare that to elected offices in this country going to not the best candidate, but all too often the candidate with the most money. I do not believe that in May our military would seize the opportunity and take over. But, it might be something to think about."

"Your crazy, our military would never do that. As a naval Officer I would never participate."

"I'm not saying that it will happen and I agree with you that it probably won't. Just a thought that's all."

They noticed that the center had rapidly filled up. There was a stirring in the center, people were standing up. Both the Garcia and Vega families had entered and were walking from table to table to thank the Officers for being there for them. Given the fact that they had just buried their husbands and father, it was classy as well as courageous.

WEDNESDAY, SEPTEMBER 30TH 08:00 HOURS.

Sean and Sean Jr. were on the road heading up to Fort Devens in Ayer,MA. for some long range target practice. This would be the last time that Sean Jr. would practice with the Boston SWAT team. His orders had been changed, and he was to report to Marine base Quantico on October 1st. Apparently General Quinn was determined to not only keep his own hat, but to win the hats of the other joint chiefs.

They had exited the Mass Pike and were traveling on route 2 when they decided to stop and get a light breakfast at a roadside stand. Fall was in the air, and a few leaves were starting to change color. Sean asked his father if they could sit at an outside table and enjoy the air. Sean read-ily agreed; anything to spend more time with his son.

Over the last few days they had spent a lot of time talking about the plans for the revolution, house cleaning, corrective action, whatever you wanted to call it.

Sean Jr. was still in a semi state of disbelief. He had always been proud of his father. If his father only knew of the hours Sean had spent in a barracks, on a training range, or mission in the desert waiting for extraction, bragging to the guys about his father. Almost as many hours as Sean Sr. had spent bragging about Sean to everyone he knew.

"Dad, you know this is going to work, everything seems well thought out. Just what happens if no Senator or Congressman will accept the Office of President under these circumstances?"

"That has been discussed. If that happens, I myself favor General Kelly, but if he or another member of the Joint Chiefs will not accept, then some in our group, well, they think that I should."

"Dad, you as president?"

"Yeah, but I don't like the idea. I'm not qualified, and it will not hap-pen anyway. Just the thought of me as president would make a senator or governor want to take the office." They both just laughed. Sean Jr. could not get the thought out of his head; his father, The President of The United States!

"We still have another 25 minutes to get to Devens, we should get on the road."

"Ok, let's go."

Upon arrival at Devens, Sean assumed his role as officer in command and checked in at the range masters office. The rangemaster was visibly impressed when Sean informed him that there was a member of the Army's Delta Force with them, who also happened to be his son. Of course the rangemaster insisted on meeting him.

Originally they were to be assigned to the Tango range. But, given that a member of Delta Force was here, they could use the Delta range, which was not only much closer, but was completely automated. Sean thanked the rangemaster and upon exiting the office observed that his SWAT team had also arrived in their semi armored SWAT truck. They all proceeded through the security gate and followed the road to the Delta range. They could hear automatic firing close by, not rifle fire such as from an AR 15, but big stuff, like squad automatic weapons maybe even a .50 cal or two. Just as they were exiting their vehicles a platoon of M1A1 tanks climbed over the hill and came down the road towards them. The tanks were truly impressive; although they were only traveling at 10 MPH, the earth shook. The barrels of the cannons looked as big as a cave, the engines seemed to growl like a wild animal, and at 70 tons there was no stopping them. They passed on by the tank commanders, giving a friendly wave.

Sean thought of what it would be like to face those tanks if... He put the thought out of his mind and gave the order to set up to fire. Everyone was getting their gear out when the rangemaster arrived.

"Sorry if I am intruding, I really just want to see your son shoot."

"You are more than welcome And maybe could you help me with this target control system, it looks like it should be on a spaceship, not a firing range." With a smile on his face the rangemaster assured Sean that it was an easy system to use. Yeah, sure it was.

The firing would be as follows: 20 rounds rapid fire at both 50 and 100 yards. Then 20 rounds, with thirty seconds to fire at 200 yards, 20 rounds with 40 seconds at 300 yards, and 10 rounds in under a minute at 400 and

500 yards. That was about the maximum range using a 14.5' barrel, with military spec. M193, 5.56 NATO cartridge.

As there were only eleven shooters today, ten from the Boston SWAT and Sean, the shooting would go rather quickly. The rangemaster programmed all of the stations into the target control system. The targets would be electronically scored by station. All shooting would be from the prone position.

Over the PA system he then advised all shooters to check their weapons for barrel obstructions and to place on their eye and ear protection. "Is the line Ready?"

"The line is ready, commence firing!" As one, the rifles started to fire; most finished firing their rounds in under 15 seconds. Sean fired his in closer to 10 seconds. The scores came in; all shooters had scored 100 on the fifty yard shoot, but the grouping of the rounds were much more spread out on some targets than on others. Sean's grouping was phenomenal. Most of his rounds had gone through the same hole, dead center in the target with the other two touching the center hole.

The same commands with similar results occurred at the 100 yard target. At the two hundred yard target, although most of the rounds were still in the black or center of the target the grouping of the shots were much more spaced out. Except for Sean's. At 300 yards Sean's groupings still were almost dead center in the target.

The range master called a two minute time out to let the shooters stretch.

"Your son can really shoot."

"Yes he is pretty impressive, I am glad he is on our side."

"I saw a press release or announcement about the SWAT military competition at Quantico, will he be there?"

"Yes, he is one of the 20 Army team members. I don't want to discourage my guys or hurt their feelings but I don't think that they can compete with the military teams at long range with the AR 15, not to mention the Barrett's 50 cal sniper rifle."

"That's impressive, wish I could see that."

"Would you like to go as a my guest?"

"Thanks anyway but I can't get away. But I'll be rooting for your son."

He called the shooters back to the line and announced that the line was hot, commence firing!

At 400 hundred yards Sean's rounds were still in the inner center circle, three of the SWAT shooters managed to keep all of their shots on the black.

"Ready commence firing", all the shooters used their full minute at the 500 yard target, even with the laser sights the targets appeared to be the size of a postage stamp.

One minute later the command "cease firing" was given. They all got up and gathered around to learn their scores, they could see the range master just shaking his head. He announced that one shooter had gotten a perfect score of 100 at the 500 yard target. They all knew that it was Sean.

While they were packing up, a column of armored vehicles that Sean had never seen before came down the road. They had no unit markings on them, nothing whatsoever to identify them by. Sean asked the rangemaster "What are those and who do they belong to?"

"Those are Street Sweeper armored cars, nasty things, they belong to the Dept.of Homeland Security. Come out here every couple of months, fire thousands of rounds and then leave. No one will tell me where they are based; I would guess on a closed military base. Our Governor Patrick and Obama are big buddies, love to know what they are up to with them. Whenever they come out here I only see one person, he comes in and registers when he arrives and checks out when they are leaving."

"What does he look like?"

"Hard to describe. Has an accent, almost sounds Russian. White guy, but with a hint of oriental in him. Never really says much." Sean had goosebumps all over him. He went over and explained everything that he had just been told to the guys. "What do any of you make of that?"

"Don't know Sir, but it's not good. Obama and Patrick, what a team, both cop haters. As an attorney Patrick has defended cop killers for free, nice guy!"

They packed up, the range officer told Sean that he would go ahead and check him out, no need to stop in, he wished them all good luck in Quantico, shook Sean Jrs. hand and said "that was some shooting and I ought to know I see enough of it."

"So dad what do you make of the Streetsweepers being there and what are you going to do about it?"

"I wish we left sooner, I should have thought of following them to see where they went."

"I guess we have to wait till Monday to find out about those Street Sweepers, first time I ever saw one. Did you notice that they each had four squad automatic weapons all protected by armour, one on top, one on each side and one in the rear. No one has much of a chance of getting close to one of them. They can probably hold at least eight or maybe ten men, in addition to the gun crew."

"Think of that name for GOD's sake, street sweeper, what would they be sweeping off the streets? People of course, American Citizens. And if they were deployed it would be in response to protest by the American people. So much for Obama defending 'the right of the people to assemble between street sweepers and drone missile strikes on American citizens in this country.' What are they up to?"

"That's easy dad, they are preparing to shoot us, we the people down, if we finally have the courage to seriously challenge them. They are afraid that one day they might actually take something from us that would be the straw that broke the camel's back and cause the people to revolt. Ironically I believe that the thing that would break the camels back is what the liberals, the democrats and their friends in the United Nations fear the most and want to take the most: guns. They can never fully enslave the American people while the people remain armed. But somehow instinctively the American people seem to know this; look at elections. Historically, and just recently again. The United States Supreme Court has ruled in two landmark cases that the Second Amendment is an individual right, not a right just for the military. So what does Obama and his allies in the Congress do? They try to enter into treaties with the United Nations to disarm the American people. Of course no nation that believes in it's own sovereignty would let the U.N. destroy it's Constitution." Sean looked over at his father, he knew the signs and could tell that a major explosion of that Cuban and Irish blood was coming. Instead Sean Sr., maybe acting Presidential, called his friend Joe Annino. Joe answered on the first ring.

"Sean, sir, how are you?"

"I am fine Joe. Actually, I'm not. I'm kind of angry, myself and my son were just up at Fort Devens, in Ayer MA. a closed Army base. While we were leaving a column of street sweeper armored cars came driving past us leaving the range. They had no unit or any type of markings on them. I asked the range master about them and he informed me that they show up at the range every couple of months, and seem to be commanded by a Russian. I know we have located some possible locations for them in other states, but I never thought that they were here in MA. And what about the Russian?"

"We both know that the Department of Homeland Security has the street sweepers, and we probably have no real idea of how many bases they have spread across the country. The Russian though, that's troubling."

"Ok Joe, we will talk later and I look forward to seeing you in a few days down at Quantico."

"So, he had no idea about the Russian either?"

"Nope, but we are going to find out about him, I promise you that!"

"Who are you calling now, on your burner phone no less?"

"Nathan Green, FBI."

"Hi Sean, what's up?"

"Nathan I think I just stumbled onto something critical, and I would like the FBI to check it out, unofficially of course. You got a moment?"

"Go ahead Sir".

Russian Army Major Peter Mikhal Kalashnikov was the great nephew of the famed designer of the AK 47 rifle, Mikhal Kalashnikov. He was in command of the Russian soldiers stationed at Fort Devens. They were part of a full division of elite Russian Soldiers stationed in the United States since the signing in 2013 of the "Security at Mass Events" agreement between the U.S. Department of Homeland Security and the Ministry.

Of course foreign troops, including Polish, Russian and Canadian, had been stationed in the U.S. since Obama's election in 2008 training in urban warfare drills. The original idea had been that of the United Nations. Foolishly the U.S. State Department released information on the foreign troops in its Publication 7277. But with the Department of Homeland Security gaining such strength and creating such impressive forces, modeled on the KGB Interior Security Forces, it had been both useful and necessary to create bases across the U.S. to train on and store the equipment.

Before his arrival in the U.S. and as part of his mission briefing, he had been informed that in the U.S. it was illegal under, Posse Comitatus, for the military to conduct police patrols. He found that funny since his troops and other foreign troops had been conducting patrols with Homeland Security units.

He was thinking of this weekend when he would go to a closed former U.S. Air Force Base outside Washington DC to visit his friend Colonel Dimitri Abramovich. He was in Command of the base where 4 full squadrons of Russian Mig fighter bombers. It was amusing, the U.S. closed their bases to their Air Force for lack of funding, but Homeland Security opened and fully maintained the bases for the Russian Air Force. The joke even got better. When Russian Backfire Bombers came into American Airspace, the American people were told that the U.S. fighters had escorted the Russians out of the area. In reality, it was Russian pilots flying Russian planes, with U.S. markings from the "closed U.S. Air Force base," that flew up to say hello and exchange pleasantries with their comrades.

He knew that the planes were based there for multiple purposes, first to protect Obama and the useful idiots in the U.S.Congress from harm; the U.S. could not be conquered without their help. Secondly, well secondly, to destroy those same useful idiots, if necessary. The thought made him laugh.

SATURDAY, OCTOBER 1ST 09:00 HOURS

They had just finished breakfast, Sean was getting ready to drive Sean Jr. to Logan Airport for his flight to Quantico.

Shannon was in Sean's bedroom helping him to pack. She was trying to hold back her tears, it was always hard for her when Sean was leaving. The hard part was not knowing when she would see him again. Finola and Heather were sitting on Sean's bed, talking about what a great visit, how good it was to have Sean home, and already knowing the answer wondering when they would see him again.

Normally Sean would also have been feeling sad about his son's leaving. However this time was different; he, Shannon and the girls would be traveling to Quantico for the shooting competition. That should be quite a surprise for Sean Jr.

With a last long hug and kiss, Shannon let go of her son. Sean then turned and picked up both sisters, one in each arm, gave them a squeeze, a kiss on the cheek and with what looked like a tear in his eye, began the family ritual, a prayer that the herd said when parting from each other. It was an old Irish prayer: "May the road rise to meet you, may the wind be always at your back. May the sun shine warm upon your face, may the rain fall soft upon your fields and until we meet again, may The Lord hold you in the palm of HIS hand."

It was a quick drive to the airport. Sean helped Sean with his bag, slipped him some money, which Sean did not want to take "Do what you are told, this is from me and your mother. Be good, see you in a few days."

"Thanks dad, see you soon."

Sean then drove over to the state police barracks to see his old friend Major Jeff.

As he entered the barracks he was greeted by a trooper. The trooper obviously remembered Sean but Sean could not recall his name. "Let me get the Major for you sir."

"Thank you."

"Deputy, please come right in, the Major is waiting for you." Sean stepped in. He always enjoyed the view of the airport from Jeff's office. Planes landing and taking off, and the view of the harbor was not bad either. "Sean how are you, what's going on?"

"I'm great Jeff, just dropping my son Sean off. He's on his way to Quantico for a police military shooting competition so I thought I'd stop by and see you."

"Well glad that you are here. What would you like water, juice, coffee, tea?""Tea would be great. Jeff have you heard anything about the Department of Homeland Security, having or basing street sweeper armoured cars in the area of Fort Devens?" "No not off hand, why what is up?"

Sean then told Jeff about the street sweepers, and the Russian. Jeff listened intently, he was going over in his mind all that Sean was saying to him and he had a growing sense of unease in his stomach.

"So, could you discreetly ask the troop commander in the Ayers area if he knows anything?"

"Yes right now."

"Paul." "Jeff. what is going on?" Jeff put the phone on speaker. "Quick question, do you know anything about street sweeper armored cars in the area of Fort Devens?" "Not first hand, but my guys go in there a lot, a couple of them have seen the street sweepers, they drive past the main gate towards the hotels and then turn into the woods, that base goes way back in the woods, who knows what is in there."

"So they are not seen on the road."

"No, there have been no reports of that, why what is going on?" Jeff looked at Sean who nodded for him to go ahead. Jeff told Paul all that Sean had told him. At the end Paul said, "Do you want my troopers to do anything, follow them?" Sean shook his head no, "Just keep an eye open and report anything to do with street sweepers." "will do talk to you soon."

11:30 hours

Sean stepped into his office and sat in his chair, gazing out the window at the minaret of the Nation of Islam mosque. The pace of things seemed to be picking up quickly. Each day seemed to bring more and more problems, everyday it seemed that the United States was in more danger than anyone ever would have believed, maybe they had to move faster, not wait until police week. In the beginning he figured that the new president and congress would repeal all of Obama's executive orders, regulations, and so on. It now appeared that his suspicions were becoming certainties, a secret political army, possibly with foreign soldiers was being established within the United States, what was worse the U.S. military might not be strong enough on it's own to stop them, how many U.S. military personnel were even in the U.S?

15:00 hours

Sean had just finished writing a memo to the group that he planned on sending out this evening over the short wave radio. He was just about to leave his office when his burner phone rang.

"Sean this is Nathan, do you have a couple of minutes?"

"Of course Nathan, go ahead."

"I was able to call in a few favors and to get a friend of mine to do multiple flyovers of Fort Devens using drones. There is a small, maybe fifty acre, active military base within the boundaries of Fort Devens. It is set back a mile and a half from the main entrance gate. About half a mile in there is a fortified checkpoint, with uniformed soldiers manning it. We are unable to identify the uniforms that the soldiers are wearing, but they are carrying M16 rifles. There is a helicopter pad, barracks, motor pool, swimming pool, obstacle course and several other buildings, there also appears to be an entrance to an underground garage. The drone recorded Russian, English and you ready, Arabic, being spoken."

"Nathan can you make several copies, I want to share them at Quantico. And share this with Joe Garcia and Joe Annino; deliver them yourself. I just want to make sure that if anything happens to me or you the video will not be lost. Can you keep the drones flying over the base?"

"We can. I could even attempt an infiltration of the base, you know the FBI works with, shall I say, many freelance ex military."

"No, any slip ups and they would be alerted. Just keep the drones flying. I will be sending out a shortwave message to the group tonight."

"Ok I will call if anything new pops up, talk to you later."

22:00 hours The Dominguez house.

Sean and Shannon both went down into the basement. Sean opened the safe and removed his radio transmitter. He had already told Shannon all of the latest news so it was no surprise to her as he broadcast his message to the group. He then closed the message with a request that all of them make every effort to attend the competition in Quantico, a group meeting was needed. He had no idea that every word was being recorded by the spy satellites.

WEDNESDAY, OCTOBER 7, 11:00 HOURS

Sean and his family arrived at the State Police Barracks at Logan airport. He had already arranged with Jeff to park his car at the barracks while he was in VA. He quickly went in to see Jeff, both to thank him again for the parking spot and to inquire about the street sweepers at Fort Devens. Thanks to the drones, he of course already knew what was going on at Devens but it did not hurt to have multiple sources. Jeff rose to meet him as he entered, they shook hands and Jeff knowing that Sean had a plane to catch got right to it.

"There have not been any sightings of street sweeper vehicles reported, but there have been two other incidents. The first, a family was out hiking in the OX BOW National Wildlife Refuge, just a mile or so from Fort Devens, when they came upon a group of 43 armed men. Nothing happened, the men just marched past them in silence. The father claimed that they were wearing military style uniforms without any insignia and were carrying rifles, he also stated that they all had long beards and, his words, they smelt like they had not washed in weeks. The second incident was just two nights ago.

In the town of North Lancaster again just a mile or two from Devens. Two guys wearing uniforms without insignia started bothering a couple of the local girls. A fight starts, only one officer was on duty in the town, so he had to call for help from other towns. By the time the police all arrive the fight is over, the soldiers are bleeding pretty good. No one wants to press charges, they refuse medical attention, a friend of theirs arrives and drives them away. A trooper runs the plate, and it comes back, "restricted access". Never heard of that from the Registry of Motor Vehicles before. Police undercover cars always come back registered to the police department, thought that was strange."

"It certainly is. Please have the troopers keep track of anything else unusual that happens up there and let me know about it." Jeff gave Sean a strange look as if to say, "What are you up to?"

"Ok Sean will do, have a safe trip." Sean felt bad as he left the office. He knew for security purposes that the fewer people involved the better but he also knew in his heart that Jeff would be with them. It was not right to take advantage of friend and a friend at that who could shut down Logan Airport if required.

16:00 hours

The flight down was quick and uneventful. As promised Joe Annino was there waiting for them as they came out of baggage claim. They shook hands warmly and Sean introduced Shannon, Heather and Finola to Joe. They filled the ride to Marine Base Quantico with small talk, mostly about the match and family talk. Joe's wife Margaret was looking forward to meeting Shannon and, with a twinkle in his eye as he looked at Sean, Joe let them all know that his sons were looking forward to meeting Finola and Heather. Shannon and the girls all laughed; Sean just stared at his friend and shook his head.

Upon arrival at the base entrance gate the MP's on duty saluted and asked everyone for their identification. General Kelly had arranged for the many members of the group, including Sean and Joe's families to stay in the one family houses usually reserved for married officers and their families. With all the cutbacks and in the military downsizing there were plenty of houses to go around. Upon arrival at the house Joe's family, Margaret and his son's Joe Jr. and Andrew, along with Joe's daughter Grace came out to say hello.

Joe was so proud of his son's, they were tripping over themselves to carry the girls bags into the house for them. Sean saw Joe laughing and walked over to him and whispered, "I have a son to you know, can't wait to introduce Sean to Grace." Joe stopped laughing.

They were still outside talking when in about 45 minutes a black shiny SUV with no plates on it stopped at their door. Two Marine MP's exited the vehicle, saluted and politely stated that they were there to transport Deputy Superintendent and Colonel Annino to General Kelly's base command center. Sean felt good, he thought to himself that it felt really great to be back in a military environment, the police world was semi military, but this was real, even as a Colonel in the National Guard Joe recognized the difference. Shannon and Margaret just smiled waved by, looked at each other and said, "Let's see if the marines left us any wine!"

They arrived at the base command center. The MP's exited the SUV and while coming to attention opened the doors for them. They were met by a full Colonel; Sean was impressed, if a full Colonel had been detailed to act as your escort, well, you were important. From the outside, the command center looked liked a concrete building camouflaged to match the color of the ground. Inside was a highly polished corridor with a slight downward incline. At the end of the corridor another set of Marines came to attention, and without a word opened the door to the Commandant of the Marines, General Wayne Kelly's underground headquarters.

The electronics in the room looked like they should have been in NASA. The walls were filled with digital maps of the world, coded in color showing where each ship, satellite and known military unit of every nation was located. On the far side of the room was the communications station from which General Kelly could communicate with not only every Marine unit in the world but also with any U.S., Navy, Army, Air Force or Coast Guard unit anywhere in the world.

The most impressive thing about the office was the people that were in it: General's Kelly, McDonald and Carpenter of the Marines, The Chairman of the Joint Chief's of staff, General Stewart of the Air Force, General Quinn of the Army and Admiral Fletcher of the Navy.

General Kelly walked up to Sean and introduced himself, then said hello to his old friend Joe. Then one by one he introduced Sean and Joe to the rest of the generals and Admiral Fletcher.

General Kelly then started the conversation. "Sean let me first say to you that I greatly admire you. You have recognized the grave danger that this country is in and you have taken action to save the country. If not for you and the like minded people that you have recruited, in all likelihood we would not be standing here today. You and the rest of the members of the Son's and Daughters of Liberty have my greatest respect. I have briefed everyone in the room about your plans as far as I know them, but I want you to personally re-brief us as to what motivated you to begin this operation, your plans and if successful your vision of what will occur after Obama is removed from office."

Sean was understandably hesitant in briefing the combined Joint Chiefs of Staff, and telling them what was going to happen. General Kelly spoke up. "Don't worry Sean, you are among friends we are not going to bite you." At that Sean began a two hour briefing, that was seldom interrupted by questions.

After his talk, the doors opened and Nathan Green entered the room, himself looking a little nervous. Sean got up and quickly introduced Nathan to everyone. General Kelly spoke. "Please play the surveillance video from Fort Devens right now." He said please, but it was an order. Now it was Nathan's turn to be uneasy.

The video was timed stamped and Nathan narrated as the video played "Sir, if you listen you will hear the Russian language being spoken, now English and now Arabic. This individual here speaking Russian appears to be in command. Just today through the use of facial recognition we have identified him as a rising star in the Russian Army, Major Peter Mikhal Kalashnikov. Just today he took a commercial flight to Washington DC. He was picked up at the airport by a car from the Russian Embassy; I had both a drone and a mobile surveillance team follow him. The mobile team had to break off the tail when the car entered the rural roads of VA by the town of Philomont. The drone of course continued to follow. This is where, in my opinion things get spooky." At that, everyone in the room sat up.

"At one point the U.S. Air force operated a small clandestine air base by Philomont. The base was officially closed in 1998 due to budget cuts. Notice now, Kalashnikov's car is approaching the entrance gate to the base. Look at the guard turned out to greet him, I count fifty men there. Now look at the hardened bunkers that used to hold our F15 and 16 planes. They now are holding Soviet Mig 21 fighter bombers, painted in U.S. Air Force paint schemes. All told there are four full squadrons of planes on the base."

"Do you know who his host the base commander is?"

"Yes sir, his photo was obtained by the drone. Colonel Dimitri Abramovich, a highly decorated pilot in his own right. Gentlemen that concludes my briefing." General Stewart looked like he was about to explode, Russian planes on one of his closed bases!

The briefing by both Sean and Nathan had been very thorough. That, coupled with the military briefings, the nightly news and their own sources of information, left them in no doubt that what they had heard was accurate.

General Quinn spoke up. " Ok I am in, so that means the U.S. Army is in. What do you propose that we do Sean?"

"Wait a minute" said both Admiral Fletcher and General Stewart, "we are in to. Can't let the army and the marines have all the fun".

"Look guys, I am not a general, but it seems to me that the military will have to neutralize these bases. I think that we all know the threat is much greater than what we thought. The police will probably need help in taking on the Homeland Security bases in our cities. The military will also have to deal with any threat from any hostile government; that would probably be the air force and the navy at first anyway. The marines, army troops at Fort Bragg, and national guard units will seal off DC and stand by to help with any resistance. Oh, and seal off the U.N. building in NY.

Speaking of sealing off. Areas of the country such as Dearborn will require special attention. As I have said before, whatever force is needed will be used no half measures. Besides overwhelming force will send a strong message to anyone, including foreign governments who might oppose us.

The air force will be given the responsibility of transporting all arrestees, politicians, media, ACLU etc to Sheriff Joshua in Arizona."

"I thought you said you were not a general; you sure sound like one!"

"No kidding Sean, you are acting more presidential than Obama has in the last six years! We have our orders sir, will you allow us to plan the operational details for the targets that we have now and any future targets?" The magnitude of that question was lost on no one —they the Joint Chiefs were treating him like he was the president.

Sean did not miss a beat, "Of course admiral, the operational details are completely up to you, the military. I would also appreciate it if you would each consider who would be the most qualified person to be the next President of the United States. You will each have one vote, the same as the other core members of the group. I will ask for your votes right after the first of the year."

"Sean who do you think would be the best person to serve as our next president?" "Well, between us, I am considering Senator Cruz from TX, former Governor Perry of TX, Rand Paul, or Senator Demint. We also will need a Vice President, maybe Alan West, Condalisa Rice...any combination of those people and I think the country would be in good hands."

General Kelly remembering his duties as host offered to get everyone a drink, an offer that was quickly accepted. The rest of the night was spent going over plans and options. They were all impressed when Joe Annino informed them that the national guard and state police from VA, Maryland, West Virginia, North and South Carolina and PA were all on board,There was speculation about what may happen state by state if the people decided to follow their example and remove, replace local and state governments. Sean for one thought that the people should be allowed to do just that. He related to them how the Massachusetts State Senators and Representatives had just allegedly spent 20 million dollars in renovating one room, one room in the MA State House. It seemed impossible to spend that much money on one room, so how much brown bag money went to each politician? Also the state of MA had one of the highest tax rates in the country. Governor Patrick and other liberals were always saying how the working class people had to pay more in taxes to help the poor, meaning those who would not work.

Admiral Fletcher said that he was really impressed by the plans to mobilize the NRA, and veterans groups.

The next thing they all knew was that it was 4AM. General Kelly said that they were all welcome to stay, but that he was going to bed. He invited them all to meet him for lunch 12:00 hours, at the officers dining hall and they were all to bring their families with them.

THURSDAY, OCTOBER 8TH, 10:00 HOURS

Sean was still sleeping when Shannon came into the room, opening up the windows, letting all of that fresh cool air and sunlight into the room. She was just bursting with energy, pulling the covers off of him and telling him to get up, join the family, his son was here waiting to see him and asking him if he knew how badly he stank. Sean just groaned he knew from past experience that Shannon was probably a little put out by his coming home a little late last night. She obviously did not understand how hard it was to organize a revolution!

Being a gentleman he was not about to argue with his wife, he already could guess how the conversation would go. After making his morning toilet he walked jauntily into the kitchen, gave the girls and Sean a kiss on the head. Strangely, Shannon did not want her kiss, well her loss. While drinking a large glass of ice water Sean announced to the family that General kelly was expecting them all at the officers dining hall at 12 noon. Sean Jr. started to say that not being an officer he could not attend, but Sean told him that not only General Kelly, but Army General Quinn had stated that they wanted to meet Sean today, so there!

Joe Annino knocked on the door to let Sean know that Sara, and two ladies had just arrived. Ed, Brian and the Chicago SWAT team were on base; Ed and Brian had a house to share. Sean's cell phone rang, it was Brandon Robinson notifying Sean that he and the Philadelphia team had arrived.

12:00 hours

Sean, his family and the Annino family, along with the other members of the group walked into the officers' dining hall. Sean saw that General Kelly, the other Generals and Admiral Fletcher were already in the hall waiting for them. They all stood up as Sean and company walked over, introductions were made and Sean was pleased that General Kelly's wife, Jeanne, was there. Both Sean's were stunned when General Quinn walked up to Sean Jr. and introduced himself. "I had a look at your record Sean, very, very impressive. I also looked up your range scores, more than impressive. I guess the two go hand in hand. I am counting on you to not only let me keep my hat but to win for me the hats of all of these other gentleman here, understand that son?"

"Yes sir, will do." He knew better than to say he would try; trying would not be good enough for the general.

"Thanks dad, now I have a general watching me."

"Don't blame me Sean, I had nothing to do with you being chosen for the army team. But after seeing how you could shoot at Devens I understand why you were picked for the team."

"Not just picked dad, I guess I'm the captain of the team. I don't even know most of them, but by their records they are a scary group of guys."

"They probably think that you must be really scary if you are the team captain."

Sean just shook his head and laughed. "Come on dad lets eat".

The food was actually very good. The women were all looking at Brian and whispering to each other. Sara quietly gossiped with them about Brian and Susan. Amanda was laughing to herself while she watched Susan, who actually looked both jealous and possessive of Brian. Amanda promised herself that she would have to meet Sean jr.

Al, Audrey,Tony and Joe Garcia, along with their teams, had just arrived. General Kelly, again being a perfect host, invited them all to his home for a barbecue at 18:00. Nathan and Joe Garcia approached Sean and asked if it was possible to speak to the group directly; a partial fingerprint had been recovered from the frame of the bicycle that was used in the Dearborn bombing. The partial print had eight matching points; nine matching points were needed in a Federal court to admit the print as evidence. The partial print belonged to Saddam Uday Daher, the suspect in the attack on the Chicago Officer.

Sean immediately grasped the significance of the recovery of the print. "Up to you whether you want to tell the people that are here now or wait till later when everyone will be here."

"I think that It would be more beneficial to share the news now, get everyone thinking. Then I will let everyone know what the FBI and ATF are officially doing. We can all meet later when the rest of us arrive to go into more details. I think I will start over there with Ed, Brian and the group at that table. After all it was their officer who was stabbed."

They walked over to Ed's table and Sean interrupted the conversation. "Nathan and Joe have some information to share regarding the Dearborn bombings. " The silence was instant; so instant that it attracted attention. Sean noticed that the generals were all looking over at them so, in order not to offend them, he asked everyone to gather around the generals table.

Nathan began to speak. "I am going to ask everyone here to not repeat this to anyone other than ourselves, and then only in a secure area. We cannot let the media find out about this. Everyone agreed?" They all nodded or said yes.

"There has been a major development in the investigation of the Dearborn bombings— Ed and Brian, pay attention. A partial fingerprint has been recovered from a part of the bike frame that exploded at the police checkpoint killing the three officers. The partial print matches that of Saddam Uday Daher, the same Daher that stabbed the Chicago Officer in the deli." Ed and Brian just looked at each other, Nathan really had their full attention now. General Quinn spoke up.

"One, I'm not a cop, but what do you plan on doing with this information? Two, it seems to me from what Sean has already briefed us on, we now have a suicidal terrorist bombing in Dearborn, and three separate coordinated attacks on police officers in three separate cities. Daher, who was the stabber of the Officer in Chicago and apparently was involved with the Dearborn bombing, is linked to Wright's church by a disconnected phone number. And the domestic terrorist bomber, Bill Ayers, attends Wright's church, and both have links to Obama. Is that accurate? And we don't even know if Daher is the true name of the suspect?" Everyone sat in silence for a minute. Everything that the general said was known to be true, but what did it mean?

"Yes general I'm afraid that you have summed it up nicely and, given the amount of information, rather succinctly."

"So what are your plans now from a law enforcement perspective?"

"Sir, can we meet later somewhere we can talk more freely and privately?"

Now at was General Kelly's turn to speak, "19:00 hours in my command center."

The White House 14:00 hours

Kalaak was furious, he had just received a call from his CAIR contact. A member of CAIR had by the grace of Allah, been monitoring the progress of the FBI investigation into the Dearborn bombings. Kalaak had nothing to do with ordering the bombings, that was a spontaneous act by that idiot Aakif, who the FBI was calling Daher. No, the bombings were not his fault, but ordering the three attacks on the police officers, that was his idea. Aakif had brought much attention to them with the bombings and killing of the three officers. Therefore, it was Allah's will, revealed to him in a dream, that Aakif must die. Kalaak reasoned that in launching a knife attack on armed officers, Aakif would be killed. But Aakif had not obeyed. Oh, he had attacked and stabbed an officer, but his orders were to attack a *group* of officers, preferably coming out of a police station all together. Surely one would have shot him to death. The other two attacks were just diversions, designed to deflect some or all the attention away from Aakif. But now, the FBI had obtained a partial fingerprint that matched Aakif's, or Daher's, print. It would be only a matter of time before they realized that Daher was Aakif... then what. No, for years Aakif had served Allah well, in Palestine, Syria and Lebanon; it was time that he enter paradise. Now how to help him on his journey? Kalaak was actually both happy for and a little envious of Aakif, soon Aakif would be in paradise with Allah and his virgins. Aakif to be soon in paradise, being fed grapes...*being fed*! That was it! Allah had once again shown him the way! Kalaak summoned his assistant; she immediately appeared wearing her Burka. She was very well trained, as all females should be. She just stood there silently awaiting his will. "You will personally go to Abdus Shaheed. You will tell him that I wish to meet him tonight after evening prayers in the usual place; he is to come alone. You will then go to the Tabriz Iranian bakery, tell the owner, Abdul Mani, that I will be stopping in this evening for a box of his special dates." She immediately bowed and left both the office and the White House. She knew she was on an important mission for Kalaak, who was Obama's most trusted advisor, and all the faithful knew that Obama was the Mahdi.

Kalaak left the White House on his way to meet Abdus Shaheed. But first, a stop at the bakery. He was instantly recognized as he entered, and all bowed to him. While England, France and other European countries tried to stop the immigration of the faithful, the Mahdi had greatly increased the number of the faithful allowed to legally, never mind illegally, enter the U.S., that coupled with the birth rate of Allah's children! Soon the Star and crescent flag of Islam would fly from the roof of the White House!

Abdul Mani himself came out and handed Kalaak the box of dates. Kalaak went through the pretense of offering to pay for the dates, but Abdul Mani begged him to accept the dates as a gift. After all Kalaak's presence in his bakery was payment enough. They spoke quietly for several seconds and Abdul Mani assured Kalaak that the dates were very special indeed. Kalaak then went on his way to meet Abdus Shaheed.

As expected Abdus Shaheed was there waiting for him. When Kalaak drew near Abdus bent over and kissed Kalaak's hand. "I am honored, oh chosen of Allah, that you would once again call on me to obey your command."

"You have proven yourself to be a most loyal and capable servant, Allah has noticed you. Your place in Paradise is assured!"

" Praise Allah and thank you, what do you need me to do?"

"You will fly to Chicago in the morning. Take this box of dates to a lawyer named William Stedman. He is one of the attorneys representing Daher. You will tell Mr. Stedman that he must give these dates to Daher and no one else. If Stedman questions you, tell him that the dates have been prayed over by a Mullah and for religious reasons must be opened only by Daher before the sun sets. Do you understand?"

"Yes my master, I understand."

"Very well go now and may Allah protect you."

The generals were all there and waiting as the Sons and Daughters assembled in the center. By the look on their faces, everyone could tell that the generals were in a very serious mood.

As soon as the door shut Sean introduced the newly arrived members of the group to the generals. Admiral Fletcher started the conversation. "Has everyone who arrived this afternoon been briefed on the latest developments? I mean everything, Fort Devens, the secret air base, Russians, the fingerprint, am I missing anything?"

Sean spoke up. "No sir, you got it all."

"Ok Nathan and Joe you have the floor."

Joe indicated that Nathan could speak for them. "The FBI and the ATF have been working hand in hand on the bombings. The ATF has just within the last hour confirmed that the explosive used in Dearborn was military grade C4 which was originally issued to the U.S. Army. However, from the incomplete records that we have been able to obtain it appears that the C4 was transferred to the Dept. of Homeland Security, along with other weapons and munitions. We strongly suspect that some quantity of them are in the Homeland Security warehouses.

I have made a few more calls to my contacts in the Mossad, Interpol, MI5, and the Egyptian and Mexican Federal Police asking, them to once again check their fingerprint databases for Daher's print. We will see what happens. I have also ordered that Major Kalashnikov and Colonel Abramovich be kept under constant surveillance, let's see if they lead us to any other bases."

General Quinn then spoke up for the Joint Chiefs. "We have ordered flyovers by both drones and reconnaissance planes of all closed military bases. Our staffs, along with some national guard staffs, are already planning for a preemptive strike on the already identified Homeland Security warehouses, the air base and Fort Devens.

Brandon spoke up, "Excuse me general, awhile ago I read an article that hikers were complaining about not being allowed into remote sections of some of our National parks. Some of the hikers also claimed to have seen soldiers marching through the closed areas of the parks, they talked about secret bases being there . Seemed crazy at the time, but now..."

"Ok let me see if we can identify any closed off areas of the parks and get some flyovers of them."

FRIDAY, OCTOBER 9TH 08:00 HOURS

Everyone seemed to be up early and they all had the same thought. Going out to the firing range and watching the various teams practice. Sean noticed that his son Sean was standing over by the shotgun range with what he assumed was the army shooting team. It was obvious by the way that the men were standing around respectfully listening that Sean was in command.

Sean wanted to stay and watch the army team, meaning Sean jr, but he knew that he had better go and join the Boston team, or he would never be forgiven by the guys...He was pleased to see that his guys were really shooting well today. Most of the other police SWAT teams were using .40 caliber Glocks, the Boston SWAT and military teams used .45s, which was a much more powerful bullet.

Sean walked up to his best long range sniper, Sgt. Frank McCarthy. "So Frank, how are we going to do? Where should I bet my money."

"Good morning sir, bet on us of course! Seriously though from what I am seeing we will do ok. I am very confident in our building entry and clearing. On the other hand the military teams, especially your son, will probably clean house on the long range sniper course, not that we will not beat the other police teams."

Sean tried to conceal his pride. "Ok Frank, let me know if you need anything or if any problems come up. Like everyone else, I will be drifting around watching you and spying on the other teams."

"Ok sir, let me know if you spot any ringers."

"Oh, last thing the competition starts for real in the morning. Make sure everyone behaves and gets a good nights sleep tonight."

Sean, walked over to where Sara, Susan, Amanda and Audrey were standing. He noticed that Brian and Ed were also walking that way. Susan saw Brian coming, excused herself and walked over to meet him, "Hi Ed, mind if I steal Brian away for awhile?"

Brian did not seem to mind the prospect of being stolen. Ed just said,"Would it matter if I did?"

He could have saved his breath; they were not listening to him anyway.

13:00 hours

They all met at the cafeteria. Sheriff Al offered to say grace before the meal. As he was praying he looked around the table and was again relieved to see that Sara was not sitting too close to Brian. After saying Grace, Nathan yelled down the table, "Al this is Federal property, you can only pray to Allah here, not GOD!"

They all got a chuckle out of that. It was Joe Garcia who reminded them that the trial for the people who were arrested in the original rock attack on the police and city workers was to begin today. Nathan then informed the group that he had run the photographs of the crowd from the day Kalaak had come to Dearborn through the FBI's facial recognition system. Out of 62 photographs, only 27 were in the system. Meaning that the rest were illegal! That kind of took the fun out of the meal. Nathan just had to add that out of the seven who were arrested and charged, only three had shown up for trial today.

After lunch they decided to head back out to the range to watch some more of the training. As a group they headed over to the shotgun range, where both rapid fire shotgun, from a standing, moving and barricade position against,both fixed and moving targets would be tomorrow afternoons competition.

The generals were out touring the range with some of their staff members. They were all very impressed by the talent on many of the police teams, and were also taking the opportunity to build good will with the police by posing for photographs and trading jokes with the officers.

12:00 hours

Attorney Stedman was reviewing the report from the ATF regarding the partial fingerprint, allegedly from his client Dahar, recovered from the frame of the bike used in the Dearborn bombing. He thought to himself that he had better go to visit Daher and ask him about the partial print.

Most probably the print was not his client's at all. Or, if it ever came to it, his client had maybe ridden the bike out with friends, and the bomber had later stolen it for the bombing. His inner office door opened and his secretary came in to inform him that a man claiming to be a friend of Daher's was in the office and wished to speak to him. Stedman sighed. What could this be about?

"Ok, show him in please."

Abdus Shaheed entered the office as Stedman was standing to greet him, and walked across the floor with a huge grin on his face. Abdus immediately noticed that Stedman was wearing a Kippah, which of course meant Stedman was Jewish. Abdus truly appreciated the humour of the whole situation; a Jew defending one of the Prophets' most deadly bombers, acting as an errand boy for the Mahdi...it was just to funny; Allah did have a sense of humour.

"Mr. Stedman, it is an honor to meet you. My name is Abdus."

"A pleasure to meet you Abdus, how can I help you?"

"Sir, I read in the paper that you are one of the attorneys representing the youth Mr. Daher."

"That's correct."

"I bought these dates for Mr. Daher, they are a traditional Arabic gift for someone who is sick, in times of death, or other troubles. They have been prayed over and blessed by the Mullahs at my mosque. Would you please deliver them to Mr. Daher for me? Myself and, ah, other members of our immigrant community are afraid to go to the prison you understand of course?"

"Yes, indeed I do understand, I would be happy to deliver them for you. Would you like me to relay any other message to him?"

"Just that he is being remembered in our prayers."

"I can do that. I was actually just about to leave the office to go and see Daher now."

"Then let me detain you no longer, and thank you again for helping Daher. You have no idea how we Muslims are persecuted in this country, and it is so reassuring to know that good people like yourself are here to help us."

"Myself and others will always be there when someone's rights are being violated. Good day to you sir, I will be sure to give the dates to Daher."

It was about a 45 minute drive to the Federal prison where Daher was being held. Stedman showed his bar card identification at the entrance gate to the parking lot, and again to get into the prison. He advised the guards that he was there to see his client, Mr. Daher, and that he wanted a private conference room to speak with him. Additionally, he was invoking his attorney client privilege and did not want to be disturbed.

He entered the conference room which, thanks to the attorney client privilege, was not monitored in any way. The door opened and Daher was escorted into the room wearing handcuffs and leg chains. Attorney Stedman immediately demanded that the chains, all of them, be removed. His client was an innocent juvenile who had no previous arrest record. Stedman let the guards know that he would inform the judge about the way his client was being shackled and chained, as if he were a dangerous animal.

The guards just looked at him, removed the chains at his request, informed him to use the telephone to call them when he wanted to leave, left the room and locked the door .

Daher, or rather Aakif, thanked Stedman for coming to see him. He once again praised Stedman for his courage in representing him, and thanked Allah and his holy Prophet for Stedman. But inwardly, Aakif was repulsed by being so close to a Jew...at least a Jew he could not kill.

Daher just looked so young and helpless to Stedman that he wished to himself that there was something he could do brighten Daher's mood. Then, he remembered the dates.

He took them out of his bag and told Daher how a nice Arabic man, he could not remember his name had brought the dates into the office. He also told Daher how the dates had been prayed over by the mullahs. Daher immediately understood. His face visibly brightened. A peaceful, almost heavenly look came over his face. Allah was not only summoning him to paradise, he had delivered him the means of his passage to paradise. And as a final gift was letting him kill one last Jew. Oh, Allah was very merciful to those who loved him.

Aakif opened the box of dates and insisted that Stedman eat many. Stedman gladly accepted; not only would it be rude not to accept, but he also did like dates and hadn't had lunch. Aakif also began to eat the dates and, while watching Stedman closely, continued to insist that his friend share in his bounty.

They talked casually for several minutes, with Stedman commenting on how delicious the dates were. That was the last comment that Stedman would ever make. The cyanide was beginning to act. Aakif too began to lose consciousness; in his mind as he began to leave this world, he saw the clouds opening and paradise waiting for him.

It had been almost four hours since Stedman and Daher had begun their conference. The day shift guards were about to go home when their supervisor ordered them to knock on the door and check on Stedman. After repeatedly knocking and receiving no answer, the guards opened the conference room door.

19:00 hours. The officers club

Everyone was kind of tired. It had been two long days, and the next two promised to be both exciting and tiring with the competition in full swing. They had all gone up to the bar and were waiting for General Kelly to arrive before beginning to eat. Nathan entered the hall and looked visibly agitated. He had just received a call from one of his agents that both Daher and his ACLU Attorney had been found poisoned in Daher's cell. What was worse was that someone at the prison had called the local media and informed them of the deaths. They, along with the national news teams, were flocking to the prison. In Dearborn there was dancing in the streets and the faithful were praising Allah for bringing his servant into paradise.

Everyone just watched as Nathan approached them. "Well, once again I get to be the bearer of bad news."

It was Sean who asked, "What happened now Nathan?" As Nathan was beginning to speak General Kelly entered the hall. Telling Nathan to wait a minute, Sean asked the General to join them after he got his drink, which an aide promptly fetched.

"There is no easy way to say this, but Daher, our suspected bomber in Dearborn, and his attorney were just both found dead in Daher's jail cell. From what I have been told, poison is suspected, but we will have to wait on lab results to be sure."

General Kelly soke. "Apparently ISIS, Al Qaeda, Obama, or who-ever it was has a very long reach. I guess someone did not want to take a chance that Daher would talk."

The national news then came on. The lead story was live from IL; the scene was of the prison itself, with the reporter breathlessly and repeat-edly telling a dumbed down viewing audience that really nothing was known other than the fact that Daher and his attorney had been found dead inside of Daher's jail cell. They then went into the fact that Daher had allegedly stabbed a police officer and that what could be a par-tial fingerprint of Daher's had been found on the frame of the bike used in the Dearborn bombing where three police officers were killed. News teams had been sent to attorney Stedman's home and office to try to get a reaction from his family and co-workers. The public would of course be informed of any breaking developments.

Joe Annino was the first to speak after the broadcast ended. "Let this be another lesson to us all: we cannot underestimate these people. Apparently the enemy army that is here inside the U.S. is as well organized as we are. That means they also have an intelligence unit. Who knows, they may be getting their information directly from our sources; just like Nathan said CAIR has access to FBI offices and communications. Look at the Fort Hood shooter and the couple of soldiers who have gone over to the enemy in Afghanistan. I think that we will all have to get with our intelligence units and try and retry to identify anyone that we are not 100% sure of, both civilian and military." "You are absolutely correct Joe, I think we have to start with recent immigrants to the U.S. that have joined the military."

"That will set off alarm bells that we cannot afford."

"Yes you are right about the alarm bells, any other ideas?"

"What about randomly increasing the use of polygraph tests for people in sensitive positions, such as intelligence and communication units? Can't hurt."

"That's one way to go. Let's think about some others."

Tony then offered, "Is there any way to have a planning session with the Department of Homeland Security and FEMA? I know we do so on a limited basis, but maybe after several meetings go out for a drink or two with them, see if we can get them to let something slip."

"You, Tony, would make a good counter intelligence officer," Sara stated.

"Ok not a bad idea, lets think about it overnight. I for one am going to bed soon, I want to be up early to have breakfast and be at the range at 08:00 for the playing of the National Anthem and first events."

"Ok with me that sounds good. After one more rum and coke."

Sean went to get Shannon and the girls. Sean Jr. had stayed with his team going over final plans for the competition. Shannon was tired and ready for bed. His girls and Joe's sons, however, seemed to be having a great time talking and dancing together. As any father would, Sean took a step in their direction, but Shannon knew exactly what he was going to do. She reached out, grabbed him by the arm, and giving him "the look" said "they'll be fine, lets go to bed my love."

The White House 19:00 hours

Kalaak had been anxious all day, sitting in his office and keeping the news on. It was on returning to his office from evening prayers that he saw the news and knew that Allah had answered his prayers. He did not know if he was happier that Aaif was dead or that he had gone to Paradise. Abdus must be rewarded!

SATURDAY, OCTOBER 10TH 07:00 HOURS

Sean was up before the alarm went off, but he was not having much luck in trying to wake Shannon. He kept prodding her, attempting to get a response, then thought of the one thing that would get her up, "Time to go and see your son." At that her eyes opened; she did not say a word, but got up to see Sean. He then went to wake up Finola and Heather— they were dead to the world, Shannon informed him that they did not get in until sometime after three in the morning. "Annino's boys, they are to blame for this," thought Sean.

Sean quickly hatched a plan for revenge. He knocked on Joe's door and let him know that they were all going to get breakfast and then go to the range. He also asked Joe to let his son's know that Finola and Heather wanted to have breakfast with them. He and Shannon, with the girls sleeping soundly, then left the house and went to the cafeteria.

It was no surprise that the cafeteria was filled. Sean noticed that Audrey was talking to several news reporters, he was both surprised and pleased that any had showed up to cover the competition not only was it good PR, but it helped to prepare the cover story for police week when the military would be joining them in DC.

The Annino's then entered all five of them, the boys had some how managed to get up out of bed. Sean wondered what could have gotten them up so early after such a late night. Sean waved them over to the table and laughed when he saw how quickly the boys got there. They were so polite, looking around the table and then searching the cafeteria while they both said "good morning Mr and Mrs. Dominguez. Is your whole family here?" Sean just smiled at Shannon and with an Irish twinkle in his eye said, "Actually no, Sean is with his team, I guess you will see him soon and the girls are still in bed asleep, apparently they came in kind of late last night."

Joe had heard the conversation and instantly knew what it was about, he roared with laughter while Margaret and Shannon just stared at him. His sons, being tired were a little slower on the uptake but then realizing that they had been foxed, also laughed. "I guess we did bring them home a little late sir, but we were just sitting on the bench across from the house, honest."

"I believe you guys, but your father would tell you the same thing, you will not understand until you have daughters of your own."

They and most of the other people in the hall were leaving the cafeteria and walking out towards the ball field. The day's events were to start with the combined bands of the Army, Navy, Air Force and Marines playing the National Anthem in unison and then each band would play their own sevices song. The Joint Chiefs had agreed that since it was a marine base, the Marine Color Guard could have the Honor of raising the American Flag.

Everyone assembled on the field facing the flag pole. Sean noticed that the camera crews were in a perfect position to record the ceremony. In silence the bands marched in perfect step onto the field . Sean, and he was sure everyone else, noticed how the musical instruments shined. The uniforms were spotless, leather gear gleamed, the gloves were pure white, why, for both the pride of the services and to honor our flag. These men and women would look this sharp everyday that they were hoisting our flag and playing our National Anthem. These were the men and women who would be the first to defend, fight, bleed, suffer and die for our flag and country.

The young Marine Officer of the parade was closely watching his watch. At exactly 08:00 he would signal the bands and Flag detail. Then the music would start to play and our flag would start to rise. At the exact same second, arms would be raised in salute and hands placed over hearts. Sean was sure that most voices would join in singing our National Anthem, he knew his would.

On the exact tick of 08:00 the Marine Officer made a quick pointing motion at the bands and Flag Detail, and then raised his hand in salute. They began to hoist Old Glory while the bands began to play, "The Star Spangled Banner". The flagpole was fifty feet high and as our flag rose, goosebumps rose on those who were there honoring their flag. The wind whipped the Stars and Stripes out fully, it was truly a combination of a religious and patriotic moment.

After the Anthem had been played and many tears had been wiped, the Navy band went first playing "Anchors Away." The last note had hardly ended when the Air Force band began playing "Off we go into the wild blue yonder." The Army then played "The Army goes rolling along", and lastly came the Marine Band playing "From the halls of Montezuma".

After the songs ended, General Kelly invited Sheriff Al, both as Sheriff and Reverend, to say an opening prayer.

Al's wife Carol Ann was bursting with pride. For weeks she had debated with herself whether Al would wear his Sheriff's uniform or a suit and if a suit what color? He had wanted to wear a plain gray simple suit. He argued with her that he was leading a prayer for the men and women of the law enforcement and the military, so he should dress plainly, so that people would hear his words not notice his uniform. Carol Ann understood his point of view and after much handwringing decided that Al would wear his full uniform. So, Al stepped out from the crowd and onto the field wearing his sheriff's uniform.

"Oh heavenly Father we invite you to join us today, to be present in our lives. To guide us and to most importantly protect and defend the men and women who protect and defend us, and our country. A country founded by your children to worship you in freedom. They were guided across the ocean by you to this the new world, you made them to prosper, you made our country to grow from sea to shining sea. You have been our shield against those who would have destroyed us. Oh Father once again your children are in danger, a domestic enemy,is attempting to remove you from our lives and our history. Save us Father so this, our country, The United States of America, will remain one nation under GOD!" The crowd erupted in applause; Al had just prayed a prayer that had been in their hearts.

As Sheriff Al prayed Sean could not help but once again think of all the military and police who had died defending our freedom and our way of life. Sean had just recently been the main speaker at the Boston Police Academy graduation. While speaking he mentioned to the graduating class that since 2011. 631 law enforcement officers had been killed in the line of duty. That figure did not include officers being shot, assaulted or other injuries. Sean reflected that he, and probably most citizens, had no idea of how many people in the military had died for us. He did remember some heroes, such as marine gunnery sergeant, John Basilone. The son of Italian immigrants, he came to this country legally and fully assimilated into American culture. John won the Medal of Honor on Guadalcanal and posthumously the Navy Cross on Iwo Jima. He was the only marine in all of the fierce fighting in the Pacific to win both medals. Basilone could have sat out the war after Guadalcanal, but no. He loved his country and was not only willing to fight for it, but as he proved to die for it. That same spirit, had been displayed many thousands of times by members of the U.S. military, including both his and Shannon's families. Although they were first generation Americans, all of Shannon's uncles, the Mulkerns, had fought in WWII: Joseph, Paul, and Francis in the Navy. Her uncle John Mulkern had been killed in WWII, while serving in the Army Air Corps. Grandfather Mulkern had begun his American journey by passing through Ellis Island. He was determined that his sons would defend the new country, a country that had given them a new life and unlimited opportunities.

The news crews were horrified . Who was this sheriff to say a prayer while wearing a uniform paid for by the taxpayers? On public property no less. What domestic enemy was he talking about? They were just warming up; if they had their way the sheriff would pay for this outrage. It was ok with them that Obama had allowed only a Muslim prayer at the Dawah summit in the White House itself. But this was a Christian prayer. A clear violation of the mythical Constitutional Separation of church and state.

Each team had 20 shooters and each shooter had to compete in at least two events. On the Alpha range teams would be competing in rapid fire handgun shooting while moving from one position to another; shooters would be scored on time and accuracy. In all events a five point penalty would be deducted from any shooter who shot the mannequin or printed target of an unarmed person.

On the Bravo range teams would begin with rapid fire shotgun drills. Not only would they move from target to target, but also in quickly moving through a house that was constructed just for the competition and eliminating any hostile threats in the house while not harming any innocent occupants.

inally on the Charlie range teams would compete with the AR15 rifle in both rapid and slow fire shooting out to a distance of 300 hundred yards. Tomorrow would be the long distance shooting out to 2590 yards or a mile and a half.

To say that there was an air of excitement was an understatement. A friendly, rivalry had always existed between the services and today was no exception. Many members of each service were present to cheer on their teams. But although friendly, the spirit of competition was fierce. The range master announced 60 seconds to live firing, everybody either put in their ear protection or made ready to cover their ears. The noise of all the different weapons firing in close proximately from three different ranges would be loud to say the least.

Sean and Shannon were watching Sean Jr. They were very impressed by the way he moved from one of his men to another, offering last words of encouragement and checking equipment. Of course Sean could not be on all three ranges at once. It appeared that he was wearing headgear that allowed him to communicate from range to range.

With 10 seconds to go the range master began the countdown. After the count of one, all three ranges erupted in gunfire, smoke, and movement.

It was amazing how quickly the different teams moved through the various courses of fire. The scoring was pretty even across the board, with the military teams having a slight advantage in the rifle event. Shotgun was pretty even and the police teams had a slight point lead in handgun shooting. Before anyone realized, it the cease fire siren was sounding and it was time for lunch.

Sean looked around and noticed that Sheriff Al was standing in front of the news crews and cameras about to be interviewed. To Sean it appeared that they were salivating like a pack of hyenas about to devour a newborn gazelle.

He noticed Susan and Audrey were standing off to the side talking to a group of people. He managed to catch Audrey's eye, pointed over to where Al was and indicated that they should join Al now.

As they approached the cameras they heard the female reporter asking Al about who he was and where he was from. Al looked completely at ease and was answering her questions about himself and today's competition. But the next question was not so benign. "Sheriff, or should I call you reverend?"

"That depends on what you want to ask me, but I am proud of both titles."

"Given the constitutional separation of church and state, do you think that it was appropriate of you to say such a blatantly Christian prayer?"

"Firstly, yes I think that it was totally appropriate, and you are factually mistaken, there is no constitutional separation of church and state. That is a made up lie! The reason it was totally appropriate is that the United States is a Christian nation, under GOD. Did you know that one of the first actions,of the first Continental Congress was to establish the office of chaplain of the army? Or that in World War II, all U.S. military personnel were issued Bibles, or that many of the buildings in not only DC but across our country are inscribed with quotes from the Bible and or prayers. The quote on the Liberty Bell itself, 'Proclaim Freedom Throughout the Land,' is from Leviticus, 25:10."

The reporter, seeing that Al was not only not going to back down but was using this as a religious history lesson, decided to cut her losses and end the interview. "Thank you Sheriff." She then turned to the cameras and droned on about the "Blatant display of militarism here today."

Al had a huge smile on his face as he walked over to them. "Do you think any of that will make the national or even local six o'clock news?"

Sean, just laughing and shaking his head, put his arm around his friend's shoulder and said, "I don't think so, I guess you didn't need our help. Sorry to have come over but you looked kind of outnumbered." "Sir, with GOD on your side, you are never outnumbered!"

There was good natured banter back and forth between the teams in the cafeteria.

Sean noticed that the Joint Chiefs were all sitting at one table together. While none of them were ready yet to surrender their hats, Sean noticed that Admiral Fletcher had a rather confident look on his face. Apparently his Navy Seals had done quite well this morning.

Most people were just having a very light lunch and were heading right back out to the ranges. The first event on the Alpha range this afternoon was the handgun competition between the Secret Service and the FBI. While on the Bravo range the ATF would face off with the Philly team on the shotgun range. The army and marines would start the afternoons AR15 competition on the Charlie range.

As Sean was passing the Generals' table, General Quinn called him over. "How are you enjoying the competition?"

"Very well general. There are some really good shooters here today, a lot of talent on display, and more importantly lots of new friendships are being formed." They all knew what he meant by that.

"I don't know if you noticed or not sir, but my son Sean will be shooting for the army now on the Charlie range with the AR15 rifle. I don't want to brag, but from the way I have seen him shoot and from what I have been overhearing about his skills the army team will score very well today." At that General Quinn had a very satisfied look on his face while the others looked a little glum. Even Admiral Fletcher was was looking a little nervous as he and the others picked up their hats to go back out to the ranges.

Sean saw his sisters' first, they were wearing the "Army Strong" sweatshirts that he had bought for them. He gave them a wave, but that was not good enough for them they ran up to him, wished him good luck and each gave him a kiss on the cheek. Then he saw his parents who were waving and smiling at him just like they had at his first little league game.

The range master gave a five minute warning, the various shooters stepped up to their shooting station and began to make themselves comfortable.

"Sixty Seconds...ten, nine, commence firing." Sean's rifle came up in an instant. The first target was 100 yards away and each shooter had 30 seconds to fire 20 rounds, then reload with 20 rounds and with 40 seconds begin firing at the 200 yard target. Finally they would reload again with 20 rounds and have one minute at the 300 yard range. Not only accuracy but speed would be factored into their scores. A total of 2 minutes and ten seconds to fire 60 rounds, while having to reload and adjust for distance and windage, a piece of cake!

The sun was shining on the targets making it fairly easy at the one hundred yard target to see where the bullets were hitting. Like many others there the Dominguez's had brought binoculars with them. As they watched Sean finish firing his first 20, rounds. Shannon, with a sound of desperation in her voice said,"Oh no, he only hit the target once." Sean, just laughed and said no honey, his bullets all went through the same hole, dead center of the target!" General Quinn was picturing in his mind how he would arrange his fellow Chiefs' hats on his wall. Sean quickly reloaded and began firing at the 200 yard target. He was a full five seconds ahead of all the other shooters. All eyes were on Sean, all of the spectators were shooters themselves and they knew that they were watching a real expert at work. Shannon said to Sean, "I see two holes on that target."

"Yes love, notice how the holes are touching each other."

"Is that good?" Sean did not have time to answer. Sean Jr., in accordance with the rules, had placed his rifle on the table next to him when he finished shooting. A full 15 seconds before the next shooter!

There was an air of excitement as the crowd waited for the scores to be totaled. The feeling in the air was very similar to that of a hometown football crowd waiting for the officials to review a close touchdown that their team had just scored. People from the other ranges had heard about Sean's performance and were drifting over to the Charlie range to await the results. After five minutes the scores began to be posted. The spectators began to clap thunderously. Sean had not only scored a perfect hundred on all three targets, but in accordance with the rules he had been awarded a point for each second he was under the allotted time that he finished shooting, so that his final score was a phenomenal new range record of 315. The applause lasted for several minutes and all of the other shooters lined up to shake Sean's hand and congratulate him.

General Quinn and Colonel Joe Annino walked out to the range to congratulate .Sean. Yes those hats were going to look great on his shelf.

15:00 hours

The matches were finished for the day. All of the spectators who had friends on the various teams were talking to them and making arrangements to meet at the barbecue. Sean and the other police officials had made plans to meet and compare scores while the military team leaders were all reporting to their respective generals and admirals, who were chomping at the bit to learn which one of their teams were in the lead, for now.

After talking with their teams the guys were all meeting by the beer wagon. Nothing like a good shooting match to work up a thirst. Ed began the conversation, "Well guys, I for one have told my guys to exchange phone numbers to talk about socially meeting for police week in DC."

Nathan then spoke up, "I am not sure if we should be pushing police week to strongly among the guys, let's just do it through our agencies, why set off any possible alarm bells?"

"Yeah, you're probably right,sorry."

Joe Garcia commented on how well Sean Jr. was shooting. Nobody disagreed with him. Then they all started to compare notes and exchange compliments on each others teams. After all was said and done there was only a forty point difference between the first and last place teams. Regardless of where their teams finished, they were looking forward to the long range course. Tony said, "Imagine hitting a target, a moving target at that from one and a half miles away! I believe that is the longest confirmed wartime shot ever made."

The smell of the food was calling to them and the lines were beginning to form at the various food stations. General Kelly and the Marine Corps had outdone themselves in both the quantity and quality of the food. The military bands had changed out of their dress uniforms into their fatigues and were beginning their own competition by taking turns playing a selection of American music from folk to patriotic songs. A bonfire was lit in middle of the field and while some people sang along with the music, others danced and everyone seemed to be tapping their feet or clapping to the music. They were truly one people here; united by a common heritage, language and shared history. Al commented that "this is what America was and in the heartland and hearts of America still is. People unashamed to show their love of country, no liberal PC here, just a good old fashioned American shindig! They all smiled and were comforted by the thought of being with other Americans. Al could not help but wonder if Barry Soetoro or whatever his real name was would know any of these American songs.

18:00 hours

Sean came by to say hello to his family and to collect his men. Most of them had already competed in their events and would not be shooting tomorrow, but they were a team, and if some of them were being sent to bed, in a manner of speaking, then the rest of them would also go to bed,

The rest of the evening quickly passed by, with the other teams, especially the military teams following Sean's example and leaving the field early. By 21:00 the field was empty. Some of the group were going to get together at Joe Garcia's house. Sean and Shannon decided that they wanted to turn in early, it had been a long day and they wanted to be wide awake to watch Sean tomorrow. As they were leaving the field Sean looked around and saw Finola and Heather sitting with the Annino boys, he was starting to walk over when Shannon grabbed his arm and said "leave them alone Sean".

SUNDAY, OCT. 11TH 07:00 HOURS

The cafeteria doors were just opening as Sean and Shannon arrived for breakfast. They were just picking up their plates when the rest of their friends started to arrive. Joe Annino walked right over to them with a huge grin on his face. "Good morning Dominguez's, how are you two doing?"

"Fine thanks Joe, why, may I ask, are you in such a good mood on this fine morning?"

"Well, because, and you cannot tell my state police this, but the army team is leading the other military teams by about 40 points. Which is mainly due to your son Sean. General Quinn must have called me five times last night trying to figure out which shooters from the other military teams might offer some challenge to Sean. The short version is, the General is convinced that he has won his bet with the Chiefs and will be leaving here with all of their hats!"

Sean could not resist tormenting Joe. "Joe, today's long distance shooting will be with the .50 cal, Barretts rifle. Sean told me that he has never fired that rifle, and that only two members of the army team have very limited experience with the Barrett."

Joe turned ashen white. The smile on his face disappeared and he looked liked he was going to vomit. "You're kidding right? What, what do I tell the general? He is going to flip out!"

"I don't know Joe, but there he is now just coming into the hall, where did those other Army Generals come from? And look at all the colonels. Wow, you don't see that much brass all in one place to often." Sean picked up his coffee mug to hide his smile.

"Oh no, he see's us, he's coming over now!" General Quinn, followed by a parade of officers, came over to Sean, Joe and Shannon.

"Good morning all, it's going to be a great day for the army, can't wait to see your son shoot at distance!"

Joe looked like he wanted to sink into the floor. Instead he stood up straight and started to say, "Sir, Sean here was just telling me—"

Sean cut him off. "Oh let me tell him Joe. General, my son was telling me that the Barrett rifle is his favorite weapon. He feels really confident in his abilities using it." General Quinn's smile could not have gotten bigger. "That's great news Sean. I want you, your family and the of course the army team to come over to my house later for an all army celebration. That includes you and your family Joe!"

Joe was just staring at Sean. "Yes sir, thank you sir, we will be there."

"Good, lets say around 16:00, see you at the range." With that and he and his kite tail of officers went to get some food.

"Sean, we've known each other for how long? How could you have tormented me like that, I thought we were friends?" Sean just smiled at Joe, revenge was sweet.

08:00 hours the Charlie range

Shannon spotted Sean right away, he was staring out into the distance, down range as Sean had called it. Holding a large pair of binoculars he watched the red flags that were spaced out every one hundred yards, for a mile and a half indicating wind direction and speed. The other shooters from the other teams were doing the same. They took seats right in front of the giant TV screen that would enable the audience to see exactly where the shots hit the target.

Shannon's attention was caught by a large, scary looking thing on the table. "Sean, that thing that's on the table next to Sean and the other guys, what is it?" Sean had to look for a minute to see what she was asking about then he realized. "That, Shannon, is a .50 cal Barrett's sniper rifle. It fires an amazingly destructive round; the .50 cal. will go through steel. It's even used to shoot down airplanes and disable vehicles, I can only imagine what it will do to a human body." With a mother's fear in her voice Shannon questioned, "And our son is going to shoot that thing?"

"Relax love, unless I am gravely mistaken, I believe he's fired it once or twice before."

The range master announced today's rules. Only one team at a time would be allowed to fire. Each team would consist of a two man team made up of a sniper / shooter and a spotter. Only the sniper could touch the weapon. The spotter could handle the ammunition and magazines and advise the sniper of wind conditions and target location. A ten point penalty would be accessed for each violation of any rule.

The sniper must fire from a prone position and could take no longer than 25 seconds between shots. Each sniper would fire a total of ten shots at each of the targets that were placed at the red flag mile markers. One point would be awarded for every hit at the half mile target, two points at the mile target and three points at the mile and a half target. Lastly, three of the ten shots from each distance would be at moving targets.

None of the police teams possessed the Barrett rifle, and therefore would not be competing in this event. Only the FBI, ATF, Secret Service and the military teams would be shooting. Today's scores would not be factored into yesterday's scores relative to the police teams. However, the scores would be factored into todays military team totals.

By luck of the draw the teams would fire in the following order. ATF, Navy, Air Force, FBI, Secret Service, Marines, and then lastly the Army.

Sean held his breath while the range master read out the order of the teams. He wanted to fire last. When the army was called last he let out an audible sigh of relief, he had gotten his wish. He then turned and gave his father and mother a big thumbs up.

Shannon and Sean both waved back.

"He never even turned around. I didn't think that he had even seen us, how did he know exactly where we were?"

Sean just smiled at her and seemed momentarily sad. He knew how Sean knew where they were, and for that matter, where everybody else was. He was a soldier, a hunter. Thank GOD that our country had men like him, but why did it have to be his son? He knew that his son Sean didn't learn and perfect the skills he was displaying by sitting in a classroom.

Others including General Quinn had noticed Sean give the thumbs up sign to his parents. That was just fine with him. If his star shooter was happy with the order of firing then he was to .

Joe Garcia was sitting next to Nathan Green as the ATF team settled into position. The spotter and sniper both looked down range, the sniper through his rifle scope and the spotter with binoculars. They consulted in hushed tones while the sniper made adjustments to windage and elevation settings on his scope.

The range master announced one minute to firing. The large crowd all adjusted their ear protection, these .50 cal. shots would sound like cannon fire. Ten seconds were counted down, followed by deafening noise. Even with a long flash suppressor and portalized barrell, the flames that shot out looked like a flame thrower. The first round struck a couple of inches above what would have been someone's naval. But it did not really matter where a human body was hit with a .50 cal., for it would rip off a limb or take out the entire chest of not only the first person hit, but anyone else behind them, even if they were behind a steel or concrete wall!

The ATF sniper then fired his second and third shots which were also hits. Then came the moving targets. As the target moved at 2 mph from the left to the right side of the range, the spotter informed the sniper of the estimated speed of the target. His first shot missed, he had led the target to much. The target then returned from the right side of the range to the left; the sniper fired and missed once again. Sean was watching both the target and wind with a detached coldly professional eye. He correctly estimated and appreciated the target's speed. After all that's about how fast an Al Qaeda fighter would be traveling up the side of a mountain. Sean grimly smiled to himself; yes he knew that speed well. The ATF shooter finished shooting at the half mile target and by Sean's count scored six out of a possible ten points. He then consulted with his spotter and adjusted his scope for the one mile target. After firing all his shots, Sean estimated that out of a possible 20 points the ATF sniper had scored eight.

The tough shooting now started. Once again the targets came in random order. After all ten rounds had been fired. Sean estimated that the sniper had scored one hit for a total of three points on the target. The sniper and spotter stood up from their prone positions, sweat poured down their faces. The crowd applauded enthusiastically, Sean was impressed, not bad shooting. The distances involved here were exceptional.

Now the Navy team, comprised of Navy Seals, stepped up to the firing position. Sean was not overconfident at all. He knew too well that overconfidence would lead to carelessness which would lead to your own death on the battlefield. On many occasions, in actual combat, Sean had seen both the Seals and Marine sniper teams in action. They were among the best in the world.

The Seal sniper began to fire. After firing at both the half mile and mile targets the Seal had a perfect score. That did not surprise Sean. Actually he would have been professionally disappointed with any less of a performance. Now came the real test. The first shot rang out at a moving target at the mile and a half distance. Through his binoculars Sean saw it was a miss. The next nine shots seemed to be over in a second, with the Seal scoring 27 out of a possible 30 points. Admiral Fletcher had a huge smile on his face. One of his staff officers was doing some rapid calculations on a pad of paper and the admiral looked pleased with the results.

The Air Force, FBI, and Secret Service teams then rotated through the event with mixed results. Now came the Marines. Once again, Sean perked up with professional interest. He and the marine actually knew each other from Afghanistan and Iraq. To put it mildly the marine like the Seal was very good.

Sean observed that the Marine had added what looked like a one pound weight to the barrel of his rifle. This was totally in keeping with the rules; a sandbag or other object was often used in the field to steady the rifle. The wind was now becoming difficult, blowing straight at the shooters at speeds from 2 mph to what Sean estimated was six or seven mph.

The range master announced, commence firing! The first shot roared out and Sean, watching closely, saw the bullet go straight through what would have been the targets left arm.. The next nine shots all struck in the target's torso area. Sean and the crowd clapped for the Marine who turned and looked at Sean.

After conferring with his spotter the sniper changed the settings on his scope and began firing at the one mile target. Several times he paused when the wind gusted and once he fired with only one second left, narrowly missing a ten point penalty. As he had at the half mile target, the Marine once again achieved a perfect score at the mile target. Everyone could sense that a master was at work.

General Quinn waved over to General Kelly "Your man is very good, did we train him?" General Kelly just laughed. Like Quinn, he was having a staff officer add up the points. If only the army did not have that point lead from yesterday. He yelled over to General Quinn, "Hey Eric you want to let our snipers decide the bet today, just on their score alone?" Everyone, including his staff heard the challenge. This was an unexpected problem. If he agreed to that, he was giving up a forty point lead, for the total, best score won. If he said no and stayed with the original bet, well then he was admitting that the marine sniper was probably better than the army sniper. Why had he opened his big mouth to yell over in the first place? His fellow Army Generals and staff officers were all giving him advice from, "don't do it general we have them beat," to the very opposite "you have to accept general for the honor of the army, our guy can beat their guy."

The marine sniper would be shooting at the mile and a half target any second. So far he had not missed; what to do? Kelly once again yelled over, "Well Eric, yes or no?" All the marines and most of the audience were waiting for his reply. Finally he answered "Ok Wayne if you want to change the bet I will go along if you agree to throw in your nameplate from your office door so that I can remember whose hat is on my shelf." Now it was Kelly's turn to think— if he lost his hat and name plate... oh well, he started this. "Ok deal." At that very second the first shot rang out at a moving target from the sniper's rifle, a miss! Kelly and the marines scowled while the army all looked very happy.

Sean started to get into his shooting vest and adjust his scope. He and his spotter had been together for a long time now— as a matter of fact General Kelly had flown the spotter in from Germany when Sean said he needed him. The marine fired his next nine shots. Although he was a very good shot, for some reason today he wasn't hitting the moving targets. He finished with seven out of ten hits, very impressive at that distance. The crowd gave the marine team quite an ovation.

Sean and his spotter walked over to their table and Sean picked up his rifle, that he had named "Gypsy" after a favorite boyhood family dog that he had. The first Gyps did not have much of a bite. But, as many had learned in Afghanistan, Iraq and several other exotic locations, this Gypsy's bite was fatal.

The crowd began to clap as Sean got into the firing position; they remembered his record breaking performance of yesterday and were looking for more of the same today.

Once again the range master started the countdown, but his voice had not subsided by the time the first bullet went through the eye of the moving target. Shot after shot rang out and bullet after bullet went through. Like the marine, Sean had scored a perfect score at the half mile target. But all knew that his shots had been deliberately placed in the chest area of the target. It was both impressive and frightening.

Sean and his spotter made their calculations and scope adjustments. Sean began to fire at the one mile target. Just as he had done at the half mile range, Sean placed each bullet into the chest. All spectators, including the other snipers, were speechless. There was something inhuman in Sean's machine–like precision. No one doubted that Sean had sent many of his country's enemies to the paradise that they claimed they longed for.

As the last shot left his barrel Sean and his spotter once again made the required adjustments to Gypsy's scope. Out at the mile and a half range the first moving target began its journey across the range. Sean followed it for about five seconds before squeezing off his first shot. A hit right in the eye. All eyes were on the viewing monitor as Sean placed shot after shot into the target. Sean had four shots left. Both the army and marines began to fervently pray, although for different outcomes, as Sean squeezed off his shots. He had three left. He could miss two and still win. The next two shots went right through the target's torso area. All knew that Sean had won, but could he make it a perfect score? As the crowd watched the last shot fire on the monitor, they erupted in applause. Sean had again set a new range and military record.

Everybody seemed to be both awed and elated. Sean, Shannon, and the girls were cheering wildly, General Quinn and the Army brass were jumping around while Admiral Fletcher, General Kelly, and General Stewart were looking at their at their hats as if they were saying goodby to a loved one. They of course would all have extra, but losing one's hat, that was hard to take. Let alone the nameplate from your office door.

Sean wanted to go over to his son, but he was surrounded by both his team mates and members of the other teams who were lining up to shake his hand or pat him on the back. Sean looked over at his parents and smiled that pleased smile that they knew so well. Sean held up four fingers and pointed at his watch; Sean understood that his father was signaling that they would meet at 4pm at General Quinn's house.

The range master announced that the army team had won the competition and that Sean had set a new military, possibly world, record. The army team all gathered together to accept the championship trophy and to have their pictures taken.

As he turned to leave he noticed that the generals were all standing in a circle talking. General Quinn was holding up his hands and shaking his head no. Sean guessed right away that he was refusing to accept the hats of the other Joint Chiefs. Sean thought,to himself, "A magnanimous gesture that might go a long way."

16:00 hours

General Quinn, along with some of his officers, were standing on the porch of his house with cold drinks, waiting to greet his guests as they arrived. He could hear the commotion from the field where the combined team members, along with their supporters, were gathering for a last social event before heading home tomorrow.

Sean and Shannon, with the other members of the Sons and Daughters of Liberty arrived at General Quinn's. The general was in a wonderful mood and greeted them all warmly. When he greeted Sean he quickly asked, "Where is my hero your son?"

"I think that he was having a hard time breaking away from the team sir, but I am sure that he will be right along." No sooner had Sean finished speaking when they all heard singing voices approaching them. Sean jr. had arrived leading the entire army team and carrying the competition trophy in both hands— it was rather large. Some of them had been a little hesitant to come uninvited to not only a general's party, but the army Chief of Staff's party, no less. Sean persuaded them by a combination of his authority as team leader, beer, and a common sense approach, asking them when was the last and next time they had an excuse to crash the Chief of Staffs party? They all saw the logic in that and hence here they were at the general's house.

General Quinn was laughing and smiling so hard that his stomach and face began to hurt. He practically ran up to Sean, who, even though they were all in civilian clothes, immediately called the team to attention. The general waved them to relax and when that did not work said, "At ease, no relax men." He then shook each of their hands and turned to Sean, "What are you going to do with your trophy soldier?"

"Well sir we, the team, figure that the trophy belongs to the army and since you're the Army's highest ranking officer, we'll turn it over to you, so that you can decide, sir." Those were magic words to General Quinn. He sent his aide in to get his camera and had multiple pictures taken of himself accepting the trophy. Then, after whispering with his aide, and signaling a nod of consent, the aide made an announcement. The general would, in appreciation of all the training they had done for the competition, not to mention winning it, be awarding them all two weeks leave. The men all thanked the general who insisted that they have a drink with him. They all quickly agreed and then Sean said, "Ok guys just one drink, we won't take advantage of the general's generosity anymore tonight." The real reason was Sean knew his team wanted to get back to the field where the real party was going on.

MONDAY, OCTOBER 12TH 10:00 HOURS

Sean and Shannon were saying goodby to the group when Sean noticed the Annino boys and his daughters were standing off to the side talking amongst themselves . Sean was trying to listen and was sure he had heard one of the boys say, "Well just ask your mother first then."

Nathan Green, Joe Garcia, and Joe Annino all came up to Sean. Nathan spoke first. "I just learned that we're having some luck with the drones following Colonel Dimitri Abramovich. If it's ok with you I will send out a message on the shortwave to the group and stop by General Kelly's office with Joe to update him."

"That will be great Nathan."

Just then Audrey came walking up to them, "Just wanted to tell you that my Secret Service friend, Carl Brown, called me to let me know that effective December 1. He will be the new Secret Service Agent in charge at the White House."

They collectively expressed their appreciation.

Audrey just smiled. "Piece of cake. I have to go and get on the bus now with my guys before they leave me, talk to you soon, stay safe."

"You too Audrey, hope to see you soon."

After looking at them all she replied, "Yes Sean I hope that you arrange for us all to meet real soon." Everyone understood her meaning.

Sean jr. came walking up the street. He was coming back from the armory where he had to go to sign in and turn over "Gypsy" and his AR15. "Well family I'm good. This was fun but I'm also glad that it is over, thank you all for being here for me. Let's get home, I think that I will sleep for the next two weeks." Shannon just looked at her son and smiled. Part of her knew that Sean was a soldier, and from what she had seen and heard here, that part of her knew that as a soldier he had seen and done things that she could not believe. But with a mother's love she just saw her son who wanted to go home and sleep. People were calling him America's most deadly sniper, but in her eyes he was just a little boy.

The plane ride back to Boston was uneventful. Sean jr. did manage to sleep while Shannon and the girls, seated together on the other side of the aisle, talked in whispers and gave him furtive looks. Sean wondered what they were up to.

13:00 hours

Nathan and Joe were shown into Generals Kellys office . The other Chiefs of Staff were also present .

"So you said this was important Nathan."

"Yes sir, I will be brief. Primarily we have been using drones to keep Colonel Abramovich and Major Kalashnikov under surveillance. But, even though limited, our human and electronic surveillance have been paying dividends. Both men have been drinking too much and, quite frankly, talking too much about the end of the U.S. and how Putin had outwitted Obama; no surprise there. Yesterday they left the base in Philomont on what appeared to be a private jet, and flew to what had been a small, closed air base by Cheswold, DE. The base had been used by the military to house any overflow from Dover Air Force base. The runway is too short to handle any big planes, but it does have a repair facility and eighteen hardened bunkers for planes. While flying over the base our drones captured video of exactly 12 Russian Army Kamov Ka -60 multi use helicopters, painted U.S. Army green. There is activity going on inside the bunkers but the drones were not able to capture what the activity is. Lastly, as you will see in the video, when Abramovich's plane landed he was met by a guard of a dozen men, all carrying Russian Kalashnikov rifles. There's also a manned checkpoint at the only entrance to the base."

There was silence in the room for a minute, then General Quinn spoke up. "So, we have evidence of at least three officially closed U.S. bases being used by foreign militaries within the U.S. At least two of these bases are capable of servicing aircrafts and are located within a 30 minute flight of D.C. Is that correct?"

"Yes sir that seems to be it."

"Very well Nathan, is there anything else we need to know about?"

"Not now sir, with your permission we will keep you updated as to anything we learn. I'm actually leaving now for a few days in New York City to visit *friends*."

"You do that. Thank you for informing us."

The door had hardly closed when General Kelly said, "The country is in much bigger trouble than I imagined. Now how do you want to play this? As I see it, we can hit these bases now. Which, if we do, means ousting Obama now and basically having a military coup instead of a joint police and military operation. Or we can use our satellites increase the level of surveillance on Abramovich, Kalashnikov, and the bases, in the hope that they will lead us to not only more of the bases but also to their superiors. Or, we eliminate both of them. However, I don't like that option. Their second in commands will take over, we won't know who they are, and they'll be on a heightened level of vigilance."

Admiral Fletcher spoke up. "I like option number two. We increase our surveillance through the use of all our resources, including human. Meaning I want to put some of our people onto all three of those bases. Let's get inside of those hangers, see what's there, and get an accurate count of the number of hostiles on the bases. Agreed?"

"Ok, but who do you want to use?"

"Come on Kevin. I know that you're in shock learning that your former air bases are housing enemy units and that you're only a flyboy, but think, sir."

"We use our 'competitive shooting teams.' The Marine recon and Navy Seal teams are still here, we'll attach some of your air team's personnel to each of them. The marines will infiltrate and recon the Philomont base. The Seals will do the same at the Cheswold base, and the army, led by a man we all know, Staff Sergeant Dominguez, will do the same at Fort Devens."

General Quinn spoke up. "That's fine. But if they're discovered they will have to be authorized to eliminate any and all potential threats."

"Agreed. It's unreal that our men will have more authority to use force here in the U.S. against our enemies, than they have in combat zones under Obama's rules of engagement."

"Ok, lets draw up the orders and get the teams in motion. I say we do this three nights from now."

18:00 hours

Despite the phone ringing, no one was moving to answer it. Sean gave them all a disgusted look. One of the problems with everyone having their own cell phones was that when the house phone rang, no one bothered to answer it. But when their cell phone rang, well, then they jumped like trained mice to answer! He picked up the phone and gave a friendly, "Hello?"

"Good evening Mr. Dominguez, this is Major Connor Fitzsimmons, how are you sir?"

Sean immediately had a sinking feeling in his stomach. "Very good Major, how can I help you?"

"Sir, I need to speak with Sgt. Dominguez, now sir."

Sean tried to postpone the inevitable. "Well Major, he's sleeping."

"Sir, I'm calling on the direct order of General Quinn. I really need him now."

"Ok Major, can't blame me for trying to keep him for a day or two."

Sean looked over at Shannon, who instantly recognized the look on his face. Something was wrong. Sean walked upstairs and knocked on his son's door. There was no answer. Opening the door, he heard Sean snoring up a storm. Despite his former training and discipline, both in the army and on the police force in obeying orders, Sean had to force himself to wake up his son. He started to gently rub his shoulder saying, "Sean there—" He had hardly gotten the words out when his son, quick as a snake, had him in a choke hold, a real choke hold.

"Sean, stop it!" Shannon was standing in the doorway screaming at her son, who was only just starting to wake up. He saw his father, or rather his father's head, under his arm. Why was dad turning blue? And why was he there anyway? Shannon pulled Sean's arm from his father's throat. Groggily, he asked his parents, "What's up?" Sean was having a hard time breathing, but managed to reply, "There is a Major Connor Fitzsimmons on the phone for you." Sean was instantly awake and ran to the phone in the hallway. "You sure the name was Major Connor Fitzsimmons?"

"Yes."

"Sir, this is Dominguez, Echo Delta five lima one, golf golf." Sean Sr. was beginning to believe that whoever was on the phone, his name wasn't Major Connor Fitzsimmons.

Sean had no idea what "Major Connor" was saying to his son, but he suspected that it was an order for duty. His suspicions were confirmed when he heard his son say, "Understood, sir."

Sean looked at his parents. "Sorry, but I'll be leaving at five in the morning."

"Ok, I will drive you to the airport."

"Thanks dad, but they're sending a car for me." Now Sean Sr. knew it was serious. "Ok pal, what do you want to do now, you hungry?"

"No dad, you just fed me two hours ago. I really need to get some sleep though." Shannon had tears in her eyes, as Sean walked away, but went to her bedroom and set the alarm for 4 AM. Her son would need breakfast before he left.

23:30 hours

True to his word, Nathan sent out a low band radio message to the group. Yet as the satellites received and computers recorded the message, Chinese Naval Captain Xi was aboard the spy ship Beijixing in the Pacific, scanning the bands. Trying to locate the conversation of a couple in Iowa, he also heard the last 30 seconds of Nathan's message.

07:00 hours

The Joint Chiefs and their key staff members gathered once again in General Kelly's office. They had much to discuss, including their already-scheduled meeting with the president in the White House tomorrow at 10AM. The previous president had always acted like a Commander in Chief, starting every day with a 7AM military briefing. Now, they were lucky to get the president to attend a meeting once a month. It was true that there was still a daily military briefing given to members of the National Security council, but one never knew what member of the president's staff would happen to show up.

General Stewart called the meeting to order. "Gentlemen please continue to have your breakfast. First, I understand that Colone Arnone from the Marines is coordinating and will speak as to operation 'Peeping Tom.'" 'Peeping Tom' was the codename given to the mission to infiltrate the three military bases.

"Colonel, please go ahead."

"Thank you, sir. As of right now we are fully prepared to execute this mission. All personnel have been either recalled from leave or were ordered to remain on base. Transportation is a go. All equipment, including night vision eyewear, silenced weapons and low light cameras have also been allocated. There will not be time for a lot of training for our teams, but they are our best and quite frankly, this is not the hardest mission that they have been assigned. Mock up small scale models of the bases have been prepared. The operation will begin at 01:00 hours on the morning of the 16th. The rules of engagement have been explained to each of the team leaders, who in turn will brief their teams. The mission will conclude no later than 04:30. Upon return to their departure base, team leaders will fully brief me, the mission commander, and I will in turn brief you. Any questions?"

"Yes, if there are casualties, and I mean mainly hostiles casualties, what is your plan for them?"

"That has been considered sir, and the means of disposal will vary depending on the location."

They all knew what that meant. "Very good, Colonel, very good. Stand by please."

"Admiral Fletcher, you have the floor."

"Thank you general. Overnight our satellites and the few submarines and intelligence ships that we are still allowed to keep in the South China Sea have reported greatly increased coded radio traffic from a large part of the Chinese Navy. As you know, China has 18 naval bases scattered throughout the area in the Indian ocean including, the bases on the West coast of Africa, the largest of which is in Somalia. They, of course, also have access to naval bases in Iran. As an aside, we know that China has provided Iran with their SILK WORM missile. It has a range of a thousand miles and was made for the sole purpose of sinking American Carriers. Remember, just a few months ago Iran built a replica of a U.S. Carrier and then bombed it. Anyway, it looks like a screen of Chinese subs is preparing to sail from their bases in Yulin, which is a nuke base, and the Hainan Island base. A second group of subs is also preparing to sail from the Zhanjiang naval base. The fourth Chinese base that we are seeing activity on is the Hambantota port base, located near Sri Lanka.

Our old friend, the state of the art "Beijixing" spy ship, has been sailing a fine line just outside of our Hawaiian territorial waters. The Beijixing is the ship that the Chinese have been using to monitor and interfere with our joint naval exercises with our allies in operation Rim of the Pacific, or RIMPAC. Satellites indicate that a large part of the Chinese surface fleet, including their fully operational Russian built aircraft carrier the "Liaoning," are preparing to set sail. While not yet fully operational, they also have the former Russian carriers, Minsk and Kiev, along with the former Australian carrier Melbourne. These carriers are capable of putting to sea and launching helicopters and Harrier type jump jets. If these ships do indeed set sail, it will be the largest single naval sortie since WWII, which was of course by the U.S. Navy."

"Admiral, is there any indication of where they will sail and if so, when? Could this be a giant exercise, the surface fleet against the subs?"

"They could be sailing anywhere and quite frankly we would not be able to stop them by ourselves. The Chinese now have more submarines than us. And while we still have a slight advantage in the number of surface ships, all of China's ships are of modern design, while ours are aging. Our ships are scattered throughout the world, while China's are concentrated in the South China sea, Indian ocean and the Southern Pacific. By 2020 the Chinese navy will be numerically larger and stronger than the U.S. Navy. As to when, if they are going to sail, and I believe they will, it will probably be within the next 24 hours. Yes, this could be a either a giant exercise or an invasion of Taiwan. I plan to ask the president tomorrow for the authority to ask our allies in the area, who have a lot to fear from China, for their assistance in aggressively monitoring Chinese naval activity. Anything else gentlemen?"

"Ok, Admiral, thank you."

Unknown to Admiral Fletcher, other participant nations of the RIMPAC naval exercise, including: Australia, India, Japan, Indonesia, South Korea, and the Philippines, were much more concerned with the activities of the Chinese fleet. They had seen first-hand the enormous growth of the Chinese navy, and many of their ships had been bullied by the Chinese. They watched with growing alarm as China encircled them with base after base. Even the tiny Vietnamese Navy was preparing their ships to sail.

In both the distant and not too distant past, several of these nations had fought wars of varying sizes with China. Historically, they knew they could count on the U.S. Navy and strong leadership from the White House to help contain the Chinese. But that wa s no longer the case. Messages began to fly; at first they were internal messages, then the various naval commands began to speak with each other. Messages then flew up the chain of command, and soon the leaders of the these nations were issuing orders for many of their ships to join up with the other nations' ships to monitor the Chinese in operation 'Mirror Mirror.' The situation was already tense and could easily escalate.

"General Kelly or Quinn, do you have anything?"

It was General Quinn who spoke up first. "Those of us who are willing to face the truth are really seeing the price for such an unknown, unqualified amateur being elected president. Obama has torn, and, with his backdoor assault on the Second Amendment in banning bullets, is continuing to rip apart our Constitution. Internationally, we are a laughing stock. Iran is conquering northern Iraq, where we not only spent so much of our national treasure, but more importantly lost so many American lives. Russia is on the march and reclaiming it's post WWII empire. Obama reportedly even threatened to shoot down Israeli planes if they attacked Iran's nuclear bomb making facilities, and is entering into a treaty with Iran to allow them to make nuclear weapons. He even wants to give Iran a fifty billion dollar signing bonus! I guess he's forgotten how Iran took over our embassy, held our people hostage for a year, and on a daily basis, burned American flags while shouting, "Death to America" the entire time. Then a foreign head of state, the Israeli Prime Minister, comes to D.C. to address a joint session of congress and Obama boycotts the speech. If it was the Iranian president, would Obama have boycotted him?

Everyone here is aware of the plans for police week. I know that we are all committed to our pledged course of action, but let us all consider what I have just said, and recommit ourselves to the saving of our country."

11:30 hours

Superintendent LaPaglia rushed to the intersection of 42nd and Madison. For years Muslims, numbering in the hundreds, had been allowed to illegally block that intersection, among others, for their prayers. Totally disrupting traffic for blocks, maybe miles around, causing hours of traffic jams. "What about the separation of church and state now, when it comes to Muslims?" she thought. When had Christians or Jews ever been allowed to block the streets everyday for their prayers?

From what she knew, a driver had driven over one of the Muslim prayer mats that they had put down in the street. Not a person, just a mat. The enraged mob of the faithful had dragged the driver, an orthodox Jew no less, from the vehicle, beat him, threw him down in the street, and driven over him in his own car. This incident had been witnessed by two NYPD Officers, who immediately called for help and charged into the mob in an attempt to save the driver. The crowd, of course, attacked the police. Several citizen bystanders attempted to help the officers, but they too were beaten by the peaceful followers of the Prophet. Now she and her Emergency Service Unit, along with every cop for miles around, were responding to not only help their brother officers and the other victims of the mob attack, but also to restore order.

The problem was that the Muslims had also been calling their mosques, friends, and by the look of it, Tehran itself for reinforcements. Now a full fledge riot was breaking out. Just like in Dearborn MI, the streets looked liked the west bank or Palestine, maybe even Paris or London during their riots; Muslim flags, uncovered and covered enraged faces screaming in Arabic, and rocks by the hundreds being hurled at the police abounded. As windows were continually smashed, Lapaglia thought to herself, "Rocks, where in the heart of downtown New York did they find so many rocks?" Audrey was forced to establish her command post blocks away at the intersection of Broadway and 42nd. With the way the riot was growing she might have to move the command post, or CP, at any moment. She had, on her own authority, ordered Time Square evacuated and had issued a mandatory level three call in order for the entire NYPD. "The Mayor and Police Commissioner will just love the overtime expense," she thought sarcastically. But strangely, the Commissioner and Mayor were not responding to the area, leaving Audrey fully responsible.

Things just kept getting better and better; now she heard that a Rabbi and Catholic Priest who were on the outskirts of the riot had attempted to save a woman from being possibly raped by the Muslim men. Apparently, a mullah had urged the men to attack the Rabbi and Priest for defending the female, whose only crime had been not wearing a burka. Audrey thought of an intelligence report she had read which said that 80% of the mosques in America preached hatred and Jiha. How benign.

Of course TV news crews were arriving in mass, and she was about to order that they be kept back away from the riot. On second thought, she decided to let them broadcast live footage of the faithful, being so peaceful and tolerant of other religions and women. The footage they took might even help the NYPD to identify and later arrest some of the rioters. That is if the media would give them the footage.

Kalaak was sitting in his White House Office when Anees Mutaa Sadat, his new CAIR liaison, called him to ask if he had been watching the news. When Kalaak said that he had not, Sadat explained that the faithful had been attacked in the streets of NY during morning prayers by Jews, the police had come to the aid of the Jews, and now the faithful were being beaten in the streets.

Kalaak was horrified. He turned on the TV and just as Sadat had stated, he saw images of the faithful being beaten by a group of police officers. There appeared to be a police officer laying on the ground, but that was of no consequence. Kalaak watched for several minutes and then walked down to the Oval Office where the Secret Service agent immediately opened the door for him. He noticed that Obama, the Mahdi, was sleeping at his desk. Should he awake him or not? Of course he should, the believers needed his protection. Obama listened while the TV was turned on. NYPD 'paddy wagons' were being loaded and filled to capacity with believers by the Jewish-controlled police.

Any resistance to Islam, especially by the police, had to be crushed immediately. If not, the conquest of America could be delayed for hundreds of years. America had lost it's national will to survive. Federal civil rights investigations and lawsuits against anyone who dared to act, or even to speak, out were constantly needed to send a message to the sheep: be quiet, accept your fate. Obama placed a call to Holder and ordered him to send a team of his investigators to NY to begin an investigation of the NYPD. Obviously, Holder was only too happy to comply. Never mind that the Officer in Ferguson was cleared of any wrongdoing, and it appeared that the Officers in Dearborn would also be cleared; they who resisted the will of Allah must be crushed.

Kalaak was almost in a panic, how could this be happening now? Now, when they were so close to fulfilling Allah's will and having the Mahdi, Obama, remain in office and declare the U.S. a Muslim nation. They had made such progress! Kalaak's handpicked Imam had, on multiple occasions now, opened sessions of the U.S. House of Representatives with Muslim prayers. Even on the White House lawn the Dar al Islam, claiming the U.S. as sacred land for Allah, had been said.

A thousand places like Dearborn, MI and Mansfield, MA were almost theirs. New Yorkers had become accustomed to having their streets taken over for prayers to Allah. In Dallas TX, Sharia law was being introduced and the national assembly of Muslims took place in TX every year. They were following the plan that had worked so well in France, England, and Belgium; take over small areas, school PTAs, then school committees, City council seats, then State Rep. seats, and so on. Obama had even announced his plan to take over all police departments. With the military so depleted, and the people being denied ammunition for their guns, the police were the only ones who could resist them. Why would this trouble have to happen now? And of course a Jew was behind it all.

14:00 hours

Superintendent Lapaglia, surrounded by her command staff of Captains and Lts., was at the point of a crisis. The crowd had been partially contained, hundreds of arrest had been made, hospitals were overflowing, and traffic was a mess. She was being urged to issue a level two call to authorize the use of pepper gas to disburse the crowd. She knew that no matter what she did, the armchair Monday morning quarterbacks would hang her. "Use the gas, this has to end! Issue the level two call in, and try to get the Commissioner again on the phone. Keep pushing the crowds back as far as you have to in order to break them up." At least someone still had some courage.

18:00 hours

With the arrival of police reinforcements, coupled with the arrest of many rioters and no small thanks to the gas, order was slowly being returned to the area. It would take days for the cleanup and investigation to be complete, but much longer if the Jewish driver died. Right now, he was just barely clinging to life with the aid of every medical device known to man. The first two NYPD Officers had been beaten horribly. Audrey both wondered why, and at the same time was thankful for the fact that they had not shot anyone. Of course she knew the answer: the way the media and Dept. of Justice had persecuted the police officer involved in the shooting of the 'gentle giant' in Ferguson, every officer in the country had been intimidated into never firing their weapon. Well, if that was how the public wanted it... Audrey was physically exhausted. She had been on scene in command all day; no other officer of her rank or above had responded to the to help. Now, one of her captains came over to her.

"Sorry to bother you Super, but there are some men from the FBI over there. They need to speak to you now."

"Isn't that just great." As she walked over to the group of agents, she noticed that one of them was also walking towards her. She looked up and smiled; it was so nice to see Nathan.

WEDNESDAY, OCTOBER 14TH 10:45 HOURS

The Joint Chiefs were sitting in the hallway outside of the Oval Office— the president had kept them waiting for 45 minutes so far. The door finally opened and Kalaak, along with some other men dressed in Middle Eastern clothing, came out of the office. The door shut and the Secret Service agent gave them a shrug of the shoulders, as if to say, "What did you expect?" At approximately 11:00 AM the door opened and they were invited into the Oval Office. Just as the door was about to shut, they were joined by the President's National Security advisor. The president was sitting at his desk. Obama barely acknowledged the military salute they gave, waving them to take a seat.

Chairman General Stewart began. "Good morning Mr. President. Sir, right now as we speak the Chinese Navy is sending a massive amount of ships out to sea. As yet we do not know the Chinese intent. In response to China's naval actions, the following nations are sending large parts of their fleets out to sea: Australia, India, South Korea, Indonesia, Japan, and even Vietnam. We also have several ships in the area. Sir, with the navies of so many nations in such close proximately to each other there is a very great chance of something unfortunate occurring." As he spoke, General Stewart realized that Obama was not even listening. He seemed bored, staring out the window onto the South lawn.

"Sir, as we discussed before, the U.S. Navy is not strong enough now to stop the Chinese Navy in their home waters. Since they also have bases in Iran and along the west coast of Africa—"

At that Obama interrupted him. "General, we have been over this before. I have a foreign policy that has not only contained the Chinese, but with the signing of my treaty with Iran will make the world so much safer that we might not even need a navy."

"Sir, respectfully, I must disagree. Everyday the Chinese are flexing more and more of their military muscle. Iran is a," he could not resist, "Muslim terrorist state."

"That is enough general. If there is nothing else..."

Nothing else? He could not believe his ears. They had been in the office for what, two minutes? Admiral Fletcher spoke up. "Sir, as part of your foreign policy, why not hold (now he could not resist) our debt to China over their heads? Tell them that we demand that we no longer pay interest on our 18 trillion debt to them. Tell them that if they do not play nicely we will cease to make any payments at all, and that for every instance of cyber attacks, spying, or counterfeiting we will fine them 10 billion dollars, which will be subtracted from our debt to them."

"That is enough, Admiral, I do not expect you, or any of you, to appreciate the fine points of diplomacy. Now if there is not anything else, I have to deal with the situation in NY. Good day then." They all saluted, were ignored, and turned to leave the office.

After the door had closed, Obama wrote himself a note to begin retiring the good Admiral and Generals, they were beginning to stand up to him and that could become dangerous, like the others, they had to go.

Obama looked at Security Advisor, in a way that said, why are you still here?

"Mr. President, you know that I am not too fond of the military, but if you don't do something and if there is trouble it might look bad for you." Obama gave a long bored groan, then asked, "What do you suggest?"

"Why not call the Chinese Premier, Li Keqiang, and ask him what's going on?"

"Ok, get him on the phone." Obama went back to gazing out the window as he waited for the call to go through. Historically when a President of the United States called anyone, they immediately picked up the phone to speak with him. After an unusual length of time of time, Obama heard his advisor ask, "Then what about the Deputy Premier? I see. We will call in your ambassador then."

Obama stared at his advisor. "What?!"

"Apparently both the Premier and Deputy Premier are too busy to talk right now. I was told that if they wish to speak with you, they will call you."

"Hmmmm, well I heard you say that we will call in their Ambassador, see if he is free to come and talk with us."

Outside, Admiral Fletcher could hardly keep from exploding, "Why that—"

"Not now, there are too many people around including that woman in the burka who started following us the second we stepped out."

FRIDAY OCT 16TH 00:45 HOURS

As they sat huddled in the dark woods, Sean checked his watch. His team had been briefed over and over on their mission. There were four ten man teams assigned to the Fort Devens operation. While a Captain would be in overall command, there were three Lts. and Sean, who had worked together in Afghanistan and would each command a team. Sean's team was assigned to recon the barracks area. If possible they would try to get a count of how many hostiles were on base and exactly who they were. Another team would check out the motor pool and underground parking area, if necessary using the drones that each team was issued. Team three would check out the kitchens and support areas, for knowing how large common spaces were would indicate of how many troops were on the base. Team four would be tasked with supporting each team if needed, keeping open their line of retreat and setting up anti tank weapons in case the street sweepers came into action. Sean would be in command of the second team. They all knew the route that their team and the other three would follow in infiltrating the base.

At exactly 01:00 hours the Captain pushed his transmitter twice, signalling for all the teams to move into the base. Things went wrong for Sean's team almost right away. All of the team members were intently searching the night for any man-made sound or smell. The point man had been scanning back and forth with his night vision glasses, the sound tech had been listening intently for the sound of a heartbeat or breathing, and the communications tech., who was also in charge of the infrared scanner, detected nothing. There was no indication of anyone being on guard in the area. The point man stepped into a fairly shallow depression where two soldiers, presumably on guard duty, were sleeping. They began to curse each other in what Sean recognized as Russian. They had not gotten many words out when both of them had their throats slashed by a combat knife. Sean wiped his knife clean, looked at the corpses and indicated for the team to move on; they would take the bodies out with them when they left the area. No plan was ever fool-proof, but although they had not wanted to kill, the mission had to proceed.

Their senses were on a heightened level as they approached the barracks. From the aerial drone photographs, they were expecting to encounter four original barrack buildings of the base. As planned, the team took a full twenty minutes to approach the barracks from all directions. Two men had been assigned to interrogate each barracks while the rest of the team stood by to provide support. The comm. tech and sound tech, taking approximately 25 minutes at each, moved from barracks to barracks. Sean could not believe that there were no guards, or dogs, patrolling the base itself. There was not even any electronic security being used. He reasoned that whoever was in the barracks assumed that no one from the U.S. military would be infiltrating them. After all, they were being protected by the highest authority in America.

They were just about to signal that they were finished when someone opened the door to a fifth, unsuspected barracks that was about a hundred feet away from the others, concealed by the trees and camouflage netting. The men were wearing their night vision goggles and so when the the light from the opened barracks door shined out, it was like looking into the sun. Fortunately for him, the soldier quickly closed the door and stepped into the shadows to urinate. He then went back inside and presumably back to bed. Sean signaled to his team to move on to the fifth barracks. He was thinking to himself how much easier it would be to just neutralize everyone in the barracks, he could do it with just his team, rather than sneaking around in the night.

Sean checked his watch and saw he had plenty of time. When they had completed their part of the mission, all of the teams were ordered to report back to the Captain, who remained at the command post. Sean used the time to message the Captain about the two KIA hostiles who they would be bringing out with them and monitor the area. At 04:00 hours they received the prearranged order from the Captain to return to their jump off point. All teams received the order to report back to the CP.

The other operations began simultaneously with the Devens op. The marines moved into the Philomont base without incident. Gunnery Sergeant and scout sniper Jack Strongbull led team one. His twenty man team entered the southeast quadrant of the base, and from there penetrated into each bunker, as the guards who should have been walking back and forth slept on their feet. Air Force intelligence Officers assigned to the marines entered each bunker, made a quick photographic inventory of equipment, and then placed both a miniature transmitter, receiver, and 8 ounces of C4 plastic explosives attached to a remote detonator under each pilots' seat.

Team two was tasked to enter the munitions bunker. Incredibly, there was no guard on duty. They quickly entered and were awed by the sight; from floor to ceiling were pallets of rockets. Air to air, air to ground, and mini cruise missiles filled the bunker. Again, the Air Force Officers made a fast but thorough inventory of the missiles, then placed a much larger charge of 100 pounds of C4 plastic explosives, connected to a receiver and detonator, in the very middle of the bunker.

Team three's mission was to evaluate the base barracks and estimate enemy strength on the base. From there they were to inspect the latrines, PX, cafeteria, base motor pool and sick bay.

Team four would provide the ready reserve and weapons support if needed.

All teams finished their assigned objectives by 03:30, and transmitted the prearranged signal to the Captain, who then signaled all teams to withdraw.

Admiral Fletcher never would have admitted it to anyone, especially his fellow Chiefs, but he was a little bit nervous about using his SEALS within the U.S. at Cheswold, even though against a foreign enemy. Oh, he knew they were the best in the world, but, well, they were just not right in the head. Yes, that was the easiest way to say it. They were individually insane and collectively deranged. GOD only knew what they might do. He knew from past experience that they were prone to use any discretion afforded them in their orders to wreak havoc.

He was wide awake in the Norfolk Naval base command center, watching the clock and praying while waiting for the mission to be completed without incident. On the stroke of 01:00 he said a silent prayer, "Oh Heavenly Father, tonight I once again beseech you, protect those who protect my country, the U.S. of America. Guide them, restrain them, and shield them against all enemies."

As with the other two teams, the mission commander and main communications team would remain outside of the base in the command post, which was really just a hole in the ground. The SEALs, along with air force personnel, were divided into four teams of ten men. As they approached the base they too utilized all of their electronics equipment to survey the area for any possible guards or electronic security barriers.

Team one had the mission of infiltrating the hardened bunkers. The team leader, Chief Petty Officer Wilbur Hernandez, had originally proposed the brilliant idea of flying the newest and smallest drones — about half the size of a golf ball and completely silent— into each bunker. That way, regardless of security, a thorough video inspection of the bunkers could be made, minimizing the risk of SEALS having any contact with enemy assets. For this reason, team one had six air force members with them. They would each control a drone so that multiple drones would simultaneously be inspecting six bunkers, greatly reducing the time required to complete the mission. Hernandez would be in operational command of the team, while the Air Force would be in control of the drones.

Team two would inspect the barracks, weapons and ordnance bunkers, and base fuel supplies. Team three had the mission of inspecting the remaining buildings including the motor pool, kitchen, latrine, and gymnasium. Team four would electronically inspect the control tower, which appeared to be operational, and the parked helicopters. If possible, they would place transmitters onto all of the helicopters so that they could be tracked even when flying below radar, as well as C4 explosives which could be radio detonated.

As team one approached the bunkers, they were immediately alerted to the presence of guards stationed at each bunker. Additional guards were patrolling past in overlapping patrol sectors; the tight security prohibited the men from entering the bunkers. But although security here was good, it wasn't good enough. The air force techs still got to work, and quickly manouvered their drones past the guards. The drones were easily moved through the spacious bunkers, which each contained one Harrier type of jump jet, multiple fight suits, tools, engine ignition machines... in short, everything to get the plane moving. The drones flawlessly transmitted the video from each bunker back to the computers each air force tech was carrying.

All teams at Cheswold had completed their mission by 03:40. They signaled to the CP and were authorized to withdraw. Once assembled, they left by the same route that they had entered by. All three teams had completed their missions at their respective bases.

04:50 hours

Sgt. Ivan Bagrov was furious— no, he was in a murderous temper. He had checked the post where those two nitwits, Privates Orloff and Prokop, were assigned. Neither one was there. For one hour now, he had been walking through the woods, branches whipping across his face, tripping over roots, looking for those two. Nothing, no sign of them. He cursed himself for being so stupid. Just weeks ago he had saved them after they had disobeyed orders, entered a local bar while in uniform, got drunk and into a fight, and got a good beating. He had narrowly arrived in time to help them avoid being arrested, driven them back to the base, got them all cleaned up and sent them out into the woods on guard duty before their Lt., Maslow, who would have hung them, found out about it. And now, how did they repay him? They had obviously left their post and walked back into town, gotten drunk and were sleeping it off somewhere in the woods. Or had been arrested. To make it worse, they had both been armed with AK47 rifles, which were probably hidden somewhere in the woods.

Bagrov was no fool; he knew the Russian army. He was the Sgt. of the guard and it was his job to have checked on them at least once an hour. Normally no one would blame him for catching a few hours of sleep. But if Orloff and Prokop were in jail and had been arrested at, say, midnight, how could he explain not reporting them absent for five hours? The Russian army was not very tolerant when it came to desertion; the penalty was either life in Siberia, which would not be very long, or a firing squad. No, if he could help it he was not going to be shot or be sent to Siberia. He got on his field radio, called Lt. Maslow and reported Orloff and Prokop absent from their posts. Maslow immediately demanded of Bagrov when the last time he had seen them was. Without hesitation Bagrov stated "04:00 comrade Lt." Now it was Maslow who was in trouble. For he too should have been out at least twice inspecting the guards, not sleeping in his bed. Maslow then stated "So when me and you inspected them at 04:00 hours, that was the last time you saw them?"

" Yes Lt., when we were together at 04:00."

"Very well sgt., you did well to report them absent so quickly. Come into my office and let's start the report!"

10:00 hours

Colonel Arnone was waiting in General Kelly's briefing room to update the Chiefs regarding operation 'Peeping Tom,' which, except for the two KIAs, had been a complete success. The door opened and Colonel Arnone snapped to attention as the Chiefs entered the room.

Arnone motioned for his aide to standby as the generals and admiral took their seats. General Kelly then said, "Well Colonel, what have we got?"

"Sir I will begin the briefing with the operation at Fort Devens. There was an unfortunate incident where two enemy sentries had to be eliminated; our men came upon them by chance, the sentries were sleeping when our men literally tripped over the. They were neutralized without any casualties to us."

"Just out of curiosity Colonel, do we know who did the neutralizing?"

"Yes Sir, I was informed that it was Staff Sergeant Dominguez Sir."

The Chiefs exchanged a quick smile. "Proceed Colonel."

When the Colonel finished speaking, there was silence in the room for several minutes, as each of them tried to wrestle with what they had just not only been told, but also seen for themselves in the videos. Admiral Fletcher wondered aloud, "How could they have gotten all of that stuff into the country?"

"My guess sir, think about all of the thousands of cargo containers that come into the country everyday from all over the world. It would only take two containers, maybe even one, to bring in one of those planes, rockets and anything else they needed. That's if some of their stuff isn't our surplus equipment that we've sold to them at a bargain basement rate."

"What about customs, wouldn't they have found some of this stuff?"

"Sir, customs is a division of Homeland Security, need I say more?"

"Very good Colonel, thank you and please tell all of the team members well done. Give them all the two week pass we promised them, starting tomorrow."

"Well the situation is just as bad as we suspected. Which one of you approved placing C4 and transmitters on the aircraft?"

They all looked at one another and laughed. "If it was not one of us, my money would be on Dominguez."

"I wouldn't bet against you. Why don't you promote that boy?"

"Are you kidding? He's already turned down two promotions, says that if he was an officer he wouldn't be able to go on as many missions with his men as he does now."

"I don't know, maybe I should order him to accept the promotion to Captain, bend the rules a little to keep him. His enlistment is up in June, I sure don't want to lose him."

"Anyway, what do you all propose?"

"Nothing for now, we keep up the surveillance on our Russian friends. I will say it again, the C4 and transmitters were a stroke of genius, gives us a nice advantage if we ever have to take them out."

"Now what about the Chinese Navy, what's the latest on them?"

"Just as we expected, the subs sailed enmass. They were originally heading straight for Taiwan with a massive amount of ships behind them. The only thing that convinced me that it wasn't an invasion force was that our satellites indicated that their air force had not shown any activity. Otherwise, who knows what might've happened."

"That was probably the Chinese intent; start a little saber rattling, see who reacts. Next time though it might not be just rattling."

MONDAY, OCTOBER 19TH 09:00

For days now hundreds of Muslims, including many females and children who would normally not be allowed to pray with the men, had been conducting a 24 hour sit-in at the intersection of Madison and 42nd streets. Aside from causing chaos with the traffic, they were behaving very peaceably in front of the many TV cameras. They were now displaying black flag draped pictures of Aakif, aka, Saddam Uday Daher, whom they were describing to the media as the latest victim of the Jewish persecution of Muslims. The "murdered" suspect in the Dearborn bombings and stabbing of a Chicago Police Officer was now a martyr.

The New York Police Dept. had concluded its initial investigation of the riot. The investigation exonerated all of the officers, including Superintendent LaPaglia, who was also commended for her decisive actions while in command of a very dangerous situation. The Police Commissioner had received multiple calls from the Dept. of Justice demanding that the two officers who were the first to charge into the crowd, thus provoking them, be terminated. Never mind the fact that one of the officers had slipped into a coma from the beating he had received from the crowd, and that the other would in all probability lose sight in his right eye and be unable to father children. The original victim, the Jewish driver, whose identity was not being released despite repeated media demands for his name, was still on life support.

To his credit the Commissioner had ordered a criminal investigation of the crowd and promised that criminal charges, including civil rights violations, would be filed against anyone who had been videotaped or could otherwise be proven to have committed a multitude of the various crimes, including: attempted murder, attempted sexual assault, destruction of property, and kidnapping.

Nathan Green could still not believe his bad luck. He had been assigned to head up the FBI investigation into both the Dearborn assault and then the bombing. Thankfully the ATF, meaning Joe Garcia, had jumped into the investigation feet first. And while the FBI had jurisdiction over the first assault, the ATF had jurisdiction over the bombings. His final report recommended no charges against the Dearborn Officers. Just as they had in the investigation of the Ferguson Police, his superiors in the Justice Dept. had tried every angle, including bending, twisting and even breaking the law, to find a way to criminally charge the Dearborn Officers. Reluctantly, they concluded that the officers had not done anything criminally wrong.

It was extremely irritating to him that even though police officers in Ferguson and other cities in the country continued to be hunted and shot, no one in the Justice Dept. had suggested that the FBI get involved in trying to find the shooters. Nathan just happened to be in the New York FBI office visiting some 'friends' when the call came in from Holder to "get a team of investigators down to Madison street now." The agent in charge knew Nathan, and given his experience in Dearborn and his expertise in civil rights investigations, immediately ordered him and his 'friends,' agents Mark Logan and Michael Jenkins, to the scene to begin.

Today Nathan would be conducting a videotaped interview of Superintendent Audrey LaPaglia. Nathan had met with Audrey the night before last and given her the list of questions that he would be asking her today. The questions were not his, but had been given to him by attorneys in the Justice Dept. They were worded in such a way to entrap LaPaglia and, if successful, would lead to the filing of criminal civil rights violations against her.

13:00 hours

Superintendent Lapaglia, accompanied by two attorneys and a total of seven Captains and LTs., entered the conference room on the fifth floor of the FBI building. The Captains and Lts. had been on scene for the riot and had been brought in by LaPaglia as both witnesses and to provide any records, such as dispatch tapes, that might be required. Nathan, along with agents Logan and Jenkins, rose to meet them.

They all gathered around a highly polished oak table, with high backed swivel leather reclining chairs. The room itself had a large glass wall facing over the Hudson river. Looking around, Audrey thought to herself, "Nothing but the best that tax dollars could buy." With the comfort of the chairs, the afternoon sun shining into the room and her feet sinking into the thick carpet, she wondered how anyone could not help but to doze off. Maybe that was the whole point. Get a person who was being interrogated (the FBI would call it an interview but it was an interrogation) sleepy so that they might make a careless or unguarded remark.

Audrey had to hand it to the FBI. Although, thanks to Nathan, she was more prepared than anyone knew, for this interview. The power that the room implied, the panel of three FBI agents, and as she knew would happen, having her MIRANDA rights read to her, all combined to put any individual at a severe psychological disadvantage. Which was exactly what the FBI hoped for.

Nathan opened the meeting by introducing himself and his fellow agents. He then informed everyone in the room that this interview was being recorded by both video and audio. He also informed everyone that since criminal charges could possibly result from this interview and the ongoing investigation he was required to read Audrey and anyone who might be questioned today their MIRANDA rights. Nathan started, "You have the right to remain silent..."

For the next ninety minutes, Audrey was grilled relentlessly. But none of them, including Agents Green, Jenkins or Logan, were aware of the fact that the entire interview had been monitored live by attorneys from the U.S. Dept. of Justice, civil rights division, and Kalaak .

As soon as the interrogation was over, Kalaak excitedly asked, "We have her, right? We can punish her?" His choice of words was not lost on the attorneys, who, despite what Holder said, were not all that legally comfortable with listening in on an interrogation without either side knowing about it.

"Mr. Kalaak, we are not in the business of punishing people. It is up to a jury to find someone guilty after a fair trial, and a judge to sentence or, as you say, punish, someone. We are not the jury or the judge." Kalaak just stared them. Obviously they would not be entering paradise, and Holder will hear of this outrage. Kalaak got up from his chair and left the room without saying another word. He walked the short distance down the hall and entered Holder's office without knocking.

Once Kallak had left the room attorney Richard Holt turned to his fellow attorneys. "Well, that's most likely the end of my career, and to tell you the truth I feel relieved. I'm tired of being used as a political hitman, being sent to destroy Obama's enemies whether they have committed a crime or not. And most have not. We go after police officers who are doing their best to hold things together while Obama's crimes, Fast and Furious, Benghazi, IRS attacks, audits and missing emails, Solandra and others go uninvestigated, unprosecuted and therefore unpunished, all by Holders orders. I've had it." With that, he picked up his papers and walked to his desk. On an impulse he picked up his private cell phone and called FBI agent Nathan Green.

"Hello?"

"Yes is this FBI agent Nathan Green?"

"Yes, who is this please?"

"My name is Richard Holt. I'm a prosecutor with the U.S. Dept. of Justice's civil rights division. I watched your interview with Deputy LaPaglia today and—"

"You watched it? How'd you do that? I was not aware that the interviewing was being monitored live by anyone."

"Come on Nathan, you were on a closed circuit system while you were recording LaPAglia, we just basically turned on our TV and watched."

"So who is we?"

"I would like to talk to you about that. I 've heard your name being mentioned around the Justice Dept. They do not like you, so if they do not like you, you must be a good guy, can we meet?"

"Sure where and when?"

"I'm in DC, how about the day after tomorrow? We can meet in New York, in that deli around the corner from the FBI office?"

"I would prefer somewhere a little further away from the office if you don't mind."

"Ok, how about by that old fort in the Bowery? We can grab something to eat at one of the food carts. Noontime ok?"

"Yes, noon is good, but I don't know what you look like."

"That's ok, I'll come up to you. This is my number if something comes up and you need to cancel. I do look forward to meeting you."

TUESDAY, OCTOBER 20TH 02:00 HOURS, PACIFIC TIME, SOUTH CHINA SEA

Chinese Fleet Admiral Bo Zheng was standing in the Combat Information Center of his flagship, the Aircraft Carrier Liaoning. It was obvious to those on duty that he was not very happy. The naval situation was growing serious. What was designed to be a three day drill for the Chinese Navy was rapidly turning into a test of wills between China and, as of now, six other nations. This drill had been planned to not only test the sea-readiness of a large part of China's fleet, especially it's submarine force, but to also test the reaction of China's neighbors.

The test had been both positive and negative. Positive in the sense that the Chinese Navy had responded to the unannounced drill better than had been hoped for. The men were highly trained and the ships were state of the art.

Negative in the sense that it had provoked such a strong reaction from China's neighbors. Especially the rebel province of Taiwan, who had sent messages to China through the Russians that they, the Taiwanese, believed that China was in fact sending an invasion fleet and that if the Chinese Navy trespassed into Taiwanese territorial waters they would be immediately be fired upon. To emphasize the point, the Taiwanese Air Force had been conducting flyovers of the Chinese fleet with fully armed American made F15 and F16 fighter bombers, while their navy was putting every available ship out to sea.

China's ancient enemy, the Japanese, were conducting an aggressive surveillance of his fleet using American made A2 Hawkeye aircraft and submarines. Japan also had a very modern and powerful fleet of their own. They had not only sent an even dozen ships to monitor the Chinese fleet, but, along with the Indian Navy, were preparing more ships to go to sea. The Vietnamese, another ancient enemy and whose navy consisted of only a handful of outdated ships that once belonged to the U.S. Navy, had also set sail. The South Koreans, who possessed a very respectful navy, had gone on a high alert both on land and sea. Apparently, they feared a Chinese invasion by sea and land.

Admiral Zheng politely snapped at his communications officer, "Where is the intelligence ship 'Beijixing' now?"

"Sir, she was only ordered to leave Hawaiian waters six hours ago. She will not be in range to provide us with effective intelligence for another three days."

"In the meantime, our most advanced surveillance planes, the Zdk-03 and KJ-200, are enroute to assist in monitoring enemy movements."

"Enemy! What enemy, are we at war? Have hostiles commenced that I am not aware of? No? Then we have no enemy." That type of thinking was dangerous and must be curbed immediately. He wanted to avoid any incidents that could lead to an escalation, and had already asked Naval HQ for permission to withdraw. Naval HQ had given him permission, but on the return voyage had ordered him to steer a course that put his fleet dangerously close to the territorial waters of Taiwan, Japan, and South Korea. He understood the reasoning of HQ. Face honor must be maintained, even if it meant a war.

09:00 Hours The White House

Obama sat half-listening as his National Security Advisor gave him a thorough briefing of the events unfolding in the Pacific. As of now no one from the Chinese government, or even the Chinese Ambassador, had returned his calls.

"So sir, the situation has reached a point where the slightest accident could provoke a serious incident that could lead to war. I recommended that we contact all of the governments involved asap and try to deescalate the situation. I have Admiral Fletcher waiting outside."

"I really don't want to see him. You know my family is waiting for me, we're going to Hawaii for a well deserved vacation."

"Yes sir, I know you could use a vacation, but could you take five minutes to meet with the Admiral?"

"Ok, five minutes."

Admiral Fletcher entered the Oval Office and saluted. "Thank you, Mr. President, for seeing me. I am sure that you have been briefed on what has become a very serious situation in the Pacific. If hostilities do occur, there is a very good chance that we could be drawn into—"

"Excuse me admiral, how could we "be drawn into," any as you term it, hostilities, without my authorizing it?"

"Sir, things happen. A stray shot, a collision with so many ships and planes in such close proximity to each other..."

"I see. Have all of our ships leave the area, that region is really of no vital importance to the U.S. And if it makes you feel any better, I have already begun communications with the highest levels of the Chinese government to resolve the situation. I have to go now, my family is waiting for me. We're going on vacation to Hawaii, so if anything I will be even closer to the situation. Keep me posted on any developments."

"Yes sir." With that Obama left the office and headed out to the South Lawn to meet his family and board Marine One, which would fly them to Andrews Air Force base to board the most comfortable plane in the world: Air Force One. It was good to be president. President for life even, only he had to decide when to tell the people. Maybe the right time would be at his State of The Union speech. He would have to think about that, see what Kalaak thought. He and Michelle just loved it when the Marines and Air Force personnel saluted him. No way was he going to give that thrill up.

Admiral Fletcher just stood in the office. Not only was he feeling personally humiliated, but more importantly, professionally humiliated. He had served for almost thirty years in the United States Navy, an institution that he loved greatly, and now for the second time in a few days his navy had been dismissed by Obama.

In his own way the National Security advisor was embarrassed. Granted Obama was of course right. And sooner or later someone from the Chinese government would realize how badly a statesman like Obama was needed to defuse and resolve the situation. But the poor Admiral, what was his name? Well, his heart was in the right place. Nevertheless, the meeting was over. "Sir, we have to go now. The Secret Service will secure the office now that the President has left on vacation."

Admiral Fletcher could think of a lot of things to say. But he didn't. "Don't worry Sir, if the President says he has it all under control, why then it is all under control."

"I'm sure you are right. Good day now, and if myself or the navy can help out in anyway, please let us know."

"Thank you Admiral, I will do that if we need your help."

Admiral Fletcher left the White House and was driven back to the Pentagon. He shut his door and immediately called the other Chiefs, inviting them over to his office to update them on his discussion with the President. On an impulse, he called his security unit to come up and perform a 'sweep' of his office, looking for any hidden listening devices. They arrived promptly and, after a complete scan, they pronounced his office 'bug' free. The Admiral thanked them and waited for his guests, thinking, "Maybe I'm getting paranoid. Then again, maybe not."

04:00 hours Pacific time

Capt. Xi was running out of patience; it seemed that every five minutes the Captain of the 'Beijixing' was calling him asking if they were yet in range to intercept any and all electronic communications from the militaries of the bandit countries that were threatening the Chinese Navy.

He had to be very diplomatic with the Captain, explaining to him that both distance and atmospheric conditions were combining to mask the transmissions from the bandits. But, maybe if the ship went faster, they would be able to get within hearing distance sooner. The Captain, not realizing the sarcasm, informed Capt Xi that the ship was responding as fast as it could to the admiral's orders! Capt. Xi needed a moment to relax. He was almost going to listen to that unusual, most peculiar, low band radio message that he had stumbled across. But no, not now. The captain would probably come in and catch him in the middle of his 'hobby,' and that would not be good. The way things looked, he would not get to enjoy eavesdropping for weeks to come, if ever.

23:00 hours the Kremlin

Russian President Putin, along with both his military and political advisers, had been in conference for hours. The situation in the Pacific had at first been of no consequence to Russia. But now things were getting much more complex.

Diplomatically Russia, while not fully trusting China, had been strengthening their ties. While they both had an interest in humbling the United States, China did not want to destroy the U.S.— at least not until the U.S. had repaid it's financial debt, which would never happen. The Chinese were happy to keep the U.S. as a vassal state. Russia remembered that she had fought several severe border battles with China, and that China was interested in expanding into eastern Russia. As odd as it seemed, Russia did not by any account want to alienate the Vietnamese. Russia had been using, and needed, the American built air bases in Vietnam to land, repair and refuel Russian Tu-160 and TU-22 long range nuclear bombers. This gave Russia the ability to project airpower far out into the Pacific. Russia also wanted access to the U.S. built naval base at Cam Rahn Bay.

Ever since the Russian Japanese War, when the Japanese had destroyed a Russian fleet, the Russian Navy had been looking for an excuse to fight the Japanese. Several times during the dispute over the Kuril Islands, they had come close to provoking the Japanese to fire. A similar situation existed between China and Japan over the disputed Senkaku Islands, to the Japanese, or the Diaoyu Islands if you asked the Chinese.

Putin sensed an opportunity. By withdrawing the few American ships in the area, Obama had clearly signaled to the world that he was not going to get involved in honoring the U.S. treaties with any of the allied countries. If he did nothing and the Chinese fought the combined navies of the allies, even if they won, China would be so weakened that the U.S. would regain supremacy in the region. No, that could not be allowed to happen. Russia was walking a tightrope in its actions in the Ukraine and eastern Europe. The Europeans had also observed Obama's desertion of the U.S. allies. They were not stupid; if the U.S. abandoned the Pacific allies, why wouldn't they abandon the European ones?

Putin and his advisors concluded that they did not want China growing so powerful in the Pacific. The decision was made. Putin picked up the phone and ordered the operator to connect him with the Chinese Premier, Li Keqiang. In a matter of several minutes Li answered the phone. Putin explained his concerns while Li listened respectfully, then asked if Putin had any suggestions. His suggestion was to withdraw from the immediate area, why risk an incident? Putin, of course, had no idea that Li had already ordered that very withdrawal. They talked for several more minutes and Li agreed that he would withdraw his navy by the route he had already ordered. Li also agreed that Putin could call the various heads of state and inform them that he had arranged to have the Chinese Navy withdraw, but only if they too started to withdraw their navies. Putin quickly agreed and thanked Li for his statesmanship in ordering the withdrawal. While Putin was congratulating himself for his handling of the situation, Li was overjoyed to have Putin's help in ordering the withdrawal. To the Asian mind, China had not only used Russia, but had saved huge 'face' in front of the rest of the world. In addition, Russia would now owe him a favor.

Putin then immediately had his aide arrange a video conference call with the nations aligning against China. Within the hour they were all on the screen and listening. Not only were they all looking for a peaceful resolution to the situation, but also they recognized the historical shift in the game of world-power which was happening before their eyes. While the U.S. was in a steep nose-dive politically, financially and militarily, Putin and Russia were gaining power and international respect in all three areas. As they all knew, with power and respect came influence. All listened with relief as he related to them his conversation with Li Keqiang, and were eager to accept the resolution that Putin had negotiated. With real gratitude, they all said goodby to Putin, disconnected from the call and issued the orders for their navies to return to home waters.

After they had disconnected from the call, Putin and his advisors congratulated themselves. They all knew that they had just solved a potentially serious situation, and that they had gained stature and influence in the Pacific region. They then began a casual political talk with their staffs, discussing how well they had performed on the world stage and how different this incident would have been if one of the Bushes, or GOD forbid Ronald Reagan, was President of the U.S. *Reagan*, that name, that thought, made them shudder.

THURSDAY, OCTOBER 22ND.
11:00 HOURS BOSTON

Sean had just hung up the phone from his official conference call with members of the group. He had arranged for the call in response to an FBI alert, reminding departments nationwide of the graffiti threats for Halloween night to be national "kill a cop night." They had discussed the measures that their departments were taking. Most agreed that they did not want to go overboard with their response, as this would only encourage whoever had made the threats. They promised to keep each other aware of any incidents in their areas. Sean could not help but think that they were missing something.

11:45 hours, New York

Nathan Green casually walked towards the old Bowery fort. He was scanning back and forth trying to spot Mr. Holt and the NYPD Officers he had asked Audrey to have in place, just in case something went wrong. He was pretty sure that he could see at least four undercover officers, including two dressed like telephone repairmen, in the area. As he was walking he saw an individual approaching him who certainly looked like a lawyer. There was just something about lawyers, they had that look!

"Hi Nathan, I'm Richard Holt, pleased to meet you."

"The pleasure is mine. Before we really begin to talk, Richard, would you mind if I asked you for several pieces of identification?"

"No problem, I actually appreciate your being so careful. Here's my Driver's License, Bar card, Dept. of Justice ID—"

"Ok that's enough." Nathan took the IDs, examined them, and handed them back to Richard. For some reason, he was beginning to like him. Instinct told him that Richard could be trusted.

"So Rich, what can I do for you?"

"If you don't mind I actually am hungry, can we get something to eat?"

"Sure anything you want, how about hot dogs? I really love a well cooked all beef hotdog."

"Sounds good to me."

They ordered their dogs. While each went to pay, Richard was just a little closer to the cashier, who took his money.

"Thanks" said Nathan, "let's sit over there on that far bench."

"Well, I have to admit that I'm eager to hear what you have to say."

"Let me start by saying I have been with the DOJ for fourteen years now. I was hired when John Ashcroft was the Attorney General. When I started, the Justice Dept. was just what you would have expected. An agency dedicated to fighting crime, protecting our constitution, enforcing our laws in a fair, legal, and impartial manner. I never once heard of the DOJ being used to attack, silence or intimidate anyone, especially people with different political opinions. Under President Bush we really had, especially when compared with the Obama administration, a scandal free presidency.

Now the DOJ and IRS are used to threaten and attack anyone who disagrees with or criticizes Obama, while Holder refuses to even investigate, much less prosecute, any of a hundred possible crimes or scandals. But Holder will use the full force of the DOJ to investigate and prosecute any police officer, or non-minority, for even an alleged allegation of racism. However, not one minority has been prosecuted by Holder for a committed act of racial assault against a non-minority. Not one. I could go on and on, but you don't have all day. There is a member of Obama's team, a special advisor, who I believe is a radical Muslim, named Kalaak."

Nathan had been paying close attention to what Richard was saying, but at the mention of that name all of his senses went on high alert. Richard spotted this and asked, "You know him?"

"Yes. Please proceed and then I'll tell you what I know."

"Well, Kalaak seems to have some strange hold over Obama and Holder. He comes and goes as he wants in the DOJ, and I presume in the White House. Kalaak was the one who pushed so hard for the investigation of the police in both the Dearborn shootings and the Muslim riots here in New York. When you were interviewing LaPaglia, myself and two other staff attorneys were in the room along with Kalaak. I actually objected to him being present. I mean, who is he to have first-hand access to a law enforcement interview and investigation? But I was overruled by Holder himself.

Kalaak sat silently during the interview, which by the way, from a professional standpoint, your team, and especially Lapaglia, all did a very good job at. It was very obvious that she was being completely truthful. Anyways, at the end of the interview, Kalaak gets all excited and demands, "We have her right, we can punish her?" I explained that we were not there to punish anyone, that it's up to a jury to determine guilt and a judge to pass a sentence. Kalaak just looked at me, did not say a word, and left the room. I was told that he walked down the hall and entered Holder's office without even knocking."

"Nothing you've said surprises me. I only met Kalaak once when he came to Dearborn, MI after the Muslim attack on the city workers and bombing which killed three police officers. He demanded access to our crime scene, not only for himself, but for Muslim leaders, so that they could handle the evidence and make sure that we were conducting a correct investigation. I told him no way was he entering the crime scene and if he did he would be arrested. He then called me an 'infidel' and stormed away."

"Well, I have to confess that I did hear something about that; a video had Kalaak calling you an Infidel on it. At the time, I was not sure what to think of it. It was just too hard to believe. But now, after what Kalaak said to me after watching the interview, I guess I believe that he called you an infidel."

"Well thanks for believing me. What are your plans now?"

"I assume that I will be asked to leave my position; that is if I am not fired outright. Then I'll go into private practice. You know, chasing ambulances." There was silence for several minutes as Nathan debated with himself whether or not he could trust Holt . He decided to take the middle road. "Richard, you might be much more valuable to the country by staying where you are, keeping your eyes open and gathering evidence that could be used to prosecute Holder, and who knows who else." Richard just looked at him, Nathan was telling him something. But what?

"I might be inclined to do that if, if I knew that my efforts would not be wasted."

"I can't say a lot, but your efforts will not be wasted."

Holt looked at him in a funny way, then said, "Ok Nathan, for some reason I trust you. I will try, at least for awhile to do as you ask, but then I'll need to see some reason to continue. Deal?"

"Deal."

"Richard, are there any other prosecutors in your office who feel the same way?" "Yes, plenty."

"If you're comfortable, try and see if any of them want to help quietly put a case together against not only Holder, but Obama too."

At that, they shook hands and then parted company. Both of them had much to think about.

11:45, the Pentagon

The Joint Chiefs, along with a number of on-duty personnel, were all in the secure and supposedly top-secret global command center, located about 200 feet below street level on the West side of the Pentagon. They were all being briefed on the current naval situation in the Pacific. The regional display of the area had the ships of each nation color coded, highlighted and displayed in geographical relation to each other.

They all scowled when they saw, approximately 600 hundred miles away from the action, seven blue blimps, which indicated the U.S. ships. Chinese ships were highlighted in red. One of the system operators called out that all allied naval units were changing course. Everyone instantly looked up at the display. After several minutes it was clear to even a novice that the ships were indeed changing course. It was also clear that some arrangement had been made to have so many ships from so many nations all change course at the same time.

General Stewart said out loud, "I wonder what, or whom, caused that to happen."

In a voice laced with sarcasm, Admiral Fletcher replied, "Maybe our Commander and Chief." This drew a chorus of laughter from all.

They were still speculating on the possible military reasons for the ships to alter course when once again the operator called out, "The Chinese ships are now also changing course." This second course change confirmed in everyone's mind that some sort of a deal had been reached.

General Kelly picked up a phone and called a contact in the NSA. He talked quietly for about five minutes, then said, "Yes Claire, I will stand by. Thank you."

In about fifteen minutes the phone rang, and was answered on the first ring by General Kelly. He listened intently for several minutes before replying, "Yes Claire, I have it. Thank you very much." He then signaled the other Chiefs to meet him in the soundproof conference room located along a wall in the bunker.

"Well, I just spoke with a contact in the NSA. The NSA had earlier recorded a conversation between Putin and Li Keqiang, and then a video conference call between Putin and the leaders of the Pacific allied nations. Apparently, a world leader has successfully resolved the situation. Anyone care to guess who the obvious world leader was? No? Well, it was a real Commander and Chief, Putin!"

Admiral Fletcher had, of course, already informed them all of his conversation, or rather *attempted* conversation, with Obama.

Wayne Kelly spoke first. "I am tired of waiting. Police or no police, hopefully with you but without you if I have to, I am going to act. I honestly think that we all have to act sooner than May. He probably already has plans to relieve us all, and if that happens it will make things a lot harder."

"Fine, we are with you, but when? We want to catch all of the Congress in one place at one time; when will be the next time that they are all together in one place?"

They all thought for a minute when General Quinn spoke up. "The State of the Union address in January. Both the Congress and the Supreme Court will be there, along with the leader of the FED, cabinet members, the National Media and on and on."

A smile came to all of their faces, which seemed to convey multiple feelings: three months, not eight months away, vengeance, resolve, relief, and yes, happiness.

General Quinn then spoke up. "Gentlemen, I suggest we quietly alert our staffs of the change in the timetable. Wayne, can you call your friend Joe Annino, see if we can get together at his cabin with Sean Dominguez and whoever Sean wants to bring? I think we should also invite the Commanders of the surrounding states' national guards that are with us."

"Fine Eric, I will do that."

FRIDAY, OCTOBER 23RD 10:00 HOURS

Sean had just hung up from a rather serious sounding phone call with Joe Annino when he noticed both Sean and Shannon looking at him.

"Well, Joe wants me and some other friends to stay next weekend, Halloween, at his cabin in Virginia. I told him I would be there. Something's up, but that's all I know for now." Sean Jr. just smiled. "I don't know for sure dad, but I would guess that something has happened to alter the plan, maybe move up the date. Just a guess."

Shannon spoke up. "We started this, I guess you better go."

"Ok then, I have a bunch of phone calls to make."

"Why not just send one message to everyone on your radio, saves a lot of time," Shannon suggested.

"Good idea. I'll still want to talk with one or two of the guys, but I'll send that now." He looked at his son. "What are you going to do?"

"Not much, I might see if mom wants to go for a walk around the island."

The phone started to ring again.

"Who *now*?"

Sean jr. just laughed. "Looks like it's your day, dad."

It was Jeff Clark. Sean knew that he had to answer. With more energy than he felt, he answered with a hearty, "Jeff, how are you sir?"

"Fine Sean. If you have a minute, I have a story to tell you about the Fort Deven's area."

Sean signaled for Sean to stay and listen. "Jeff can I put you on speakerphone?"

"Sure fine with me. This started several days ago. Some of the locals have been calling the state and local police to report many men going through the woods. They seem to be moving in a line, almost like they were searching for someone or something. I don't know what to make of it, but you asked me to let you know of anything unusual happening up there."

Sean was looking at Sean jr; he had that same look on his face that he had had as a child that said, "How did you find out about *that*?"

"Ok Jeff, thank you for keeping me informed."

"Oh, one more thing about the street sweepers. The night before last, the troopers assigned to that area reported that at 3AM there were fifty of them going about 60mph down route two. They traveled about ten miles, turned around doing 60 again on the way back, and entered into the base. Which should've been closed for the night."

"Eh that is interesting."

"Sean, what's going on up there?"

"Jeff, let me get back to you to set up a time to meet."

"Ok, I'll look forward to it, bye."

Sean stared over at his son. Sonny-boy had been listening intently as Jeff spoke, and at both the mention of the possible search party and streetsweepers he had detected a visible reaction from Sean.

"So, do you care to enlighten me about what you know about both the streetsweepers and the possible search parties?"

"Sorry dad, can't say a word."

Sean decided that one, he was not going to push for an answer, and two, he probably would not like the answer if he heard it.

Sean went down the cellar, opened the gun safe and took out his radio. He thought carefully about the message that he was going to send. In the end, he decided to make it short and sweet. "Urgent meeting on 10-31-15 in VA. Please plan on attending. Call me for further details, or if you absolutely cannot attend."

The NSA and the Chinese added another of the group's messages to their computer hard drives.

13:00 hours Fort Devens

Major Kalashnikov was in a terrible temper; in fact, he had been ever since he returned on the 19th and was informed of the two missing soldiers and their weapons. He had delayed one day in reporting the desertions in the hope that the two privates would be found. He had done everything that he could think of. But, after an extensive search of the woods in all directions, phoning the local police to see if they had been arrested, even calling the local hospitals, nothing. He knew the Lt. and Sgt. were lying to him about the times they checked on the two deserters, but that was almost irrelevant. The men and their weapons, which they probably sold for traveling money, were gone. The men had deserted. The time of their desertion did not really matter, and if he turned in the Lt. and Sgt., well, that just made it appear that his entire command, and he himself, were unreliable. No, better to let the blame rest on the two peasant soldiers. He counted himself lucky that he had been away from the base on an official inspection with Colonel Abramovich himself.

Kalashnikov also knew that he was fortunate the desertions had happened when they did. He was not privy to exactly what was occurring, but he knew that Colonel Abramovich was on edge. After leaving the Cheswold base, Abramovich had flown on to FEMA area six for a meeting, commanded by his rival, Colonel Tapac Sabantsev. Sabantsev was one of General Pyzik's favorite area commanders, and Pyzik was the Supreme commander of all Russian forces inside of the U.S. Kalashnikov knew from Abramovich that all of the commanders from the ten FEMA areas were also attending the meeting. Each FEMA area contained approximately two thousand Russian military personnel, and at least one air base with anywhere from 12 to 45 Mig fighter bombers. When ordered, their mission was to launch a preemptive strike on nearby U.S. airfields and aircraft, and support Homeland Security. For now, he would count himself fortunate that his superiors seemed to be busy and therefore not paying too much attention to him. He hoped.

It did not take long for members of the group to start calling Sean. Sara was first. She did have family plans for the weekend, but would come if it was important. Sean told her what he knew, and that the meeting was important; she agreed to come.

The next five hours were spent on the phone with Sheriff Al, Nathan, Joe Garcia, Brian, Ed, Tony and the rest of the group. They all promised to be there. Audrey called later in the day to report that the situation with the sit in had been slowly improving, with fewer and fewer Muslims coming every day. The weather had been getting colder, so the evening and night sit-ins had been canceled. Audrey was still the on-site commander; at the direct order of the PC himself, she had to spend the majority of her working time monitoring it. She was going crazy. Anyway, Audrey wanted to bring Carl Brown to the meeting. Sean hesitated, then said he would check with their host first.

18:00 hours

Without exception, they were all going to attend on the 31st. Joe informed Sean that his friends from the area state police and national guards would be there also. Sean learned from Joe that the marine wanted to move up the date of the operation, but Joe did not know anything more than that. They also discussed the advisability of inviting Carl Brown to the meeting. After going back and forth, they decided that it would be better to have him there. Sean then called Audrey, apologized for keeping her waiting, and extended the invitation to Carl.

Sean had a migraine; he had spent hours on the phone basically having the same conversation with countless people. He needed some fresh air. No one was home, he hadn't even noticed when they had left. There was a note on the counter from Shannon, short and to the point: 'went to the mall with Heather, back around six. Love you.' He knew six could mean seven or even eight PM. He decided to sit on the front steps, have a beer and get some fresh ocean air.

WEDNESDAY, OCTOBER 28, 17:00 HOURS, THE WHITE HOUSE

Kalaak was in a foul mood. Earlier in the day he had learned that Atif Khayyam, a high ranking member of the Department of Homeland Security, had, for the last few nights, been broadcasting a reminder on his internet show *Jihad Tomorrow*: Halloween, the promised 'national kill a cop night,' was fast approaching.

Kalaak did not care about cops being killed, not with January so near. Obama had hinted to Kalaak that during the State of The Union address he would announce his intention to remain in office as president for the rest of his life. Upon hearing this, Kallak had experienced a religious fervor, understanding the Mahdi's plan. It was as if Allah himself had spoken to him. The Caliphate would soon be established here in America, and then the rest of the world. That was precisely why Kalaak was fuming. Not only did he not want any more trouble, but he was also doing everything in his considerable power to prevent it. That was why he had issued orders for the New York sit-in to end. Now Khayyam had to go and put the police forces across the country on high alert. Fox News had even reported on Khayyam's call for violence, and was speculating on why the FBI and FCC had not taken action against Khayyam. Now Fox was reporting that they were trying to verify reports that Khayyam was an actual employee of the Dept. of Homeland Security. When, not if, they confirmed that, it would bring a great deal of unwanted attention on Muslims in general, and the Dept. in particular. If there was violence when that was reported, all of Christian America would be getting out their rifles. If that happened... No, Khayyam, faithful servant that he was, he had to be silenced for good. Allah would provide other faithful servants. Kalaak sat thinking for a moment and then decided to call his old and trusted friend, Abdus.

FRIDAY, OCTOBER 30, 12:00 HOURS

Joe Annino, along with his aides Vince and Chris, arrived at his cabin. They had a lot to prepare, from making the beds in both the cabins and Winnebagos to stocking the refrigerator. In addition, they set up video equipment and folding tables that would be used to lay out the maps and build mock ups, unit locations, and a hundred other things. Lastly, they had a mobile field communications unit set up.

14:00 hours.

Joe looked up and was pleasantly surprised to see his close friend, Colonel George Palmer of the Maryland National guard, getting out of his truck. "Hello Joe, how we doing?"

"I am fine George, just getting things set up for our meeting."

"I noticed that there are several of your state troopers stationed at the turn off into your place."

With a smile on his face Joe replied, "Really? They must be running a radar trap there."

"Yeah, and checking IDs on anyone who turns down this road, what a coincidence!" "Can't be too careful George." They both just laughed.

"I think some of the other guys are planning on arriving today."

"Great, we'll be ready for them when they get here."

"Oh, I brought some provisions, where do you want them?"

Shortly after Walter May and Stephen McCain from West Virginia arrived, followed by John Piffer and Justin Thompson from South Carolina. Sean Dominguez, along with Audrey LaPaglia, arrived within the hour. Right around supper time Edward Johnson and Kevin Wickens from PA came in.

The food was cooked, and since the night was getting chilly, everyone settled around the fire. It seemed that no one wanted to start a serious conversation. But of course it happened. Piffer could not resist asking Audrey to brief them on the situation in NY, from start to finish.

Audrey gave a silent sigh. She could not be rude, and so proceeded to narrate the entire incident.

Piffer then spoke up. "You know Audrey, if you did not have the courage to give the orders that you gave, calling in more manpower and using gas, the situation would have spiraled out of control. I had already been contacted by the Charleston Police and asked to be prepared to send in state police. The Charleston PD had taken the sensible step of beginning to monitor several of the mosques in the city. They noticed a big surge in the amount of Muslims entering. I believe that when they saw how tough you and the NYPD were in responding, they decided not to start additional protests. If, on the other hand, the NY Police response was weak, I believe that we would have seen Muslims all over the country taking to the streets. Well done, Audrey."

Joe Annino spoke up. "I guess from what Audrey said our group has begun looking out for each other. It was very nice of Nathan to help you the way he did. Even being innocent and having two attorneys with me, I wouldn't have wanted to sit before a panel of three FBI agents being grilled. By the way, do you know when Nathan will arrive?"

"He told me that he plans on driving from NY to Washington, picking up Carl Brown, and getting here late morning or early afternoon."

"That will be great, the Chiefs are planning on arriving around 10 AM."

"By the way Joe, are your troopers out there tomorrow?"

"They will be out there 24 / 7 until I relieve them, and that will be when I leave. Believe me, they are all good people and will be with us when the time comes."

Sean spoke up. "You just hit the nail on the head. The time, seems like that's what this meeting will be all about."

"Which would, I believe, leave us all with the conclusion that something has occurred to make it imperative that the time table be moved up. I guess we will all find that out sometime tomorrow."

They heard a car coming, then were blinded by headlights, which were quickly turned off. Sara Mahoney and Susan Nguyen stepped from the vehicle.

"Hello all, Joe you need to put up some street signs to find this place. If it wasn't for the troopers out there, I would have driven right by."

It was Audrey who spoke up first. "Well girlfriend you're here now, so relax."

"I intend to. It's a long flight here from San Diego. Is that a margarita? Can I have one?" They all welcomed her as if she was family while Joe went to make the margarita.

SATURDAY, OCTOBER 31ST. 08:00 HOURS

Joe had the coffee brewing both on the stove and over an outside fire. Breakfast sandwiches would be cooked outside while a full breakfast —pancakes, omelets— would be served inside. They heard a car coming down the road, and were pleased to see that both Conor Evans and Matthew Forcioni from North Carolina had arrived.

Joe was making introductions and taking breakfast orders.

"Joe, if this doesn't work out you can always get a job in the prison kitchen," Ed commented. Nobody thought that that was very funny, and Ed soon found himself being bombarded with cups and anything else non-lethal that they could find to throw at him.

About 10 AM, Brian Olofson, Ed Larkin, Joe Garcia, Brandon Robinson, Tony Lee, and Sheriff Al all arrived. They had coordinated their flights so that they could drive down together.

Nathan Green was ahead of schedule. He had picked up Carl Brown at 9AM and should be arriving at Joe's place by 11AM at the latest. He phoned Audrey to let her know where they were, and was surprised to learn that everyone other than the Chiefs had arrived. At 10:45 he pulled off the two lane road. As he came to the turn off into Joe's place, he noticed the VA troopers blocking the turn into Joe's property. He thought to himself that this was either a very good or very bad sign. He was stopped, showed his ID, and was allowed to proceed. A very good sign, he decided.

Audrey greeted them when they arrived. She seemed to be especially happy to see Carl. "What might be going on there?" Nathan wondered.

At 11:45 the Joint Chiefs of Staff, accompanied by Marine Generals Carpenter from Camp Pendleton and Paul McDonald from Parris Island, along with six aides, arrived. Everyone came out to greet them, and any needed introductions were made.

Commandant Kelly spoke up. "Folks, let's all take 30 minutes, grab something to eat or drink, and meet in the big cabin. I will begin the briefing then. Sean, can we have a few minutes of your time now?"

"Of course General."

They sat down, and General Kelly gave Sean a heads-up that he was going to suggest, no, *order*, that the operation be moved up to January. There were issues, not the least of which was operational security arising. He would explain fully at the briefing. Since Sean was the one who originally got this operation in motion, he wanted to give him a little advance warning. Sean thanked the general, stating that he was looking forward to what promised to be an exciting afternoon.

They walked into a beehive of activity; aides were just finishing setting up video screens and laying out maps, both on the wall and table. There was a respectful silence and everyone took a seat as General Kelly walked to the front of the room.

"Ladies and gentlemen, for the following reasons I propose that the operation originally planned for May of 2016 be advanced to January of 2016." Everyone knew that no one was going to seriously disagree with the general's proposal. Most of the people in the room were stunned. It had seemed to some of them that May was coming much too soon, and now January!

"What I am about to share with you is *top secret*, and I mean that. Outside of a very few members of what's left of the U.S. military, no one knows what I am about to tell you."

He looked around the room for telltale signs of fear, nervousness, or even to see if someone was looking at the door and thinking of fleeing. He saw no signs that anyone was having second thoughts; rather, just the opposite. Everyone was leaning forward in their seats with expectant looks on their faces. He wondered for a second if these same looks were worn by the original Sons of Liberty when they assembled in Independence Hall, Quincy Market, or a hundred lesser known locations when they were planning to create our nation and give us the freest form of government ever known to man.

He recalled how, in a negative way, President Bill Clinton described the priceless gift of freedom given to us by the Founding Fathers as "radical". Then, he thought of the words of President Ronald Reagan, and his never ending work to downsize government and defend freedom, not only in the U.S. but the entire world. He remembered when he stood just out of camera range when Reagan gave his 'Evil Empire' speech. And when Reagan called on Communist Party General Secretary Gorbachev to "tear down this wall," resulting in the reunification of Germany and the collapse of communism in Russia. Lastly, he remembered how Reagan had said, "Government is not the solution, government is the problem." As usual Ronald Reagan had it right, especially when he thought of Obama's government. Well they were going to solve the problem, once and for all.

He remembered that in every cause, and especially the cause of freedom, there were always leaders and followers. Here in this room were the leaders, he knew that in his heart. But he hoped that there were still a majority of Americans who were willing to stand up for their freedom. That was another lesson from the Founding Fathers: the people had to be the final defenders of freedom.

Did the American people remember the words and spirit of Patrick Henry when he asked, "Is life so dear, or peace so sweet, as to be purchased at the price of chains and slavery? Forbid it Almighty Father, I know not what course others may take, but as for me. Give me liberty, or give me death!"

"We have just recently discovered that as of now, there are ten of our former military bases, which we believed were closed, that are operational and being used by Russian military personnel here inside the U.S. These bases all contain either fighter bomber aircraft and or helicopters, and also rockets. In addition, as most of you know, Homeland Security has another 10 known locations where they have stored streetsweeper armoured vehicles, weapons, and we now believe explosives. Each base contains at least 250 enemy personnel, with Fort Devens in Massachusetts containing as many as 500, including what we believe are Muslim soldiers.

The Russian bases are all in close proximity to operational U.S. bases. Each of the ten FEMA districts contains at least one base and district number three, which includes D.C., has two air bases which contain Soviet multi-use helicopters and I think the number was 43 fighter bombers. From what we have been able to gather by both human and satellite intelligence, something is about to happen. Two weeks ago we followed one Soviet Major from Fort Devens, who led us to a Soviet Colonel, who in turn led us to a meeting with a Soviet General by the name of Pyzik. He is known to have served in Afghanistan, advising the Mujahideen and Taliban fighters on tactics in our war against them. He has a reputation for ruthlessness that any KGB officer or ISIS fighter would envy. The two Colonels that we have identified are also the cream of the Soviet military and are being groomed for promotion. In short some of the Russians most promising officers are here in command of secret bases, why?

Besides the bases, we have identified four possible sites within our National parks. Namely Yellowstone, Great Smoky Mountains, Denali in Alaska, and Olympic in Washington, where there is possible enemy activity occurring. Now listen to this. Under a 1972 United Nations treaty the U.S. and other countries gave control of our National Parks to the U.N. The U.N. has set up 'buffer zones' around many areas of our parks and has declared "biodiversity' sites in many parks. This means that American Citizens are not allowed into these remote areas, and as a consequence no one seems to know what's going on inside of these closed or off limits areas. All of these closed zones happen to be within quick striking distance of American military bases.

So as you can see the situation is very serious. We believe that there has already been at least one test-run to the Homeland Security weapons sites. That, coupled with the meeting of the Russian brass foreign troops stationed here, leads me to believe that time is running out for us to act. We have learned that it was Russian President Putin who stepped in and peacefully resolved the situation in the Pacific. This was and is a huge blow to American influence in the area. To tell you the truth, even though we could not stop the Chinese ourselves anymore, with our allies we would have sent a strong message to them. Now, if we ever get a strong president again, it will be difficult for him to convince our allies that we have regained our national will."

"Right now I want you to watch approximately 30 minutes of video from our recon. of Fort Devens, the base in Philomont and the base in Cheswold. We used regular military personnel to recon. the bases, as you can see here at Devens...

General Kelly then went on to give them a briefing of what was found on each base. While he spoke, the digital map which was hung on the wall would glow at the exact point that the general was describing. There were audible gasps when the Mig fighter bombers were shown. When the briefing was finished, General Kelly made the comment that the equipment at Devens was of particular concern due to the fact that from Devons the streetsweepers could quickly reach several major cities. Their appearance in those cities could encourage opposition forces to rally around them and counterattack us. Right now he and his staff were considering options such as a bombing of the base by air force or navy planes. Devens, he added, would be an important top tier secondary target. The Russian planes and rockets would have to be taken out first. As the General spoke, Sean was beginning to have an idea. The Massachusetts National Guard contained four of the oldest still active units in the military, operating since The War of 1812. He knew that his friend Jeff Clark of the MA State Police had strong ties with the MA National Guard. It might be time to recruit Jeff.

Audrey raised her hand. "General, I might be getting ahead of myself, but how are we going to get thousands of cops to DC in January? What will be the pretext to get them there? Also, with the winters we've been having, the heavy snows, I don't know if the highways will even be passable or the airports open. "

"Well Audrey first we will not need thousands of cops right away. I would want you all to be in DC with, say, between you all one thousand officers. More officers can be called in if needed. Don't forget that at least initially, there will be a certain hesitation among some police officers in the country to join us. They will be thinking of their pensions, their jobs. At least initially some will put their own needs before that of the country, their own freedoms or even the future freedom of their children. But as time goes on, and especially if we are prevailing, they will join us. Also, the military is not very strong right now. Even with the combined national guards of all of the states that are here we will have a hard time destroying the enemy bases that we have identified. Don't forget Homeland Security units that do not join us. Let alone opposing any resistance from the civilian population, which includes enemy sleeper cells that we know are in the country.

However, I do not anticipate any real opposition from our citizens, just the opposite. As we talked about in prior meetings, most Americans are still very patriotic. They will come to the defense of the Constitution. Especially the groups we already planned on: the NRA, veterans, and just hard working Americans. When they hear of our plans to cut taxes, investigate congress, strengthen the military, take a meat cleaver to the Federal budget, end Obama phones, Obama Care, the welfare state, and close the borders to illegals and the drug cartels, they will, as Americans have always done, rally to the Flag. We will get this done, our mission will be accomplished!"

Sara then spoke up, "Sir when will we take action?" "I was just coming to that. Tuesday, January 19th, 2016, the day of the State of the Union Address. It meets several of our top priorities. One, the Congress will all be in one place and therefore easily arrested. Two, we know Obama will be in DC, along with Biden, and not on some vacation. Three, the National Media will already be there to broadcast the speech. So, we will be able to broadcast live from the Capitol building. I think when the American people see the Congress being arrested, along with the announcement that Obama has been arrested, it will have an important psychological effect both on citizens that support us and those who might oppose us. Our supporters will be greatly encouraged, and our potential opponents will be greatly discouraged. Remember, the Americans have always come together in times of national emergency. Once people see the videos of Russian planes and troops, along with Muslim fighters on our soil, and learn that we are attacking them, I believe that nothing further will be needed to have them join us." The general was a powerful and motivating speaker. A leader had to be. But there was more than that; simply put, the general was speaking the truth, and there is no more powerful weapon than the truth.

Again Sara spoke up. "Maybe we can still use the ruse of having our pictures taken with Congress as an excuse to have officers from our departments in DC for the speech. Maybe combine the pictures with the idea of our officers being present in the chamber to show law enforcement's support for Obama. Just a thought. "

"I like the general idea of that, give it some more thought, and let's see what happens."

Carl Brown then raised his hand. "If I may, from the perspective of the Secret Service, anytime the President travels anywhere, even to the Capitol building, it is a big deal. Not only the extra limo but Marine One will be standing by to transport the President as a backup if needed. So I assume we will arrest both Obama, Biden, and anyone who is with them, in the White House itself. I will arrange for the agents that I trust the most to be on-duty inside the White House on the 19th, especially those agents who will be manning the portable anti-aircraft missiles. My other agents in the White House, along with the marines, and whoever else from our group is there, will arrest Obama. I would suggest bringing him to Camp David and holding him in the underground bunker there. I also think that the arrest should take place approximately two hours before the scheduled State of the Union speech."

"That sounds perfect Carl. We will have to go over that again and again fine tuning it, but I think your plan itself is great."

"We have to be exact on the timetable. From the White House, we will be sending out orders to all national guard and reserve units from all the services in the entire country to report for duty. In other words we will Federally activate them."

Nathan then spoke up. "Make sure that when the arrests are made, Kalaak is also arrested."

"Don't worry Nathan, if Kalaak is still alive and in the White House, he will be arrested."

"Moving on, in cities like New York, Boston, Chicago, Philly, and Atlanta where we have already identified the Homeland Security warehouses, he sites will be cordoned off at least one day prior to the State of the Union speech. We'll use some kind of a ruse, gas leak, hostage situation, etc. That way, the local police departments will already have a perimeter established to keep anyone from using the equipment. I'll also send demolition experts to each location with enough C4 to collapse the building, if any determined effort is made by the hostiles to gain access to the site.

The air force and navy will move assets into place that, if needed, will destroy any Russian or hostile forces that mount a counterattack. If things go according to our plans there will be no time for any other country to decisively intervene on Obama's behalf. The navy and air force will, however, also be tasked with defending our territorial waters, and the U.S. itself, from any outside interference. The National Guard units from WV, NC, SC, MD, and PA will move with the state police to cordon off D.C. They'll establish a ring of artillery bases around DC, just in case they're needed. I believe the staffs from all of the guard units have already allocated roads, and determined the location of the artillery bases.

As soon as we enter the Capitol Building, our troops will immediately surround the building. All emergency bunkers and escape routes will be blocked off. At the same time, we will enter the chamber and order them all to their seats. We will then announce that Obama has been arrested and removed from the DC area. Then, based upon their own voting records, inform them whether or not they are under arrest. If they are arrested, they'll immediately be transported to Andrews Air Force base by bus. From there they will be flown to Arizona to be Sheriff Joshua's guest. Whoever we elect to be the next President and Vice President will be respectfully asked to come with us to the office of the Speaker of the House. At that time, we'll answer any of their questions truthfully, and hopefully they'll accept the office of President and Vice President. While this is going on, one of us will address the nation and inform the country of what we have done and the reasons for it. That is the general outline of the plan. As with any plan, the devil will be in the details. Any questions?"

"Yes when will we decide who will be President?"

"Sean, will you answer that for us?"

"Originally I wanted your votes right after the first of the year. Now however, in light of the new date, we will all vote at 10AM tomorrow morning. Everyone gets one vote, whoever gets the most votes is President, the 2nd most Vice President and the third most is the alternate in case either of the first two refuse. We will count the votes immediately after the last person votes."

"Who will address the Nation?"

"Myself and Admiral Fletcher will remain in the White house to coordinate any military movements. General Quinn and General Stewart will be at the Capitol building. We will of course be in constant communication with each other. As to who will speak to the Nation, that is up to you. But my vote would be for the man who brought us all together, who made us realize our duty to our country and it's history, Sean Dominguez."

They all rose and gave Sean a short but heartfelt standing ovation. Sean just sat there in shock. Speak to the entire nation, with the whole world watching, as to why they were revolting and restoring freedom in America... well, he could not very well refuse. He just stood up and said, "Thank you I would be honored."

13:00 hours Hawaii time, 7AM EST

Obama sat relaxing in his chair under a large umbrella. "What a perfect day," he thought.

The sand was not too hot, and he was quite comfortable in the shade. Waves were crashing on the beach just a few feet away. He told his aides not to bother him for anything. He was still congratulating himself on solving that little problem in the Pacific. Obviously everyone in the Chinese government, from the Premiere down, had been afraid to take his phone call. When they were informed of his traveling to Hawaii they were so intimidated they instantly ordered their ships to retreat, or whatever it was that ships did. Yes, it was good to be President. The country, no the entire world, would be lucky to have him remain as President for the rest of his life.

He laughed to himself about the irony of his life and his journey to the White House. Nobody knew the real truth about him. He had been pushed, pulled, and carried all the way to the White House. He had even told the American people how he would change their country. Yet, they still voted for him and, unbelievably, had re-elected him. Michelle had also told the people how they both felt about America when she said, "For the first time in my life I am proud of my country." He reflected that here he was within minutes of Pearl Harbor, where in order to destroy the U.S. Pacific fleet, the Japanese had started a World War. He congratulated himself on the fact that without firing a shot, he had destroyed more of America's military power than had all of America's combined enemies since the founding of the country. In addition, he had bankrupted the country, destroyed the very national identity of the country by allowing in millions of illegal non-English speaking, unskilled immigrants, dramatically increased racial divisions, and the best was yet to come. The useful idiots in the Congress and his lapdogs in the media were next. After all, who needed idiots around? And lapdogs, well, they were just dogs. Soon, he would establish Allah as the only god in America, and that filthy jew star would be removed from the dollar bill. Yes, the best was still to come.

13:00 VA

"Ok, let's all take a break and get something to eat." Sean watched as the group members broke up into smaller groups to talk. He figured that it was the same with the original founding fathers. He realized that if they were successful in saving the country, future generations would consider them the second group of founding fathers. Thanks to the modern age they lived in, in future generations would hear their voices and listen to them as they explained the state of the country and the reasons for their actions. That is, if they lived. He then noticed Sara and Susan laughing together as Brian walked over to them. They spoke politely for under a minute, then Brian and Susan turned and walked away leaving Sara standing alone. Just as Sara looked his way, Sean realized that he too was standing alone. They walked over to each other.

"So when's the wedding?"

Sara had that look about her that females have when matchmaking. "Soon I think. Come on, let's get something to eat. You know, organizing a revolution and planning a wedding all at the same time makes a girl hungry!"

14:00 hours

Lunch was over and they went back to their seats. Tony started off with a question. "If any in Congress try to resist arrest, what force will be used to arrest them? You know, several of the big anti-gun grabbers, like NY Senator Chuck Schumer, actually carry guns for their own protection?"

"As we talked about before, whatever force is required. We are not playing here folks, you have to understand that. If we lose, they will not only give us the death penalty, but will use us as the excuse to declare martial law and really turn the U.S. into a dictatorship."

Joe Annino spoke up. "Guys, some of you are making me a little nervous. Straight from the shoulder, stop thinking like cops about excessive force, civil lawsuits, civil rights. *This is a war*. If we lose, everything you have will be taken, including most likely your life. If we win, there will be nothing to worry about. We will all be given a complete total pardon along with what will be almost a total rewrite of all Federal and State laws regulating law enforcement. All the laws relating to police liability will be changed. Just like a judge, an officer who acts in a good faith and a reasonable manner will have immunity from all civil and criminal action. So toughen up, don't worry about anything but winning!"

General Quinn interrupted. "I think that we have gone over everything as far as we can. Now the military has to fine tune the movement, mission and targets of our units, including national guard units from all fifty states."

"Hey, remember when Obama said that there were 57 states during his first campaign and he still got elected!"

"Yes I do, as usual the media covered that up for him. Each of you must develop a plan of action for your departments that can be implemented by someone you trust, a second in command, if you will. If you are in DC for the speech, then someone in your department has to be on scene in your city.

15:00 Washington D.C.

Kalaak stood outside of the National Cathedral as the faithful were entering for afternoon prayers. He was envisioning the architectural changes that would be required once the Cathedral was officially turned into a mosque and dedicated to Allah. Thanks to Allah and the Mahdi, they had come so far, and so fast. Soon, just like in Bethlehem itself, there would not be a Christian church left in America. Soon, very soon.

16:00 hours

General Kelly rose to speak. "Ok I think we are all getting a little tired, it's been a long day. Let's call it quits for now. Remember, we also have an election in the morning. We all need to give a great deal of thought as to who we will entrust with the Presidency. Talk about it among yourselves, share any facts about your favorite candidate. As for me, I am thirsty and getting hungry and that fire looks good."

The talk around the fire was friendly but spirited; it was obvious that they all wanted to elect someone who loved America as much as they themselves. It was surprising how many names were being mentioned as possible candidates. In and of itself, it was a good sign that there were still so many nationally known political figures that the group felt were worthy. Several times the name of Senator Cruz was mentioned. Sean did not want to squash anyone's favorite candidate, but he had to say something.

"Guys, I greatly admire Senator Cruz, and he would probably be a great president, but he was born in Calgary, Canada, and until recently, been a dual citizen. Therefore, constitutionally, he cannot hold the office of President of The United States. His father, like mine, was born in Cuba, but I do not believe that Mr. Cruz ever became an American Citizen. So, is Senator Cruz a Canadian, Cuban or American? We're not going to do what the democrats did and violate our Constitution by knowingly placing on the ballot someone who the Founding Fathers said couldn't hold office."

There were several groans as a few people said, "I didn't know he was born in Canada."

Sean then called his friend Jeff Clark. Jeff didn't answer, and so Sean left a message for Jeff to call him back to arrange a meeting time.

As he walked back to the fire Sara, who loved to tease Sean, said, "Quiet everyone, here comes the president."

Sean just stared at her. "Not funny, buddy."

19:00 hours

Joe Annino was carrying out a portable television that he placed on the table. In a loud voice he said to them, "You guys might want to come and watch the news. Things are getting bad in a couple of cities."

Fox news came on and showed the scene from Dearborn. Huge crowds, mostly dressed in Middle Eastern clothing and wearing face masks, were throwing molotov cocktails and rocks at several Catholic Churches. Firefighters who had responded had been attacked by the mob. Police officers who had tried to help the firemen were also being attacked. At the front of the crowd of rioters was a row of women who were chanting, "hands up don't shoot" while the men behind them continued to throw rocks and set fires.

The scene then switched to Detroit where Halloween had long been known as "devil's night." Not that there was much of the Democratic party's stronghold of Detroit left to burn, but the crowd was doing it's best; several buildings and numerous vehicles were in flames. The few firefighters and police still employed in Detroit had been ordered not to interfere, and were moving back several blocks in an attempt to form a perimeter and contain the crowd.

A second large crowd dressed in Middle Eastern clothing, wearing face masks and carrying pictures of the 'martyr' Saddam Uday Daher, aka Aakif, had formed in front of the Arab American Museum. With women in the lead, the crowd began to march down Schaefer Highway towards Dearborn.

Chicago, Boston, New York and Los Angeles were all reporting civil unrest to one degree or another, with ISIS flags being carried in both NY and LA. In LA. the crowds had nicknamed Halloween "sheet night," and were wearing white sheets over their heads and bodies. Either they were unaware of, or were intentionally mimicking, the KKK's infamous white sheet costumes. Several shots had been fired at police officers in LA, but as yet no officers had been injured.

A breathless reporter from Dallas then interrupted. A large crowd had been gathering since around 5pm in front of the Dallas Museum of Art. Like many museums in the country, the Dallas museum had been gathering "art" from the Arab and Muslim worlds. For a long time, Muslims had been protesting that the museum had been displaying Muslim art in the same building as salacious Western art. Tonight, hundreds of Muslims had attacked the museum and stolen "their art," then had started fires inside to cleanse it of its decadence.

The crowd was quickly growing, and police now numbered it at an estimated 1000 people. Led again by women, they started to march down North Harwood street tipping over cars, smashing store windows and shouting "Allah Akbar." Several dozen infidels were attacked, and the crowd was working itself into a state of religious ecstasy. All of a sudden, the crowd came to a halt. In front of them they could see what looked liked hundreds of armed men and women. Not police offices, but armed citizens blocking their path. Store owners and employees were coming outside of their businesses with shotguns in their hands. The scene was being repeated all along Harwood street, as well as all the parallel streets. As rioters gazed down the intersecting streets, more and more people were stopping their cars and pickup trucks, and stepping out of them with firearms. The crowd of rioters quickly quieted. Many began to look for an escape route. Some actually got on their cell phones and called the police for protection. The anti gun reporter covering the scene informed the cameras that he could not understand why the crowd had stopped. He quickly passed coverage back to LA.. There was no way in the world that he would mislead the public by letting them form an erroneous conclusion that guns, in the hands of law abiding citizens, had stopped the rioters.

Ed spoke up. "Hurray for the Texans! See, I told you that the American people still had courage!"

Joe Annino, quickly agreed. "You're right, Ed, but don't forget they were only able to stop the Muslim rioters because they were armed. Thank GOD for our second Amendment."

"Amen to that" Wayne Kelly affirmed.

"All in all, the night was not as bad as it could have been. A couple of derelict buildings in Detroit, and maybe 20 cars, were burnt. No one was killed. Some damage in Dallas, including the museum, but that could have been much worse. Even though a few shots were fired at the police in LA no officers had been shot.

But most telling of all was the burning of Catholic Churches in Dearborn; so much for tolerance and diversity on the part of Muslims. Even the riot in Dallas was caused by Muslim intolerance of other art.

"Remember that so called art display years ago that traveled around the country, with a picture of a Crucifix in a jar of urine? That was even paid for with taxpayer money. But no liberal protested the fact that taxpayer money was used to attack Christianity, no Constitutional violation there, no sir. And no Christians rioted or burned down the museum."

20:00 hours, The White House

Kalaak was beside himself. Not only had his orders been disobeyed, but also the media actually showed Muslims rioting and destroying property. What was even worse was the scene in Dallas. Kallak was not stupid; he knew that all of America had seen the faithful stopping and acting like sheep when confronted by armed citizens. All of America had both seen and heard the message: "Defend yourself from the radical Muslims, confront them, stand up to them and they will act like sheep." Kalaak was thinking of sending the FBI to investigate, but investigate who? The Texans had broken no state or Federal laws, but the Muslims had. Even if the FBI investigated, it would only bring more attention to the fact that guns in the hands of free people had stopped them. Khayyam would soon pay for this. That is if Abdus had not yet already found him.

SUNDAY, NOV. 1ST. 10:00 HOURS

Sean was standing outside staring into the fire. He had purposely brought with him an old wooden ammunition box for the ballots to be placed into. He saw a certain logic in using an ammunition box. After all it was GOD, guns, and guts that had made America great. They were certainly praying to GOD for His Divine help. Guns were going to be used, and a gun needed both ammunition and guts. He was lost in thought contemplating not only the reasons why they were doing what they were doing, but why it was right on so many levels. He remembered a verse from the Irish song, *A Nation Once Again*, "for freedom comes from GOD's right hand." He knew history, and remembered what a positive effect the United States had on defending freedom, giving hope and providing opportunity for so many millions of people around the world. He wondered what effect their actions would have on the world. He decided that the effect would be as, if not more, positive than the first revolution. He heard a gentle cough behind him and in turning around he saw everyone quietly standing there, waiting on him. Sean was overwhelmed. The respect being shown to him by people for whom he had the utmost respect was emotionally paralyzing. He looked at them all. How many times in history had a small group of people risked everything for freedom, and how had their courage, even in death, changed history? The Founding Fathers themselves, the Alamo, the battle of Thermopylae, the battle of the Bulge in WWII, the last stand of Fox Company during the Korean war...it went on and on. It occurred to Sean that one lesson from all of history was that freedom was not free. It had to be purchased in blood, and defended by the sword unto death.

He looked up at them; boy was he proud of them all. "Ok, we each put our ballot into the box. When all the ballots are cast, we will jointly count them. Well, let's get started and may GOD guide us. Ladies first."

Audrey was the first to drop her ballot into the box, followed by Sara and Susan. The rest of the guys walked up dropped in their ballot and walked away. Sean was the last to vote.

He knew it was silly, but he rolled up his sleeves before reaching into the box. Voting was such a precious right. A gift of freedom that had to be honored, that had to be free of any taint of fraud. Without saying a word he reached into the box, stirred the ballots, and pulled out the first one. On impulse, he handed the ballot to Sheriff Al. Al grasped Sean's meaning and with a tear in his eye read the first name. In a clear voice he announced, "Senator Rand Paul." Sara, acting as Secretary, wrote down the name. The next votes read: Condoleezza Rice, Rand Paul, Allen West, Rand Paul, Rand Paul, Rand Paul, Rick Perry, Alan West, Rick Perry.

When the votes were all counted, Sara, with obvious emotion in her voice stated, "We have a clear winner. The next President of The United States will be Senator Rand Paul from KY. Our next Vice President will be Governor Rick Perry, and the third place alternate is Condoleeza Rice."

For a second there was absolute silence. Everyone of them realized that they had just made history; the significance of their vote was not lost on them. They had done exactly what the Founding Fathers had done when they elected George Washington as our first President. Then they all burst into a sustained round of applause. Only one more little thing to do!

Wayne Kelly then asked them to gather round. "Ok folks, I think like me you all feel, recognize, that something, I guess you could call it historical, mystical, patriotic, religious or a combination of all, has happened here today. In the interest of history, I am going to ask Sara to not only keep custody of the ballots themselves but to write a record of what occurred here since we first assembled. Now, things are really going to heat up from here on out. For security reasons, we need to cut out any back channel communications. Official communications between departments are fine. Unless something comes up to require it, really try to cut down on contacting each other. Sean mentioned, and I agree, that we should all try to get together in December maybe around the 15th, to go over our plans for January. Any questions?" No one had any questions or anything to say. "Oh and it goes without saying no one is to contact Senator Paul, Governor Perry or Ms. Rice. I myself will say so long for now, all of you be safe and GOD Bless." They all said bye and General Kelly, along with the other Chiefs and their aides left the camp. One by one, with hugs and handshakes the rest of the group made their way out of the camp.

20:45 hours

Abdus, and as he liked to think of them his gang of "cut throats," had been watching Khayyam all through evening prayers. Abdus really enjoyed being here inside of the Islamic Cultural Center in New York City. As he watched him he felt a feeling of pity for Khayyam. Abdus did not know Khayyam personally, but he had seen him on the internet praising Allah and preaching Jihad. He wondered what Khayyam had done to displease the Mahdi so much that the Mahdi had directed Kalaak to order him to send Khayyam to paradise.

Prayers ended and as Abdus and his cut throats watched, Khayyam stopped to speak with several men. The conversation did not last long; Khayyam then exited the mosque and turned right on third Ave. Abdus and company followed a short distance behind. Just as Khayyam was approaching a darkened driveway used for deliveries to the building Abdus called out to Khayyam.

"Brother please stop and interpret the word of Allah for us." Khayyam could not for any reason refuse his brother's call for guidance in under-standing the Koran. As they came up to Khayyam, Abdus began to call down the blessings of Allah on him. When within arms reach all five men attacked Khayyam, gagging him and dragging him down the driveway. Khayyam struggled with all of his strength but was no match for the cut throats. Abdus did not waste words, "You brother have been sentenced to die by the Mahdi himself, may Allah grant you entrance into paradise."

With that Khayyam was pushed to the ground and held firmly as one of the cut throats began to saw through his neck. While the blood spurted and Khayyam gagged they all chanted "Allah Akbar" over and over again. After the beheading they placed Khayyam's head on his chest, admired their handiwork and left the area in a state of religious euphoria.

23:00 hours

Ethan Williams was walking down the driveway to the employees' entrance at the back of the building. For several days now he had been feeling the flu coming on. His wife had told him to stay home and go to bed. But with a wife and three children he had no choice but to go to his second part time job as a night custodian. As he approached the bottom of the driveway he noticed what at first appeared to be a rug, no a body. No, it had to be a sick Halloween joke. The body had a head sitting on it's chest— it had to be his co-workers from the evening shift. Well, they could pick up their little trick. On second thought, it would be funny to sneak in on them and throw the head at them. He bent over the body to grab the head and at the same time he felt his foot slide. As he grabbed the head in his hands he felt something wet and sticky. With a feeling of absolute terror he realized that this was no Halloween joke. He dropped the head and began to scream. Trying to back away, his feet slipped out from under him and he landed in a puddle of blood.

His screams attracted several pedestrians who were walking by on the sidewalk at the top of the driveway. Of course, no one came down to see what was happening, but several people did get on their cell phones and dial 911. They informed the operator that it sounded like someone was being murdered and, no, they did not want to give their names. More and more people stopped and were staring down the driveway. A passing NYPD cruiser was flagged down and the crowd all screamed at the officer to "Do something, someone was being killed down there!" The officer called into the dispatcher, gave his location and asked for another unit to respond to the scene. He then activated his cruisers takedown lights, high beams and spot light. As he drove down the driveway the crowd began to follow him. The lights all combined to turn night into something like approaching daylight. The officer could not believe his eyes; there on the ground right in front of him was what appeared to be a headless body, over there was what appeared to be a head, and sitting right there in and covered by all of the blood was the sicko who had done this. He immediately notified the dispatcher of what he had and requested a rapid response from his fellow officers. At the same time he drew his firearm and pointed it at the suspect while ordering him not to move.

For his part, Ethan was paralyzed with fear. All he could was sit in the blood and scream. Just then two of his co-workers opened the double delivery doors to push out a cart full of trash. They saw it all in a second:

the lit up police car, the body, the head, and Ethan sitting in the middle of it all screaming.

Turning to each other, Lou said to Henry, "I told you he was a nut." They quickly backed into the building and locked the doors.

MONDAY, NOVEMBER 2ND 09:00 HOURS

Inspector Lapaglia was just walking into her office when a sgt. came up to her and asked if she had heard about the beheading last night right by the Arab cultural center. Audrey said no, then called the chief of detectives. She was informed that the scene was still being processed but that security cameras had captured four men carrying what appeared to be the victim down the driveway and beheading him. The individual that the media had wrongly identified as the suspect, was in fact a night janitor who had been going into work when he came across the body, thought it was a joke, and then slipped in the blood and went "kind of cuckoo." He was ok now, but had been admitted to the hospital where he was sedated and was resting. The victim had been identified as a Dept. of Homeland Security Director and a radical internet talk show host named, Atif Khayyam.

Audrey thanked the chief and asked him to keep her informed. She then wrote a brief message and sent it out to the group on her low band radio. As soon as she sent the message she remembered what had been discussed about not sending messages on the low band. Well, it was too late now. Unknown to her the satellites had already recorded it anyway.

10:00 hours DC

Kalaak was dumbfounded, how could Abdus have been so stupid as to behead Khayyam less than a full block away from the Arab Cultural Center, on film no less? There was not much doubt as to where the investigation would begin. The Mahdi would be furious. He picked up the phone and called his contact in CAIR. He instructed her that she was to hold a press conference demanding the arrest of the murderers who had killed a peaceful Muslim man coming from prayers at the cultural center. She was to explain to the media that the suspects had, during Halloween, dressed in Middle Eastern clothing in order to lure Khayyam to his death. This was just another example of the persecution being directed at Muslims in the U.S. by Jews and those that did their bidding.

10:30 hours Boston

Sean sat waiting at the end table for his friend Jeff Clark. He knew that Jeff suspected that something serious was going on in the area of Fort Devens. Not only had Sean asked him about the area, but also the troopers had observed on several occasions Streetsweeper armoured cars racing down route two, and large search parties going through the woods looking for someone. Jeff would have to be told something or else he might start an investigation of his own. If that happened, who knows what could come of it. He looked up as the door opened and Jeff came in wearing street clothes. Sean waved him over to the table and the waitress came over with coffee and ice water.

Sean began the conversation by asking Jeff about his family, to which Jeff replied, "Thanks, they are fine. Now Sean, the truth about what you know about the happenings at Fort Devens."

"Ok Jeff, Obama has built his own private secret army, consisting of personnel from Homeland Security, FEMA, Middle Eastern Muslims and best of all regular Russian Army troops. Planes, rockets and who knows what else at multiple closed former military bases in the U.S."

Sean sat back to await Jeff's reaction. Surprisingly Jeff was silent for several minutes; Sean could see the wheels spinning, Jeff was no fool.

Finally, Jeff said "That does not surprise me one bit. As a matter of fact, it just confirms what myself and some friends have suspected for a while now. Ever since Obama said he wanted an internal army as strong as our regular army the alarm bells went off in our heads. You know, for years we haven't had a federal budget, just continuing resolutions to fund the government. That of course is totally unconstitutional but the Congress went along with it. That way they could spend money wherever and for whatever they wanted and there was no way to really track it.

Friends of mine who work for a major firearms firm have told me that the government is buying thousands of M16 rifles and more ammunition than you could imagine. At the same time, the military has been gutted to the point that they do not need the rifles that they have, let alone all of the new ones. So the question is, why buy the rifles, and what are they doing with them?"

Sean remained silent, just waiting to see what Jeff would say next.

"Sean, why do I get the feeling that you know even more than you are letting on and that you are also up to something?"

"Well Jeff, this gets complicated. Let me ask you two questions. One, what do you think should be done with the enemy force at Devens? Two, how far will you go to protect, preserve and defend the Constitution?"

"Let me answer the second question: I will do anything to defend my country. I am just about ready to retire, I have saved my whole life to be able to retire in some kind of comfort, but I will risk all of it for my freedom and the freedom of my kids and grandkids. I still remember President Kennedy's speech where he said, 'The price of freedom is always high, Americans have always paid that price.'

The enemy force must be either contained or eliminated. If they are as strong as you say it will take either the national guard or regular army to do either. Are you sure that there are Muslim soldiers there?"

"Yes absolutely sure. Why?"

"One of my Lts., Colin Fleming —I think you met him— anyway, between Iraq and Afghanistan he's served three tours and is always going on about radical Muslims. He watches this website called 'Jihad watch' and claims that he has proof that there are Muslim Madrassa schools that are actually terrorist training camps being operated on Federal land inside of our national parks. He has the coordinates of the schools and has sent them to the FBI. I used to think he was kind of nuts about the Muslims, but now... I even vetoed his getting command of our SWAT team because I thought he would fly them all out to Yellowstone or someplace and attack some park ranger barracks out there. Now I feel terrible."

At the mention of the national parks and the coordinates being sent to the FBI, Sean had a knot in his stomach. The group was already concerned about Russian or foreign troops in the parks, and Nathan had told him how CAIR could and would intercept police communications at the FBI office in DC.

"Jeff, two things. I want to talk with Fleming and get those coordinates from him— I actually believe that he is right. Second, are you sure that you are ready to risk all for our country? And if so, are you ready to listen to our plans and help to bring about a revolution or, as we are sometimes calling it, a 'house cleaning'?"

"Yes to both." At that Sean started to talk for the better part of an hour. When he was finished Jeff rolled up his sleeve and showed Sean a somewhat faded tattoo of a paratrooper. Above the soldier was written 101st Airborne and below the motto, 'Rendezvous With Destiny'. Jeff looked into Sean's eyes.

"Let's go meet our destinies, count me in."

12:00 hours Washington DC

Brad and Philip were just entering the private cafeteria reserved for members of Congress and their staffs. Brad was wondering if today was lobster or prime rib for lunch. Philip was sure that it was both, a surf and turf lunch. Brad then turned to Phil and said, "I heard that they are raising the price of the lunches at the cafe next year from, what do we pay now, $2.50 a meal, to $2.75 beginning in January."

"They can't do that, how are we supposed to live? Well they had better increase our bonuses or base pay in order to make up the added cost."

They both laughed. Why not laugh, they were sure that their raises would cover the extra $3.25 a week. They picked up their surf and turf and were waved over to a table of other hard working, dedicated Congressional staffers. As they approached the table everyone burst out in laughter.

"Ok, what's so funny you guys?"

"I was just telling the guys how we got an invitation from the police to not only attend a group picture taken on the Capitol steps during police week in May, but an individual picture with Senator Schumer. Those cops must be daft, they actually thanked him for all of his support over the years!"

"Oh, I can't stop laughing, it hurts! Schumer supporting cops! It's just too funny, the cops are like kicked dogs, they always come back for another kick."

250

"What are you saying, Chuck kicks cops and dogs?"

They were all laughing hysterically; several Congressman turned to look at them, wondering what was so funny. Brad made a motion of taking a picture.

"Police week pictures, smile for the camera!"

Many in the room joined in the laughter, Senator Warren from MA, the Indian girl, who was also laughing, said to the comedian Senator Al Franken, from MN, "I just can't wait for police week, those morons, talk about dumb donut eating cops!"

They all got a good laugh at that.

19:00 hours

Sean had just hung up the phone from talking to Colin Fleming. He was stunned. If Colin was right about the Madrassa schools, and Sean had no reason to suspect otherwise, then... Sean went to his safe, took out his transmitter, and sent a long message to the group. He gave the coordinates of the Madrassa schools and requested that surveillance by drones be conducted on them.

Once again, the satellites relayed the captured message to their computers.

TUESDAY, NOV. 22ND 11:00 HOURS

Sean was sitting in his office when the phone starting ringing. No matter who it was, he was determined not to answer. He just had to get through these reports. But when he looked at the phone saw that it was Sean Jr., he instantly answered.

"Hi tiger how are you? Where are you?"

"Hi dad, I'm fine, and as a matter of fact I'll be landing in Boston about 2PM. Sorry for the short notice."

"No problem, I'm free. Will be there to pick you up."

"Thanks dad. I also have some news to share from some of your friends. See you soon."

"Ok Sean, can't wait to see you, so long."

He then picked up the phone and told Shannon that Sean was coming home at 2PM. He barely finished speaking when she began.

"Ok let me go, I have to run to the store to get a roast beef for him, bye."

He thought to himself, "I wish he'd come home more often so that I could get a roast beef dinner once in a while."

14:20 Hours

Sean was at Logan airport standing outside of his take-home cruiser waiting for Sean Jr. when another unmarked cruiser pulled up right behind him. A quick glance told him that Jeff Clark was driving and who was the passenger. Jeff got out.

"Sean, what a surprise, what are you doing here? You remember Colin Fleming."

"I most certainly do. Myself and Colin were just talking last night as a matter of fact. And I'm here to pick up my son, he just called me at 11AM to tell me he was landing at 2PM. As usual though, I don't know where he's coming from. Well speak of the devil, here he comes now."

As they looked over at Sean Jr., Colin exclaimed, "I didn't know that your son was a captain!"

Staring at his son, Sean blurted out, "Neither did I."

Sean Jr. walked up to them and immediately gave his father a hug, then shook hands with Jeff and introduced himself to Colin.

"So tell me my son, when did you get promoted from staff sergeant to captain?"

Looking kind of embarrassed, Sean replied, "They wanted to promote several times over the years but I always turned them down. Now with the way things are, General Quinn not only ordered me but convinced me to accept my promotions retroactively on paper and here I am, Captain Dominguez."

As always, Sean could not have been more proud of his son.

"Speaking of General Quinn, how is he?"

"Fine dad, as you might imagine rather busy right now. As a matter of fact my orders from him are to brief you, dad. I also know Jeff's one of us and has already recruited LT. Fleming. So where can we all talk privately?"

"How about my office, Captain?"

"That will do just fine Sir."

When they arrived at Jeff's office he immediately ordered the trooper at the desk to hold all of his calls and not to allow anyone, meaning *anyone*, into his office. They entered, took seats and waited for Sean to begin.

"Well first, acting quickly on Colin's intelligence regarding the Madrassa schools, we did obtain photographs from our satellites that confirm that three of the locations are actively being used for what appears to be military training. Another four locations show indications of being recently used, and the rest we still have to check on. When the time comes the air force will hit each of these bases with a MOAB. That is our largest non nuclear bomb— believe me, nothing will be left of the so-called schools."

Sean went on to speak for another twenty minutes; he had additional information to share with his father that he had not been authorized to share with Jeff or Colin. When he had finished, Jeff turned to Colin.

"I am going to arrange it so that you can take our SWAT team down to DC to help out."

Colin answered with an enthusiastic, "Yes sir."

Jeff then addressed Sean.

"Sean, there are only about seven thousand of them now. But the Massachusetts National Guard contains the oldest units in the entire U.S. military. For example, our 101st field artillery, 101st engineers, 101st infantry, 181st infantry, and 182nd infantry were all originally formed in the year 1636. They are not only the oldest units in the country, but they are the only army units still in service that fought in the war of 1812. My old unit, the 211th MPs, was formed in 1741. They have a combat history older than the country itself of protecting and defending the people who would go on to become the first Americans. Not to mention defending the nation itself. So, what I'm getting at, what I am asking, is let us have the mission of taking out the force at Fort Devens."

As Jeff spoke there was obvious emotion in his voice.

Captain Dominguez thought for a minute.

"Are you sure that you can get the national guard to attack the base before they are Federalized? The base must be taken out before they can even begin to organize any resistance to us."

Without the slightest hesitation, Jeff replied.

"Yes sir, just leave it to me."

"Very well, but I want to know your plan by 12-10, at the latest . In the meanwhile I will inform General Quinn of what you have told me."

"Yes Captain, and thank you."

They talked for another 30 minutes, then Sean Jr. said, "I think that covers everything for now. If you need to communicate with me please do it through my father. I don't know when we will be able to meet again, maybe not until our mission has been accomplished. But please know that it is an honor to serve our country with men like you."

With that they all shook hands and the Dominguez's left the office. When they were gone, Bill looked at Jeff.

"I don't think that I've ever seen a more squared-away soldier in my life; bet you a dollar he becomes a general.

"You're right though, there is something special about that young man. His father too."

17:00 hours

Shannon was sitting on the arm of the chair, staring out of the window waiting for Sean. When she saw the car stop in front of the house she went flying out the door to see her son. For his part, Sean was overjoyed to see his mother. They hugged and walked into the house, leaving Sean Sr. outside and having to carry Sean's bag in. "Nice to be loved," he thought to himself.

SUNDAY, NOV. 22ND 17:00 HOURS

Wayne Kelly fully realized the psychological strain that was put on men and women who were going into combat. Even in an organized unit of soldiers who have lived, trained, worked, slept and eaten together, the strain was enormous. Soldiers who have been psychologically prepared by the military to act as a team, a *machine*, who know that they are not alone and have the comfort of being surrounded by their comrades, have been known to break under the strain. He could only imagine how, especially as the time grew closer, the stress was or would be taking it's toll on the Son's and Daughters of liberty. They must be reminded that they are not alone, that they are part of a much larger group. Which was one of the reasons that, true to his word, he was organizing a Christmas party. Not a holiday party, a *Christmas* party with a real *Christmas* tree, for Saturday the 12th of December at his private home in the DC suburb of Falls Church. He had already contacted several hotels in the area and reserved rooms for the group. Unfortunately, he himself would not be able to sponsor the rooms. But if they chose to attend, there was a room waiting for them. He and his wife Jeanne had just finished stamping and stuffing all of the invitations with a combination Christmas/ invitation card and a list of the hotels where rooms had been reserved . He also requested an RSVP from all those planning to attend.

SATURDAY, DECEMBER 12. 18:00 HOURS, THE KELLY RESIDENCE

As with any family that were about to receive their guest, the Kelly family, Wayne, Jeanne, their son Wayne Jr. and daughters Julia and Cecily were giving the house a last inspection, making sure the food was all out and hot, plenty of ice, and so on. The doorbell rang, and Wayne and Jeanne went to the door to great their first guest. They opened the door and were pleased to see that the Annino's, Dominguez's, and Garcia's had all arrived together. Hugs, handshakes and greetings of "Merry Christmas" filled the house as everyone stepped inside.

Although this was a Christmas party, General Kelly had not over-looked the fact that pretty much the entire leadership of the Sons and Daughters of Liberty were all gathered together, and thus would make a tempting target to anyone who had learned of their plans and who might be inclined to try and stop them. Accordingly, he had not neglected to have security in place.

Even as they had pulled into the driveway, Sean noticed approxi-mately seven young athletic looking men and women, who had a military bearing, standing by in the driveway to act as "valets." Upon entering the home, Sean observed another six young men and women with similar bearings acting as greeters collecting coats and waiters. "Wow, I feel important," Sean thought with an inward laugh.

Other guests started to arrive and Sean was not surprised to see Audrey and Carl walk in together. Sara, Susan, and Amanda came next, with Susan looking a little out of sorts.

"Why the long face, it's Christmas?" Sean asked.

Amanda, with a coy look on her face, quickly spoke up.

"Oh her little Brian couldn't make it, they have to spend their first Christmas together, apart, so sad!"

Susan just gave her a look. Amanda, spotting their hostess, quickly changed the subject.

"Jeanne I brought an ornament for the tree."

The Christmas music was playing and toasts were being made. The room was full of laughter; just as Wayne had hoped, everyone appeared to be relaxed. He looked up as the door opened and saw Eric Quinn, his wife Stephanie, Al and Carol Ann Thomas, and Sean jr. entering the house. Wayne walked over to greet his guest and congratulated Sean on his promotion. He could not resist saying in front of Eric, "Sean if you transfer over to the Corps I will make you a Major."

They all laughed, but Eric was sure that Wayne meant it. Talk about corporate raiding.

Sean looked around the room and spotted his parents talking to a group of people, including two very pretty young ladies. Amanda looked up.

"Look over there girls, who's the hunk?"

All the girls quickly looked, with the guys turning a few seconds later. Susan looked right at Amanda.

"I don't know, but I'm going to find out."

"Hey you have what's-his-name remember, Brian? Look he's coming this way."

Shannon, probably like all mothers, immediately began to evaluate both Susan and Amanda for a possible match with her only son. With a sly smile on her face— she was enjoying herself— Shannon said, "Ladies, I will be happy to introduce you to my son Sean. You never had the chance to meet him at the SWAT competition." Shannon thoroughly enjoyed the embarrassed look on their faces; both of them looked like they wanted to sink into the floor. Amanda wasn't sure if Susan meant it or not that she wanted to meet Sean, but she was not going to take any chances.

As soon as Sean walked up and Shannon made the introductions, Amanda intertwined her arm around Sean's, saying, "Why thanks Sean, I would love to get a drink." She then smiled at Susan and gently pulled Sean, who was more than willing, towards the bar. Shannon enjoyed the show, and the look on Susan's face told her that there would be an act two.

22:00 hours

Wayne quietly rounded up both Seans', Carl Brown, Joe Annino, Nathan, the other Joint Chiefs and several of their top aides. They all went upstairs to a room that Wayne called his "study." After closing the door, he got right down to business.

"We have just about one month to go till the State of the Union Address. Does anyone have any concerns, any issues, questions, anything at all no matter how small you might think it is? I, we, want no surprises. Timing is everything, so let's briefly touch on the main points. Two hours before the State of the Union, Carl and his Secret Service Agents, along with my marines, will arrest Obama in the White House..."

Wayne was conscience of the fact that the other guests would be missing them. He quickly went over the rest of the timetable, and when there were no questions he said, "I just have one question. Captain Dominguez, are you sure that the guard units can handle the assault on Devens?"

"Yes sir I am. Between the ground units, the MA Air National Guard, plus MA State Police that will be on hand to assist if needed, they will be able to get the job done."

"Ok Captain, we will take your word for it, but just as a reserve we'll have a B52 and naval bombers assigned to provide support if needed. If that's all, we should probably get back to the party."

FRIDAY, DECEMBER 25TH. 13:00 HOURS

Kalaak and 20 other mullahs were waiting in the East room of the White House for the Mahdi to arrive so that they could begin afternoon prayers. The door opened and the Mahdi entered, resplendent in his new green robes with gold trimming. They all bowed low, and were honored when the Mahdi bowed to them in return. Kalaak had already ordered the Secret Service to spread the prayer mats. They were all waiting respectfully for the Mahdi to take his place in the center of the row. When he did, prayers commenced.

After the prayers they all sat silently in a circle with their legs crossed, as the Secret Service brought in fresh fruit and water. Obama signaled for the agents to leave the room and then began to speak.

"My brothers in Allah, I have great news to share with you. Our beloved Prophet Muhammad himself has appeared to me in three dreams. He has commanded me in the name of Allah to proclaim the truth to the world, that I am the Mahdi." At this there was a cry of excitement. A look of religious fervor came over their faces, and cries of, "Allahu Akbar" filled the room. Matt Anderson and Alan Wainwright were the Secret Agents standing outside of the door. They heard the cries, but they had been hearing that cry now for seven years in the White House. They just looked at each other. "What else is new?"

"The prophet has ordered me to inform the world that I am indeed the Mahdi and to also proclaim the Caliphate during my State of The Union speech on January 19, 2016. Only three weeks from now my brothers!"

More cries of, "Allahu Akbar" sounded. As he spoke, Obama's voice rose in volume.

"I will remain in office as the President of the United States for my entire life." "Allahu akbar, Allahu akbar, Allahu akbar!" filled the East room.

"You all know what is expected of you. Do not tell the faithful what by the will of Allah I have just shared with you. But," at this he looked directly at Kalaak who was sitting on his right side, "tell the faithful to be prepared, tell them to watch my speech. I do not want them to take to the streets or begin to convert the infidels until I give the word. Our allies are to be alerted, but are also to remain on their bases unless I summon them. I do not want to encourage any resistance to us by showing too much force. The flag of Islam will fly from the roof of The White House, and the name of the Christian GOD and all references to HIM on all public and private buildings will be obliterated. Christian Churches will be closed, bibles will be destroyed, Islam will be taught in all schools, alcohol will be outlawed, and Sharia law will be the law of the country. The burka will be worn by all American women. Pork will be prohibited in the entire country. Jewish Temples, schools and clubs will all be cleansed by fire; the Jews themselves will be cleansed by fire."

"Allahu Akbar" again resonated.

"Go my brothers, heed the word of Allah."

They practically ran from the room to alert the faithful. Obama had held Kalaak by the arm; he did not want him to leave yet. They sat back down on the mats and in low tones began an intense talk. Matt and Alan had been hand picked by Carl Brown. Listening through the door they had not only heard most of what the 'Mahdi' had said, but had recorded it.

"Wait until Mr. Brown hears that."

SATURDAY, DEC. 26, 09:00

Carl could not believe it. Why was his work phone ringing on his day off, and at 9AM? This had to be important, for somebody's sake.

"Carl Brown."

"Good morning boss, this is Matthew Anderson."

"Hey Matt, what's going on?"

"Sir you have to listen to this, it was recorded yesterday in the East room of the White House about 14:00 hours. I didn't want to bother you on Christmas day with this but.."

"Ok, Matt, play it for me please."

Brown instantly recognized Obama's voice as the CD played. He was stunned by what Obama had said, it was beyond belief. A bare two hours after his planned arrest, Obama had planned to declare himself the 'Mahdi and President for life. The timing of this was something from medieval times, when the king learns of his nobles coming to kill him and with just minutes to spare, locks the castle gate.

"Matt, I want you to personally bring that CD to me now, tell no one else about it. On second thought, who was with you when you made the recording?"

"Alan Wainwright, sir, no problem there."

"That's good, bring Alan with you now please. And Matt, bring the names and background information on every one of them that was in that room."

"Yes Sir, see you in about one hour."

Brown decided that he might as well start his day now. "Being divorced had it's privileges," he thought. "At least I won't be waking anyone up." He banged around the kitchen putting on the coffee and getting out a couple of frying pans; he figured the least he could do was make breakfast for the guys. In a little over an hour his doorbell rang. Upon opening the door he saw Matt and Alan, standing there like two little kids about to go into the principal's office. He quickly invited them in, telling them to relax and come into the kitchen.

"Sit down guys, I figured that I owed you both breakfast. Let me get you some coffee and I'll start the eggs. All I have for meat is ham steaks if that's ok?"

"That will be great sir."

"So while I cook, read me the names on the list."

Matt started. "Kalaak, Abdus..."

Carl was quiet for several minutes after all of the names were read, then said, "I recognize most of those names, several of them I know are on the terrorists watch list. You guys have done well, I promise you that I'll remember this."

"Sir, what are we going to do? We can't just stand by and let this happen."

"No, we can't do that. Trust me, when the times comes, and it is coming, I will make sure that the two of you are involved, deal?"

They exchanged a glance. Matt spoke for the both of them, simply saying,

"We trust you sir."

"Thanks, that really does mean a lot right now. Leave the CD and list with me." After finishing up their breakfast, they went back to duty at the White House.

Carl then went to his closet and took out his low band transmitter. He sat there for several minutes composing the transmission that had to be both relatively brief, but also contain all of the pertinent facts and names. When he was done typing, he was surprised that almost two hours had past. Not that it would take nearly that long to read.

It took the satellites just seconds to reconfigure the message and to relay it down to the computers in both China and Washington DC.

Shortly after the message was sent, he received a call from Nathan on his burner phone.

"Hi Carl."

"Hey Nathan, I assume you just read my message."

"Yes, and please do not take offense, I know that you know all about handling evidence, but I have a friend in the Dept. of Justice that is preparing a legal case against Obama and the rest of them, and that CD will be the nail in the coffin in so many ways. Please make sure that the CD and list of names are placed in a very secure location, and tell me where the location is. You know, just in case anything happens to you, my friend."

"Geez thanks for the good wishes Nathan, I love you too. There's a hidden safe under the floorboards in my walk in closet, it's buried under a pile of shoes. The combination is 78M1*. That's where I will keep them for now anyway."

"OK I have that. I'll call you back."

The phone was hung up before Carl could say, "See ya".

13:00 hours

Nathan called Sean on his burner phone. He hated to bother him on the day after Christmas when he knew that Sean and his whole family were together, but this was important. For his part, Sean was more than surprised when the burner phone rang. "Now what?" he thought.

"Hello Sean this is Nathan, I need to talk to you, now."

The phone ringing was disturbing enough, but the obvious anxiety in Nathan's voice set off all of his alarm bells.

"Sure Nathan, go ahead."

"Real short, go check the message from Carl on your radio. Call me back if you want or need to. I would suggest that you call our military friends and ask them to listen to the message now."

"Ok Carl, talk to you soon."

Sean got up and signaled for his son to follow him.

"What's up dad?"

"That call was from Nathan. Carl Brown just sent us all a message on our radios and Nathan asked that I listen to the message now and then call our military friends."

Sounds serious."

They went over to the gun safe and took out the radio. They had to listen to the message twice in order to fully comprehend the magnitude of it. One by one, Sean then called each of the Joint Chiefs and ask them to check their radios for the message. He could only imagine the impact that it would have on them. He was actually surprised when he received a message from Wayne to all members that the operation would be advanced by three hours. That was it.

General Kelly called the other Chiefs and requested that they meet the day after tomorrow, Dec. 28th., 10 AM at his home, to discuss developments. In his mind, he already knew what he wanted to do. The people on the list —especially Kalaak— were the obvious leaders of the Muslim forces, and also the ones Obama trusted the most. They had to be detained and arrested before they could issue orders to their people to resist. But not too early that their disappearance would raise any alarms. Probably the night before on the speech would be best; he knew just the people to carry out the arrest.

MONDAY, DECEMBER 28TH 10:00 HOURS

The doorbell rang. Wayne was walking up to the door as it was opened by one of the same young men who had worked as a "valet" at the Christmas party. As Eric entered he laughed to himself at how well a "valet" could stand at attention. Especially with a .45 caliber handgun tucked into his waistband. At least Eric assumed that it was a .45, not some pop gun. With a smile on his face Wayne walked up to take Eric's coat and escort him into the living room. They had only taken a few steps when they heard the sound of several car doors being shut. The valet opened the door before either Andrew Fletcher or Kevin Stewart could knock. They all exchanged greetings while Wayne also took their coats and handed them off to yet another valet.

"Being a little careful aren't we Wayne?"

"Not at all. I suggest you all take your personal security a little more seriously, at least until the op is over. If we are making plans to arrest the enemy leaders, what makes you think that they aren't making the same plans for us? I don't think they have caught on to us yet, but if they do..."

"Let's go up to my study. Tommy would you please bring up the coffee, tea and food?"

"Yes general right away sir."

They entered the study and each chose an oversized leather chair that had been arranged in front of Wayne's desk. Tommy and another valet entered and placed the trays on top of the table. They then silently left the room, shutting the heavy study door behind them. The study was to all appearances just that, a study, but Wayne had told all of them at Christmas that it was in fact a "panic room." The walls had been reinforced so that nothing short of a bulldozer could come through them. The carved interior wood panel window shutters actually covered a thick layer of bullet proof kevlar material, the same that was used on military helmets and ballistic vests. Wayne also had a very respectful amount of firearms in the gun safe that was mounted inside of the closet. Best of all, the room was soundproofed and protected from electronic surveillance.

After they had helped themselves to coffee Wayne started the meeting.

"Thanks to Carl Brown, we have all heard of Obama's conversation with his mullahs in the East room of The White House. On Christmas day no less. So what I propose is that we arrest everyone on the list and anyone who might happen to be with them the night before the speech. We will use not only our own MP units but officers from the various SWAT teams that our police members will be bringing to DC."

"Won't that set off the alarm bells if all of the mullahs go missing all at once?"

"No, I don't think so. They have, on the Mahdis orders, already started to tell their followers to watch the State of the Union Speech and be ready, but thankfully take no action. I'm willing to bet that they are saying more than that. Probably bragging about their relationship with the Mahdi and how they are on some kind of secret mission for him. So that if they disappear, their people will think that they are on a mission for Obama."

"Where will they be held?"

"We have a Sheriff friend in Arizona who is more than willing to have them as guests." This brought on a chuckle from them all.

"Now, the so-called Madrasa schools in the national park. As we agreed, the air force will hit each one with a MOAB. Granted a little bit of an overkill but I do not want to take the chance of any of them surviving, and then launching terrorists attacks inside our country. After the MOABs detonate, local national guard units will enter what is left of the buildings and collect any evidence or survivors. The air force will also hit all of the interior Russian bases that we have identified in the FEMA districts. Again, after the air-strikes the bases will be entered by national guard troops, who by then will have been federally activated. Fort Devens will be assaulted and neutralized by the MA National Guard and the MA State Police. We will also have the air force and naval air support on standby in case it is needed. The navy," at this Wayne looked over at Andrew, "will hit the bases at Cheswold and Philomont with carrier based planes flying from the, I love this, the U.S.S. Ronald Reagan and Abraham Lincoln. Because both of these bases have hardened aircraft bunkers, an infantry assault will also be mounted against both. The Army will assault the Philomont base and the Marines will take out the Cheswold base. I want all of the bombs to be on target at exactly 06:00 hours. The infantry will move in immediately after the bombs explode.

After the bases are secured, the FBI and ATF investigators assigned to each will begin to gather any evidence and document anything they need to in order to prove that Russian and Muslim soldiers were in fact at these locations. We want as many prisoners as possible, but if we have to kill them all so be it. We also want to capture as much equipment as possible to offer as proof to the American people the danger that the country was in.

Now regarding the night of the speech. The first thing we must do is to provide security for our next President, Senator Rand Paul and Vice President, Rick Perry. I believe we should meet with them around noon-time. Explain everything to them, let them listen to Obama's speech from the East room. If that does not convince them I don't know what will. I think that we go with a modified plan of Sara's. We call the members of Congress that are to be arrested out in small groups. We tell them that Obama is downstairs and wants to get some small group pictures before giving his speech. We'll ask Carl Brown to relay the message. Presumably they will all voluntarily walk down, and from there will have their cell phones taken from them, be placed on the buses and be transported to Andrews for the flight out to Sheriff Joshua's hotel. Any questions?"

"A few, but first I would like to hear the recording of Obama from the East room."

"No problem, I have it right here. A copy for each of us, along with a copy of all of the names of the mullahs that were there, courtesy of Carl Brown and the Secret Service."

They all sat in silence as the recording played. Being told about the recording and even reading the printed copy of it in no way compared to the shock of hearing it.

"We will have to play this for the American people, and the whole world, to hear. Just think... a matter of hours. That's how close we came to losing the country or having a massive religious war."

"It's been more than a matter of hours, ever since the 1960's, with the exception of the Reagan years. The country, the people, have been losing freedoms. Don't forget what I consider to be the greatest, or at least the first greatest, seizure of freedom by the Federal government: forced busing. Many communities where it was implemented, such as South Boston, fought very hard, not against integration, but against having their children taken from them and transported to wherever some Federal Judge decided to send them. I remember saying to my friends if the government can take your children away from you, then they can take anything!

Look at the result of that liberal social experiment. Another epic failure of the Federal government. No government program has ever succeeded. Be it racial quotas, or as the *progressives* like to say, affirmative action. Busing, social security, they all sound great when first proposed, but as the years go on and it's evident that the experiment is failing. What do the progressives do? Why, they come up with another social experiment that is even more dangerous than the previous ones. For example what we're going through now with open immigration or Obama care.

Of course the liberals never admit to being wrong they just need more money. Which since the Federal government neither earns or produces anything, means that through a thousand different taxes; the government just takes more and more from the working people in this country. Which just hurts the working people more and more. Usually, years or maybe decades later, it becomes evident to even liberals that the experiment has failed. By then the liberals that originally implemented the experiment are dead and not around to see the disaster that they created.

"And don't forget us, the military, and I suppose law enforcement. We are the ones who serve, defend, bleed, suffer and die for our country. We are not only the first but usually the only part of the Federal budget that suffers huge cuts. There, sorry about the speech, I just got on a roll."

"No one disagreed with you or interrupted you Eric, you were preaching to the choir. If that's allowed anymore."

TUESDAY, JANUARY 5TH 2016 18:00 HOURS

Steve walked into the corner bar in Watertown, MA. It was just about two blocks away from where the police had a shootout with the Muslim Boston Marathon bombers. He was just coming home from his weekend drill while serving in the Massachusetts National Guard's 101st infantry. The division's motto, Sempter Paratus, meaning "always prepared," was stitched into the divisional patch on his shoulder. His friends, several of whom were also in the guard, ordered him a beer as soon as they saw him walk through the door.

"So how was the weekend?"

"Actually kind of fun, we did more firing and practice assaults this weekend than we have in a long time. The 126th aviation unit was also practicing close in airsupport with us; it was cool to see those jets screaming by just over the treetops. Then when we were leaving they said we're having another drill on the 18th. We will be taking a lot of equipment up to Devens, I heard a lot of other units are going up there too."

"Yeah my unit, the 101st field artillery, has already been ordered up there for the 18th with our guns, and Roger's unit the 181st infantry is also going."

"Don't forget us, the 211th MPs, we'll be there."

"Wow I don't think this many units have manouvered together since we were getting ready for the Gulf War, I wonder who else might be coming?"

Unknown to them, similar conversations were taking place in other national guard units in seven other states, all getting ready to move on the 18th.

MONDAY, JANUARY 19TH. 17:00 PACIFIC TIME, 05:00 IN WASHINGTON, D.C.

As he leaned over the railing watching the coast of China and the ZhanJiang naval base fade slowly away, Captain Liu Xi was at peace with himself. The last few stressful weeks and what turned out to be a totally unnecessary cross-ocean mad-dash to monitor the navies that were monitoring the Chinese Navy were behind him now. The entire crew of the Beijixing had been given leave while the ship spent a week in port. He had even been able to visit several family members in the area. Though he was back at sea on the Beijixing, he contented himself with the knowledge that he could once again begin to listen to that naughty couple in Iowa, or listen in on his friends from MIT. Oh yes, he had almost forgotten those low band radio messages that he was about to listen to before all the commotion. Yes, that's where he would begin his listening pleasure. The thought comforted him, and so he decided, why wait? He then went downstairs to his domain, the intelligence center of the ship. The sailors on duty stood respectfully as he entered the room. When Xi turned his back and sat down, they grinned at each other. They all knew that he was a little strange. It did not take Xi long to locate the file that he had started on the low band messages. Amazing how many of them there were now.

He kicked off his shoes and placed his feet up on his desk. Leaning back in his chair, he placed on headphones and pushed the play button. As he listened to the messages his throat went dry, no it could not be, the last message of Obama speaking in the East room almost convinced him, no, a revolution in America, with cops and the military both involved? Should he go to the Captain now? No, he had better listen to the messages again, make sure that they were not a hoax. That would take another hour. He reasoned with himself that time could be of the essence, but if he was wrong, his career would be over and that meant he would have to leave his computers. Why would he have to say anything anyway, no one would ever know. What to do? Would they call him a hero if he reported it? Or would they court martial him for taking so long to discover the messages. Oh, what to do?

07:00 Washington DC

Sean was in command of the teams at his location. Ed Larkin, six marine MPs in civilian clothing and another ten SWAT officers, five from Boston and five from Chicago, were with him. They were spread out in four vehicles parked throughout several streets bordering the mosque of the martyrs on 16h street, watching for any of the twenty known Muslims who had been in the East room for the Mahdis speech on Christmas day. A total of twelve teams were watching other mosques and the known residences of the mullahs. So far, despite the fact that there had not yet been any sightings of Kalaak, things were going well. Six different mullahs had been taken while coming out of their residences, presumably while on their way to morning prayers. Reports stated that they had offered no resistance. But, confronted with overwhelming force so early in the morning, and then having a needle full of the sedative Fentanyl plunged into them, how much resistance could they have offered? As the arrests were made, each team crossed the names off of their master list and drew an 'X' through the picture of the mullah.

As Sean watched, he heard his team members on the north side of the mosque where the parking lot was located say, "Bingo" over the radio. Abdus and three other mullahs were all entering the lot now. Since there were four of them together, Sean ordered team two to assist team three in making the arrest. Team three's leader came over the radio.

"We are moving now before they enter the mosque."

Team two replied, "Be there in 30 secs." Ed wanted to go over to help, but Sean overruled him.

"We have to watch this entrance both for the mullahs and for anyone going to the parking area."

Ed reluctantly agreed. Shortly after came the report over the radio.

"All four in custody, taser guns and Fentanyl used."

"Oh well" thought Sean, "that's what they get for resisting!"

"This is team three. We are transporting to Andrews, team two thanks for the help." Sean advised the other teams of the arrest and crossed off the names and pictures. But where was Kalaak?

Sara, Audrey, Tony, and Brandon all had command of their own teams. So far only Audrey's and Sean's teams had made any arrests. There were still ten mullahs unaccounted for. While she was thinking, she heard her team one leader come over the air.

"Abdul is coming down his front stairs now, we are moving in."

Abdul's sixth sense must have kicked in, for as the van approached him, without even looking up he turned and began to run back towards his house. He would have done better to run in the opposite direction he had been walking in.

Abdul was not in the best state of physical fitness. That, coupled with trying to run in robes, resulted in his not going very far before the Philly SWAT Officer Richard Ryan reached casually out of the window and, in a remarkable display of marksmanship with a taser, hit Abdul in the right side of his neck and right face cheek. Abdul went down hard, splitting his forehead wide open on the sidewalk. Team members quickly jumped out, picked Abdul up and without any ceremony threw him into the van, where Brandon immediately gave him a needle full of Fentanyl in the leg. They then advised the other teams of the arrest and the fact that they were heading to Andrews to drop off Abdul. Ryan did not have very much pity for Abdul, but all the blood was making a mess. Ryan reached down and tore Abdul's robes into several strips, which he then tied tightly around Abdul's wound. "Not very sanitary but at least the bleeding stopped," thought Ryan.

But where was Kalaak, the prize that they were all hunting for? By 10:00 hours, a lucky 13 out of the 20 mullahs had been arrested. But still no Kalaak.

10:00 hours Camp Edwards, Cape Cod, Massachusetts

The adrenaline was flowing in almost 5,000 soldiers as they loaded up truck loads of ammunition. Attached were the trailers that would carry the 155 mm howitzers to the 2 1/2 ton trucks, known as deuce and a halfs. They filled the trucks with fuel, mounted .50 cal machine guns onto humvees, loaded hundreds of cases of MREs, tents, medical supplies and a thousand other items that an army would need to fight a battle. Several sergeants were running back and forth, screaming at the men to get a move on while others were inspecting body armour and personal medical kits. Steve was working alongside of Tony. He had been on both drills and real deployments before, and knew the difference in the preparations, the feel in the air; this was real. He looked over at Tony.

"Where do you think that they are sending us? This feels real, you know?"

"Yeah no kidding, I was just thinking the same thing. But what's throwing me off is if we were going overseas we wouldn't be taking artillery with us or, look over there, tanks all loaded up on their transport carriers."

Just then, a flight of F16s from the 126th aviation wing thundered by overhead. Then they heard another type of screaming; Sgt. Cerilli was coming towards them, yelling something about anti armour DRAGON and TOW rockets. Yes, things were getting real.

This same scene was being repeated at national guard bases in seven states, with close to 30,000 national guard soldiers all asking the same question, "Where are they sending us?"

11:00 hours Camp Steuben, PA

Captain Lucas Wheeler of the PA National Guard's 28th Mechanized infantry division was inspecting his company of Stryker Armored personnel carriers. He had just finished talking to his chief mechanic, Master Sgt. O'Neill. O'Neill had assured him that everything as far as the engines and operational capabilities of the Strykers went were just fine. That was what Wheeler expected to hear. His Stryker's would be transporting the 56th combat brigade, but to where? All he had been told was that they were moving out at 01:00 hours on the 19th. "Strange," he thought.

11:00 hours Fort A.P.Hill, VA

Colonel William Christian had just hung up the phone with Colonel Joe Annino. He was still laughing to himself. Annino was insisting on leading the VA Guard units into DC. When he was reminded of their orders to seal off DC Annino simply said, "Fine, the men can seal off DC. I'll go in with the marines."

Knowing Joe, he meant it. Christian, the commander of the 116th Infantry Brigade, nicknamed "The Stonewall Brigade" after the famed Confederate Civil war General Stonewall Jackson, who just happened to be Christian's great, great grandfather, was a very proud man. He looked out of his office window, watching his men loading their equipment onto the trucks. Loading anti armour FGM-148, Javelin missiles, and a variety of other deadly munitions that he hoped would not have to be used, at least against American citizens. His old commander and trusted friend, Eric Quinn, had fully briefed him on his mission. He was to rendezvous with elements of West Virginia's 30th heavy combat team, 201st field artillery, 150th cavalry regiment and 19th special forces. They were to form a ring around the southern and western approaches to DC. At that time, he would take command of the combined forces and standby for further orders. He was also authorized to act independently to repel and destroy any hostile force, civilian or military, attempting to enter DC.

"What a strange world it could be, and how history repeats itself," he reflected to himself. 150 years ago his hero, great, great grandfather Stonewall Jackson, along with another hero and fellow Virginian, General Robert E. Lee, had on several occasions attempted to capture both Washington DC and Abraham Lincoln. Now, he would be moving his brigade basically over the same roads they did during the civil war, again to capture Washington DC and a man who held the office of President. But who in Christian's mind had betrayed that office. Yes, it was a strange world. He even appreciated the historical irony of the fact that while he was sealing off the southern approaches to DC, the Maryland 115 armoured regiment, along with their 58th combat brigade, 110th and 224th, field artillery, 175th and 115th infantry would, along with the Pennsylvania units, seal off the Northern roads. They would be meeting his troops at the Western approaches, just as they had done during the Civil War to stop great, great, grand dad. Of course their main job was to destroy any military or hostile forces that would attempt to reach DC. The State and local police depts would be responsible for all traffic and local issues.

13:00 hours Washington, DC

Ensign Michael Wong and Lt. Jg Justin Hamilton, along with a combined force of exactly 200 Navy Seals and U.S. Marines, were in the Washington Navy yard. They were loading the hovercraft that Wong would captain with all of their equipment. All military planning anticipated and provided for any possible contingencies that could arise. Therefore Wong's and Hamilton's mission was to secure and deny access to any crafts attempting to come up or down the Potomac river past the Lincoln Memorial. Their mission was basically a precaution, a safeguard against the impossible possibility of either an attempted escape or rescue mission via the Potomac by hostile forces. If needed, reinforcements would be readily available from any of the army or marine units that would be in DC, not to mention that the U.S.S. New York herself. With her bows made of steel from the World Trade Center attack of 9-11, she was stationed just of off Bolling Air Force base and the Anacostia Naval station. All in all, a quiet assignment.

13:00 Fort Bragg, North Carolina

The world renowned 101st Airborne division was once again put on ready alert, meaning be ready to move in 12 hours. Her sister Airborne division, the famous 82nd Airborne, had been stripped of her proud Airborne status due to budget cuts enacted by Obama, leaving the 101st as America's only Airborne division. General Sheldon Sheffield, in command of the division, had received his orders directly from his West Point roommate of many years ago, General Eric Quinn. Another member of their West Point class, General Alexander Campbell was in command of Fort Hood in TX. Sheffield and Campbell had just hung up the secure line from talking to each other. Sheffield was envious of Campbell. While he and the 101st. remained on ready alert and anxious for battle, Campbell at least had his orders. The same orders as Marine General Carpenter at Camp Pendleton had: be prepared to move to and seal off the Mexican border.

13:OO hours Marine Bases Quantico, Parris Island and Cherry Point Naval air station.

Colonel Barry Hamilton's helicopter had just landed on Parris island. His assignment from General Kelly was simple: make a visual inspection of the preparations underway at Cherry Point and Parris Island. As expected, things had been all squared away at Cherry Point. He was not at all surprised to see the base commander himself, General McDonald, moving through the mass of organized confusion, randomly stopping an officer or sergeant and asking a question. No doubt about the readiness of the men and equipment. Hamilton walked up to the general and gave a salute.

"Things are looking great sir. I am just coming in from Cherry Point, all is a go there."

General McDonald gave a little smile.

"You are here as a spy for Wayne, aren't you Barry? You go back and tell him that I personally promise him that my base and my marines are ready."

"Yes sir, will do, good luck sir."

"Good luck to us all Barry, I guess we will all know in about 24 hours or so."

With that Colonel Hamilton got back on his chopper and headed back to report to the Commandant.

13:00 hours Washington DC.

Sean looked at his watch. Afternoon prayers had long ended and they still had four of the mullahs plus Kalaak to arrest. He knew that one plane had already departed Andrews on it's way to Arizona with sixteen sleeping mullahs on board, none of whom had objected to being fingerprinted and giving DNA samples while they slept. He decided that they all needed a break. Over the radio he relieved all units for two hours.

"Freshen up, eat, brush your teeth, sleep, I don't care what you do, just be back on station at 15:00, especially at their houses."

"OK mom, we all have that" came back at him over the radio.

15:00 hours Pacific time 03:00 hours EST

Captain Xi had reluctantly concluded that he had to report his suspicions about the low band messages to the ship's Captain. Let him decide whether or not to bump them up the chain of command. He had already printed out the messages and as he looked at the dates on them he was wondering again if he would be in trouble for not intercepting the messages months ago. With a knot in his stomach he climbed up to the bridge to see the captain.

"Excuse me sir."

"Yes what is it Captain Xi?"

Even as he began to speak Xi wished that he had never decided to bring this to the Captain, but it was too late now.

"Sir, I have intercepted some transmissions from unknown individuals in the United States that may be of supreme importance. Sir, may we speak in private?"

After a moments hesitation Captain Chow said, "Of course, why don't we go down to the officers wardroom and have a cup of tea while we speak."

"Yes sir, that would be most welcome."

As they entered the wardroom several officers stood up and the captain asked them politely if they would mind if he and Capt.Xi spoke privately. The officers bowed and left the room. After getting tea for the both of them, the Captain then asked, "So Xi, what is it that you think that you have found?"

Xi began to speak, handing each message to Captain Chow in chronological order as he did. He could see the color draining from Chow's face, and was not at all surprised when Chow said, "Start again from the beginning and go slowly."

An hour and a half later, Chow was both convinced that the messages were real, and that his career was about to either end or he might soon be at the top of the promotional list for admiral. Thinking of admirals, Chow realized that fate or karma had taken over and that he had no longer had a choice. He picked up the intercom and ordered his radio operator to immediately connect him with Admiral Zhang at fleet head-quarters at Zhanjiang naval base. He also ordered XI to transmit copies of the messages to the admiral. The admiral's aide came on the line and demanded to know what was so important. Chow was normally patient with pompous desk jockeys, but he had no time now.

"Tell the admiral it is about a revolution in America that will be start-ing in a matter of hours."

There was silence on the line and after thirty seconds or so, "Stand by, I shall get the admiral now."

Zhang answered the phone with an abrupt inquiry.

"Chow what is this nonsense, have you been drinking?"

"No sir, please listen, I have already sent all of the messages to you but this is the story..."

Now it was Zhang's turn to worry about his career. He knew that if this story was true, there was literally no time to waste. He had only one option: he ordered Chow to stand by, and then had his aide place a priority call to the Chinese Premier, Li Keqiang.

TUESDAY, JANUARY 19, 03:00 HOURS, CAMP EDWARDS

It was a beautiful, cold, clear New England January night. The stars were shining brilliantly. What appeared to be a hundred Massachusetts State Police cruisers were waiting outside of the main entrance to the base to escort the convoy to Fort Devens. With the tank carriers and trucks, the trip should take just under three hours for the eighty mile drive. Major Jeff Clark was standing outside of the gate talking to Colonel Brett Davis, the National Guard Commander. Jeff and Brett had served together Afghanistan; both of them realised that the enemy from Asia had come to America.

"You know old friend, it seems anywhere in the world— Asia, the Middle East, Europe, Africa, and now here in America, wherever Muslims are there is fighting, political unrest and outright war. That seems to be their history."

"You won't get any argument from me Brett. We had better get the convoy started, we have a mission to accomplish."

Brett motioned with his hand and the MPs opened the gates. The noise from the engines of so many powerful trucks was deafening. The lead State Police cruisers, with blue lights flashing, began to lead the way as the first of the convoy passed through the gates.

The men did not know it, but along the East and West coast in Texas and PA, convoys similar to their own were also beginning to move. At six different U.S. Air Force bases, bombers were being loaded with both MOABs and a variety of smaller bombs. In the Atlantic ocean flight crews and plane handlers were bringing naval attack aircraft to the decks of the U.S.S. Ronald Reagan and the U.S.S. Abraham Lincoln, fueling and loading them with ordnance. Inspired by the nation's police, at long last, what was left of the U.S. military was once again going into combat to defend freedom. But this time, within the boundaries of the United States itself.

03:00 Philomont PA

Approaching from the South, Captain Sean Dominguez silently led his company of marines through the woods to within a half mile of the Philomont base. Normally the marines would resent being led by a soldier, but Sean's status as a member of Delta force, plus the reputation he had won both in combat and at the Quantico sniper shootout silenced any misgivings that the marines might have had. A second company was approaching from the East. Their orders were simple: after the navy bombed the base they were to move, prevent any surviving aircraft from taking off and take as many prisoners as possible. After the base was secured, Sean and his company would be helicoptered back to DC to stand by for orders.

Sean signaled for sentries to be posted and told the men to get what rest that they could. Sean and Lt. Ed Arce had just met for the first time earlier in the day. As officers, they both felt that they should remain awake and vigilant. To pass the time they talked in low tones, and Sean mentioned that he was from Boston, MA. Arce, who was from Miami, stated that he would love to visit Boston sometime and to see for himself all of the things he had read about from American history: the Freedom trail, Bunker hill and even the Kennedy library. Sean then mentioned how another building was being erected for Ted Kennedy right next to the the President's library, and that the seventy four million dollar cost for the building had been taken from the military budget. With a smile on his face Arce asked, "Do you think they will have a Mary Jo Kopechne room there? You enter it by walking over the original Chappaquiddick bridge and if you get lost on the way in you call a justice of the U.S. Supreme court for directions." Sean just laughed to himself, he would have to recommend Arce to General Kelly.

03:00 Cheswold

Lt. James Nelson of the Navy Seals was leading his combined arms company, made up of Seals and Marines, in a wide arc around to the East side of the base. Capt.Wil Anderson of Baker Company, 2nd battalion, 82nd infantry division, was right behind him. The plan was to form up in one extended skirmish line and move onto the base after the

Navy bombers had dropped their bombs. Once they were in position outside of the lethal drop zone of ½ mile. They posted sentries and tried to get what sleep they could while waiting for the planes. Chief Wilbur Hernandez had been a member of the original team that had scouted the base and placed C4 explosives into the helicopters. So Nelson figured that it was only fair that in the event that the helicopters had to be blown, Hernandez would have the honor of destroying them by blowing them to kingdom come. He also kind of suspected that Hernandez would enjoy himself while doing that.

17:00 hours Beijing, China, 05:00 EST

Li Keqiang was screaming at his staff, which included the top commanders of all of China's military branches.

"How could you have not detected this before now? If anything happens to Barack Hussein Obama and the Democrats, we could lose everything that we have been working towards! We have to save Obama!"

"Sir, could we not attack the U.S. now?"

"Idiot, we cannot destroy the United States! Why would we want to? We own them, they work for us now, the 460 billion dollars a year they pay us in interest alone on their debt to us is what buys your new planes, ships, tanks and everything else you want. Look at what just happened in the Pacific, Obama would not even let the U.S. Navy ships sail with the allied nations, he ran away. No way in the world will he honor the U.S. treaty to defend Taiwan, or any other nation for that matter, and they all know it. Even if we were able to destroy the U.S. we would basically be destroying our own property at least 18 trillion dollars of it. Think, will you?"

"What troops do we have in the DC area?"

"Counting embassy staff and security, and our operatives posing as business men, students and so on maybe 5000 in the greater DC area."

"Excuse me sir, here are the latest satellites photos of the DC region. There appears to be an unusually large number of military vehicles on the roads heading into DC. In addition there is a high level of activity on the local marine bases and at Fort Bragg. Also, the U.S. Navies aircraft Carriers the Ronald Reagan and the Abraham Lincoln, along with their battle groups, have moved unusually close to the East coast of the U.S. Right by DC, as a matter of fact."

Li Keqiang was in a panic. By all the gods, Obama must remain in office. If China could not act alone...

"Get me Putin on the phone now, Russia has as much to lose as we do if Obama is forced out. Tell whoever answers that it is critical that I speak to him at once."

Within several minutes Putin was on the line. Time was of the essence and Li Keqiang was frustrated at the delay, however slight, of having to use interpreters. Without any diplomatic niceties he explained the situation to Putin and the fact that it was now close to six AM in DC; they had only hours to do something. Normally Putin, like most active or former KGB officers, was known to have ice in his blood. But, as he listened to Li Keqiang, the ice started to melt and he felt a growing pain in his stomach that was matched by a sense of desperation in his mind. He, Russia, was so close to regaining all of the lands of the former Soviet Union plus some. Meanwhile Obama wasted time and attention trying to negotiate a treaty with Iran, giving them nuclear weapons no less. A treaty that Iran had no intention of honoring, as they would soon use the weapons to destroy Israel. He and Russia had grown stronger and stronger while the U.S. had grown weaker and weaker in so many ways.

His aides that were sitting around the table and listening to the conversation watched him intently. They had never seen such a confused look on his face before. If they did not know better, they would almost think that he was close to panicking.

"I understand Li, yes I agree it would be a disaster for us to lose Obama or to have the Democratic party weakened in any way. Yes, why don't we both call Obama now and warn him? Maybe he can flee the White House or hide in a bunker until we can think of some way to save him. I have some assets in place; let me see if I can launch a rescue mission to get Obama to a place of safety. We will talk when either of us has some definite news." Putin hung up the phone.

"Get me General Pyzik on the phone now."

05:50 The White House.

The Marine and Secret Service agents manning the main entry gate of the White House saluted as the armoured humvee carrying General Kelly and Admiral Fletcher passed through the gate and entered the White House grounds. A long line of armoured vehicles containing hundreds of police and military followed the general's humvee, while many more vehicles containing thousands of military and police personnel took up positions for blocks around the White House.

As General Kelly and Admiral Fletcher, followed by Sean Dominguez and Joe Annino, walked up to the front door, it was opened by Secret Service Agents. Both Carl Brown and Nathan Green were standing in the lobby waiting for them. Without any preamble Brown stated, "He's upstairs in bed."

Wayne just nodded.

"Keep me informed of his movements; he's not to make any calls and any visitors are to be detained. We will be downstairs in the situation room. I want to watch the operation from there, call me if anything comes up."

For his part Sean was overwhelmed. This was the first time that he had ever been inside of the White House. He actually had tears in his eyes as he thought of the history here, from the war of 1812 when the White House was burnt by the British to the great Presidents, Lincoln, Reagan, and Teddy Roosevelt walking through what Sean considered to be sacred halls. Wayne looked over at Sean and sensing what was going through his mind said, "Come with me Sean, later on you and if you want all of the Sons and Daughters of Liberty, along with all of your families, can spend as much time touring the White House as you want to, but right now let's go watch what we've set in motion."

Without a word Sean, Joe and the rest of the group followed them onto the elevator and rode it down to the command center.

06:00 hours

Sean and Ed were listening for the sound; there it was, growing louder every second. A sound that Sean had heard many times and was always grateful for. American jets were coming in. He knew these particular naval bombers were coming from the U.S.S. Ronald Reagan. He looked around and saw that all of his men, that he could see anyway, were looking up at the sky. Some of them were combat veterans, and for the others this would be their first taste of combat. Someone yelled, "There they are!" Sean could see two distinct flights of planes coming in with maybe 20 seconds between them. High above them he could see contrails in the sky that told him F22 Raptors were flying high cover. The noise was more than deafening, it was painful. "Just wait a second," he thought to himself, "it gets better."

They passed overhead in the blink of an eye. Sean had already warned his men, but he began to scream, "Get down, get down, get down!" Then he took his own advice and hugged the earth. As the ground shook, the noise of huge explosions coupled with the sound of the jets filled the air. Sean knew the second round of explosions was coming in about ten seconds; he kept hugging the earth, bombs had been known to fall far short of their targets.

06:00 hours Cheswold

Lt. Nelson looked over at Chief Hernandez and shook his head.

"Wilbur, put the transmitter down now please, and don't touch it again until I say."

Chief Hernandez looked liked a kid on Christmas morning whose parents had just told him that he could not yet open the big box. Then they heard it, the sound of thunder growing louder and louder. Navy jets from the U.S.S. Abraham Lincoln came streaking in. The explosions were deafening. Then came the sound of smaller explosions, followed again by the Navy bombers. As the explosions began to subside, Lt. Nelson both yelled and signaled to his men, "Move in." As they began to move in, they could hear the klaxon sounding the alarm.

Military precision was a term that was often bandied about by TV reporters, most of whom had never served in the military, and thus something that they had no personal knowledge of. Yet to see it unfold, the years of training, discipline, professionalism and above all patriotism, all come together in exactly the right place and in exactly the way that it was planned was, even for generals, gratifying and awe inspiring.

As General Kelly and Admiral Fletcher stood in the command center, both watched and listened to the digital displays that showed the planes' locations and to the radio traffic between the planes and the men on the ground. They were as proud as parents whose child had just hit a home run. After all, these men and women were to all intents and purposes their kids, and they sure were hitting home runs today.

06:05 hours

Sean and his men were advancing at a slow run. This was a free fire zone; anything or anyone before them was considered hostile. They approached to about two hundred yards to the base perimeter, and the scene was one from Dante's inferno. Men were laying on the ground screaming in agony, fires and smoke were everywhere, the smell of burning flesh mixed with whatever else was nauseating.

Sean was using the scope of his .50 cal sniper rifle to assess the scene. All of the buildings, had been completely destroyed, but there was very little damage to the aircraft bunkers or the planes themselves. He noticed one man, obviously a high ranking officer and perhaps the base commander himself, calmly giving orders: pointing with his hands, stopping some men and sending them on some assignment. While he was watching, another man, and from viewing his epaulettes another officer, walked up, saluted and began to speak urgently to the first officer. Sean also noticed that men, probably pilots, were running to some of the planes and that crews were starting to remove the small unexploded cluster bombs from the runway in preparation for the planes to take off.

Sean's orders were to take as many prisoners as possible, but no one said that they could not be wounded. For Sean a shot at two hundred yards was easy, he thought to himself, "Why not get two for one?" He aimed his rifle at the rear right leg of the man who he assumed was the base commander, just below the knee, which was lined up perfectly with the front of the left leg of the second officer. Sean squeezed off the shot; in less than two seconds both officers were down on the ground, one missing a leg below the right knee and the other missing a leg below the left knee. As soon as he saw his shot hit, Sean yelled "Advance!" and two hundred men moved forward as one. Colonel Abramovich and Major Kalashnikov were both laying on the ground, each semi-conscious and bleeding profusely from the loss of a leg. They looked up and saw Captain Dominguez standing over them.

The Russian troops saw the Americans coming, for who else could it be? Several attempted to fire on the Americans but were quickly killed by the advancing marines. One brave pilot was moving his plane out from it's hanger when the front wheel hit an unexploded cluster bomb, and then erupted in a giant fire ball, killing perhaps a dozen of his ground crew and comrades. After that, the few surviving Russians, dazed and petrified, raised their hands in surrender.

06:05 hours Cheswold

LT. Nelson was impressed; the navy had certainly done their job. All of the helicopters had been destroyed, buildings all down in a blazing heap of rubble. Off to his right he heard the sound of both AK47s and M16s firing. On his radio he heard that several of his men had been hit by fire from what had been an unidentified bunker. His men were reporting that groups of Russians were organizing a defense from the various plane bunkers. The navy jets were returning to take care of that bunker. His men were moving back away and taking cover, evacuating the kill zone. The whoosh of the hellfire missile being fired was audile even with the engine noise. In a second the bunker and all those anywhere near it were vaporized. He heard a cheer from his men and saw that once again, the marines were advancing. Chief Hernandez had stayed right by his side, he had that look on his face. "Why not," Nelson thought, "he deserves it."

"Ok, chief blow them away."

Hernandez's face lighted up with the look of what could be called a holy rapture. He then took out his transmitter and pushed the first button; instantly a MIG plane blew up in one of the hangers, killing everyone inside. Hernandez then began to repeatedly push the button, causing plane after plane to explode into a fireball. After ten of the planes were destroyed the remaining Soviets dropped their weapons and raised their hands in surrender.

"Stop chief, we need to capture the rest of those planes."

Hernandez looked at him like a teenager who was told that he could not use the family car that night. In an effort to cheer him up, Nelson added, "Come on chief, not only did you just blow up billions of dollars worth of planes, but I am pretty sure that you're the first Navy Seal in history to become a double ace! Congratulations!"

06:08 hours

Beginning at 04:00 hours, planes from six different U.S. Air Force bases had swept into the sky on the way to their various targets, which included all ten headquarters of the FEMA zones, plus each Russian base that had been identified within each zone. The first of the MOABs began to fall exactly two minutes ago, just as the call to morning prayers was sounded at the three active madrassas in the national parks. Hundreds of the faithful were coming out of their barracks, AK47s slung over their shoulders. All heard the sound; some thought of it as a loud whistling wind, others as a freight train. Regardless, when the MOABs exploded, they were all sent together on the trip to paradise.

The large secondary explosions from the FEMA headquarters were duly noted by the flight crew and videoed by the plane's camera system. All of the planes radioed in that their mission was accomplished and returned to their home bases to refuel and rearm.

06:08 hours

General Pyzik was rushing to his communications bunker. His aide had violently awakened him two minutes ago to inform him that President Putin himself was on the phone and wanted him now. With a feeling of dread Pyzik raced to the bunker, if "Vlad the impaler" himself was calling, well, things were not good.

"Yes Comrade President?"

"Pyzik, right now, and I mean *right now*, you are to enter the White House with as many forces as you can and protect President Obama from a coup, do you understand?"

"Yes Sir."

"Call me back the second that Obama is safe, I will call him now and tell him to expect you."

With that he hung up the phone. If Putin had stayed on the phone for another six seconds, he would have heard a very loud explosion.

06:08 hours The White House

The emergency direct line from the Kremlin was ringing in the command center. Everyone present, including General Kelly, stared at it. With what could be described as a cynical smile on his face, Kelly walked over and picked up the phone. Before he could say hello, he heard a somewhat hysterical voice say, "This is Vladimir Putin, put me through to President Obama now, that is an order!" General Kelly chuckled.

"Sir this is Wayne Kelly the Commandant of the United States Marine Corps." As Putin listened he had a sinking feeling in his heart; he knew they were too late.

"First, Mr. Putin, with all due respect, the United States Military does not take orders from you. Secondly, Mr. Obama cannot come to the phone now, how may I help you sir?"

There was no longer any doubt in Putin's mind; Obama was no longer president. Still, just to be sure, he asked, "When will he be able to come to the phone, General?"

"I am afraid Sir, that Obama has developed a phobia regarding phones and he will not be talking on the phone for a very long time to come."

"I see. In the event that I needed to talk to someone in the U.S. government on any important issue that might arise, whom should I ask for?"

"For the present Sir, that would be me. Oh and sir, I think that it would be very advisable not to have any of your bombers or ships anywhere near the international borders of the U.S.; we do not want any misunderstandings right now, do we?"

"I understand perfectly general and I share your concerns. I am sure that you are most busy right now, please feel free to call me when you desire to talk."

"Thank you sir, excuse me, but I have a lot to attend to right now. Have a great day."

With that General Kelly hung up the phone, and Putin hurled his crystal glass full of water off of the door to his bunker. He then picked up his phone and called Li Keqiang. When Li answered the phone Putin began by saying, "We have a big problem."

06:30 hours

As the MA National Guard approached For Devens, they knew that they were slightly behind schedule. The convoy stopped on Route 2. and began to unload tanks and men. Overhead jets from the U.S.S. Ronald Reagan flew in circles, waiting for the order to attack. Massachusetts State Police had stopped traffic miles away in both directions. Infantry from the 181st and 182nd divisions began to move into the Ox Bow wildlife preserve and towards Devens in order to cut off any escape from hostile forces.

The 101st. Artillery began to set up its guns a mere three miles from the target area.

The 101st infantry, the 211th MPs and the Massachusetts State Police would directly assault the base after the bombers had done their job.

At 07:00 Colonel Brett Davis received word from his staff that all units were now in position. Colonel Davis picked up his handset and called in the planes. The Navy A5s, along with A10 Warthogs from the Vermont National Guard, swept in like hungry hawks. Each of the first five planes had been assigned a particular barracks to bomb. The second flight of five planes would standby in case the targets needed to be hit again or the soldiers needed air support. The Warthogs' mission was to destroy any and all Streetsweepers or other armoured vehicles that might be used by the hostiles.

07:02 hours

While most of the Russian soldiers were sleeping in the Muslims soldiers, many of them combat veterans and recent arrivals from Afghanistan and Yemen, along with three of the recently prisoners from Guantanamo Bay, had just finished morning prayers. They instantly knew that the approaching planes were bringing death, and that after the planes came the American soldiers. They were not stupid, they knew there would be no second chance for them; the roar of the jets told them that death was seconds away. They pointed their rifles into the air and began to fire, just hoping to hit the planes. The planes released their bombs from an altitude of only 2500 feet, which hit the barracks within seconds of being dropped. The second flight of planes and Warthogs turned in a tight circle over the base, hoping to be called in. As the tanks drove up to the underground garage and barracks area, they received some small arms fire. Their 120 millimeter main cannons quickly silenced their attackers. The infantry and state police quickly arrived, rounded up any survivors and secured the garage full of captured streetsweepers that now would never be used against the American people.

09:00 hours Washington DC

The security ring around DC was complete. Artillery positions had been established and fighters were patrolling the skies. The local and state police departments were stopping all vehicles attempting to enter or leave DC, checking the names of all persons inside against the names of those wanted for betraying their oath of office. Columns of tanks and armoured vehicles, along with thousands of armed soldiers, stood by to render any aid that was required of them.

The situation inside of DC was much the same. The DC Police, along with Police Officers from Boston, San Diego, Chicago, Philly, Atlanta, and

New York, along with state police from surrounding states, were patrolling the streets while military vehicles stood by.

09:00 hours

Along the Mexican border from Imperial Beach in CA to Brownsville, TX, U.S. Marines from Camp Pendleton and U.S. Army troops from Fort Hood were beginning to seal off the Mexican border. Assisting them were the Texas dept. of Public safety, U.S. Border Patrol Agents, armed American citizens, local police and sheriffs depts.

09:00 hours

In Boston, Chicago, Philadelphia, San Diego, Richmond and Atlanta police moved into position to seal off the streets for a two block radius around the Homeland Security warehouses. Military personnel wearing civilian clothing, including ordnance technicians, moved into the warehouses. Local fire departs. responded and curious news crews were informed that there was a possible gas leak in the buildings.

09:00 New York

The fire alarm sounded inside of the U.N. building. As diplomats, staff members and employees exited the building they saw a large number of police officers from both the NYPD and the New York State Police who appeared to be forming a cordon around the front and, from what they could see, the sides of the building. From around the corner a convoy of buses came into view. An FBI agent was announcing that he apoligised for any inconvenience, but no one would be allowed to reenter the building and due to the weather they would all be transported by bus, with a police escort, back to their own embassies. Employees and U.S. citizens were free to either take a bus now, or leave the area by other means. Other FBI agents who were assigned to counterintelligence operations noted the look of dismay on the faces of known KGB agents and agents from China's Ministry of State Security or, MSS.

There was of course outrage on the part of many officials but FBI agents, dressed in heavy winter coats with hats and warm gloves, politely yet firmly restated that they could not reenter the building. Soon the freezing cold January weather came to the aid of the FBI. The diplomats, while promising to report this outrage to their governments and to Obama himself grudgingly boarded the buses, while the few employees and U.S. citizens who were still there either also boarded the buses or walked to the public transportation entrance.

The buses departed the area with a police escort. As soon as they were out of sight FBI agents, along with agents from the NSA, CIA, and military intelligence entered the building to begin gathering information as to the spying activities within the U.S. of every nation on the earth. In time, many spies would be identified, both foreign and Americans who had betrayed their country.

09:00 hours Alexandria VA, the home of Senator Rand Paul.

The convoy of black SUVs and police cars pulled up into and outside of the driveway to the Rand residence. Carl Brown and many other agents exited the vehicles. While Carl walked up to the door and rang the doorbell, other agents and police officers formed a protective ring around the house. The door was opened by several children who, with a look of pure joy on their faces, said,"Oh wow, cool!" Despite the seriousness of the day Carl could not help but laugh. Before he could ask to speak to their father, Senator Rand came to the door and warmly asked Carl, whom he knew from previous occasions, to step inside. In doing so he looked out the door and saw the small army of agents and police, along with what looked like enough SUVs for a presidential motorcade. He was confused, and temporarily speechless.

"Well Carl what have I done this time? Looks like I'm in real trouble?"

"No sir, just the opposite. Would you please get dressed and please come with me to the White House?"

Rand's wife had joined them in the hallway.

"Please tell us what is going on?"

"Ma'am, I really cannot say anything right now. But Senator, if you will come with us, everything will be explained to you at the White House. It is urgent that we get you there sir, it's about a forty minute ride as it is."

"Will my family be ok?"

"Yes sir they are well protected."

"Give me ten minutes to get a suit on please."

"Yes sir, I'll be right here waiting on you."

Rand and his wife went upstairs where Rand quickly started to get dressed.

"I wonder what this could be about, turn on the TV news will you? I've never heard of anything like this happening to a Senator before."

The news came on with a live report of the story of the evacuation of the United Nations, and was then followed by a report of all the soldiers and police officers from all over the country who were in DC itself, as well as on all of the roads leading into and out of DC.

They looked at each other in silence, then, "That Secret Service Agent was very deferential to you downstairs."

"They're always like that, always very polite."

"No honey, he spoke as if was talking to, you know, the president or something."

"Don't be silly, I have to go now, I promise to call you as soon as I know anything."

Along with her kids, she was looking out of the window as Rand left the house. She noticed how the agents surrounded him, walking him to the third SUV. She saw how they held the door open for him, and how one even buckled him into his seat.

"What's going on?" She watched as the motorcade sped from her driveway. She was even more confused when she observed that many police officers and agents were still in her driveway and all around her house. The doorbell rang again. Upon answering it another very polite agent asked her if they could please use a room with a table to set up some equipment. She just pointed into the room on the right, then asked if she could make coffee or tea for them all.

"That would be very kind of you ma'am, it is rather cold out there."

"Well tell all of them to come into the house whenever they want to warm up."

"Thanks again, I'll let them know."

"It'll be nice working for someone who's so considerate," he thought to himself.

09:00 hours the White House

The Obamas had slept late, not getting up until 08:30. He had already canceled his military briefing and other meetings for the day; after all, tonight would be a huge night for him and the world. He also suspected that it would be a late night, what with taking all of the calls of congratulations from every major world leader who would begin calling probably even before the end of the speech. He needed to rest up and practice reading his speech from the teleprompter.

Their breakfast was brought in to them, and they all sat down to eat. He casually picked up the remote control and turned on CNN for his morning news. The scene from the U.N. did not really interest him, and he smiled at the report of extra police and soldiers in and around DC. Obviously Kalaak had ordered extra security for him due to tonight's announcement. They heard the helicopter Marine One arriving, but this was not at all unusual. However, it was unusually loud. He looked out of the window and saw not just Marine One but many other helicopters both landing on the White House lawn and circling above. Kalaak had definitely gone overboard, but his heart was in the right place.

Obama picked up his cell phone to call Kalaak, but it was dead. He thought that he must have forgotten to charge it, and tried the phone in the residence; also dead. He was more annoyed than anything. He walked out into the living room and saw several Secret Service Agents there. "Funny, usually they remained outside in the hallway in front of the residence door. Oh well, extra security," he thought.

"Guys my cell phone and my house phone are both dead, get them fixed ASAP." Both agents Matt Anderson and Alan Wainwright answered.

"Yes sir."

09:00 hours

General Kelly took the call from the White House situation room or, as it was also commonly called, the command bunker.

"Sir, they have just finished their breakfast and he has begun to watch the news. We also saw him looking out the window at the helicopters; sir he has tried to make several phone calls and has found out that his phones are not working."

"Ok thank you Matt, you Alan and the other agents just keep him there. I will be up shortly, tell the pilot of the marine copter to stand by please."

09:15 hours

Kalaak was just waking up in the Lincoln Bedroom. His head was pounding, he had consumed too much of that Russian vodka last night. It really wasn't his fault, the girls in that club, they just kept pushing them to drink. Oh why last night of all nights, he knew how important tonight was. Some greasy eggs, a soft drink or two and then a steambath, and he would be as good as new.

What was that noise? Was it, a helicopter? No, too loud for a helicopter, and Obama had not told him that he was going anywhere today. Why wouldn't the noise stop, the thing had to have landed by now. Kalaak got up and looked, then stared out of the window. It looked as if the entire sky was full of helicopters. But wait, why were all of those soldiers on the White House grounds and outside of the main gate? Kalaak was seized with a thought; panic and terror quickly filled him. He heard a large group of people coming quickly down the hallway towards the stairway to the private residence. If he was right...Kalaak quickly made the bed and then hid in the closet. As he heard the group passing by the door, he breathed a sigh of relief. Now he must find out exactly what was going on and plan from there. He quickly turned on the TV and knew that his worst fears were realized.

General Kelly, accompanied by another dozen individuals including Sean Dominguez and Joe Annino, approached the door to the private residence. The door was opened for them and they entered the residence. Obama looked at them.

"What are you doing in here I have not summoned you, get out now!" He demanded.

They just stood there staring at him. Obama repeated himself in a much louder voice.

"Get out."

General Kelly did not say a word. As Obama watched dumbfounded, Kelly pushed the play button. Obama heard his speech from the East room of the White House to the mullahs. A frantic look came over him, as he screamed at the Secret Service and FBI Agents.

"Arrest him, get them out of here!"

No one made any move; Obama sank down onto the sofa and began to whimper.

"I am The President of The United States."

They all just stared at him. General Kelly spoke in a voice filled with contempt. "You were never worthy of holding the office of president of this great republic. In the name of the *people of the United States of America*, I arrest you and charge you with treason, with failing, no not even failing, with deliberately *lying* to the American people, violating our laws both knowingly and intentionally, and I will tell you, coming very close to destroying this country. Get him out of here."

As soon as the general spoke, Secret Service Agents grabbed Obama by the arms and pulled him to his feet. Obama fell to the floor and cried hysterically. The agents picked him up bodily and carried him out to the waiting marine helicopter; he would not be traveling on Marine One or Air Force One ever again. The Obama family had watched in silence as the scene played out before them. They silently followed the agents out to the helicopter and, along with a dozen agents, boarded the copter that would take them to Camp David where Obama would be held in isolation until the next president decided his fate.

As the copter was lifting off from the White House lawn, a motorcade carrying Senator Rand Paul entered the White House grounds.

09:40 hours

Vice President Biden was staring happily out of the window of the Blair House looking at the clouds. When the door opened and his Secret Service detail, along with a large group of men, entered the room.

"Yes what is it, do you want to look at the clouds with me?"

"No, we are here to arrest you. You are no longer the Vice President of The United States, please put on a coat."

"Oh are we going somewhere?"

"Be gentle with him, get his coat and let's get moving."

10:00 hours

Traffic was backing up for miles on all of the roads leading into DC. Many Congresspeople and Senators rolled down the windows of their limos to stare out at the police and soldiers. Senator Schumer called out of his limo to an army officer.

"You, what is going on here?"

"Who are you?"

"I am a United States Senator from NY, Chuck Schumer."

The officer checked his list.

"Yes senator, excuse me, you are on the list. Please sir, hand me your gun."

"My gun? No, what are you talking about, I have a right to carry a gun." "Obama's orders sir, no one can carry a gun."

"That does not apply to me, to us lawmakers, important people. And besides Obama was not going to announce gun confiscation until the speech tonight."

"I do not know about that sir, my orders are to confiscate your weapon."

Schumer was about to argue further, but noticed that several soldiers with rifles were coming towards the limo. Well, if Obama ordered it, then it must be ok. And besides, he knew that he would get his gun back later. He then handed the officer his .45 cal handgun. Ironically this particular brand of firearm was illegal to own, even with a license in both NY and DC. Schumer rolled up his window and was waved through the checkpoint.

10:00 hours the Oval Office

As the door opened and Senator Rand entered the office, General Kelly, Sean, Nathan, Joe Annino, Sara and Al all stood up. Carl was the last one to enter; he gave orders to the agents at the door, then came in and took a seat.

General Kelly began to speak.

"Thank you for coming Senator."

"Excuse me general, but I do not understand this, where is President Obama and what is going on here?"

"Sir, Obama is no longer the president."

"Well who is then?"

"That, sir, is what we are about to determine. We have removed Obama from office for what I believe are obvious reasons that are known to all Americans, and for this."

He then placed the CD player on the table and pushed play. For several of them, it was the first time that they had heard the speech to the mullahs. When the speech ended, Senator Paul stated, "That speech, that is treason."

"Yes sir it is. Now we in this room, along with some others who you will meet later, held an election a little while ago. As a result of that election you were elected president and Governor Rick Perry was elected vice president. However, first, we want to go over some very important national security and social issues with you. Depending on your answers we will or will not offer you this office. You of course have the right to refuse."

Senator Paul was overwhelmed to say the least. First he is informed of a, well, a revolution, and secondly he is offered the office of president. All within five minutes! He collected his thoughts.

"Very well general please proceed."

"Sir, we request straight answers to straight questions. We will expect you to repeat these answers to the people of the United States tonight during the State of The Union address if we offer you the office. Ready?"

"Yes please go ahead."

"Sara why don't you start."

"Sir, most importantly I am a citizen of the United States, made in the image of my creator Who, as you can see, decided to create me as a black female. I am married to a white male and have two mixed race boys. I despise having to and have refused to answer questions on civil service exams for instance regarding race. I and my husband also refuse to answer questions regarding race for our sons. I believe in complete equal opportunity for all. I believe in the words of Martin Luther King Jr. when he said, 'I dream of the day when my children will be judged based upon the content of their character and the level of their ability, not on the color of their skin.' So, sir, will you oppose the use of racial quotas and defend equal opportunity for all?"

"That one is easy Sara, absolutely, I will do that."

Joe Annino spoke out.

"I will go next if that's ok. Mr. Paul, where do you stand on the Second Amendment?"

"Joe I am a Constitutional fundamentalist. I believe in the original intent of the Founding Fathers. I truly believe in the right of the people to keep and bear arms. That is, as long as they have not committed a crime of violence and therefore individually forfeited *their* right, not mine or yours, to possess firearms. I will live up to my oath of office to protect, defend and *preserve* the Constitution."

"My turn," said Sean. "Sir, what about illegal immigration and the welfare state?"

"I will seal the borders against all illegal entry. That might cause a big delay for people legally coming into the country, but so be it. I will build a border fence and yes, I will order all illegals out of our country. As far as the welfare state, once the illegals are gone many jobs will open up for Americans. They might be low paying, but people will have their dignity, pride and self reliance back. Anyone on welfare will have to be recertified to be eligible and will have to work for their welfare, whether sweeping streets, answering phones, or whatever; the free ride is over. For instance, there will be no more Obama phones. Oh and I will insist on drug and alcohol testing for anyone receiving public assistance."

Al spoke up next.

"Sir in addition to being a sheriff I am also a reverend in my church. So, do you believe that the United States is one nation under GOD? Do you believe that the U.S. was founded as a Christian nation? Do you know that there is no such thing in the constitution as the separation of church and state? And lastly as we look around the world, and unfortunately even in our country, are you aware of the danger that radical Islam poses to anyone who practices any religion other than Islam, as well as to democracy and freedom in the world?"

"Al, that was a lot. As far as I was able to follow you, the answer is yes to everything you asked. Religious freedom is an absolute right in this country and we, I, am not going to be intimidated by any group into surrendering my religion in favor of theirs."

"Sir I forgot to ask, how do you feel about English as the official language of the country?"

"Sean, the first continental congress had that vote over two hundred years ago. By one vote English won over German. A nation has to have one language that is spoken by all of its citizens, at least in the mainstream public, business, politics. A language unites a country and a people; the Romans understood that perfectly and insisted that all citizens of Rome speak Latin for the official language of the empire. It is fine with me if people speak a native language in their home, church, social club, or elsewhere, but in public and in business we must all speak the same language, English."

"My turn. Sir, what about the U.S. military? Whenever we have a Democratic president the military suffers heavy cuts. Under Obama we have been decimated. Where do you stand on how strong the military should be?"

"General, I agree with Ronald Reagan when he said that we need peace through military strength. Reagan wanted the military strong enough to fight two major wars at once. He built up our military to the point that no one, no enemy, would ever dare to attack us. If I am president my first priority will be to substantially build up all branches of the military so that once again the U.S. military will be the strongest in the world."

Nathan and Carl just looked at each other, and Carl nodded for Nathan to go first.

"Sir, for the first five years of his presidency Obama blamed George W. Bush for every problem in the country, and was constantly threatening to appoint a special prosecutor to investigate Mr. Bush and Mr. Cheney, among others. I myself believe that the Bush administration was one of the most honorable administrations that we ever had. However, from a law enforcement perspective, Obama and Holder have been a disaster. From Solandra to failure to investigate much less prosecute anyone in any of the missing emails scandals, IRS attacks on conservative groups or political opponents, the fast and furious gun running conspiracy, Benghazi and on and on the Obama administration is probably more corrupt than the Clinton administration was. On the home front Holder or Obama never once prosecuted a minority for a civil rights crime against a non-minority. I have a friend who is a career prosecutor in the Justice department. He and some others have been gathering evidence against Holder and Obama. Will you appoint him and whoever he needs to aid him as special prosecutors to investigate Holder and Obama?"

"Absolutely, and if your friends have already begun to gather evidence they can be, if not the special prosecutor himself, then members of his team."

"Let me just add sir, that the Secret Service has the list of hundreds of persons on the terrorist watch list who have been admitted to the White House. I think that needs to be investigated also."

"I fully agree with you on that point."

There was a knock on the door and a U.S. Marine Corps Major entered the office.

"Excuse me General, you asked for a status update."

"Yes go ahead Major."

"We have searched the White House and have arrested many staff members. We also caught two Muslims sending copies of national security documents from their office computers, not sure of who the documents went to yet, but we know what was sent. Oh and still no sign of Kalaak. Marines from Camp Pendleton and Army personnel from Fort Bragg have reached the border and have begun to close entry points to all but U.S. citizens, and we are using helicopters to patrol along the entire border. Reports indicate that U.S Border Patrol Officers are enthusiastically cooperating with our troops. There have been no major incidents at any of the checkpoints going into or out of DC. Our counterintelligence people began their investigations at the U.N. by going to the Russian and Chinese missions. They report that they found most of the computers still on, so there was no need to figure out passwords. The fire alarm apparently worked better than we counted on. The bases at Philomont and Cheswold have been neutralized with very few casualties to us. Many of the prisoners are wounded and being treated; we even captured a full colonel and a major, both of whom suffered the loss of a leg from being hit with a .50 cal round from a sniper rifle. FBI and ATF agents are taking lots of pictures and gathering evidence from the bases.

The FEMA headquarters and madrassa schools were obliterated by the MOABs, but again FBI and ATF are going over the scene. The first planes from Andrews are on their way to Arizona. As you requested, TV news crews are being admitted to the East room to set up for coverage of the speech you plan to give at 20:30 hours . Eric Holder was arrested outside of his home, he is now on his way to visit Sheriff Joshua. I think that about covers it for now sir, any orders?"

"No, major. Sean, you know what you're going to say at the press conference tonight?"

"Yes Sir, it will be short, sweet and to the point."

"Mr. Rand, if you are the next President of the United States, you will address the nation and what is left of the congress tonight from the Capitol Building. Oh and we insist on this, not that any of us feel that we have done anything wrong by saving our country, but we insist on a complete and total pardon for any real or implied criminal or civil act that happened by anyone who was acting under our orders or for all of us ourselves, all of the Sons and Daughters of Liberty. Do you agree to that sir? We need an answer right now."

"From what I have heard General, no one involved in this needs a pardon, but yes, a complete and total pardon for all."

11:00 hours

Kalaak knew that he had to move, as sooner or later someone would enter the room. Quickly, using the knife that he habitually carried, he cut his chest length beard, which fell in a heap into the sink. But in his haste, he made a cut on his left cheek that began dripping blood onto his robes. He then used one of the razors that was provided in the room for guests to remove the remnants of his beard. The blood on the front of his robes would be a problem. He briefly thought of attempting to reach Obama, but then decided that Obama would have to look out for himself; after all Allah wanted his servant Kalaak to live to fight another day.

Hearing footsteps coming down the hall, he opened the door a half of an inch and saw a lone soldier, who appeared to be about eighteen years old, coming towards him carrying several boxes. This was his chance. As the young soldier was passing the door, Kalaak sprang from the room and placed the knife against his throat. Kalaak dragged the soldier back into the room and with the knife still against his throat ordered the soldier to take off his uniform. Kalaak noticed that the soldier's dog tags had a Christian cross stamped into them. He hesitated a second, and then rammed the knife into the soldier's throat. He then took off his robes and put on the soldiers uniform, picked up the boxes and began to walk down the hallway. As he was opening the door to the stairs he heard a voice from behind him.

"Hey, please hold that door for me will you?"

Another soldier, who was also carrying several boxes, was coming towards him.

"Sure, no problem, after you."

Kalaak followed the soldier down the stairs and out the side entrance, where the boxes were being turned over to the FBI and loaded onto trucks as evidence. An army officer noticed the cut on Kalaak's cheek.

"Hey soldier, how did you cut your cheek?"

"On the corner of the box."

But Kalaak made a mistake.

"You meant to say sir, correct soldier?"

Kalaak was close to running away.

"Oh sorry sir, the pain, you know."

The Lt. hesitated a second; something did not seem right, but then again what was right about today?

"Ok soldier head over there to the medics, let them look at your cut."

"Yes sir."

11:15 hours

Nathan, Carl and Joe Garcia, along with several agents, had just left the Oval Office. All of them were satisfied that Senator Paul would be the next president, and they were still the agents in charge of the scene for the FBI, Secret Service and ATF. There was still a lot to do. In Nathan's mind nothing was more important than finding Kalaak. As they were passing the Lincoln Bedroom one of the agents said, "Look there, is blood coming from underneath the door?"

They all stopped and looked down. Without a word guns were drawn and the door was pushed open. The scene spoke for itself; a soldier, his dog tags visible in the blood, had been murdered, his uniform had been stolen, robes with a decent amount of blood on them were on the floor. They quickly searched the room, under the bed, closet, and bathroom where they saw the pile of facial hair and the used razor lying in the sink. Nathan immediately knew.

"Kalaak!" he screamed. Nathan got on his radio. "This is FBI agent Green, there is a man, possibly Kalaak, wearing an army uniform and possibly bleeding. He has murdered a soldier and stolen his uniform. Close all gates, do not let anyone leave the grounds." He then ordered the Secret Service and marines assigned to the White House to begin a level-one search for intruders inside of the White House. The Lt. was still standing at his post by the trucks when he heard Nathan's radio message. Instantly he both began to run towards the medical tent and got on the radio to spread the alarm, advising all personnel regarding Kalaak heading towards the medical tent with a cut on his left cheek.

Kalaak knew his luck could not last. He looked around the White House grounds and saw hundreds of soldiers, tanks, humvees, and trucks. With mounting panic he quickly walked towards the gate and saw that they were beginning to close. He started to run, then heard shouting from behind him. Unknown to him, it was the 'infidel' FBI agent Nathan Green. Soldiers from each side began to run towards him; the soldiers at the gate were un-slinging their rifles,

Kalaak swerved to his left and headed for the fence. The human will to survive gave him the strength to scale the fence at a run. Kalaak did not know it, but he was running towards the Potomac river, on whose banks Michael Wong was standing with the marines and seals. They all heard the alert from Nathan, but thought no way would he make it out of the grounds. Then came the calls stating that Kalaak was heading towards them. They all quickly grabbed their weapons and in a line moved towards the White House. Seeing them coming, Kalaak turned to his left and then his right. From both directions men and women in uniform were running towards him. From behind came more men and women, some of them in suits . He was trapped and he knew it.

Kalaak sank onto the ground and began to cry; he was so frightened that he could not move. Looking up, he saw they were forming a circle around him. Nathan Green pushed through the crowd to stand over Kalaak. Kalaak recognized Nathan from Dearborn; his fear grew to the point that he actually wet his pants. Many saw Kalaak's pants grow wet. No one laughed, no one even gave a smirk. Before them was evil, true evil, and it was disgusting to them to see how evil, when challenged by men and women of courage, quickly turned into cowardice. It was a lesson that seemed to have to be learned over and over again. Dictators, mad men such as Hitler or Hassan Rouhani could not be appeased, could not be reasoned with; they understood only force. Kalaak sat there in his soaked pants crying and begging for mercy. Nathan looked down at him and in an instant remembered the dead police officers in Dearborn, the people killed and injured in the bomb blast at the church, the dead soldier lying in a pool of his own blood in the Lincoln bedroom. The World Trade Center, The Boston Marathon bombings, the mall shootings by Chechnyan Muslims, the murdered school children in Russia and Israel and the reign of terror that he knew they were planning for the United States. No, they must be stopped. "An eye for an eye, a tooth for a tooth and a life for a life. And what good was having a full presidential pardon if you were not going to use it?" Nathan thought to himself.

Calmly, Nathan drew his gun from his holster. Everyone knew what he was going to do, and no one tried to stop him. He looked down at Kalaak and then shot him three times in the chest. He holstered his weapon and then walked back to the White House; he had a lot of work to do.

20:00 hours

The sound of many helicopters approaching once again filled the air around the White House. The lead helicopter landed, and Captain Sean Dominguez calmly exited the copter and entered the White House. A marine Lt. was there waiting for him, and the two exchanged salutes.

"This way sir."

They walked into the elevator and went down to the situation room. Sean had expected a mad house, but given the circumstances, things were busy but obviously under control. He quickly spotted his father, who was wearing his full Boston Police uniform, bent over a desk and absorbed in reading something. He looked around and saw General Kelly, who had ordered him to report to the White House. He walked over, saluted and was surprised to not only receive a salute but a warm handshake in return.

"Sean, I am very happy to see you. I heard that you and your men did a great job at Philomont. I want to talk with you in the next few days and hear all about it. I also want to get a written report from you soon. Hey, what's this I hear about a Russian Colonel and Major both losing a leg to a .50 cal round? You know anything about that?"

The smile on Sean's face was answer enough.

"Sean seriously, I would like to have every member of the American military here tonight. GOD knows they that have done so much for us all deserve to be here. Anyway, I want you and a few more of our military personnel to be front and center tonight as representatives of the entire military, standing right next to our police officers."

"Thank you general it will be an honor."

"Good, now go say hello to your father, I think he's kind of nervous about his speech tonight."

20:30 hours

The East room of the White House was packed with reporters. Every major network and news station was present. The noise, mostly in the form of loud complaints from the media, was deafening.

The door opened, the cameras turned and the room became very quiet. In walked a line of police officers and members of the military. The first was Sara Mahoney, followed by Capt. Dominguez, then Nathan Green, Joe Garcia, Susan Nguyen, Brian Olofson, Sheriff Al Thomas, Joe Annino who was wearing his military uniform, Audrey Lapaglia and Tony Lee. The rest of the Sons and Daughters came after.

Deputy Superintendent Sean Dominguez was the last to enter. He walked up to the podium, and absolute silence settled. Sean was wishing he was somewhere else, but he had started this. The cameras began to roll and all over America, viewing was preempted on every network. This also meant that the speech would go world-wide to anyone who was watching American television. Except in the U.S. Capitol building, where a blackout on all television and communications had been placed.

"Good evening ladies and gentlemen, and to all of my fellow Americans. My name is Sean Dominguez, I am a Deputy Superintendent with the Boston, Massachusetts Police Department. I am also the leader of a nation wide organization of law enforcement officers, from the local, state and Federal levels, known as the Sons and Daughters of Liberty. Along with the active assistance of the United States military, we the Sons and Daughters of Liberty have carried out a revolt against the Obama administration and the illegal usurpation of power by Obama. Our actions, authorized by the Founding Fathers themselves, were required due to the fact that our leaders in Congress not only failed to stop, but in many cases such as in Obamacare have actively supported, Obama. Remember Pelosi's comment before the vote on Obamacare, 'You have to vote for it before you can know what's in it.' This and the below examples are some of the reasons for the revolt. These words that I am about to read might sound familiar to many of you, taken as they are from our Declaration of Independence.

The New Declaration of Independence

When in the course of human events it becomes necessary for the People of the United States to dissolve the political bands that have bound them to and with a government that has lost sight and respect for the intent put forth by the original Founding Fathers of this great Republic which were granted by God, it is fitting that the causes which bring to fruition this separation be stated. WE hold these truths to be self-evident, that all citizens are created equal, that they are endowed by their Creator with certain unalienable rights that among these are Life, Liberty and the Pursuit of Happiness, that to secure these rights, Governments are instituted among men and women, deriving their just powers from the consent of the governed and not the reverse. That whenever any form of government becomes destructive of these ends, as this government under its current

leadership has, it is the right and in fact the obligation of the
people to alter or abolish that government and to institute
new government laying its foundation of such principles
and organizing its power in such form, as to them shall seem
most likely to affect their safety and happiness and in fact
the safety of the citizen population as a whole. That this
decision to purge the current leadership and replace it with
those 'of the people' is not an action that should be taken
lightly or at whim. An act such as this should be undertaken when the United States of America is in danger of
being destroyed from enemies both foreign and domestic
because of the policies of the entrenched leadership which
was the state of this nation and which required immediate
corrective action. The policies and illegal, unconstitutional
actions and activities of the administration of President
Barack Hussein Obama, and it's minions, complicit members of congress and a subversive anti-American news
media required immediate corrective action if the Republic
was to be saved for future generations to live in freedom
as envisioned by the original Founding Fathers. To prove
this, let the following facts and reasons be submitted to
a candid world: Barack Hussein Obama has refused to
Assent to Laws, the most wholesome and necessary for
the public good. They have refused to secure our Nation's
borders, a must and requirement for any sovereign nation
if it is to survive. They are attempting, at every opportunity,
through illegal methods and executive actions to dilute,
diminish and eliminate personal and individual freedoms
guaranteed to Americans by the Constitution of the United
States. The First and Second Amendments among other
rights are constantly under attack. They have encouraged
and assisted in the illegal immigration of tens of millions
of foreign nationals; many of them convicted criminals,
while also refusing to deport and providing American jobs
for millions already illegally here and have used American
tax dollars for this purpose. They have ignored or refused
to adhere to the American concept of State's Rights and

*have illegally imposed his/their authority by executive
action to disregard such rights of the states. They have
systematically and methodically weakened and reduced in
size the United States Military and by so doing has rendered
its capacities far less effective than needed, placing the
entire country and its national security in danger from
foreign enemies. By their inept in appearance and subversive by design, they are appeasing and emboldening our
nation's hostile enemies while causing our allies to distrust
America's resolve and dependability. They have disre-
garded legal decisions of American courts; ignoring and
dismissing the American rule of law and the Separation of
Powers. They have turned the ever increasing power of
modern technology against the citizenry for the purpose of
invading the private lives of individual Americans in ways
that have little or nothing to do with national security. They
have used powerful American Agencies such as the IRS,
The NSA, The Justice Department, Homeland Security and
others for political advantage over individuals and organization who hold opposing views. They have infringed
on the Freedom of Religion; particularly members and
organizations in the Christian and Jewish Faiths, by executive orders and fiats; actions which attempt to force, with
threats and action of penalty, members of those faiths to
adhere to policies that clearly go against what their faith
requires. They have undertaken the task of dismantling the
finest healthcare system in the world and replaced it with
an inferior; government run and controlled substitute and
illegally required citizens to purchase the product; often
against the will of citizens. They have in secrecy, armed
federal agencies with military grade equipment and weap-
onry for no apparent but suspicious reasons. They have
been proven to have lied consistently to the populace on
matters of vital economic and national security issues with
intent to subvert American law. They continue to block,
with all of their power, the development of production of
energy which is resulting in the continued dependence*

on foreign fuel causing economic and well as national security vulnerability. They continue to yield by increments, American sovereignty and self-rule to the corrupt, one world tyrannical United Nations. They have imposed burdensome taxes without the consent of the people. They are using the Justice Department to harass and undercut the nation's police forces while enabling violent mob rule to go unpunished and undeterred and even to be encouraged. They have attempted, with much success, to cause racial and economic class divisions among Americans. They are methodically imposing; by design, Socialistic economic policies with the goal of replacing the free enterprise system that has kept American prosperity second to no other nation. In every stage of these oppressions and dictatorial acts, Americans have petitioned for redress in legal and responsible ways; only to be ignored, rebuffed or retaliated against for daring to question or speak out against these clear injustices and illegalities. A president whose character is thus marked by every act of a tyrant is thus unfit to govern the people of a free nation. We have reminded them constantly and respectfully of the illegality of their actions and the dangers their policies; both foreign and domestic are bringing upon the United States of America and its people who have a right to demand our country remain free and prosperous and strong. We have appealed to what should be, but is apparently not, their sense of justice and patriotism, but they have been deaf to the appeals of the people and arrogant and tyrannical in their response. The people therefore, must step up and take action and return our great nation to its long held position of prominence; the greatest nation in the history of the world. We therefore, as patriotic Americans, look to guidance and God for his assistance in this action to return our country to its rightful owners – the American People; released of dictatorial bonds, independent from the control and influence of any other nation with a people who cherish, respect and defend freedom at all cost for every citizen.

20:30 hours The U..S Capitol Building

The cameras were all off. That was the agreement that had been in place for many years between the media and the Congress. No need to let the American people see their masters and their allies in the media drinking champagne, eating lobster and other delicacies that were all paid for by the American taxpayer. The irony was that due to high taxes, most working Americans could not treat themselves to this lifestyle.

Carl Brown looked at his watch. As he circled the room all around him he heard snippets of conversations.

"Have you heard from Obama today?"

"What is he up to that he needs all of these soldiers in DC for?"

"Do you think that he will finally announce it tonight?"

Brown could have answered all of these questions, but why spoil the surprise?

Time to begin. He walked over to where Nancy Pelosi was talking to all ten of the FEMA governors that had been appointed by Obama. Harry Reid and his close friends and political allies, Mitch McConnell and John Boehner were also standing in the circle. They all knew who Brown was, and as he approached they all stopped talking.

"Excuse me folks, but President Obama has asked me to invite you all upstairs for a private talk and group pictures."

They all knew that there was a hierarchy within the congress and they thought that it was just their due to meet with Obama first. They followed Brown to the large, thickly carpeted, mahogany paneled elevator that they assumed would be going up, but were only mildly surprised when it went down, Brown must have gotten his directions mixed up.

It would be an understatement to say that they were shocked as they stepped off of the elevator. Instead of seeing the presidential limousine, there were buses. Instead of the press corps, there was an army of police and soldiers.

"What is the meaning of this?"

It was Carl Brown who answered.

"The meaning of this, Nancy, is that all of you, along with Obama, are relieved of office for treason and for breaking your oaths of office."

It was a statement in and of itself that none of them denied the charges. They just stood there like deers in the headlights, not knowing what to do.

"Please step onto the bus now."

They obeyed; they still could not understand, fully comprehend, what was happening. As they took their seats on the bus, army medics came down the aisle and gave them a little shot of Fentanyl to help them sleep on the plane.

Brown then went back upstairs to use the same ruse on Obama's Czars, cabinet members and the next level in the Congressional hierarchy, a ruse that he would use many times in the next 30 minutes.

There is a total of 100 U.S. Senators; fifty four were Republicans, forty four were Democrats and two were independent. Twenty four of the Republicans and thirty seven of the Democrats, along with both of the Independents, found themselves boarding buses for Arizona.

There are only 435 members In the U.S. House of Representatives. Two Hundred and forty five are Republicans and one hundred and eighty eight are Democrats. Ninety eight Republicans and one hundred and twenty three Democrats also found themselves taking an unplanned trip to visit Sheriff Joshua.

21:30 hours

The remaining Senators and Congresspeople sat silently in a very empty congressional chamber. They looked around the room and saw that all of the Joint Chiefs of staff were present, along with five members of the U.S. Supreme Court. To the left of the speaker's desk, members of the Marine Corps band were standing by. They noted that there were many police officers from all over the country and a large number of armed military personnel in the room. Strangely, no one from the leadership of either party was present. For some reason the wife and children of

Senator Rand Paul were sitting in the visitors gallery. There were, however, a great deal of cameras from many different networks in the room. They sat in silence waiting.

As the cameras rolled, a Marine Colonel in full Dress uniform, along with Colonels from the Army, Air Force and a Captain from the U.S.Navy, also in dress uniform, entered the chamber. Behind them marched the Sons and Daughters of Liberty, and then a large number of police officers. The Colonels and Captain took seats behind the Joint Chiefs. The police officers filled all of the empty seats both in the chamber and visitors gallery then stood up along the walls.

The Sergeant at Arms of the United States House of Representatives then entered the room. They all watched him as he announced, "Ladies and gentlemen, The President of The United States."

They stood as the Marine band played Hail to The Chief for the first time to President Rand Paul. Many if not all of the members of Congress, plus all of the military and police in the room, gave the new President a rousing and heartfelt greeting.

President Paul made his way down the aisle, shaking hands and looking into his former colleagues eyes for what, support, sympathy, jealousy, friendship? He was not even sure himself.

He stood at the podium, glanced up at his family, and began.

"My fellow Americans, for those of you who do not know me, my name is Rand Paul. I am a former Senator from Kentucky and I am now the new President of the United States."

In the chamber itself as in living rooms, DAV posts, corner bars, in the Kremlin and in the government halls of the People's Republic of China, you could have heard a pin drop.

"I come to you as your President, as the result of a revolution that has removed former president Obama, his Czars, FEMA governors, cabinet and many members of both the congress and senate from office on the charges of treason and of betraying their oaths of office. The proof of these charges is overwhelming and will be presented to the people of the United States within the next few days. One of the more insidious examples of this treason was allowing foreign troops to establish secret military bases here within the United States. Earlier today, these bases were attacked and destroyed by our military and police officers. Another example was the creation of a private army within the United States, paid for by your tax dollars, under the auspices of the Department of Homeland Security and FEMA. Additionally, Obama had recruited many individuals from the ranks of illegal aliens and radical islam to serve in his private army; they were to be armed from strategically placed ware-houses within our cities with weapons again paid for by your tax dollars.

Earlier today the Commandant of the Marine Corps, General Wayne Kelly, whom I am instaling as of now as our new Secretary of Defense, issued an order Federalizing all state national guard units and activating all of our military reserves. I am now expanding that order to all veterans and members of the NRA who are physically fit to serve to report to their local sheriffs, where they will be sworn in as deputy sheriffs. I am also authorizing all citizens of the United States who have not been convicted of a violent felony to arm themselves, in accordance with our constitution, and stand by to assist law enforcement when and if called to do so.

I am ordering that all illegal aliens, no matter how long that you have been in the country or no matter if you have children who were born in this country, to leave the country immediately. I am ordering that starting twenty four hours from now civil rights will no longer be afforded to illegal aliens or anyone who harbors them. My fellow citizens, let me make it perfectly clear that this was not a military coup. This action was led by the police and only by a matter of hours was Obama's takeover of our country averted. You, the citizens of the United States, failed to live up to your duties under our Constitution of being the ultimate guardians of liberty. You have gotten lazy, you have taken for granted our freedoms and as a result you have come very close to losing your freedoms and those of your children. It is up to you to clean your local and state govern-ments of all those who do not love America. All those who have betrayed the voters trust and have broken their oaths to protect, defend and pre-serve the Constitution of the United States should be removed from office and arrested. It will be up to you to decide who will replace them within your own communities.

For a long time now, the nation's welfare program has seen widespread fraud and abuse. We will restructure welfare from the top to the bottom. Anyone who does receive temporary public assistance will work for it in community programs. The days of working people supporting those who *could* but *won't* work are over.

I will introduce legislation to increase the number of the members of Congress from its current small number of four hundred and thirty five to twenty times the current number, to a total of eight thousand and seven hundred members. The Senate will increase from its constitutional limit of one hundred members to two hundred members, with each state having four senators. The proportion of senators and representatives per state will remain the same, but the increase in numbers in both the senate and congress will make for a much more diverse and representative government. For both the House and Senate, term limits should be established, possibly four terms in the House and two in the Senate. Congressional perks will be all but eliminated. I intend to once again make the government of the United States a government of the people, for the people and by the people!"

In the house chamber and all over the country patriotic, hard working Americans were standing and cheering. The President was sweeping away their individual feelings of helplessness, the feeling that they could not change anything, that government was too big to fight.

"Ladies and gentlemen, facts are facts and the historical fact is that we are a nation that was created by Christians in search of religious freedoms; we are one nation under GOD. While we have tolerated and respected the religious beliefs of others, we will not have our beliefs destroyed by any group of religious fanatics that we have allowed to enter our country. Religious freedom is for everyone who chooses to practice their religion or to not practice it. No group will introduce their own religious courts or laws into our country or demand that we accommodate their beliefs at the expense of our own beliefs. I will have much more to say on this topic in the coming weeks.

Finally, to the rest of the world, let me remind you of the words of former President Kennedy: 'Let every nation know, whether it wishes us well or ill, that we shall pay any price, bear any burden, meet any hardship, support any friend, oppose any foe, to assure the survival and the success of liberty. This much we pledge and more. To those old allies whose cultural and spiritual origins we share, we pledge the loyalty of faithful friends. United, there is little we cannot do in a host of cooperative ventures. Divided, there is little we can do— for we dare not meet a powerful challenge at odds and split asunder.'

"So bearing in mind President Kennedy's words, I would like to remind our old allies, in particular one in the Middle East and the other in Europe, that although the previous administration put great strains on our friendship, to the point of actually insulting you, that has changed. My administration will remember our old friends and will make every effort to renew and strengthen our old friendships. To our enemies, and yes I know that we have enemies who truly desire to destroy us, let me remind you of how the people of the United States have always rallied, as I suspect they are already rallying, to our flag, Old Glory, in times of danger. Our military stands ready and I promise you starting tomorrow will be growing stronger and stronger every day. I can hear the Liberty Bell ringing. I see Lady Liberty waking up, stretching and limbering up to once again walk forward from the shores of America, shining the light of freedom before her, to light the way on the path of liberty for all of the peoples of the world."

At this point in the chamber and from all across America, applause echoed once again. American soldiers, whether they were standing on a flight deck or patrolling the DMZ in Korea, once again felt strong. Their morale soared, and it was evident to all that "a new birth of freedom" was happening in America.

"Thank you ladies and gentlemen. Good night and may GOD continue to Bless and protect the United States of America."

In the Kremlin, a dejected and worried President Putin looked at his advisors.

"We have a huge problem. I now know how Gorbachev felt, Ronald Reagan is back."

In a small DAV post in the town of Arlington, MA, a group of veterans had sat spellbound as President Paul spoke.

"Well you heard the President, it is up to us to clean up our local and state governments of those who don't love America. Remember how the school committee and that principle down at the high school tried to stop that kid from saying the pledge of allegiance, even though it's a state law that the pledge be said in school everyday?"

"Yeah we remember, we talked about it enough."

"Ok then, let's finish our beers and go arrest them."

Some people go through life quietly, never creating any commotion, minding their own business. Other people go through life creating trouble for others, doing whatever they can to get ahead. And a select few use their life to make a difference, doing whatever they can not to live long and quietly, and not to get ahead, but to advocate for a cause greater than themselves. This was Sean's life.

AUTHOR BIO

Lawrence, (Larry) Mackin is a police officer and former probation officer with 30 years of law enforcement experience. Larry was born and raised in South Boston, MA and is part of a large family, many of whom have served in the U.S. Military and as police officers. A life member of the NRA and political conservative, Larry has campaigned as an independent candidate for the Office of U.S. Representative and Sheriff.

Larry was the founder and President of Citizens against Reverse Discrimination, an organization that filed a Federal Reverse Discrimination lawsuit challenging the use of racial quotas in the City of Boston's Police and Fire Departments. The lawsuit went through the Federal Court system up to the United States Supreme Court.

In addition to many newspaper and magazine interviews, Larry has appeared on numerous national television shows such as, 48 hours, World Monitor, Phil Donahue, Oprah Winfrey, Sally Jesse Raphael, among others. Larry is married to his wife Jeanne of 28 years. They have three children.